I0658305

The Scoundrel's Trespass

The Scoundrel's Trespass

Men of the Marque
Book Two

a Regency-era privateer tale

by

Sandra Sookoo

This is a work of fiction. Names, characters, places, and incidents either are the product of the author's imagination or are used fictitiously, and any resemblance to actual persons living or dead, business establishments, events, or locales, is entirely coincidental.

All rights reserved. No portion of this book may be reproduced or transmitted in any form or by any electronic or mechanical means, including photocopying, recording or by any information retrieval and storage system without permission of the author.

THE SCOUNDREL'S TRESPASS © 2016 by Sandra Sookoo
Published by New Independence Books

ISBN-13: 978-0692664223

ISBN-10: 069266422X

Contact Information:
sandrasookoo@yahoo.com
newindependencebooks@gmail.com
Visit me at www.sandrasookoo.com

Edited by: Michele Jensen

Book Cover Design by David Sookoo

2012-ROM14-JKL-181 | Illustrated Romance, Jenn LeBlanc

Lighthouse by yelenayemchuk | 123rf.com

Publishing History:
First Digital Edition, 2016
First Print Edition, 2016

Other Regency romances by Sandra Sookoo you might enjoy

Scandal in Surrey series

Lady Parker's Grand Affair
The Bride's Gambit
Misfortune's Lady
Miss Bennett's Naughty Secret

Scandalous Shorts (tie-ins to the Scandal in Surrey series)

Library Tryst
Bedroom Assignation
Staircase Encounter
Garden Affair (coming soon)

Darrington family series

Marriage Minded Lord
To Bed or To Wed
The Bridal Contract

Other Regency-era pirate romances

Act of Pardon
Angel's Master
Storm Tossed Rogue
Once a Pirate

Praise for Sandra Sookoo's Regency work

Sandra Sookoo has created a strong and independent heroine who never expected to find herself in the position she is in. However, once in it she does not give up or give in to her circumstances or love very easily. I would recommend this book to readers who love an adventure and to romance lovers who enjoy a strong female heroine to match up against a sultry bad boy hero. -- Kathryn Bennett, Readers Favorite (for *Act of Pardon*)

There is something to be said about a romance book that can keep you enthralled page after page where everyone is fully clothed and no one is cursing. This was truly a delight to read, and it reminded me that there used to be a simpler time, a purer time, where people thought about family and obligation and not just lust. The book wasn't full of contrived drama or misunderstanding after misunderstanding. This book was an easy read, but a nice one. – Peyton, The Romance Reviews (for *Marriage Minded Lord*)

I was swept along with this story and the characters' grand affair and passions. It is a lively love story but starts off very carnal… The characters are full-bodied and well-developed. Maggie is passionate, scandalous, stubborn and strong-willed, while Stephen is a rogue in every way and both are sure they will not fall in love. – Linda, The Romance Studio (for *Lady Parker's Grand Affair*)

Dear Readers,

This story was done mostly on a dare. One of my beta readers put forth the idea that the follow up to *Storm Tossed Rogue* should feature a threesome as well as a spanking scene. I didn't know how that would play out... until I began outlining *The Scoundrel's Trespass*.

The captain is brother to the man you met in the first book, and as with brothers, he's very much his own person. He brings a whole lot of flaws with him, but perhaps it's his wife who can ultimately help put his pieces together.

Add to that the glimmer of second chances as well as a bit of adventure and you have the makings of a great romance.

I hope you like my *Men of the Marque* series. I've populated it with strong, stubborn men and stronger, independent women who are all looking for love even if they don't know it yet. They're connected by the sea as well as intrigue and the rabbit holes of human nature.

Happy reading!

Sandra

Dedication

To Paula. Thanks for everything.

Blurb

The heart wants who it wants, and sometimes that means sharing the love despite the scandal.

Caroline Montmorency, ten years an assumed widow, is on the verge of having her sea-faring husband declared legally dead. While the country is embroiled in a maritime war with England, all she wants is to wed her longtime friend, Paul Douglas, and begin life anew. But those plans are broken when her husband unexpectedly returns.

Captain Adam Montmorency is an adventurer, privateer and general ne'er-do-well — at least, he was. He's come back to Maine with his memories of how he treated his wife missing. After guarding his emotions during endless days of British torture, he'd like to repair relations with Caroline and gain acceptance for the man he is now — reformed and ready for domestication.

Paul has loved Caroline for years but waited to declare himself out of deference to Adam's memory. She's promised him her hand, but he's faced with the loss of his lady to Adam, so he does whatever it takes to win — even if it means betraying his best friend to the British.

While Caroline has mixed feelings about having Adam back in her life and bed, she won't give up Paul. Before any of them can grasp a happy ending, they'll have to survive a fight with the British and muddle through the aftermath of Paul's deception.

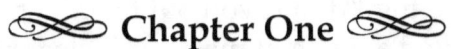

Chapter One

Mid-January 1813
Gull's Island off the District of Maine's coast, America

Caroline Montmorency shivered as she walked through her snow-covered garden. Though the sun rose as it did every day, the gray skies and thick clouds hid the evidence. She wrapped her wool cloak more tightly about her body, neither caring that the hem of her skirts trailed in the snow or that her toes were beginning to smart inside her boots from the cold.

When she came upon a wrought iron bench beneath the bare branches of a sugar maple tree, she dusted off the snow as best she could, then perched upon the frigid metal. Errant snowflakes decorated the black wool of her cloak. She smiled at the tiny pieces of dainty artwork before they either took flight again or melted. Such was life. The dearest of everything was only in your possession for but a moment.

Hadn't life taught her this more times than she cared to remember?

Instead of dwelling on that heartache, Caroline glanced around her surroundings. The wintery world always calmed her. Snow laced the naked branches of trees and shrubbery, which would be full of life and green in the summer. Evergreen trees, with their soft blankets of white, stood as silent sentinels everywhere she looked. That blanket of white blotted out every imperfection. A fresh start—for a little while. Out of the corner of her eye, the red flash of a cardinal added brilliant color to the landscape. A sigh left her lips and her breath frosted in the cold air. Here, in her dormant garden, even in the dead of the year, she found peace.

"I had a feeling I'd find you out here." The soft British accent added a touch of magic and elegance to the frozen sanctuary.

She startled at the intrusion into her solitude. When she looked up in expectation, another sigh escaped her, but for a completely different reason as she met his gaze. So easily could she lose herself in those warm, brown eyes — in him. But stubbornly, she clung to old vows by circumstance. The needs of her body and heart had to be ignored. "Hello, Paul." It wasn't unexpected to see her greatest friend on the island, since he visited three times a week. "You're early." Usually, he appeared after the noon meal, but his presence never failed to lift her mood. He had an uncanny knack for joining her when her spirit flagged. Often, they'd spend hours tucked away in the library, reading, he on a winged-back chair and she on a settee, as if they'd been together a lifetime.

Perhaps they had.

"I had some free time. Plus," he reached into the inside pocket of his greatcoat then pulled out an envelope of stiff, ivory vellum. Creases and several smudges marred the surface. He held it up in his gloved hand while a grin split his clean-shaven face. "There was a letter waiting for you in town."

A host of flutters moved through her belly. She'd thought this reaction had died years ago, but always there was a small hope it was word from her missing husband — word that would allow her to move forward in her life instead of living this shadow existence. "News of Adam after all this time?"

"Doubtful." He handed her the missive with surprising disappointment. "I'm sorry to disappoint."

"Forgive me." How could she explain her fractured thoughts? Part of her wished her husband would return for the excitement he used to bring while another part wanted the blessed relief of knowing if he was truly gone.

"There is nothing to forgive."

Dear Paul. He never failed. She laid a hand on his forearm. The muscles tensed beneath her fingers. What passions lay hidden beneath his calm façade? From her position on the bench, she looked upward into his face but couldn't help that her gaze lingered on the broad sweep of his shoulders. Too bad the greatcoat hid his form. He was most pleasing to observe and she'd wiled away many an afternoon dreaming about being in his arms, his bed. She sucked in a breath as guilt stabbed her. It would do no good to harbor such inappropriate thoughts about her husband's best friend. After all, didn't she still have vivid dreams of being naked and entwined with Adam?

I've been too long alone.

"I'm merely unsettled today." As a persistent, languid heat slid through her veins, she shook her head then cast her attention to the letter in her lap. It was addressed to Mr. Adam Montmorency. She turned the letter over. A seal of brown wax held an "M" in scrollwork. An "M" for the family name? Her heart beat faster.

"I can understand that." He paced the area just in front of her with his hands clasped behind his back. "Tomorrow will be ten years, won't it?"

"Yes." That one little word threatened to choke her. She swallowed the thickness. "Ten years since his ship came home without him on it." There had been no word about him since. It was as if he'd vanished from the face of the earth.

"Perhaps it is time to give him up to the sea." Paul availed himself of the spot on the bench beside her. With a finger beneath her chin, he tipped her face upward. The hood of her cloak fell back. She shivered as the chill of the winter air rushed over her head and ears. "You need to live again. I detest seeing you waste away, hoping for something that might never happen when there are others who wish with all their heart they could have you."

She gasped at the intense emotions roiling in his eyes. Even through the fine kid of his glove she swore she felt the heat of his hand on her skin. "I know, but…"

His jaw worked. He dropped his hand. "Yes, you wish to honor your vows, but damn it, Caroline, it's been ten years. If he was alive, he would have shown up. Not that he was such a great husband to you anyway."

The bitterness in his voice surprised her. Did he care for her as more than a friend? Her pulse picked up once more. "Adam had his moments." Though he'd been a harsh and disagreeable man, in bed they had found a common bond. That passion had burned bright and been all-consuming. Often, they'd succumb to frenzied lovemaking as an alternative to arguing. Even now, all these years later, her body ached for his touch, especially when he'd roused her desire to fever-pitch with spanking sessions. "Yes, he had his moments." Her face warmed. He'd taught her much regarding how relations between a man and a woman could be. Perhaps she missed that the most about his absence.

"What, three of them in the month you were married before he abandoned you for the sea?" His frown was fierce. "I'll always regret introducing you at that rout."

"You couldn't have known. Men behave differently around other men than they do women."

"He certainly took to you. I'd never seen anything quite like it."

"Why? Was it so odd?" Adam had called the very next morning then every day afterward.

Paul shrugged. "No. There was certainly chemistry between you, embarrassing almost, but then he showed what sort of man he really was beneath the flirting and attraction."

"It matters not now." She chewed her bottom lip. "I'd hoped if he'd spent more time on the island, with me, that perhaps he'd mellow or mature." She refused to dwell on the cruelness his nature had often taken beneath that veneer of handsome deviltry. "Now we'll never know what could have been." A tiny flutter moved through her belly. Gah! Hadn't she worked hard to banish the wistfulness after all these years?

"You've wasted too many years on his ghost." He shook his head when she murmured a slight protest. "Perhaps we must face the overwhelming facts. His ship limped home, barely seaworthy."

"That doesn't mean anything. Miracles happen."

"True, but the storm they encountered, coupled with the battle afterward, decimated the crew. The remaining ten gave up their horror stories. You know that. You've heard them time out of hand. If Adam was swept overboard like they claimed, in all likelihood, he would not have survived."

In her head, she knew this. After all, it had been ten years with no word. Caroline heaved a sigh. She broke the letter's seal then pulled out a single page of stationery. "I know." How many nights had she lain sleepless in her bed, trying to puzzle out what had happened to him? Was he truly dead, resting quietly at the bottom of the sea he loved more than life itself, or had he survived and discovered that he could essentially live his life away from the wife he hadn't really loved? Her stomach clenched, despite the vast length of time she'd had to acclimate to

5

either scenario. It had been their secret, for Adam had told her often enough that he'd married her for convenience's sake and the property she'd brought to the union. Her parents had protested the match. So had Paul. No sense in showing they were all right.

She peeked at him. Had his best friend known of her shame? "But I do wonder. I cannot help it." Deep down, she'd imagined that if Adam came home to her they could have worked on being a happily married pair, that she might grow to love him and he her.

Especially after the horrible, wrenching pain of losing that other, sweeter dream.

"We both do." Paul launched from the bench and returned to pacing. "About many things, actually." He dropped his voice. "We need to talk."

"We are talking." She unfolded the paper then rapidly scanned the page, anything to distract her from thinking of the babe she'd lost to cruel fate. Her arms were empty, and no longer would she ever hold her husband or their child again. Yes, the desire to be a mother would never leave her, but she couldn't forget her vows, no matter how horrible the marriage had been. As long as she held hope he would return and she could temper him, she could never move on. The longing for love crashed into her with the force of a vigorous wave, and she stifled a sob. There hadn't been enough time to know if Adam would have ever grown affection for her, but Lord how she wished they'd had the chance to try. "This is from Adam's brother, Clinton. Dated nearly six weeks ago."

"Ah." Paul faced her. "I assume since he's written, he's now somewhere on land?"

"Apparently so. In Cornwall, at the family manor." She read a portion of the missive aloud. "'Brother, now that I'm settled, I want to invite you to return to England's shores if you can manage to bring yourself to set foot on

British soil once again." A slight smile curved her lips. It had been no secret Adam despised the overwhelming reach of the Empire. "No doubt you're happily ensconced within the American navy. Or have you capitulated to the lure of privateering?'"

Paul snorted. "As if Adam would ever do something that benefited anyone beside himself. If he was alive, he would be a privateer, pirate really. Even now, I can easily envision him marauding and thieving off His Majesty's ships or anyone else for that matter."

"Behave, and no more interruptions. If that is true, then you both have something in common — capitalizing on this British maritime war." Her smile grew. He and Adam had always been competitive and like-minded in all aspects save one: Paul's loyalties firmly lay with the British while Adam had fought for independence in every aspect of his life. No doubt he continued to owe allegiance to no one. Her husband's greatest regret had been America's continued dependence on England's exports even if he used to sail under Britain's marque. *And now, here we are, in the midst of yet another war with Britain, with our harbors patrolled and supply lines disrupted.* Though, in recent days, the waters around her little island had been free of any sighting of England's presence. She cleared her throat then continued reading. "'In any event, if you are home and this letter reaches you, please consider a visit. I am soon to be wed to the most marvelous woman. She's unlike anyone I've ever encountered and I would like you and your lady wife to be present for the nuptials. It's quite time we reconciled the family.'"

Her stomach quivered. His brother had found love. Even on the page, she sensed the sentiment through the strong handwriting. "At least the Montmorency name will continue, since I failed in that." For one mad second, she considered leaving her secure little island and heading for the mists of Cornwall, for nothing else than companionship and to learn more of Adam's people. Then she shook her head. Her life, such as it was, lay here. "I'm happy for him."

"I must say I'm shocked," Paul stated as he faced her once more. "The elder Montmorency is even more extreme than Adam was."

Calmly, Caroline folded the letter, tucked it into its envelope then sighed. "Obviously, he has either changed or the woman he'll marry has worked magic." A small laugh escaped. "There is always hope."

"Sometimes, that hope is false and becomes a prison." He reclaimed his spot on the bench beside her. "Caroline." He took her hands in his, regardless of the letter that fell to the snowy ground. "Darling, surely you must know my feelings for you by now."

A host of tingles raced down her spine. He'd never used an endearment with her before, though there'd been times when she couldn't help noticing his passionate regard when they were together. Not one time since her husband went missing had Paul made an advance. Of course, neither had she, and there had been times she'd desperately needed to feel the touch of a man again or give in to the glory she suspected would be in Paul's kiss.

"Caroline?" Concern rang in the soft utterance of her name.

She refocused on him, on his dear face with its classical, strong lines, his sensual lips always with a ready smile for her. "You've not said anything regarding them." The words sounded harsh to her own ears.

"I didn't wish to frighten you, and besides, you would have been cross with me for encroaching on your marriage vows." He left the bench. "Like I said before, it's been ten years. If he were alive, he would have returned by now."

"What exactly are you trying to say?" If her heart pounded any harder, it would fly right out of her chest. She clenched her hands in her lap to stay their shaking.

"I adore visiting you as well as helping your parents with the lighthouse."

"Yes." She nodded even though he was faced away. Not only did he bring supplies to her home on the island, but he also kept an eye on the lighthouse her father maintained. "Paul, enough flowery words. I cannot bear to have such a thing drawn out."

"I agree." He whipped around, grabbed her hands then tugged her into a standing position. "In short, I'm in love with you. I have been for years. I think it's past time for you to let Adam go." His gaze bore into hers and she desperately wanted to drown in those depths. "It pains me to see someone so vital and so beautiful wasting away by herself on this island, hoping for something that will never happen."

"There's the lighthouse. When Father goes—"

"Pish posh, Caroline. That's too great a job for a woman." Even though he said it in a respectful tone, the implications rubbed her the wrong way.

"You don't know I couldn't or that Adam—"

"I do," he blurted, holding her hands tighter. "Even if Adam would return, you already know what sort of man he is." Paul searched her face, looking for God only knew what. "I refuse to see you mistreated by a man who won't respect you. Let me love you like a real man should, give you babies. You're still young yet."

Unexpected tears stung her eyes. When she would have pulled her hands from his, he held on. "Oh, Paul." Besides her parents and the few servants who helped at the house, no one else knew of her heartache about her child except him. "I'm thirty. Surely too old to bear children."

9

"Nonsense." He tugged her closer to him, held her in a loose embrace. "You're a vital, desirable woman still." His eyes darkened with need. "You look as you did ten years ago."

Flutters tickled her lower belly. Oh, it had been such a long time since a man had flirted with her or held her in a manner that had nothing to do with support. "You're a charmer." Yet, she couldn't help but fall for his flattery.

"It's nothing but truth. That's the real reason I didn't wish to see you with Adam. I wanted you for myself."

"You didn't say anything about it." She frowned.

"I didn't know it until a few years ago." His hand at the small of her back held her steady while he cupped her cheek with the other. He stood a couple of inches taller than Adam, and she rather liked the added height. "We get on well together, your parents like me well enough, and I'm over here all the time, so there's just one thing left for me to ask."

She trembled. She'd not been this nervous when Adam asked for her hand. Back then she'd been reckless, even stupid as only a girl of twenty and thinking herself in love could be. Now, she knew better, had more experience, had come to depend on and care for the man before her.

His expression softened. There was no mistaking the love shining in his dark eyes. "If we go through the proper channels and petition the courts to have Adam declared legally dead or even initiate a divorce on the grounds of desertion, Caroline, will you marry me?"

"I... I'm not sure—" She attempted to extricate herself, but he held her fast. A shiver wracked her shoulders and she wasn't completely certain it was due all to the winter chill.

"Do you feel anything for me, beyond friendship?" His whisper skated across her cheek as he drew a gloved thumb over her bottom lip. "There are times when I've caught a look on your face that gave me such hope…"

Why lie? There was simply no need for it. She sighed and went so far as to rest both her palms on his chest. "Yes, I will admit I've often wondered what it would be like to have you with me for longer than a few hours at a time."

"Any woman could say that." He pressed a gentle kiss to the corner of her mouth. That tiny action warmed her blood and made her forget about the cold. "I'm asking, from a man to a woman, how do you feel about me?"

"I…" Her words trailed off as she gazed into his eyes. It was as if she stood on the edge of a great precipice, about to fall off, and all she knew was Paul would be there to catch her before anything horrible could occur. Caroline bowed her head. "I am tired of living a lonely existence and hoping for what's little more than a dream." She played with a button on his coat. "But—"

Paul lifted her chin then tilted her head back. She had no choice except to stare into his face. "Perhaps this will sway your decision." He lowered his head and claimed her lips in the first proper kiss she'd had in nearly ten years.

She gasped, but when he cradled the back of her head and fit her more snuggly against the hard wall of his body, she sighed and relaxed. Oh, it was just as wonderful as she'd thought it would be! The firm pressure from his mouth against hers invoked heat in her veins. If it weren't for their heavy, outer clothing, would she be able to feel the evidence of his arousal for her? The knowledge that the length of her body mirrored his sent tremors between her thighs. She clenched them in an effort to prolong the exquisite sensations.

"Oh my." Caroline pulled slightly away and held his gaze. "I knew it would be like this between us, but I'd never hoped to experience it." Fearful that he'd change his mind, she looped her hands around his neck then tugged him down until their lips met again, this time in frenzied need. Their tongues dueled, thrusting back and forth while she tried to wrap herself around him. Why had she not encouraged his kiss before now?

"You consume my thoughts." Paul groaned. He slipped his hands beneath her cloak then slid them up her body.

She shivered, wishing he wasn't wearing gloves or that they weren't clad with so many clothes between them. Still, when he cupped her breasts and brushed his thumbs over her nipples, the buds hardening regardless of all the layers. Heat ignited along her skin. She arched into his hold with a moan of her own. Ten years had been too long a time to remain celibate.

All too soon, he released her. His breathing was harsh and labored, the expelled air crystalizing in the cold. He looked at her with a rakish grin. "Can I consider your enthusiastic response as an answer in the affirmative?"

"Yes." She didn't care that warmth blazed in her cheeks or that she probably looked as if she could eat him up in one gulp. Perhaps it was time to move forward with her life. Or else lust had run away with her. "Will you accompany me to the mainland at the first opportunity? We'll consult my father's man of business, unless you can recommend someone better?"

"Absolutely." He squeezed her hands. "Whatever you need, I'll supply it." He brought one of her hands to his lips and placed a kiss upon her gloved knuckles. "You have made me the happiest of men, Caroline." Then he offered her his arm. "Shall I escort you back to the house?"

She nodded and the thought of Adam and what he'd taught her regarding sex and bedsport came to mind once more. *Oh bother*. She bent and retrieved the dropped letter. Her heart trembled. How wonderful and exciting all at once to be on the verge of beginning a new chapter in her life, but would Paul be able to satisfy her in the way only Adam had? "I hope the courts don't linger upon their decision."

Surely they'd be mindful of what she'd already endured. After all, ten years was a long time to wait to have a man by her side again.

 **Chapter Two**

Mid-January 1813
Portsmouth, New Hampshire

Captain Adam Montmorency heaved a sigh as he came upon the inn. On the wooden sign hanging over the door, the words "The Red Pony" met his tired gaze. After being on a ship for the last six months, with no other goal except to return to his home shores, being so close yet so far from that goal tightened his chest.

Now, if only he could remember what had occurred in his life beyond the sketchy patches of memory that flashed back into being here and there.

He pushed open the door and the rays of the setting afternoon sun slanted inside, cutting the dirt-stained floor with a puddle of yellow light, which was abruptly stifled when that same door closed behind him. Immediately, the warmth from the large fireplace at the far end of the common room enveloped him. The hearty scents of roasted meats teased his nose. Ribald joking and congenial conversation flowed around him as he made his way to a scarred, oak bar.

"Help ye with somethin'?" A burly man behind the counter placed a pint of ale in front of another patron. "Need a pint, a room, a woman to help take away the winter's chill?" A smirk slid across the man's pockmarked face and revealed a missing tooth in the front of his mouth.

"A room is all, thank you." Adam paused. "And perhaps a private bath if available." His stomach rumbled. "And a meal."

The other man nodded. "We have one room left but plenty of ale and food."

Adam sent a glance around the common room. Sea-hardened fishermen mixed with merchantmen, but in one corner a handful of British navy men clustered. Odd, that. It wasn't long ago that England's forces had been beaten off by New Hampshire folks. Why, then, were they here? They kept much to themselves, not that the rest of the men gave them much notice anyway. *Bastards. If I ever engage another damn piece of British shit it'll be too soon.*

"You let trash like that into this establishment?" he asked in a low voice.

"Their coin spends same as yours, I except." The barkeep kept his answers to a whisper. "Thanks to this God damn war, we're seeing their ilk more and more through the District of Maine's shores. Figure trouble's gonna brew up again soon. Getting supplies in is harder than ever. Hurtin' honest businessmen around these parts."

"Aye." Adam gave a quick nod. "Thank goodness for smugglers." Of which he was one, or he had been not long ago.

"Smugglers." The barkeep spit on the floor. "They're worse than the British, for they ain't got no loyalties 'cept coin."

"Can you blame them?" When he would have slammed a fist down on the countertop, he stilled it at the last moment. "Twelve shillings for the lot of services."

"Shillings? Is this not America?" Though he'd been born an Englishman, circumstances over the years had him enthusiastically adopting America as his new country. Adam dug into an interior pocket. He withdrew a few pieces of paper currency. "This should cover it." He offered it to the other man.

The barkeep shook his head. "No reminder notes." He shoved the papers back. "Not recognized here these days by most. Acceptable payments are English currency only. More stable. Though if it were up to me, I'd take both." He cast a glance to the grouping of British navy men who did nothing more harmful than drink and converse. "Bunch of dubbers."

"Bastards." Adam unbuckled a worn leather satchel hidden beneath the greatcoat. He plunged a hand in, closed his fist over a cold coin then withdrew it and flipped the blunt to the barkeep. A flash of gold in lamplight caught his eye before the other man caught it.

"A guinea?" He held up the coin then just as quickly it disappeared into a sleeve. "Too much."

Adam shrugged. "Consider the extra in good faith I'll return to your establishment." Not for worlds would he let on his satchel contained many more guineas as well as other various treasures he'd collected during his most recent travels. Some were thieved off any British navy man he'd come across since he'd escaped the last stinking prison they'd thrown him into. "It's well worth my appreciation to be home."

"You from around here then?" The other man rummaged in a pocket on his stained apron then brought forth an iron key. "Room seven's yours for the night."

"Aye, in a roundabout way, through marriage you could say."

"Oh? You're friends with someone 'ere then?" Interest hung in the inquiry.

"You could say that." No sense in giving away his exact identity prematurely. He grabbed at the key as if he'd be cheated out of the luxury if he didn't hurry. "It's taken me years to return, but here I am."

"Goin' where?"

"Maybe Gull's Island. Heard there might be work." He frowned. Should he reveal who he was? "Don't know if there's anything left there though." Or even if his wife still occupied the area. If she did, would she even want anything to do with him now, so many years later?

The barkeep's gray eyebrows hit his thinning hairline. "Gull's Island, you say?" When Adam nodded, the man continued, "Not much down that way. The widow Montmorency lives there as do her parents, near the lighthouse. Got a handful of servants between them."

His chest tightened. "Oh? A widow, you say. Her husband dead?" News to him.

"Ayuh. Or assumed, I'd say. Departed nigh on ten years now. Ship went down and he never turned up."

"She's never declared her husband officially deceased?" He closed his fingers over the key so tightly that the metal bit into his palm. What better way to figure the lay of the land than indulge in gossip? All this time and Caroline had remained true? His heart lightened. It was hard to find such loyalty.

"Guess not. From what I've heard, she's always thought her husband might return someday. God knows why she'd still be hungering for him." He shrugged. "You know how women are. Romance and hope, they're full of."

Did he? Thanks to repeated blows to the head at the hands of the English navymen, his memories were scattered and shredded into bits a pieces that surfaced without any sense of regularity. He only remembered her in the vaguest sense. What little he did recall was mixed up with nightmares from his time in British custody and snatches of his travels since then. "Never remarried?"

"Nah. Can't from all accounts, since there's no proof the man died. But the she's a real looker still." The barkeep shook his head. "Only man I know of who she sees regular is Mr. Douglas. He goes out a few times a week to take supplies and such."

Adam gripped the counter with his free hand as shadowy memories danced through his mind. "Paul Douglas?" When the other man nodded, he blew out a breath. "I know of him." Of course he did. Paul used to be his closest friend in the world — until they'd argued and Adam took himself off for adventure on the sea, while Paul had decided to remain and sort out the estate left to him when his father died suddenly. Though Paul had also been born and bred on English soil, his father had holdings around the world, and the American shipping company made him a fortune twice over. No way would Paul have tossed that to the wind.

"Aye, that's him. Don't know why they haven't made a match of it. Everyone knows he's two sheets to the wind over her, though he tries to hide it." He laid an elbow on the counter. "Me and my mates got a wager goin' as to whether the man's tuppin' her on those visits. Would be a gaumy dub if he wasn't."

"I suppose he would be." Deep in his murky memories, he knew her thirst for satisfaction in bed had no equal. His heartbeat accelerated. He hated to ask the next question, but he had to know. No one, not even his damn best friend, had the right to share her bed, not while he was still very much alive. "What became of her husband?"

"That blighter?" The barkeep shrugged. "Lord only knows. Hope he ended drawn and quartered somewhere. She's better off without that culch."

What the devil did that mean? He'd been away from the Maine coast so long he'd forgotten most of the colloquial language. It could also be the old injury that had stolen his memory. He fingered the scar on his right temple. *Damn British scum.* His confusion must have shown, for the other man continued on.

18

"Man of low esteem he was. Treated her worse than a dog, I heard. Tossed her aside for the thrill of the sail shortly after they'd wed." The bigger man's gaze bore into his. "It's said he did privateer work for England 'for he got lost in a storm. Rumors too of him sailing for America too. Still, don't need more of his kind here if he does dare show his face 'round these parts again."

"Ah." Adam refrained from tracing the paperwork residing in the interior pocket of his coat.

That letter of protection, the marque from the Crown, meant safe passage for privateering, except, he'd turned against the British years ago and now remained their most wanted man for atrocities he'd committed. No doubt the paper was useless now.

In truth, he could have such a position within the American navy; however, the thought of war turned his stomach. He much preferred smuggling and blockade running, especially if it meant fleecing the British from their coin and supplies. But if there was a chance to pirate, well he wouldn't have turned it down.

Next to the marque, his most treasured possession was the act of pardon, signed by President Madison himself. Adam had promised to renounce all ties to England and give up any and all secrets he had against the same, and in return, the American government agreed to overlook all crimes he'd committed in the name of the King while in their employ against American maritime interests. And they were quite fond of what he'd brought to America's shores.

That was just how he liked it. Gladly he'd help put an end to the British maritime operations.

He'd memorized the words, for fear of forgetting them. As soon as he was able, he planned to ask for an audience with the President and talk until he was hoarse. The man had been unavailable when the pardon had been issued, and even that was on the open sea, delivered by a trusted admiral. That was where his allegiance lay — ridding the nation of the British threat. Ruling by intimidation and might was no longer the only way, though for all accounts, it would seem there was a faction here who weren't going down without a fight.

Realizing he owed the man a response, he nodded. "Supporters of the British need to be run out of town, tarred and feathered preferably."

"That they do. 'Cept, there's rumors about regarding Mr. Montmorency."

"Oh?"

"Aye. There's talk that says he's got a bounty on his head, wanted by the highest British officials, so he musta done somethin' to piss 'em off right good. Mayhap he's changed sides after all."

"Sounds like." Adam fought to control a smug grin. Obviously, the British navy took exception to his parting gifts.

"Well, if that's the case, it might go more favorable for 'im if 'e returns." The barkeep grinned, showing off another gap in his teeth. "If you're fixin' to visit Gull's Island, ye'll need a ferryman and a guide up to the Scoundrel's Trespass."

He flinched. His pulse rushed in his ears. That used to be the name of his privateering vessel — until the damn British plucked him out of the sea following a battle. He never saw any of his crew or the ship again. "I beg your pardon?"

"That's what the widow named her place. Said it had significance but would never say why."

Adam reeled. Was that out of respect and homage to him, or was it for some sort of vengeance? He had no idea, since he'd never bothered to learn about Caroline as a person, aside from their mutual enjoyment of the marriage bed. He'd merely wanted the property from her dowry and the coin that came with it to finance the first part of his voyage. As for his interaction with his wife beyond bed sport, that remained a dark haze. A scrap of conversation or an angry word or two was the most he could recall. Perhaps he didn't want to though he'd had ample time recently to dredge up those recollections from the dark scramble of his brain.

He shook his head as the snatches of memory washed over him. *Am I that person still?* He had no idea about that either, since the last few years of his life had been spent as a prisoner of the British then fleeing from them. "I see." He cleared his throat. "If this man should return, I assume a contingent of men from Portsmouth would rush to the widow's aid?"

"In a heartbeat." The other man's eyes glittered. "That woman's a prime article. Real nice and gentle, always helping where needed. No task is beneath or beyond her. Many's the time she's kept the lighthouse lit when her father was away. Saved lives, that one."

"As it should be." Caroline should have such staunch support. Perhaps it had been a mistake to return to the life he'd known before the sea. If he didn't have such a hatred of the English, he could have gone to Cornwall. Didn't his family have holdings there of some sort? Even now, his brother could command the property if he'd come home from the sea himself. His chest tightened. Being around family right now would have been the ultimate comfort. *Maybe I've made the wrong choice.*

"I've got duties." The barkeep's words jarred him back to the present. He jerked his thumb in the direction of a narrow, wooden staircase near the British-occupied table. "Room's last door on the left. End of the hall. I'll have vittles brought up."

"Right." When the other man turned away to chat with another patron, Adam wound through the maze of tables and chair groupings. The old wound in his left foot throbbed and made progress painful, but finally he gained the stairs. Once he moved upward, he kept his face averted from the British men with a reminder that he needed a haircut and shave to prevent easy identification if any became too curious.

Gull's Island, District of Maine

Knots tightened in his stomach the moment Adam set foot on the small dock of Gull's Island the next day. Gray skies accompanied him, the same as yesterday, and heavy, snow-swollen clouds stacked on the horizon that promised a coming storm. He'd arrived around noon, to no fanfare and no greetings. As he strode the wooden walkway that led around the whitewashed lighthouse, he ignored the slight pain in his foot. No one stirred at the lighthouse or around the modest cottage that rested nearby.

He settled the strap of his knapsack more comfortably on his shoulder and hurried past the weathered residence as a gust of bitter wind blew into him. It clawed at his newly trimmed hair, though he couldn't bear to bow to conventional style. The length he'd tied with a bit of leather at his nape. Though he'd retained a close-trimmed beard, without the heavy mass he'd sported for the last year or so, the chill cut into his skin, but he didn't break his stride. The last thing he needed was for Caroline's father to stop him, or worse, deny him access to her. He hunched his shoulders and continued forward then stumbled to a halt when he realized the house they used to share sat a good five miles inland from his present location.

"Damnation." There wasn't much else for it except to keep walking until he arrived. This wasn't exactly how he'd hoped his homecoming would go, but it wasn't the worse day of his life either.

A little over two hours later, Adam arrived at the house. Done in the Colonial style, it featured a rather square shape with all windows on the brick, a two-story frame featuring gray-painted shutters, which were closed against the wind. Whitewashed iron balconies decorated a few of the rooms, while large brick chimneys flanked each long side. Smoke curled out of one of them.

His heel ached and his ears tingled from the cold. He couldn't feel his toes anymore in the scuffed and worn boots, but he was home. Well, at least the last home he could remember. Each footstep crunched through the snow. Soon he'd be able to prop his feet at a hearth and let the fire's warmth seep into his bones. Adam heaved a sigh when at last he touched the handle on the gray-painted front door. He pressed the metal then pushed open the wood panel.

"Hello?" His voice sounded scratchy and hoarse.

"Take your boots off and leave them in the dooryard." The sweet, feminine voice was full of warmth and… anticipation?

Still, Adam paused. What the hell was a dooryard? "Uh, pardon?"

"Leave your boots at the door then come find me." There was a definite smile in her voice now. "I'm in the kitchen. I wasn't expecting you today, but I'm glad you're here."

Was she some kind of witch? No matter. Perhaps reconciling with his wife wouldn't be so bad. As fast as he could, Adam toed off his boots then left them just inside the door once he'd closed it. A groan of pure relief escaped him. Damn, it felt good to be free of the confines of those boots. He shed his greatcoat and dumped it on top of his boots. After that, he dropped his knapsack as he sniffed the air. The aroma of just-baked bread hit his nostrils and he stifled a groan. How long had it been since he'd enjoyed the simple pleasure of fresh bread?

Not one to waste time, Adam set off through the house, thankful the dwelling didn't have many rooms or hallways. When he arrived in the kitchen, he paused in the doorway. *Caroline.* She stood with her back to him as she sliced a loaf of bread. An apron tied at her trim waist only emphasized the rounded curve of her hips. Red hair, gleaming in the light of the healthy fire nearby, held his attention while he followed the long line of the plaited tresses as they snaked down her spine, a pleasing contrast to the gray wool dress she wore.

Need slammed into him. Heat rushed through his veins. Vaguely, he remembered her as the young woman he'd wedded so long ago. Beyond that, he had no recollection, but he wanted to renew their acquaintance.

Silently, he approached her and when he came close enough, he slipped his arms around her waist then pulled her back flush to his front. She murmured something too low for him to catch. His cock swelled. It had been years since he'd known the warmth of a woman's pussy. "It's been a long time," he whispered. Adam put his lips to her nape and kissed the silky skin there. He nibbled a path to beneath her ear as a flash of memory surfaced. Hadn't she enjoyed him teasing this exact spot?

A tiny moan left her and she stretched, offering more of her neck to him. "What are you talking about?" She wrapped her arms on top of his. "I saw you yesterday. Do you not remember or could you not wait for another kiss?"

24

Anxiety had his chest tightening once more. What was she on about? He'd still been at sea yesterday, didn't pull into Portsmouth until late afternoon, and he certainly hadn't kissed her since he'd left her for the sea. Were the rumors true? Had she taken up with his friend? Then the rose scent of her hair pulled him under her spell and he thrust the troubling thoughts from his mind. "I'd remember better if I knew such a fine woman was here, waiting for me to come home."

"Come home?" The words were so soft he almost missed them.

"Yes. Don't you recognize my voice?" She'd matured during their absence, and he very much appreciated the woman she was now. He slid his hands along her ribcage, stopping just shy of cupping her breasts. Did he dare? Would she grant him the liberty after all this time?

"Your... voice? You sound so much like Paul... I thought you were he..." Her sharp intake of breath was his only warning before she spun in his arms, snatched up the knife she'd previously been slicing bread with then waved it at him. "Who are you?"

Adam jumped back just in time to avoid being nicked. "Who am I?" He frowned even as he raked his gaze along her body. Other memories of her, naked and begging, surfaced. The front of her was just as delightful as her backside. Breasts more full than they'd been when she'd been a youth had his desire soaring again, but it was her rosy lips and her eyes as blue as the patterns on English Wedgewood china that captivated his attention. "I'm your husband, and you did invite me in."

"What? I did not." Her eyes widened. Her grip on the knife never wavered. "I assumed you were Paul..."

His frown deepened. She thought he was Paul, his friend, the man who'd apparently picked up the pieces after he'd gone to sea. The man who'd moved in on a wedded woman. He couldn't wait to meet with this paragon of a man again, just for the pleasure of landing him a facer. "Of course. How silly of me to think you'd be pining for your husband." Then an unexpected ache stabbed through his chest. No one had ever been happy to see him over the years. He'd always left pain, death, broken promises or broken hearts in his wake. Why should his own wife be different? "Sorry to disappoint you."

✄❦ **Chapter Three** ❦✄

Caroline stared at the man before her. Well, gawked really. Was it truly possible this man was her husband, home after all this time? She renewed her grip on the kitchen knife as emotions swamped her. Elation that he was alive chased after shock at seeing him again after ten years, and both collided with throbbing need. Then, finally, anger welled. Hadn't she just accepted a proposal from Paul the day before? As her chest heaved and her mouth opened and closed before she shook her head.

"Adam?" *No, no, no! This can't be happening.* She'd given Paul her promise and she intended to start a new life with him. She'd laid Adam to rest in her mind. He just couldn't be standing here!

But that tiny niggle of hope deep in her chest that had never died flared suddenly to life as she continued to stare. His clothes were this side of shabby and could belong to anyone, but he'd recently been shaved and his hair was cut in the latest style. Yet, it was the stormy gray eyes that told the tale. She'd only ever seen one man with those same color eyes. Her hand trembled as she continued to look her fill. "Is it truly you?"

"In the flesh." He propped his hands on his hips while a mischievous grin curved his lips.

Where had the broad shoulders come from, the barrel chest, the muscled thighs that showed to perfection in the tight, fawn breeches? Even those were a few years out of style. The last time she'd seen him, he'd been lean and thin, almost awkward, not this work-hardened man. Tingles swept through her belly when she spied a bit of dark chest hair peeking out from the vee of his linen shirt as well as the tanned skin. Obviously, he hadn't lingered in winter-ravaged New England. Again, that little patch of hair caught her attention. The man didn't wear a cravat, damn his eyes. Wherever he hailed from, did they not follow proper dress codes? She let her gaze drift farther down his body. From the worn waistcoat of blue silk to the brown jacket a few seasons out of style, it was if he'd stepped out of the past and was no less potent as he'd been the last time she'd seen him.

"And it seems your appreciation of said flesh hasn't lessened in the time we've been apart." A smirk accompanied the statement. As that little gesture wreathed his face, the skin at the corners of his eyes crinkled, which pulled her notice to the crescent-shaped scar at his right temple to his sideburn, so white against the darker skin. "We used to be good together. Remember how we rarely spent time out of bed those first days?"

The knowing tone in his voice yanked her out of her musings even as heat and goose flesh crawled over her skin. Of course she remembered. How could she forget? Especially since those memories had kept her warm during the cold nights of winter. Their blazing passion for one another had been the only thing she'd thought fondly of from their union. Well, that and the child they'd made. "Yes, I remember." Flutters moved through her core so sharp she caught her breath. What sort of woman was she that the slightest touch from him or his whispered words could awaken that old longing?

I want Paul now. Didn't she? Hadn't she just wondered what he'd look like *sans* clothes yesterday? Hadn't she looked forward to making a life with him, the man who'd been there for her when times had been tough and her grief threatened to bury her? He was the man she deserved.

Almost as if she couldn't help it, she swept her gaze over Adam once more. Why he dressed as if his pockets were to let, she didn't know. Those first few years, he'd sent packages to her that contained naught but coins, paper money, or trinkets and treasures from his travels. Even now they rested in a cupboard in the cellar. She'd refused to use any of his largess, refused to feel beholden to a man who'd not loved her anyway. After his fifth year gone, he'd not sent her any more, which brought home the feeling he'd been killed.

"Have you nothing to say to your husband, woman?" A hint of the old command rang in his voice and it transported her immediately back to his arrogant, lordly ways when they'd first wed.

"I'm stunned." He'd been away for ten years, yet here he was, seemingly hale and hearty and apparently thinking he could take liberties wherever he pleased, as if he hadn't left her to fate, as if she'd forget his cruel words as he walked out of their house that last time. She narrowed her eyes and straightened her spine. "Why are you here?"

"Do I not live here?" He took a step toward her, and she slipped away, still brandishing the knife.

"You did. Briefly." She tacked on the last so he would know exactly how he'd left things. "You only married me for this property, remember?" She gestured around her with the knife. "When you left, you said you never loved me and hoped I'd understand that you loved the sea more, that I couldn't possibly compete with such a mistress." A sob caught in her throat. So much for hoping she'd buried those old hurts in the mists of time. The urge to tell him exactly what she thought of him, wound him with all the hurt she'd struggled with, grew strong, but she tamped it. She'd bite her tongue in two before she'd allow him access to her emotions.

Pain clouded his eyes. Adam took a step backward. "My memories are not what they should be."

"Ah, from guilt, I assume." Was that why he'd returned, he'd felt guilty and had decided to do his duty?

"No, due to injury." He touched a finger to the scar on his temple before dropping his hand. "Some are there, some are not, some stronger than others. Flashes come and go. Make me think upon them until I do remember."

A bit of her ire faded. What he said made too much sense to ignore. The scars wouldn't like. "Were you hurt in the storm that ravaged the *Scoundrel's Trespass*?" Two of the ten surviving crewmembers had given her their personal accounts, and she had no reason to doubt their tales.

"How did you know about the storm?" His eyes were wide and filled with confusion.

Dear Lord, he had no idea his ship had returned. Her stomach clenched. "Ah, your ship did eventually limp home, barely seaworthy. Only a portion of your crew survived."

"I see." He bowed his head. "I hadn't heard, and I suppose even if I had, the likelihood of my remembering it was slim." He blew out a breath. "What happened to the ship after that?"

She shrugged. "I believe they hauled it to the south side of the island. I haven't been down there in years, but the last time I was, the *Scoundrel* lay like a skeleton on the sand."

"A testament to days gone by, when life was not necessarily better but different." His eyes were haunted. "There were years when I buried thoughts deep in my mind, for they attempted to use everything a man was against him."

What did that mean? Despite her annoyance, curiosity regarding his travels overwhelmed her. Surely they'd have to be extraordinary if he stayed away so long, and he sounded so broken they couldn't be fabricated tales. Her chest tightened. If this was how her wish to see him a better person came about, she was sorry for ever uttering it. This ragged, changed man bore only a trace of who her husband used to be. "I apologize for the bad news so soon after your arrival."

"Think nothing of it." His jaw worked. He shoved a hand through his hair, leaving the locks in furrowed waves. "In answer to your question, I survived the storm. Swept overboard due to the storm surge, but it was during the battle following that I encountered trouble." He remained quiet so long she feared he'd finished. "However, I was plucked from the sea by hands on the British vessel, *Monitor*."

"They returned you to England?"

A bitter smile touched his lips. "Oh, if only it were that easy." The haunted light in his eyes grew. "No, I never made it back to England. In fact, the journey after that was quite long and extremely arduous as well as painful, both physically and mentally, even emotionally."

Yet he didn't share details of what had happened to him. She relaxed her death grip on the knife. "You're here now." But why?

"I am." The dark mask left his face. "It took me five years, but here I am."

"Why did you stay away so long?" She couldn't let the subject drop. How could she, when waiting for his return or word of his demise had made up such a large part of her life? "Obviously, the British had something to do with it, but why?"

"They did quite a bit more than capture me, in fact, but that is a story for another day." He stood stiffly three feet away from her as if he couldn't decide to run or remain.

Her heart hammered in sympathy, but his words didn't convey enough information. "Is that a lie? Perhaps you stayed away so long because you'd found comfort in another woman's arms." She hated that her voice wavered. After all, it had been ten years. Of course things had happened in both their lives. She'd changed. No doubt he had too. But how much and for how long would it last?

"Not in the last five years."

She forced a hard swallow. "Then, you broke our marriage vows before that? How long after we were wed did you last?" When she wanted to sound hard and angry, she feared her words merely rang of tears instead.

"Honestly? I don't remember." He tapped his temple with a shaking hand. "The wound leaves me with fleeting and inconsistent memories, though I'll endeavor to remember."

How convenient. Caroline stared at him with a growing frown. How much of what he said could she believe? How much did she want to? "Yet you seem to remember you're married to me and where to find me."

"I can't pick and choose what I recall." His jaw worked. "Some I choose to never remember, for those dark days would consume me and fill me with terror and hopelessness all over again." He lifted his still-haunted gaze to hers. "I doubt I'll ever be free of them. They slip through in low moments."

"I..." Really, she had no idea what to say. She didn't know what had happened to him, couldn't begin to guess. "It's such an unexpected thing, having you here, seeing you in my kitchen." Another gesture with the knife brought his attention to the blade. "There are so many questions."

"I'd much rather converse about my homecoming." A mischievous twinkle appeared in his eye, but it didn't quite banish the darker emotions. "There are things we should discuss."

Caroline spun around, suddenly unable to look upon him. Already, the heightened awareness that slid through her body had her on edge, and if she continued to talk to him, trying to understand what had happened to him, she'd lose herself—in him—in what they'd been together only in bed. That passionate side of him had always been intense. One touch, one kiss, and she'd forget the heartbreak he'd caused, the agony he'd continue to bring. "Perhaps you should come back later. I'm not quite feeling myself." Which wasn't a lie. Seeing him again threw her into the drink of comprised emotions.

"I can make you feel things beyond the ordinary," he whispered from directly behind her. She stiffened as he slipped his arms around her. "Leave off with the knife, Caroline, and let us reacquaint ourselves."

"That's not a good idea." Oh, in so many ways it was not. Yet, he didn't release her. Of course he didn't. When had he ever followed her dictates?

"Put down the knife." He brushed the bottoms of her breasts with his thumbs. "You don't wish to harm me."

A tremble danced down her spine. His nearness heightened her need, but she did put the knife on the cutting board. What would she have done with it anyway? Stab him? It was entirely possible. "Adam, please."

"Please, what? Do this?" He boldly cupped her breasts and gave them a gentle squeeze. "Have you missed me in this way, sweet Caro?" A nip to her earlobe followed the question. "Your beauty hasn't faded one whit since I married you. It's only deepened."

No one had ever called her by the nickname except him, and in the whispered baritone, with his lips forging a path down the side of her neck and his thumbs creating havoc with her tightening nipples, her resistance to his return crumbled. Desire zipped through her veins, hot and overwhelming. Her knees weakened.

With a half sob, half sigh, she turned in his arms. She raised her gaze to his while every nerve ending screamed for more of his touch. The stark hunger in those gray depths only added to her longing. "Adam, we can't. We're strangers."

"We can. We'll talk and come to know each other again." He fingered the neckline of her dress then slid his hands around to work the line of buttons at the back.

"We shouldn't…" Her words trailed away when the dress came undone and he shoved the fabric down her arms. Her breasts, though covered by her stays and shift, were exposed.

"We should." He arched a bushy eyebrow. "However, if you say the word, I'll leave you unmolested. The British may have taken many things from me, but my ability to remain a gentleman is my own."

Who was this man? For he certainly wasn't the husband she remembered. That man wouldn't have given thought to her sensibilities regarding bed sport or her wifely duty. That man would have simply thrown her onto the table and had his way, no matter that she'd enjoyed it and even encouraged him until his desire took control and swept them both away. She parted her lips, prepared to cry off then hide behind her closed bedroom door, yet she hesitated.

With a huff, she placed her palms on his chest, intending to push him away. There were too many unanswered questions. Their courtship had only lasted a few weeks before they'd married in haste. Logic told her she shouldn't make that same mistake again. For all that they remained legally man and wife, she didn't know him and certainly didn't understand the man he was now. And what of the promise she'd given Paul? "I don't think—"

Adam claimed her lips in a hard kiss. "Then don't think," he murmured when he allowed her air. "I suspect you've done more than your fair share of that over the years." Then he resumed his domination of her mouth.

She surrendered with naught but a sigh. Her traitorous body plastered itself to his hard frame and she looped her arms around his neck in an effort to anchor herself closer. His kisses held a desperate edge, an intensity she hadn't known before, and she rather enjoyed it. Each thrust of his tongue, each tangle with hers, sent her senses soaring into danger and urged her to taunt him into claiming her again. Then her mind reeled and she gasped. This embrace was much different than Paul and his courtly genteel overtures, sharing such things with Adam made her feel alive, vital, wanted in a primal way, as if she were a flame that burned bright just for this purpose. Paul, on the other hand, gave her safety and security.

Neither were bad, only different.

"I dreamed of you early on." He wrenched away enough that he could peer into her face. "Then, the nightmares came and I didn't remember for a while."

"Then perhaps now isn't the time to remember either," she whispered before she encouraged his lips to hers once more. She didn't wish for him to talk; she wanted him with all the longing and hoping she'd had pent up for ten years.

Perhaps she didn't wish to remember either. For one, tiny sliver of time, she wanted to throw her cares and concerns to the side and merely live.

With a cry, he jerked away. Then just as roughly, he took the neckline of her shift in hand and ripped the bodice. When she gasped, he grunted then yanked down her stays until her breasts popped free. "Yes," he murmured and buried his face between them while fondling both.

Caroline's pulse thundered. As he took an aching nipple into the warm cavern of his mouth, her breath shallowed. "Adam…" Though her brain screamed to put a stop to such foolishness, her body urged her to grant him further access. She ignored the warning. Instead, she guided his lips to the neglected nipple. "Oh, Adam." There'd be plenty of time for regret in the morning. She needed the release he gave, the rush only he could bring. A moan burst from her lips at the exquisite torture. Need throbbed through her core. The want to have him filling her multiplied. She tugged on his hair. "Where…?"

A growl left his throat. He grabbed her waist then lifted her and shuttled her across the floor. "Are any of those dishes heirlooms?" Strain graveled his voice as he jerked his chin toward the sturdy oak table.

"No. Why?" Her teeth jarred together when he deposited her rear on the tabletop. She flinched as he swept the everyday plates and mugs she'd set out earlier off the surface. The crockery crashed to the floor and broke into several pieces.

"This is as good a bed as any."

She gawked while he fumbled at the buttons on his breeches. When the flap fell open, he shoved the fabric down. His cock sprang free and the proud, rampant length jutted outward from a nest of black curls. "You mean to do this here?" On the table her father had built from a tree he'd cut on the property? The table she ate upon every day and would forever recall what they'd done on it?

"Why not? It's sturdy enough." The wicked grin he shot her held some of the old edge about it. "I rather doubt we'd make it upstairs in time." He urged her backward on the wooden surface. Her legs naturally parted, and he shoved up her skirting until she lay fully exposed to him.

The cool air against her opened folds sent tremors into her core. "That is indeed a sight for sore eyes."

Caroline gave into the shiver that coursed down her spine. How decadent to be on display before him, a virtual stranger, her husband. It made her feel desirable again, needed and more alive than she'd been in a long time. "The maid could come—"

"Let her watch." Adam leaned over her and his cockhead kissed her already wet opening. "I want this more than you need privacy."

And there was a glimpse of the old Adam, but she didn't care as the haze of lust and passion fell over her. She reached for him, fisted a hand in his shirt, and reeled him in closer. "You know how I like it." God, she hoped that wasn't something lost to his faulty memory.

"Indeed." He moved between her splayed thighs, encouraged her legs around his waist then with one flex of his hips, he penetrated her and buried himself to the hilt.

A swift gasp left her on the heels of pain from his passage. "It has been a long time," she whispered.

"Good to know." And he pulled out then thrust in more gently the second pass. "No doubt we'll adjust to each other in short order."

"Yes." She briefly closed her eyes on the heel of a moan as he moved. Sensations swamped her as she acclimated to the feel of him, the experience of having a man's member deep in her passage, of being so close to this man who'd been absent from her life so long. "Dear Lord." Tears misted her eyes. He was so thick, so satisfying. Her inner walls convulsed around him. It was almost too much, too quickly. And different. The old Adam would not have cared if she'd felt pain or discomfort. "I'd forgotten…"

"Hush." Adam pulled out and the returning invasion was no less forceful than his initial thrust had been. He braced a hand on the tabletop and dug the fingers of his free hand into her hip. "It'll go fast. Been awhile."

"I don't care." And she didn't. She merely wanted the act, to abandon herself in the pleasure of it all. "Make me fly like you used to." For once, she didn't want to think, she merely wished to be selfish.

He moved in earnest then and drove into her as if she was the last woman on earth and he the last man. The table legs knocked and squealed along the floor. Each pass, the scrape of his coarse hair and the brush of his member put friction on her swollen button. Every push filled her beyond what she'd thought possible. Had it always been so wondrous with him? Bands of pleasant pressure built and quickly stacked inside her.

Caroline gripped locked her ankles tighter at the small of his back. She levered upward in order to caress a hand up the powerful expanse of his thigh before his next thrust laid her flat again. She intended to do so much more than let him lay claim to her, but once more her body betrayed her. Before she was ready, warning flutters moved through her core. Then she came undone as waves of release rippled over her.

The cry that left her throat was a keening sort. She couldn't decide if it was disappointment the rushed coupling had ended or for the wash of emotions overwhelming her. "Adam!" His next thrust sent him hurtling into the void with her, and she sucked in a breath while another band of pleasure caught her in its pull.

He continued to drive. As the hot jet of seed spilled, he ground his hips into hers. Then, finally, he collapsed onto her and she wrapped her arms around him and didn't release her ankles. She clung to him as she'd longed to do for so many years. His ragged breathing steamed her ear. "Thank you."

Caroline froze. The frantic beat of her heart kept time for a few seconds. Never had he said such a thing. Usually, once the deed was concluded, he'd either roll off and succumb to sleep or he'd leave their bed for other pursuits. She brushed her fingers through his hair. He stiffened when she glanced over the scar. Before she could change her mind, she pressed her lips to the spot. "You're welcome."

She closed her eyes and basked in the brief calm. For the moment, her husband was home. She'd decide what to do about that once she could breathe properly and think clearly again.

❧ Chapter Four ❧

Adam heaved a shuddering sigh as he pulled away from the tangle of Caroline's limbs. His pulse galloped through his veins. What the hell sort of man was he that he'd instigated relations with this woman mere minutes after entering her home? As quickly as he could, he stuffed his now flaccid cock into his breeches then did up the buttons. One thing he knew for sure: the woman before him gave as good as she got. Given the chance, how would she act if they'd been in a proper bed without clothing in the way? Heat clawed at him. His wife was a mystery he'd enjoy solving—providing she didn't throw him out after this.

He couldn't resist staring at her. Caroline still lay on the table with her skirts rucked up around her waist, her lush breasts spilling out of her bodice and a rosy flush over her chest and neck. The same high color blazed in her cheeks while the red sweep of her lashes presented half-moons on her cheeks as her eyes remained closed. Never had there been a more beautiful sight, and not wholly because it had been a long time indeed since he'd been with a woman.

All too soon she stirred. Her eyes popped open and she zeroed in on him as she struggled into a seated position. Horror clouded her blue gaze. "What have I done?"

How well did he know that feeling? He tucked his shirttail into his breeches as he backed away another few steps. "The passion of the moment is heady and leads to haste and perhaps regret." A flash of memory came over him, of Caroline laid out over his knees while he'd spanked her, not into obedience, but in order to stoke her fiery temper and passion before they'd succumbed to lovemaking. He glanced at her with speculation. Would she still enjoy such a thing?

"But, my life cannot lapse into the past." She hopped off the table then spent a few moments righting her clothing. "We shouldn't have indulged."

Perhaps she would not. "Little point in shame now." He rubbed a hand along his jaw. "Caroline, regardless of what we've just done," or what he hoped they could still do, "we do need to converse on a few things."

She didn't answer. Instead, she turned her attention to the wreck of the crockery on the floor. "I need to tidy these up before—"

The arrival of another woman interrupted her excuse. "Ma'am, is there trouble in here?"

"No, no trouble, just had a clumsy moment and dropped the dishes. It was such a surprise…" A weak excuse to be certain, and even more so made in Caroline's breathless voice, but the maid seemed to believe the explanation.

"I wasn't aware you had company." The woman gawked at him with wariness. "Do you require tea?"

"No, thank you, Jane. We were merely talking."

"Ah." The tone of that little word proclaimed her disbelief.

Adam shifted his attention to the other woman. "Hello." Who the devil was she? The damn woman looked blasted familiar. He narrowed his eyes as he wracked his fractured memories until something useful appeared. "Mrs. Montmorency's maid?" When the petite woman nodded and wrung her hands in the wrinkled, white apron, he continued, "Capital timing. I'm Captain Montmorency, Caroline's husband."

A gasp escaped the younger woman. Her jaw sagged as she stared at him with shock then fear on her face. "We thought you were dead, but here you are, in the flesh." Her rounded gaze flitted between him and Caroline, who'd stacked several large pieces of broken dishes. "You've returned. Glory be." Except, her fearful expression suggested anything but. What had the woman witnessed him do and how could he change her opinion? Even more startling, why did he want to? "Shall I go for your father or ready the guest room, ma'am?"

"I... I'm not sure." Though Caroline's responses were softly worded, she did a remarkable job at not giving away her confusion, but he caught her biting her thumbnail—a classic tell she had when she couldn't muddle through a problem. "I cannot imagine what my father will say, or even Paul." She raised her gaze to Adam. A wash of tears shimmered in her eyes. "Dear Lord, Paul. He'll never understand and will be so hurt."

Why should Paul be hurt? Adam frowned. What he and Caroline had shared wasn't illegal, and they were married besides. None of it concerned his friend beyond natural curiosity. Unless the barkeep's rumors were true and his friend wanted Caro for himself. "Where is Paul, by the by?"

"Probably on his estate. Perhaps at his shipping offices. I really have no idea." Caroline stood and brushed off her hands. Her eyes were wild. A flush stained her cheeks. "Jane, will you please see to this mess? I need to... Oh, dear God, living arrangements." The flush faded and left her face ghostly white while the muscles in her throat worked with a hard swallow. She studiously avoided his gaze. "I need to be alone. I have to get away." With that, she fled the area.

Left with only Jane as company, Adam frowned. "Should I go after her?"

The maid shrugged. "I couldn't begin to say, Captain."

"Does she do this often?"

"Only when she's upset." She knelt on the floor near the broken dishes. "Or if she's troubled."

How often was she upset and why? "I see." Even though he did not. He scratched at the stubble on his chin. "Does she have a particular place she occupies when emotions are too high?"

The woman avoided looking at him. "No doubt you'll find her in her garden. That's where she goes until she calms, no matter the weather."

"Very well." Not that he had a clue where to locate the area. "Thank you."

Jane finally lifted her head. Her thin lips formed an "o" of surprise. "You're welcome, Captain."

Had he really been such an ogre before that even the niceties escaped him? With a frown, he returned to the hall then donned his boots, greatcoat, and battered tricorne hat. All in all, the homecoming wasn't the worst reception he'd expected.

It wasn't difficult to find her garden after all. Perhaps fifty feet from the house, it backed a few stands of fir trees. He followed a snow-covered walkway that wound through bare shrubbery and a few evergreen bushes. In a clear section, amidst squares of white-blanketed vegetation and raised flower beds, Caroline sat on a wrought iron bench, her focus far away as she gazed into the distance.

"Caroline?" He kept his voice low and steady, as if trying to earn the trust of a skittish animal. The last thing he wanted was her flight again.

She jerked her head up. Tears streaked her face. "Go away, Adam. This is my private retreat. No one bothers me here."

Yet, someone had, and recently. He glanced at the boot prints in the snow that wandered all about the immediate area—boots large enough for a man. Along with them were smaller prints—no doubt hers—and not far away, the footsteps nearly joined, close enough to indicate there might have been an embrace. His chest tightened and jealousy gripped him, but he shoved it away. There was no proof, and what did he expect? It had been ten years.

"Be that as it may, you and I still have business to attend." He paused five feet away from her, not wishing to crowd or become overbearing. "Perhaps you should explain your sudden descent into sixes and sevens."

"I'd rather not." She fumbled at her throat then latched onto a silver chain and wrapped her hand around a pendant he'd not noticed when he'd ravaged her in the kitchen.

"I'll not apologize for what we did," he began as he clasped his hands behind his back.

"Why would you? I wanted that coupling just as much as you." Briefly, she met his gaze before focusing on the pine trees. Then she heaved a sigh and her breath crystalized in the chilly air. "Apparently, I lost my mind."

As if losing one's mind is an excuse for anything. Unbidden, images of broken and beaten men—fellow prisoners—flitted through his mind's eye. Their dying screams still echoed in his ears. He shook his to banish them. "It's nothing to make jest of, especially if it truly did happen to someone you know."

She trained her attention back on him. Questions shadowed her blue eyes. "I apologize for my insensitivity."

"It's all right." Adam couldn't fault her for not knowing the mind-numbing, soul-sucking torture he'd received at the hands of the British navy. The likelihood of ever being free of those nightmares was slim. He shook his head in an effort to not only forget, but also to steer the conversation into a different direction. "What is your pendant?" Perhaps if he introduced a banal topic, he and Caroline could find common ground. "Does it have special meaning?" It seemed familiar, but then, so did many things since arriving here.

A bitter laugh left her throat. She opened her hand. A piece of blue-green glass, shaped into an irregular oval, rested within a delicate filigree of silver. "You tell me. Did it have special meaning when you gave it to me?"

Adam narrowed his eyes as he advanced another few steps. "Sea glass?" He'd seen the smooth jewels of the sea many times. In the right light, they sparkled and glowed brighter than any fine bauble. When she nodded, he closed the distance then took the pendant in hand. "I gave you this."

"Yes. On our wedding day." When she caught his gaze, hers was as hard as the pendant. "In lieu of a ring. Do you remember that?"

A knot formed in his stomach. "Vaguely." He didn't recollect why he hadn't given her a ring, but there were glimmers of him tossing a jewelry box her way during their wedding breakfast. Heat rose up the back of his neck. Good God, he hadn't even put it around her neck. "I apologize for my treatment."

She waved a hand. "It no longer matters."

"It does." He gingerly smoothed his thumb over the cold surface. "Obviously, it does if you still wear the trinket." He marveled over the fact that she had kept it. "Caroline, *why* do you still wear it?"

45

"It's none of your concern." She pulled away from his reach and the necklace fell against her chest with a thump.

"I'll wager it is, since I'm here now and you're wearing my pendant." It was quite the puzzle, but it left him feeling more hopeful than he had in a long time. He gestured to the empty portion of bench beside her. "May I?"

A half-shrug lifted her shoulder. "As if I could stop you."

At the last second, he stifled a sigh of annoyance. "If I could take back my ill treatment of you, I would. I hardly remember those times, and even if I did, I rather doubt I'd want to." Adam took the seat beside her. A sliver of hope stabbed his heart when she didn't shy away. "The fate I was dealt while I've been away has made me a different man." He shook his head. "I don't know if it's a better man, but I'm changed from the one you married. However, we are *still* legally wed."

"Don't you think I'm well aware of that fact?" Her words, though low, were couched with heavy emotion he couldn't identify. When she turned toward him, her knee knocked against his. A jolt raced up his leg. "How am I supposed to conduct my life now?" Anxiety lined her face. "For ten years I'd been left to fend for myself while you chased adventure."

He expected anger, but the tinge of jealousy in her voice brought him up short. Had she wished she'd gone on the sail with him? Never had he thought to ask. He'd merely assumed she'd prefer to stay on land, tending house and hearth. But then, that was his mistake to make such an assumption about her or any woman. "I'll admit, a life on the sea is the most freeing experience a man can have, but my adventuring, as you call it, was brought up short five years into the stint."

46

"Yet you had five years living with wild abandon, not caring about anything you left behind. Not caring about *who* you left behind. I could have filed for divorce when you'd stay away after that time."

"But you didn't." Why?

"No." A wash of tears shimmered in her eyes, magnifying the blue, but she didn't drop her gaze from his. If anything, she notched her chin up slightly in defiance.

"Caro—"

A strangled sob escaped her. "I wed you with all the hope and enthusiasm a young woman could have. Such naive dreams, I now see. I'd hoped you'd come home, wished you would, so we could attempt to repair our broken relationship. So you could once more set me awash in passion." Her chin quivered. "I stupidly thought you might grow to love me more than you loved the sea and your ship."

"That's why you continued to wear the necklace?" When she nodded, the blood froze in his veins. "Did you love me?"

Her gaze wavered then dropped to the trampled ground. "I was young. I thought infatuation—desire or even the feelings of release—were love." She drew her cloak tighter around her. "I suppose I was flattered you'd taken notice of me at all… until I came to realize when you sailed away that my dowry to fund your voyage meant more than having a mate."

Sour bile hit the back of his throat. God damn, why did no one simply put a bullet through his head? "Yet, we had heat in common." He could barely get the words past his tight throat.

"We did. Apparently still do." She sighed, but he caught the blush on her cheeks. "How silly that was the only way we could relate or communicate, but then, if it wasn't flattery to try and make me spread my legs, you didn't indulge in it." Another laugh left her throat, this one wry. "We had very little time together, and quite frankly, I was curious about the marriage bed more than I was cautious."

The enthusiasm she'd brought to their couplings had been as fiery as her hair. Her thirst experience the pleasure brought on by spanking had matched his own. He'd be the first to admit he hadn't been thinking all that clearly during those days. With the excitement of the sail in his blood, visions of the fortune he'd make, and a brand new marque letter in his pocket from his last privateering engagement from England and permission to pirate against France, Spain and even America, he'd been arrogant and too proud. Most decidedly cocky and headstrong. Nothing could defy him or defeat him all those years ago. His lips twisted with bitter remembrance. The British made sure to beat that out of him until he eventually broke.

Adam's chest tightened. *God, I must have been such a bastard.* "I don't know what to say."

"Why say anything?" She launched from the bench in favor of walking the paths between the winter-dead plants. "That was a long time ago. It's not our life anymore."

"Except, part of it is." He had no choice except to follow her. They couldn't very well yell across the garden space. "We're still wed." The cold made the old ache in his heel worse, but he'd rather die than let on to her he was less than strong.

"Are we, Adam?" She caught him by surprise as she whirled around so fast her skirts flared around her ankles. "Are we really? Perhaps we are in the eyes of the law, but you've been gone for ten years. I'd already buried you mentally. I'd made my peace with your absence, and now here you are—a ghost from my past."

"I'm here now." Yet with his very presence in her life, he was once more causing her turmoil. Mayhap it would be better for him to leave and let her be free at last.

"You weren't there when I needed you the most." Her shoulders sagged. "What were you doing when my grief nearly swallowed me whole?"

"Damnation, woman, I was being tortured and wishing for death!" He held up a hand when her eyes grew large at his outburst. "I find myself needing to apologize yet again. I didn't wish for you to grieve for me." Had she cared for him that much? "I had intended to return in a few years, with a fortune and tales to entertain you."

Her jaw worked as if she searched for words. "At first I did mourn for you, for…" Caroline fisted her hands in the folds of her cloak as her words drifted away. "If it wasn't for Paul's friendship, I don't know what I'd have done. He's always been there for me when I need him."

Another swift stab of jealousy speared his gut. Just what exactly was Paul to her? Her pussy had been to tight and tried, so his friend hadn't laid with her. Was he courting Caro now? "And then?" Something about her tearful countenance and wobbly voice had him on edge. There was something she wasn't telling him.

"I discovered I was with child two months after you'd left."

"What?" Shock ricocheted through him. There was a child from their union? "A boy or a girl? Will you allow me to meet him or her?" He had a child. *I'm a father.* Warmth slid through his chest. Never did he think he'd live that particular dream.

"A boy." Her chin wobbled and she blinked back another round of tears. "Come with me." She took off down another pathway. Snow clung to the hem of her skirts and cloak.

Adam followed, trying to match her quick, efficient pace, but soon gave up the effort. His joints just weren't accustomed to the freedom of movement being on land gave him. It would take some time to work out the kinks and stretch them into the proper workings he'd once enjoyed. Finally, she came to rest at the back of the garden, near the tree line. "What are you doing?"

She'd knelt on the ground then dusted off the thin blanket of snow from an object before her. "Introducing you to your son."

"I don't understand." He frowned as he approached her. Then, when he peered over her shoulder at a brass plaque set into the earth, the brief joy he'd known shattered and broke into a million shards. Aloud, he read, "Here lies Jonah Adam Montmorency, aged six months. Beloved son of Captain and Caroline Montmorency. Coo to the angels, my love. We shall see you again one day."

His heart squeezed. For years he'd perfected the art of hiding his emotions in an effort not to appear weak or give the enemy a foothold. Showing emotion meant a man could be broken, so he'd taught himself simply not to feel anything deeply. But this... He clenched his teeth so hard pain lanced up his jaw into his temple. Outwardly, no one, not even Caroline, would know this affected him. As much as they were wed, they were very much strangers, and she might use his grief against him.

He'd had a son, who'd died. "You named him after your father."

"Yes, and you as well." She kept her gaze focused on that tiny name plate. Beads of melted snow marred the shiny surface. "I had such high hopes for him; he was a happy infant."

"What happened?" He could barely force the words out of his constricting throat.

"The doctor told me it was failure to thrive, that it sometimes happened to babies, boys especially." Caroline rose to her feet but kept her head bowed. "I was weak for a while after he was born. And he had trouble nursing." She shook her head. "Mother wanted to call for a wet nurse, but I refused. I just couldn't have a strange woman providing my baby what I should be able to give." Finally, she raised her tear-streaked face to his. "No matter what I did, he'd only eat sparingly."

He had no knowledge on the care or upbringing of children. When he reached for her, she shied away. "I'm so sorry."

"It was a long time ago." She took a shuddering breath then pulled herself together—or retreated into herself. Perhaps she, too, had learned how to guard her heart and emotions. "I had him for six months, held him and loved him the best I knew how. Then I had to give him back to God."

"You have the advantage on me, for I never met the lad." He wished he'd had the opportunity, but he hadn't known of the pregnancy. And what would he have done even if he had? Back then, he probably wouldn't have cared, for the life he'd been living was exponentially more exciting than anything domestication could give him.

I was a bloody fool.

"That was the choice you made. Nothing can change it." Caroline wiped at the moisture on her cheeks. "Just like nothing will ever take away the feeling that I somehow could have prevented his death. It took a few years, but finally Paul convinced me I should begin to live again, for me, in honor of the boy. I'll always hold Jonah in my heart."

"Just how big a part of your life is my dear friend Paul?" Adam couldn't help the sarcasm, but he was bloody tired of hearing about how heroic his friend had been to *his* wife.

"I depend on him for many things. He's one of my dearest friends, perhaps more." Her bowed head and quiet voice shot more pain through him than the crack of the whip across his back.

"Ah." So that's how the wind blew, eh? He'd need to have a talk with Paul at the first opportunity. He softly cursed. And say what? Ask the man what his intentions were toward *his* wife? Not bloody likely.

"Like I said, you've been gone ten years and I waited for you for many of those years. Recently, I'd decided it was time to let you go." Another shuddering breath followed. "After all, one must live regardless of what happens."

There was no greater truth than that. He'd come to the same decision even in the worst of the torture. "It seems we've both lived two lifetimes since we've been separated." This time when he put out a hand, she let him grip her cold fingers. She hadn't worn gloves in her haste to flee. "I am here now. Nothing can replace those lost years or what occurred during them, I know that. But you and I can begin again." Is that what he truly wanted above all things—a wife, a marriage, perhaps a family?

"Ha!" Caroline shook her head so violently the hood of her cloak fell down. She yanked her hand free. The grief fled from her expression, replaced by another wash of righteous anger. "Are we supposed to pick up where we left off then? Where was that, exactly? Will you order me about, use me as your plaything while you spend your coin on God knows what? And will this homecoming only be for a short while until the wanderlust strikes again?"

He had no answer for her, nor did he have the fortitude to counter or comfort the angst she exhibited. He just couldn't, especially not when he didn't know how to show any of that himself. Yet, he had no accounting for the deep lounging that filled his soul, a yearning for something he had no idea he'd wanted until he set foot in the District of Maine the day before.

"I can guarantee you that I have no desire for the sea any longer." Oh, to be sure, he could never live so far inland that the roar of the waves and the pound of the surf couldn't be heard. He'd always need to see the water and taste the salty spray on his lips, but to tackle the ocean in a captain's capacity onboard a ship? That love had died a few years ago while he'd been locked in the belly of a British prison vessel. "I'm here for the duration, come what may."

"Then you're welcome to build your own house on the island, or you can take up residence on the mainland, for you will not be staying beneath my roof." There was no mistaking the determination in her statement as she stormed past him then marched along the path toward the house.

Quick anger exploded inside him. Why wasn't she willing to start over? "Madam, your facts are quite eschewed, for this island and everything on it came to me upon our marriage."

"No. That's not true. The island and house, perhaps," she flung over her shoulder. "But the lighthouse belongs to my father and will be mine upon his death. You will never have possession of that. No one will."

"You're wrong, unless he's made a special concession, and if he has, you would have told me straightaway." The victory he expected died beneath cool worry. That light was the most important piece on the island. Not for his ownership but for someone to keep it out of British hands. "Nevertheless, I will, indeed, reside beneath your roof, and I'll do so from beside you in our bed!" Damnation, he sounded like a prick, but he had nothing left to fight for. The British had seen to that.

No, that wasn't true. He'd fight for Caroline. She was the reason he was still here. Adam shook his head as he set out after her.

❧ Chapter Five ❧

Adam listened at the door to the bedroom he should be sharing with his wife. As she conversed with her maid, he ran his thumb through the course bristles of the hairbrush Caroline had thrown at his head the night before. As unobtrusively as possible, he peeked around the doorframe. She stood in front of a cheval mirror while Jane finished lacing her stays.

"I suppose this means I can do away with wearing half-mourning clothes."

"That's a good thing, ma'am," Jane returned as she finished with the stays then moved off to contemplate the interior of the clothes press. "Black, gray and even lavender don't give you the vibrancy you need, and what with your husband returning, there's no need. You must be a happy woman."

In the hall, Adam strained to hear her reply. *Was she pleased?* Aside from the incident in the kitchen yesterday, he'd argue the point.

"I agree with you about the clothing color. Still, I'd rather not have to don brighter clothes simply because *he's* here now." She stepped into her petticoat then tied it about her waist.

He rolled his eyes. Well, now he knew. He gripped the silver-backed hairbrush tighter as memories of her high spirits glimmered at the edges of his consciousness. It was good she had a backbone. She'd need it after this night.

Her maid snorted. "Begging your pardon, ma'am, but your husband is quite interesting." Jane retreated from the press with a dress of deep purple wool in her arms. "He even thanked me for cleaning up, as if it wasn't my duty, though it seemed he had no idea who I was." She shook her head. "Before, he never acknowledged my existence."

"Yes, it's exceedingly odd. He'd been solicitous toward me as well."

Had he been such an ogre before? Adam narrowed his eyes. Perhaps not knowing was a good thing. He didn't wish to be that man again, not anymore. After seeing cruelty beyond measure from the British, he wanted no part of it in himself and he'd worked hard not to be that sort of man, even if it had meant giving up the thirst for revenge.

The soft conversation in the room focused his attention back to the ladies. "They say people can change, ma'am," Jane said. "Perhaps the captain isn't who he used to be. Ten years is a long time, and no doubt his stint away made an impression."

"Perhaps. But mayhap I want something different now." Caroline's answer was so low he nearly missed it.

"You speak of Mr. Douglas." The maid's matter-of-fact tone indicated Caroline often talked of his friend.

Another swath of jealousy cut through him. He needed that particular issue cleared up as well.

"Paul has become an important part of my life, especially in recent years." A small smile lifted the corners of her lush lips. Devil take it, was his wife in love with the man? That would be unconscionable. "I had thought he and I would have a future together, but now…" She fluttered a hand. "I'm not certain what will become of him, of us."

"I can't say what's in your heart, ma'am. Matters like that are complicated things." Jane did up the short row of buttons on the back of the dress. "Shall I brush out your hair now?" She lifted a mass of Caroline's hair that had been released from its bindings already.

Adam's chest tightened to see those locks loose and flowing in shimmering waves down his wife's back. What would that vibrant mass feel like in his fingers or brushing over his bare skin? He stifled a groan. Damnation but he needed to tamp his reaction. Though he'd like nothing more than to burst in, throw Caroline onto their bed then shove into her tight, warm heat again, such a thing couldn't happen until they'd come to an understanding. He wasn't in the habit of forcing himself on women—not that he'd had to yesterday. That brought a smile to his face. She really was well-matched to him in temperament and passion.

And suddenly, he needed to be near her. Before Caroline could answer her maid, he entered the room. "No need for that, Jane. I'll see to Mrs. Montmorency's tresses this morning, thank you." He held up the silver-backed hairbrush. "I believe that's what this message from last night meant. Unless, of course, you'd like me to put it to a different use." So easily he could envision her over his knee and him applying the etched back of the brush to her tender bottom. Only this wouldn't be in cruelty, but in a torture of a whole different kind. His cock twitched in anticipation then cold dread slipped down his spine. Would laying a hand on her, even for sexual teasing, put him in the same camp as the British? Where did a man draw the line, and if he didn't, would it speak of violence and send him into a dark place?

Slowly. Go slowly.

"Adam." The word escaped her in a breathless croak. High color infused her cheeks as she glanced at the brush. "I don't need your assistance, Captain."

He took a few steps into the room. "That will be all, Jane." His tone brooked no argument. He wanted his wife all to himself and neither of them would leave the room until a new direction for them was forged.

"Very well." The maid glanced at her mistress. "Is that what you wish?"

"Yes. It's all right." The words came out barely more than a whisper. "Mrs. Abbottson should be here soon from the market. I left her a note, asking if she'd do the food for tea this afternoon. I want her to prepare some of Mr. Douglas' favorites." She shot a victorious glance at him. He narrowed his eyes. The woman expected to play on his jealousy. "See that she receives the note." When Jane hurried out past Adam, he gently closed the door. The soft click was the only sound in the room for many seconds. "What are you doing here? I thought I made my stance perfectly clear last night."

"You did, but that was in the heat of the moment and borne of many different emotions. In the cold light of day, things will be different."

"My feelings won't change."

"That may be so." He advanced into the room while feeling quite smug. She wouldn't soon forget how he made her feel, how he could play her body. "However, I have my own stance and the fact that it lies opposite yours makes little difference. Of course, it makes it all the more interesting, but we'll get to that." He couldn't help the no doubt cocky grin that curved his lips. "We are married and as such, we will come to some sort of agreement. I'd prefer not to be at odds with the woman I'm leg-shackled to."

"Ah, so that's what I am to you then? An obligation? A weight around your ankle?" She popped her hands onto her hips, which only focused his attention on them and how they'd felt when he'd held her yesterday as he'd claimed her body.

Oh, she'd be a challenge even greater than navigating a ship through a squall on an angry ocean, and one he couldn't wait to conquer. "Aye, you are." He savored the surprise that widened her eyes from his blunt surprise. "As you said yourself, we're strangers though we're wed. At this moment, we're stuck with each other by law, so unless you'd like to work with me, you're against me. Ergo, it's in your best interest to square with me."

"Or?" Her breathing shallowed the closer he came to her.

"We'll see." He tossed the hairbrush into the air then deftly caught it. If he spanked her, would it arouse her passion or fuel her anger? "I gave you your space last night, but that concession will not extend to today. I'm here for the duration, Mrs. Montmorency."

"God, you haven't lost that arrogance."

"I have not. There were times when the arrogance and the rage were the only things that kept me alive."

She thrust out her jaw. The tendons in her throat worked with a hard swallow. "In any event, you have no right to make demands. It was you who left ten years ago. It was you who chose to abandon our marriage in favor of the sea." She crossed her arms over her chest, but the swells of her breasts over the bodice sent curls of heat through his belly. "So, tell me again who is making concessions with your return."

"We both are." He rather enjoyed having her on the defensive. "Or we can call it compromise." When she darted her gaze to the door, he anticipated her flight and placed himself in her direct path. "In order for us both to live harmoniously together, we need rules and guidelines."

"Rules?" She snorted. "Since when have those applied to you?" Her eyes flashed blue fire.

"You have no idea what drives me now." If she was lucky, she never would. No one should have to fight the demons he did. And he had no right to share them. "However, rules are necessary for living in any situation." As his jaw tightened, he made a conscious effort to relax. "We may not like each other, but we can certainly respect each other."

"Don't be a bigger ass than you can help, Adam. You've never respected me. I doubt you will now." Caroline made a move to forge past him, but he captured her wrist in his free hand and stayed her flight. "Let me go." Irritation shot from the command.

"I don't think so." If she wouldn't respect *him* enough to listen to what he had to say, perhaps he needed to try a different tactic. He pulled her over to the dressing table. She fought him with every step, but he was stronger. He sat upon the crushed velvet bench, then tugged her down and arranged her so that she was draped over his knees, her top half dangling downward.

"What do you think you're doing?" Righteous indignation oozed from her words.

Adam bit back his amusement. "Gaining your undivided attention." They'd never been able to converse like civilized people out of the bedroom. So be it. If that was the only way still, he'd be certain she wouldn't forget. He held the hairbrush in his left hand and smoothed his right over her rear. The soft wool beneath his palm provided a pleasing contrast to the brush's bristles he'd touched before.

"This is ridiculous." She struggled but couldn't quite lever off his lap. Finally, she twisted and looked over her shoulder with a glare that could flay flesh from a man's bones. With her fiery hair and reddened cheeks, she could easily be mistaken for a vengeful witch. "Leave me be this instant." Her gaze fell to the brush and she licked her lips. Raw need lingered in her eyes.

Adam fought off a grin. She remembered too. What was more, she wanted his touch as much as she had back then. "Not until I've had my say and you listen." Before he could change his mind, he took the brush in his right hand then lightly smacked her bum with the flat back. Her gasp sounded louder than the connection of the brush. "Are you willing to give me a few moments of your time?"

"You intend to hit me, beat me?" The words were small and tinged with fear.

His chest squeezed. God, what a prick he must have been. Renewed disgust for himself, his situation, his past rolled through him. He shoved it away to deal with at a later time—when he allowed everything else bubbling inside out. "No." The word was raw and seemingly ripped from his throat. "No longer do I raise a hand against anyone in anger or hate." At least, he tried. Where the British were concerned, it was a near impossible endeavor.

"Then what—?"

"Getting through to you the only way I know how, the only way you and I are accustomed to communicating, the only way you're craving."

"You wouldn't." Gone was the fear. In its place was excitement.

"I will indeed, unless you can promise you've never thought about me doing this again." When she remained silent, Adam yanked up her skirting and bunched it at her waist. The white globes of her arse beckoned. He rested the silver-backed brush against one smooth cheek. Was it cool to the touch? Did the anticipation excite her? "Will you hear me?"

"Yes." She braced herself on the floor with her hands. "But the second you're finished I'm lea—"

He cut her off with a swift stroke of the brush against her skin. Faint redness marred the ivory beauty of her arse cheek. "What was that, wife?"

"I said I'll leave once you're done." Her voice was more breathless than it had been before.

Adam shifted to accommodate his hardening cock. "Then I haven't properly convinced you that I'm in earnest." Again, he brought the back of the brush down on her pretty rear, this time with a bit more force. The resulting *smack* echoed in the immediate silence. "I wish to make amends, Caro. With you, with everyone who I wronged all those years ago."

"Yet you come in here acting the lord of the manor and you think deference will follow?"

Perhaps he had been high-handed in his approach. She brought out so many raw emotions in him, he could only react. "Caro, please listen to me. I don't wish to impose my will on you if you have other plans." He hated the plea in his voice but couldn't recall it.

"Very well." Her words sounded small but strong. "I agree to listen. What do you want of me?"

"I want to see if we can live together as man and wife again." He gave her another firm spank, this time to the other cheek. Now both were faintly pink. "If not as friends, then as respected acquaintances."

"Will we live together then?" Her panting breath gave away her need.

His desire roared to life in a hot wave that pounded in his temples. "We are husband and wife. It's expected."

"You will not share my bed."

"Oh, I think I will." This time, instead of one stroke, he delivered a series of short connections, being sure to cover both buttocks with attention. "I am your husband, for better or for worse. My place is by your side whether you wish it or not, both in bed or out." No matter what, he wanted her.

Something suspiciously sounding like a moan escaped her. He couldn't hold back his grin. "We will not indulge in relations though."

"You're right." His next spank was firmer than the others, and it hit soundly in the middle of the globe. Then he followed it quickly with a matching one to the other buttock. Her arse glowed a healthy rose, and he'd never seen a more appealing sight. That was his mark on her flesh and she'd remember. "I can honestly promise I will not molest you in a carnal way again unless you give me permission. If we come together, it will be at your command and your desire. You'll need to make it abundantly clear that's what you want."

Keeping his word would be torture, especially since his prick was already so erect he'd be surprised if he didn't spend in his trousers. Yet, it was the only way they could dedicate attention to their relationship. There had to be more between them than heat. If not... He shook his head in an effort to force back the thoughts. If not it would be a long life indeed when all he wanted since his return was a deep connection with someone—with her.

"Adam..." Caroline's thighs parted. She squirmed on his lap, which only sent his cock into higher realms of urgency. "I need—" She bit off the words. Did she perhaps realize her weakness?

That glimpse of pink, wet flesh fringed with red curls had him wanting to abandon his new rule, but he firmly kept himself in check. "I refuse to have you state later I manipulated you."

"I agree, and you're correct. I wanted this as much as you." She twisted around and glanced at him from over her shoulder. Desire shadowed her eyes. He ignored that too. "Are you quite finished with my," she swallowed hard but her gaze remained firm, challenging even, "persuasion, husband?"

"Are we of an accord?" He pushed the words out through a tight throat. God, how was it she could goad and affect him so quickly?

"Then we're essentially playing at housekeeping?"

"Yes." He smoothed the back of brush over her rosy arse cheeks and was rewarded by a full body shiver from her. "You will tell your parents and whoever else asks that your husband has come home at long last and you're thrilled about the development."

"And if I don't?" She caught his gaze. Hers twinkled with deviltry.

Adam delivered two sharp smacks with a tad more force than he had with the others. Her skin went from rosy to red. Caroline closed her eyes. She didn't try to hide her moan this time. Her acceptance of his spanking ramped his need. He took deep, measured breaths to stave off the inevitable. "Then all hopes of coitus, even if you beg, are off the table. Do you understand?"

"Yes." The damn woman ground her hips against his leg, no doubt to encourage friction on her button. He put a staying hand on her back. If he couldn't come, and he wouldn't due to his freshly laid down rules, neither could she, unless she asked. "Oh no you don't." He captured her hand when she would have shoved it between her body and his legs. "I don't intend to bring you completion and you don't get to send yourself during this session."

"Always so arrogant, Adam." She squirmed then squealed when he brought the hairbrush down hard on first one buttock then the other. Was her skin tingling, burning? Would she beg him to finish her or would she require more incentive? "You want the release as much as me."

He held back a groan when she parted her thighs more. Her moist pink flesh beckoned. The wench was as

64

blatant at teasing as he. Of course she knew her pussy would be on full display to him. God, it would take nothing to abandon the brush and fondle her until they were both panting and spent.

"Be that as it may, we've already established how things will work going forward." *I'm such a fool.* His cock shoved tight against the front of his trousers. He shifted again, but to no avail.

"As you wish." He could just imagine the pout on her face even though he couldn't see it due to her position and her free falling hair. "Paul is coming to tea this afternoon." Blatant teasing rang in her voice. Did she wish to provoke him? "Perhaps I'll undress him with my eyes and pretend his fingers are bringing me to pleasure instead of my husband's."

"Does he often come to tea?" The change in topic was enough to cool the dangerous edge to his arousal and he rubbed a thumb over the brush handle.

"A few times a week, or as many times as I need him." Her tone was as breezy as if they discussed the weather. "My parents adore him."

"I see." A muscle in Adam's cheek twitched. "Have you let him... has he taken liberties with you that he shouldn't because you're married?" Though there were more than enough signs she and Paul hadn't indulged, he wanted to hear from her own lips.

"Why should I tell you?" She twisted again to meet his gaze. Hers glittered with emotion he couldn't identify, perhaps didn't want to. "After all, we're only just beginning to know each other, and that's a rather private and personal conversation."

"Yet I'm the one doing the spanking."

"Whose fault is that?" When he released her hand, she gave a nonchalant shrug. "Paul is very dear to me. Let's just say he was here when you weren't."

What the devil does that mean? He studied her for long seconds. Had she lain with the other man and broke her marriage vows or hadn't she? The anger and frustration glinting in her eyes, but doubt niggled through his gut, cooling more of his ardor. His own insecurities grew and he renewed his grip on the hairbrush's handle. Perhaps he wasn't as good or noble as Paul, but he still didn't deserve to be tossed aside. He lifted his hand. When he would have brought the paddle down on her again, he tossed it away. It skittered into a corner. No longer did he react with anger.

"Then I look forward to renewing my friendship with Paul." Adam abruptly stood and dumped Caroline from his lap. She tumbled to the floor in a flurry of skirting and limbs. "It's been ten years, so you can imagine how anxious I am to hear of his adventures." With that, he strode across the room, never looking back at her. At the door, he yanked it open then all but fled down the hall. She couldn't see how much her words had hurt, had wounded him. No matter how much a monster he'd been in the past, didn't he deserve a second chance now? Hadn't he learned all too well that any emotion made a man vulnerable and open to attack?

Somehow, it hadn't been Caroline who'd been schooled in the morning's lesson.

Why the hell did I come back?

❧ **Chapter Six** ❧

"We should probably go downstairs. No doubt Paul is simply pining for you to make an appearance." Sarcasm threaded with jealousy in Adam's voice as he popped into their bedroom.

"I would have greeted him sooner had you not insisted we make a united front," Caroline replied in a sing-song voice. She met his gaze in the mirror over her dressing table and tingles invaded her lower belly. Even in his clothing that was a few years out of fashion, he cut a striking picture. Though his boots were scuffed and his topcoat worn at the hem and elbows, his bearing was proud and proclaimed him a captain of the sea. The shadow of stubble clinging to his jaw only added to the image.

She gave into a shiver. Desire climbed her spine. The unresolved tension left behind from his little stunt of this morning made her breasts ache and need throb in her core. One thing was certain. He remained the same passionate and insistent man he'd been before he went away, and he'd remembered how she'd adored being spanked and how she'd verbally tease in order to bring him to an aroused state. He grinned, that cocky, smug smile as if he knew exactly what she thought, and even that intensified the plague of strain. *Bastard.* "I hope you're pleased with yourself. We could have both had a lovely morning." But the damn frustrating man hadn't bedded her.

"I am." He came up behind her and peered into the mirror while adjusting the already perfunctory folds and knots of his cravat. "But then, I was quite satisfied with the outcome of this morning's conversation."

Liar. The closer she looked, the more she noticed the lines of stress around his eyes and mouth. He'd wanted the release the same as she. Yet, he hadn't taken the play to the next level and had, instead, abruptly quit. Why?

He arched a bushy eyebrow. "By the by, it could have ended much differently for both of us if you'd said the word." He tweaked the already straight sapphire stick pin within the ivory fabric. "One little word and I would have been between your thighs in a heartbeat."

"That will never happen again." At the last second, she rolled her eyes at her own haughty tone. But, oh, how much differently she'd thought when she'd been over his knee, anticipating, craving, nearly begging for each swat to her bottom. She'd been so close to flying, and he'd not once touched her sex or penetrated her. Involuntarily, her gaze fell to the dressing table and when it landed on the brush in question, a fierce blush raged in her cheeks. *Drat the man.*

"We'll see." Another knowing smile crossed his face.

"I suppose we will." As much as she hated sniping at him, or even deliberately trying to wound him earlier that morning, she couldn't help it. Something about him brought out a beastly, primal, powerful side. Perhaps she wasn't completely done with being annoyed at his absence or mayhap she was still at sixes and sevens from his return.

She didn't know and was loathe to try to analyze it for fear of what she'd come away with. He was here and he was staying. Now she had to learn how to live all over again — with him in close proximity. Her pulse accelerated as she caught a whiff of his orange and clove scent. Dear Lord, what had she done agreeing to his plan? There'd be no way she'd survive having him underfoot all the time. Sooner or later, her body would crumble and she'd plead with him to bed her.

Adam Montmorency, you are from the devil.

When he still said nothing, she huffed her annoyance. He couldn't know how much he affected her. Perhaps if she didn't succumb to his charms, he'd go away again and leave her to her life. That was what she wanted, right? Except, she could hardly have him declared dead when he was anything but. That complication seriously halted her newly made plans with Paul. A tendril of guilt slid through her chest. What sort of woman was she to even wish to continue on with another man when her larger than life husband was right here? The urge to taunt her husband caught flame once more. "Paul will be surprised regarding your return." She fussed with the clasp of a bracelet. Each time she attempted to catch the claw into the metal loop, she failed. "I've instructed both Jane and the housekeeper not to mention it to him." In a perverse way, she wanted to see Paul's reaction. The same way she wished to torment Adam with Paul's presence. For the first time in her life, she felt desired beyond measure, by two men to boot, and wanted to enjoy it for a little while. At the back of her mind, she worried that it made her heartless or a tempter of fate. That wasn't true. She cared desperately for Paul and she couldn't bear to cause him pain by throwing him over simply because Adam had returned.

What, then, should I be doing?

He failed to let her bait him. Instead, he gestured to her wrist with his chin, the same dratted chin that had the same dratted cleft in it that made her knees weak. "Would you like assistance?"

"I, uh…" It would have been a waste of time to deny him since he'd already captured her wrist in his large, warm grip. Wordlessly, she handed him the delicate silver piece of jewelry—the one that matched the pendant he'd given her. Of course, he made the connection almost as if he'd read her mind, for his gaze went from the bracelet to her neck. He let his attention linger at her bodice before he met her eyes once more.

"Tell me the story of this." He held up the chain and it sparkled in the afternoon sun.

Damn his eyes. Why'd he have to be so observant? "The third year you were gone, I'd commissioned one of the jewelers to make me a matching piece, somehow hoping if I thought of you, you'd return..." How stupid was she? Renewed heat flooded her cheeks. And even now, telling him the tale didn't make her any more intelligent. "Of course, that didn't happen."

"I'd like to tell you where I was then, but I have no recollection of those early voyages." Where she'd thought he'd make elaborate excuses, he merely clasped the bracelet around her wrist, and then he took her in hand again. "Did you have an accident around the homestead?" He fingered two round, white scars about the size of the blunt end of a pencil.

Low-grade tingles slid up her arm from the point of his touch. She dropped her gaze to her wrist where he drew tiny circles over the old injuries with the pad of his thumb. "No." Did he truly not remember? "We'd been married all of three days when you took me to the mainland. We came upon a dog in the fishing village. I bent down to pet him, but he attacked me, latched onto my wrist while shaking." She tried to pull away from him. He held tighter.

"What happened then?" Adam put his free hand beneath her chin and raised her face until she looked at him.

The concern in those stormy gray eyes sent confusion coursing through her veins. "I pleaded with you for assistance, but you only laughed. You said it was my fault I'd been attacked because I didn't wash off the smell of breakfast." She swallowed around the tears gathering in her tight throat. "The dog bit down and one of his fangs punctured my skin. Thankfully, it avoided the artery."

Shock and disgust lined his expression. "Did I at least bring you to a doctor?"

"No." Caroline shook her head. "Actually, you left me at the docks. I had the ferryman return me to the island, where my mother tended to the wound. Eventually, it healed." Never would she forget the embarrassment or humiliation she'd known that day, or all the fishermen who stood gawking at her long after Adam departed. A few had come forward and offered to render assistance, but she'd been scared and angry and had refused.

Shock and disgust lurked in his eyes. "I apologize for my barbaric treatment." Still holding her gaze, he brought her wrist to his lips then placed a kiss on the inside, directly over first one scar then the other. "Believe me, if I could remember such abhorrent things, I'd be on my knees begging you for forgiveness. No man should treat a woman with such carelessness." Again, he brushed his lips along her sensitive skin. "I hope my abject apology now will suffice."

She trembled, whether from his words, the intensity of his gaze or his actions she couldn't say. The man she'd married would never have done something so gentle or looked at her with such horror in those brilliant eyes. "It was a long time ago. There is nothing left to forgive except memories." And if he had difficulty remembering, what was the point of reminding him?

"Undoubtedly, there is." He kissed the scars once more then nibbled a path up the inside of her arm, while he slid his other hand around her waist, drawing her closer. "I will apologize for every slight if you'll tell them to me."

Who was this man? Staring at him, being so close and so intimate, made the accumulated hurts ease slightly. "Adam, I—"

A soft voice cleared at the doorway. "Ma'am, Mr. Douglas grows restless," Jane interrupted. "He asks if he should return at a more convenient time."

Caroline sprang from him then was immediately contrite when hurt shadowed his eyes. She hadn't done anything wrong, but that didn't keep more heat from invading her body. "Thank you, Jane. Tell him we're coming down right now." Once the maid departed, she pressed shaking hands to her burning cheeks. "He must think I have atrocious manners. After all, I did ask him here today special." Of course, she'd thought they'd be planning what she'd say to a solicitor in regards to her missing husband or even dreaming together of their new life. Now she contemplated committing adultery...

In some distraction, she smoothed her hands down the front of her gown, fussing with a few wrinkles in the watered blue silk Jane had insisted she wear, to bring out her eyes, the other woman had assured her. Right now, she felt far from confident.

Some of the tenderness left Adam's expression, replaced by... hopelessness? "Surely, a friend as close as Paul is to you will understand you were sharing a private moment with your husband," he growled as he swept past her and out of the room.

The spell broke and her husband returned to the boorish man she'd known so long ago. She took a deep breath then let it out. Too bad her confusion wouldn't leave her as easily as mere air.

"Good afternoon, Paul," Caroline greeted the second she entered the parlor. A quick glance around the room didn't reveal Adam, and she let out a tiny sigh of relief. Perhaps he wouldn't make an appearance at tea.

"Caroline." Paul stood as soon as he caught sight of her. "Is everything all right? It's not like you to be so tardy." He crossed the room in haste and then took her hands in his while searching her face with his warm, brown gaze. "You appear frazzled."

Her heart squeezed. He knew her so well. "Think nothing of it. I've been thrown for a loop, but otherwise well." She raised her face to accept the kiss he dropped on her lips. Tingles glided through her lower belly. Where Adam was forceful and his whiskers had scraped her skin, Paul's gentle overture and clean-shaven upper lip aroused her in a completely different way than her husband did.

Oh God, what sort of woman am I that two men can excite me? Shouldn't her loyalties lie with one man only?

"What has occurred since my last time here? It's not like you to extend a special invitation when you know I'll come by anyway." He took her hand and drew her over to a settee. "You haven't changed your mind about us, have you?" When she perched upon the edge of the furniture, he sat next to her, his knees touching hers.

"No, I haven't changed my mind." The fact she clung to his hand should have given him a clue. She frowned at their entwined fingers. In her confusion and haste to follow Adam, she'd forgotten gloves which allowed their skin to touch. Paul's hands weren't work roughened like Adam's and didn't provide that added awareness when his fingers slid over the sensitive palm. "I want to be with you—"

"Except, imagine how awkward that will be since her husband has returned," Adam interrupted as he made his way into the room, all rash and swagger and very much on the defensive. "Attempting to claim another man's wife is quite scandalous, don't you think?"

Paul's eyes widened. Shock shadowed his expression. His jaw went slack before he collected himself into his customary unshakable calm. "Adam?" He slowly rose, his gaze firmly on the newcomer. "Damnation, man, is that really you?"

"Who else would it be?" As Adam joined them, Paul extended a hand. The two men clasped forearms before Paul pulled her husband into an embrace. They gave each other perfunctory pats on the back then released. "No doubt you assumed I'd died," Adam continued with no mirth in his tone.

"I did." Paul gestured to a settee opposite the one where Caroline sat. She held her breath. Would they fight? When Adam dropped onto that piece of furniture, she resumed breathing normally. "What did you expect? You'd been gone for ten years without a word." He raised an eyebrow then resumed his seat. How exceedingly odd it was to sit next to this man with her husband opposite. Odd but somewhat thrilling at the same time. "In all that time you couldn't see fit to dash off a quick note and post it when on land?"

"Thank you for judging me based on my inability to keep up with my correspondence." Adam met her gaze across the table before she busied herself with pouring out three cups of steaming tea. "Next time I find myself engaging in sea battles or holding my own against pirates, the elements, or even the threat of mutiny, I'll be sure to set aside enough time to pen a letter to my best friend, the same man I didn't expect to steal my wife out from under my very nose."

Caroline's cheeks warmed, but she didn't dare look at either of them. Her hand shook as she offered a cup first to Paul then another to Adam. Based on her husband's reasoning, it made sense why he didn't write. And from his own admission, he'd been captured later. Of course he couldn't write then. Some of her anger at him faded. Perhaps she wasn't the only one wronged in this whole debacle after all.

"Be that as it may, the fact that you neither returned home nor wrote indicated you'd died or didn't wish to come back to the wife you pointedly left behind without second thought," Paul rejoined in a steady voice, as if he were well accustomed to conversing with people who were previously thought as ghosts. "Caroline and I have grown close in your intervening absence."

She nearly jumped off the settee when Paul put his free hand protectively over hers where it sat in her lap. The second she opened her mouth to add to the conversation, Adam cut in and annoyance warmed her chest. Why wouldn't he allow her to speak her own mind? Glaring, she picked up her tea cup.

"While I'm grateful you filled the gap I stupidly left, that doesn't give you the right to appropriate her affections." He dropped a lump of sugar into his cup then topped it off with a splash of cream. "I am here now, and I have no intention of leaving or of seeing her bed another."

Caroline choked on the swallow of tea she'd just taken. The conversation was rapidly growing out of hand. "Enough." She laid the cup on the table and cleared her throat then accepted the handkerchief Paul handed her. After delicately wiping her lips, she sighed. "I'd rather you both not talk about me as if I'm not in the room. I'm part of all this," she gestured between them, "whether you want to believe it or not."

"It's perfectly acceptable if you'd like to excuse yourself," Paul told her in a low voice, effectively sweeping her into the realm of inanimate objects. Her ire grew, now focused on him. "Obviously, there are a few things I want to say to your husband. No need to put yourself in an awkward position." There was no mistaking the annoyance rumbling through his voice even if his expression didn't show it. His grip was steady on her head. "I'd rather spare you any unpleasantness."

Should she flee and let the two men perhaps come to fisticuffs over her? Desire flared. What would witnessing such a thing be like? "I appreciate that, but I don't need to be spared anything. This is my life as much as yours. However, I would like to hear whatever you'd say to Adam." When she shot a glance to her husband and caught his frown as he stared at her hand within Paul's, she quickly tucked the handkerchief into her sleeve then just as quickly stood. Immediately, she missed the warmth of Paul's touch as their contact broke. "On the other hand, mayhap it's best I leave you to it." This meeting would be ugly and she didn't want her views of either man destroyed by words that couldn't be recalled.

"Don't let his opinion color what you'd like to do." Adam brought his tea cup to its saucer so hard, the resounding *clink* echoed in the room. He shot to his feet and came around the low table between them, being sure to put himself in the middle of her and Paul. His bulk ate up the slight space. "I'd prefer to have my wife by my side." The dratted man slid an arm around her waist then pulled her roughly to him.

Her bottom still faintly burned from where he'd paddled her with the hairbrush. It wasn't something she'd forget soon. No doubt he'd known that. *Damn him.*

"She shouldn't forget the vows she took."

"That's a bit of the pot calling the kettle black, eh?" Paul gained his feet with much more grace and dignity than her husband had shown. But then, they were two different men, in looks, temperament and carriage. "Did you honor those same vows while you were away?"

Hurt sprang into Adam's stormy eyes. It vanished just as quickly. "That is none of your business, Douglas." Was that a growl in his voice?

She peered into his face and was struck again by just how rugged he seemed with the light beard and skin tanned by the sun. Being in his company gave her a sense of excitement and made her feel desired in a raw, primal way. "Adam." She tried to infuse a warning into the word, conveying in tone that there were other ways to come to an understanding. He didn't look her way.

"It is now," Paul replied. He gained her other side. "Caroline and I will no doubt move forward with our own plans." When he met her gaze, she stifled a sigh. How elegant and refined Paul was, how dashing and wholly British. With him, she couldn't help but feel respected and protected, cherished even. "We had intended to have you declared legally dead. Now that you are most certainly alive, we will petition the courts for a divorce."

She gasped. "Paul!" She wanted to stamp her foot in frustration. How dare these men try to decide her future as if she were naught but a piece of cattle?

Adam snorted. "You'd have better luck attempting to stitch Gull's Island to the mainland." He tightened his hold on her waist. "On what grounds would you file—her infidelity?"

A mask of irritation twisted Paul's features. "Your abandonment of her for one. After all, you were away for ten years, yet still able-bodied enough to return, though you chose not to."

Dear Lord, surviving the gossip and judgment of such a thing would be worse than the drama of petitioning the courts. "I don't think—"

"The only thing more ridiculous than your smug attitude is your erroneous beliefs on why I stayed away." The low tone of Adam's voice sent a shiver up Caroline's spine. It meant danger. How well did she remember that? "You have no idea what happened to me out there, and at the hands of your precious British heroes."

"Assuming that's the truth. Why did you not return before then?" Paul countered.

"You weren't there!" Adam's roar echoed in the small room. For one wild second, she thought he'd spit on Paul's feet. He glared at the other man over her head. Paul returned his glare with one of his own.

"Gentlemen!" Caroline turned to her husband. She planted her palms against his hard chest. His muscles clenched. "Adam, stop." When Paul inhaled, she spun and laid a staying hand on his chest, just as solid but not as wide as Adam's. "Paul, you behave as well. I promise, we will move forward with our plans, just don't do something rash."

"Perhaps you should leave, Douglas," Adam suggested. He stepped closer to her and his front brushed her backside. "This is *our* home, after all."

Paul narrowed his eyes. "It hasn't been your home for ten years, Montmorency. If you think Caroline owes you any sort of allegiance, you've exceeded the level of idiocy I've thought you capable of." He crowded into her space as well, and soon she became wedged between the two men and their volatile tempers.

"Stop it." Since her skirts hindered movement, she glanced at Adam once more. "Both of you." Every breath she took brought her into contact with one or the other of them. Confusion poured through her veins even as the first tendrils of arousal bloomed. Never had she been so close to two men she held affection or desire for. Her mind skittered into a dark place she'd never imagined she'd venture into.

What would it be like to have both men in a different setting, perhaps a bedroom and all three naked and ready to indulge in illicit passion? Her nipples tightened as she envisioned both Adam and Paul pleasuring her at the same time. *Oh dear heavens. I'm going mad.* She shook her head to clear her thoughts, but in the process caught her husband's gaze. His eyes had darkened with familiar desire. Did he feel the energy between them, as if a storm over the ocean brewed? "I mean it, stop this foolishness or so help me, I'll unearth the pistol my father gave me and run you both off the property." When Adam had set out to sea, her father gifted her with the weapon, as well as a rifle, as a means of defense against animals on the island, even though he and her mother lived at the coast, and could be accessed by horse or carriage fairly quickly.

For several moments, the sound of the men's heavy breathing filled the sudden silence. From her position in the middle, she trembled, whether from her wild thoughts or the tension in the room she had no idea.

Finally, Paul came to his senses. "You are correct, darling." He backed away, but only a few steps. "This problem won't resolve with brute force, as *some* seem to think."

"She is not your anything." A rumble came from deep within Adam's chest. "And *some* people need to remember their manners when they're a guest."

"You two are acting like children and I'm rapidly running out of patience with you." Their posturing would end with one or both of them being hurt — perhaps she would be as well. "I refuse to have you fighting over me."

Even though a part of her thrilled at the attention, another part worried what would happen if their jealousy and possession went over the edge. "Yes, we need to talk about our plans, but we need to do so in a civilized fashion. Right now, the two of you can hardly be in the same room without wanting to kill each other. I'm leaving." She'd not taken more than two steps when Adam caught her hand then hauled her against his chest. Could these men not treat her more than an object? In the coming days, she'd voice her opinion about that.

The desire previously in his eyes shifted to concern. "For you, I promise to converse with *my friend* without violence, but I want a kiss before you go."

"Uh…" She had no time to fend him off or even deflect the embrace. He simply lowered his head and claimed her lips, quickly deepening the kiss until it became something heady and drugging that her knees had trouble keeping her upright. Would that display make Paul jealous? Would he fight all the harder for her because of it? When he released her, she stumbled backward a few steps. *Lord, I'm not better than they are.*

"I…" Heat overtook her body. She looked from him to Paul then back again. "You… We should…" Oh, why wouldn't words come? Instead of stuttering like an old teapot, Caroline fled the room with burning cheeks.

How had her life tumbled into such a confusing morass all in the span of one day?

❧ Chapter Seven ❧

"That wasn't well done of you, old boy," Paul mentioned in a droll voice as soon as Caroline quit the room.

"What wasn't?" But there was a smug grin playing about Adam's mouth that signified the other man knew exactly what Paul meant.

"That blatant need to show your claim." Though it did trouble him. He'd seen the flare of desire in her blue eyes and had witnessed the answering emotion in Adam's expression. The knowledge of that connection between them churned anxiety in his gut. Hadn't she pledged her fidelity to him just a day prior?

"Well, she is *my* wife, after all." He crossed his arms over his chest.

"Indeed." And there was the rub. Not only had he returned after such a long absence, but also he was still legally wedded to Caroline. One tiny matter of his coming home had thwarted Paul's own plans. "Same old Adam." All the years he'd been in love with her and Adam had swept in to deny him his long-awaited prize.

"How's that?"

"Never caring what anyone else wants." Despite the annoyance that squeezed his chest, Paul would honor Caroline's wishes. This meeting, at least, wouldn't end with him planting Adam a facer, but he couldn't promise what another might bring.

His friend's glare deepened to something dangerous. "Ah, and that would be my clue to bow out because you want Caro."

Paul clenched his jaw so hard the tension pounded in his temple. He reminded himself to relax. "She prefers Caroline. Detests the shortened version, actually."

"Interesting. She didn't have issue yesterday when I called her that shortly before we became more intimately reacquainted."

This time he fisted his hands in annoyance. What did that mean? Had he taken the lovely Caroline to bed? Had he forced himself on her? The bastard! "You would keep up your brutish ways." Ever so slowly, he unclenched his fingers before he lashed out. "Like I said, same old Adam." The lout. Did he honestly presume to waltz back into her life and take up as if nothing had occurred in those ten years? Did he care nothing for the woman she was now or what she'd been through? Not if he had anything to say about the matter.

"Contrary to your opinion, there is much about me that's changed. Some you will probably never see or know about."

For the first time, Paul noticed the slight limp in his friend's stride as he regained his seat. He frowned. "You were wounded?"

"I was."

"In battle?"

Adam followed Paul's regard. "The heel, yes. The others? Not quite." His eyes glinted as he offered a chilly grin before taking a sip of tea. He stuck out a booted foot. "This is but one of many souvenirs I was given at the hands of the British. Took a ball to the heel during an engagement with a French frigate the British vessel I was on wanted to take." He wriggled the foot. "Never did heal correctly once the ball was removed. No time to rest it proper while at the helm I guess." The weight of the other man's angry gaze rested on him. "I suppose you're still loyal to the Crown?"

There had been a time when they'd both happily sailed under British protection, both as ne'er do well captains, taking what they would wherever they were. When had circumstances changed for him? "I am. You are not?"

A bitter laugh left Adam's throat. "God no. Any man wearing British colors is the enemy."

"Might I ask why?" When he peered into Adam's face, he saw the memories that haunted his friend's eyes. What exactly had happened to him while he'd been away?

"I cannot stop you from asking your questions, but I can decline to answer." Shadows clouded his eyes as he looked away. "Those are not times I care to relive through telling tales. Suffice it to say, it's enough I have to live with everything done to me." When he slammed his gaze back to Paul's, the emotion had passed, replaced with the disdain he'd assumed since meeting for tea. "Why do you continue to pledge life and limb to them?"

Of course Adam would never understand. He'd lived his life in black and white. Things either were or they weren't. There was no in between, excuses or alliances. "For the moment, it's easier to side with them than to fight them." Against his better judgment, Paul returned to the table, took up his abandoned teacup then sat upon the opposite settee. He sipped the now room temperature beverage as he stared at his friend. Before Adam had succumbed to the lure of the sea, it had been him who'd introduced Caroline to the privateer come pirate.

He'd honestly thought Adam would suit the girl Caroline had been back then. He'd fondly thought the man would tame her wild spirit while she would provide stability to his friend's wayfaring life. Ideally, he would have enjoyed having them both close as a couple, for he'd never forgotten he and Adam had been the best of chums. The bald fact was, he missed the friendship he'd had with the other man when Adam left. But then he'd argued with Adam shortly before his friend had sailed while Caroline withdrew into herself. When he'd wished to comfort Caroline and give in to the deeper feelings that he'd harbored for her, the time for a possible romance had passed — even if he'd been free to court her.

He shook his head, determined to shove those thoughts to the back of his mind. "You and I used to fight for the same side."

"Things changed while I was out there. Once the savagery of human nature gets hold of a man, his loyalties shift and change."

"Apparently, and that puts us at odds." Despite his best efforts, he'd gone and fallen in love with Caroline several years into Adam's stint at sea. It would seem where Adam's wife was concerned, she was now another reason to feud. Deep in his heart of hearts, Paul knew he wouldn't relinquish his interest merely because Adam had returned.

"We are. On a few things it would seem."

"You sailed under England's marque at one point." The Montmorency clan still had their family seat in Cornwall if he wasn't mistaken. Hadn't that been where that letter from his brother originated?

"I did. Two years after I left here, I gained that all-important act of pardon with the *Scoundrel* after a particularly spectacular fight with a couple of their best ships." Pride threaded through his words. "I had two, maybe three years of privateering for the Empire before everything collapsed." Adam contemplated the tray of seed cakes and other sweets. He selected one of the honey-drenched cakes. "I owe the British nothing, and if I have my way, our paths will never need to cross again."

Paul snorted. "A tad difficult to do since our countries are at war once more."

"Not quite in this area it would seem, though I did spy a band of the British in a tavern before I came over."

"That's odd. They'd been soundly defeated months ago." Of course, the British were still everywhere in New England as trade hadn't died even with the war, and the Americans as well as Canadians weren't willing to give up creature comforts even if the American navy tried to prevent shipping.

"Yes, well, smugglers on both sides are largely active, so there would have to be some sort of preventative measures."

"This is true." He surrendered his cup to its saucer on the table. "I've heard rumors British ships monitor a few large harbors between Boston and the Canadian territories. Bribing maritime officials is commonplace and knowing someone who can run the blockades, or find a way around the first two makes a man valuable."

"Aye. For a while I made a fortune running blockades and smuggling goods. The damn British should just retreat now that they have the chance." He savagely chewed the cake he'd popped into his mouth then washed it down with a swallow of tea. "They won't give up easily. All because the Crown is still nursing a flaming bum from when the Americans declared independence. No doubt rogue factions will try and strong-arm their way into taking control of small, key ports or lights." He snorted. "Still, in this climate, I'll wager folks like you have no issue. You've always done it too brown where authority is concerned." The contempt in his tone turned Paul's stomach.

"How so?"

Adam rolled his eyes. "Men like you who've given up on scruples and morals simply to do it up brown to those in power."

He fought off a flush. What did Adam know of the situation here anyway? In a fight for survival, yes, he had no issue admitting knowing which side of his bread the butter was on. And coin was coin. Did it matter that most of his came from keeping ties with British companies? "While it's difficult to find some staples, I will say the British are given certain concessions. For which I'm grateful, since if it weren't for my connections, Caroline and her parents would eventually be forced off this island and onto the mainland. I provide them supplies, so that life continues unbroken here, but also the lighthouse stays operational. As I do with many families who don't want Massachusetts to keep them from the comforts they've become accustomed to. Everyone remains safe."

"What else do you provide for my wife?" Adam wiped his fingers on a linen napkin then tossed it onto the table. "How long have you been fucking her?" The words were low, dangerous, the same tone he'd used the last time they'd argued.

Paul flinched at the vulgarity, but he didn't back down from the steely glare the other man threw him. "I have not, as you so indelicately put it, been fucking your wife." Though, now the bald subject had been broached, he couldn't think of anything except doing exactly that.

"Explain then. The way she speaks of you indicates it's not merely a close friendship you share."

She'd talked to her husband about their relationship? His lips twitched with the beginnings of a grin. Wisely, he tamped the urge. "Very well. I won't deny that my feelings for her are decidedly amorous. Our friendship has deepened into something bigger over the years. I suppose it was only natural that it should happen when two people spend as much time together as Caroline and I do." He rubbed a hand over his jaw as he considered how best to impress upon Adam why such a thing had occurred. "At least I was here for her when she needed someone the most." His chest tightened with the anger he'd had to suppress in front of Caroline on her behalf. "Where the hell were you, Adam, when she cried herself to sleep every night when it appeared you wouldn't return? Where were you when she had to bury her only child?"

"How do you know she cried herself to sleep?" Adam's eyes shot gray lightning. "Do you often stay the night?" He curled his hands into fists.

"No, I never have, but I've been here early enough in the morning to note the signs." The jealousy took him by surprise. Did he have feelings for her he hadn't had before? Perhaps so, for even a lout could be possessive. "So, yes, it signified that I would ask her to marry me. We both need to move on to the next chapter in our lives—and I intend to do that by Caroline's side." He made certain there was no room for argument in his tone.

"In this you'll be destined for disappointment, for I have no plans to give her up." Adam scrambled from his spot. He paced the length of the room, only his slight limp marring his proud stride.

"What do you care?" Not to be seen in the weaker position, he came to his feet and clasped his hands behind his back. "You didn't value her when you married her. Why would you want her now, when you could easily cut all ties and vanish? You could be a free man."

"Free? That depends on your view of freedom. I'll never be free of what they did to me." Bitter defeat oozed from the words. "The answer to this problem isn't that easy either." Adam paused by the window. He braced his palms on the sill and focused his gaze to the woods beyond the property. His shoulders hunched and he hung his head. "That storm the *Scoundrel* hit was fate's way of smacking me in the face, as a warning of sorts. My life didn't improve after that point."

Though mild curiosity circled through Paul's brain, he didn't wish to become sidetracked. "What does that have to do with Caroline?"

"More than you could know." When Adam turned, desperation and desolation lined his expression. "She was the only person I thought about during the long years of torture and capture I endured. A vision of her was always in my mind as a distraction from the lashes of the whip or when British naval officers threw their shit on me, or even when I lay on the rotted straw in the prison ship chasing blessed sleep that wouldn't come because I hurt so badly." Raw emotion underscored his voice. "Each time I contemplated killing myself merely to make everything stop, I'd picture her in my mind's eye, and I continued to endure for the hope of seeing her again."

A shudder ripped up Paul's spine. Something in the other man's voice filled him with unexplained horror and dread. "I'm sorry for your misadventures, but don't lay them on my doorstep as guilt, for I had nothing to do with them."

"Ha. In a way, you did. Had we not argued that day, had you not provoked me, accused me of not being worthy of Caroline's regard, I might have delayed my departure. As it was, I wanted to prove myself, and Caroline's dowry was too tempting not to leave immediately."

"How convenient for you." Had he truly changed from the bastard he was?

"I'll admit that it was and that I deserved every bad thing I encountered as penance for what I did." Adam shook his head. "But please, don't try to patronize me and what I went through by calling it something it wasn't. It was torture, plain and simple. Whatever else I used to be was beaten out of me. I'm not the same man I was when I married her." A muscle in his cheek twitched. "Those last two years, my only goal was to return here, to Gull's Island, the only place on this damn earth that I'd ever felt a connection to, and Caroline."

"Why her? You'd only been wed for a few months and had treated her with contempt and arrogance worthy of the worst peer in England. What difference did she make?" Despite his interest in her, he couldn't help but want to hear the remainder of Adam's tale.

"God only knows." Adam shoved both hands through his hair. "I only know that when I thought of her, I had hope and that was hard to come by in those dark days. I don't wish to throw that away again." He raised his haunted gaze to Paul's. "Do you understand? I want Caroline if she'll have me. Don't take that away from me."

Damnation. What was he supposed to do now? The man sounded genuine, but could a man really change? After all, he'd been away for ten years. Perhaps the words were only a ploy to return into Caroline's good graces. Would he treat her poorly once more if everything settled to his advantage? Paul softly cleared his throat. "I see." His mind spun. Honor demanded he step aside and let Adam resume and possibly repair his relationship with Caroline, but pride ordered him to crush his rival. Trust was hard to come by. That last entreaty made his friend vulnerable. Would it be easy to convince him Caroline had no more feelings for him or that he simply wasn't any more worthy of her affection than he had been back then? He must tread lightly as he pondered, for his first priority was to protect Caroline from further hurt. "Come. Let's finish our tea." He gestured at the table. *I need more time.* The best way to ensure that was a distraction. "Do you remember when we used to sail together?"

"Vaguely." Adam smoothed his fingertips over a scar at his temple. "My memories are faulty due to too many beatings. Though I have flashes of things from the past, I'm afraid my brain will never be the same."

"Well, suffice it to say, we had many a friendly competition during those days—in sailing, in strength, in speed—all things, really. Many women succumbed to our charms before you went and leg-shackled yourself." He resumed his seat then refreshed his tea. "You used to be quite the charmer." Perhaps if he talked about the old times, Adam would recall them with fondness and forget about this nonsense of trying to win back his wife.

"I don't know about that." Finally, Adam came across the room. He sat in his previous spot, but his body remained tense as if ready for flight. Perhaps he didn't know how to relate to the genteel side of life anymore. "Though I do have shadowy images of two blonde twins, naked and giggling in a bed." He cocked an eyebrow and laughed. "Is it possible we were both pleasuring them at the same time?"

"We were. Being away from conventions and rules meant we were governed by whatever we desired." Paul grinned. How many times on those early voyages had he and Adam competed for the attentions of a woman and how many times had they both ended up in bed with said women—together? "It tended to be a particular game of ours, that sharing of women when we couldn't decide." God, those days seemed so long ago now.

Surprise lined Adam's face. "Why did we stop? From all accounts and the light in your eyes, it had been the ideal life."

He shrugged. "Reality interfered, I suppose." He sipped his tea. Truth be told, he missed those days, missed the comradery. Adventure on the high seas and sharing a willing woman with his best friend. Life had been full then, and though there'd be uncertainty, it was a different sort than now. "I was obliged to hurry here and take up the reins of the shipping company once my father passed, while you," his hard swallow of the now tepid beverage threatened to choke him, "became fascinated with a local young lady with fiery red hair. You begged me for an introduction."

"Caroline." Adam rubbed his temple once more. "Not having the ability to recall everything is a bugger. I suppose I should thank you for not taking advantage in my absence." His grudging tone sounded forced.

Guilt warmed his chest. "I had not even kissed her until yesterday when I asked for her hand. But the thoughts were there. I wouldn't be a man if they were not." Paul frowned. How was it that the two things he wanted the most — Adam's return and Caroline's love — were now the two things warring with each other? "The longer I interact with her, the greater the hardship becomes." He stared into the amber depths of his cup. "I've waited an eternity to wait to claim the woman I love." His chest tightened as he raised his gaze. Damn, but he hadn't meant to reveal that to his rival, but it couldn't be helped.

"Aye." Adam's eyes took on a faraway look. Had he even heard that declaration? "I can relate. Five years was an eternity to escape British captivity, but I eventually did it." When he finally returned to the present, shadows remained. "Regardless of whether you claim to love my wife or not, I will do everything I can to repair our union." He drew in a deep breath then expelled it slowly. "I've had worse challenges."

"Oh, I don't doubt it." Paul frowned again. Obviously, the man had been through hell and back if his hints were to be believed. Yet, he was the biggest obstacle in his own path to Caroline's affections. Would it be fair to further destroy him?

How much do I want Caroline more than Adam's friendship? It was a sticky wicket life had dropped into his lap.

Adam narrowed his eyes. "I should take her to the mainland, give her every kind of gift I should have all along, treat her like a lady."

"You have the appropriate coin to do such a thing? Goods don't come cheap during wartime and especially not here. You'd need a bigger harbor city for luxury."

"I do." A ghost of a smile crossed his face. But he didn't elaborate.

"No doubt if that's true you've hidden away those ill-gotten gains." Another innocent confidence that could be used against the man. Paul tucked that tidbit away. "But, you have reservations?" He paused with his cup halfway to his lips. "Why do I feel that there is a reason for your hesitation at going through with your plans?"

"The barkeep at the Red Pony mentioned there was a bounty on my head put forth by the British navy." He rubbed a hand over his face. "I refuse to put myself into their path or tease a chasing tiger as it were, no matter how much I'd like revenge on any of them. Caroline deserves more than another stretch of years parted from me, this time in exile. So it's just as well the British don't maintain a presence here." Adam connected his gaze with Paul's. "My first and foremost duty now besides winning back her love is keeping this island safe—as well as the lighthouse—and out of British hands."

"And you assume the British have interest in this island? They haven't made an overture for it before."

"Never trust the British, Paul. Just because you don't think they have an interest doesn't make it so."

"You're nothing if not loyal to a cause." He snorted as he returned his teacup to its saucer. "There are a handful of such islands off this coast alone. The British are more concerned with the harbors and waterways. If they control all those and cut them off up and down the seaboard, the Americans will be crippled."

"Gull's Island is the largest at ninety plus miles. The light keeps the harbor safe. Imagine what would happen if it wasn't lit."

"Yes, but I fail to see a significance." Paul sat back against the hard cushions of the settee as he contemplated his companion. Wanted with a bounty on his head. Interesting. How easy a few well-placed words into the right official's ear it could be to rid him of Adam's complication. His gut clenched. What sort of man would he be if he were to send his friend back to that tortured life where Adam would no doubt meet with death this time?

A desperate man, that's what. He didn't wish to contemplate how Caroline would react to his part in such a betrayal.

"I'd think the lighthouse alone would be worth something. No doubt they'd want control over it instead of an older couple who might not be as loyal to the cause as someone hand-picked by their officials. Or worse, folks who wanted out from under Massachusetts's control as well. There is much riding on this war. If the light were out, who knows how many British vessels would find themselves dashed upon the breakers." Adam launched to his feet with the air of a man who was used to constant activity instead of sitting in a parlor. "No matter. Speculation is just that. Whatever the cost, we have to keep the British scum off this island. That small faction at the tavern concerns me."

"Where does that leave me, then?" Paul didn't like the dark thoughts swirling through his mind, yet if he could remove the problem of Adam…

He dragged his gaze up and down Paul's form. "I'm barely tolerating you here. Folks who'd rather rely on the British are just as bad as the navy in my estimation."

A snake of self-loathing slid through his gut. He'd chosen to side with the British as a matter of conveyance. Now, when seen through his friend's eyes, perhaps it had been the coward's way out. "Arrogant as always." Paul hid his grin and his confusion behind the guise of wiping his mouth with a linen napkin. "However, I agree with you on keeping the island safe. It's too quaint an area to see it turned into a military supply dumping ground." Plus, he wanted Caroline's life to remain as normal as possible. The war had already disrupted enough lives. His political affiliations aside, his first priority was keeping Adam away from her as much as possible.

In this, he would win. He had to. Victory had always come easy to his friend. For once, Paul wished to know a taste of it. But could he go through with a betrayal of that magnitude to reach his own goals?

"It's perhaps one of the reasons I remained alive through everything the British committed against me. Arrogance is harder to beat out of a man than hope." Adam strode to the door. "If there is nothing else, I desire some fresh air. All of this drama in such a short time has muddled my already much-addled brain."

Paul stood. He gestured at the door. "By all means. We will speak again soon, no doubt." When his friend quit the room, he clasped his hands behind his back.

Interesting indeed. Adam had returned and had a mission on his mind. If his friend thought to steal away the only woman he'd ever loved, he was sorely mistaken. He'd worked hard to win Caroline's regard, and he wasn't about to walk away from that good thing merely for the whim of a wandering adventurer with haunting memories and a rebellious streak.

He paused by the window and marked Adam's progress through the side yard. One little slip regarding the whereabouts of the biggest thorn in the British navy's side and the knot that was Adam would be unraveled.

But first he'd need to decide if such a betrayal would swing Caroline's embattled feelings more toward him or farther against him. There was much to mull over indeed, not the least of which was whether he could live with himself in the aftermath.

✂ Chapter Eight ✂

Adam stared at the shadows as they played over the plaster on the ceiling. Snow fell outside and the lacy pattern their ghosts made through the moonlight gave off a comforting air. He'd never thought he'd see snow again in those dismal days as a hostage. Hell, at one point, he'd been convinced he'd die on that stinking prison ship with no one the wiser. It was a strange concept, indeed, to carry gratitude in one's heart instead of the arrogance people thought they saw. He grinned into the darkness. Let them think that. The only person he needed to convince of the change inside was him.

Not even that bounder Paul had his trust any more. As bad as the British he was. He shook his head. Where had they both gone wrong? It didn't matter. He'd been given one last opportunity to make things right, to grasp at the dream he'd buried in his heart. He'd overcome the odds for the chance to be exactly where he was now — in bed beside his wife. For the moment, he put Paul out of his mind. Nothing good would be gained while thinking about his friend and the possible threat to his marriage.

Caroline's rapid breathing was the only sound in the quiet bedroom. She hadn't spoken to him since they'd both turned in once Paul had finally quit the island well after dinner. That had been a tense meal. Adam stifled a chuckle. No way did he plan to bow out and let Paul step into his own life in his place. Caroline might be leery of him, but he'd been schooled in patience over the years. He had the time.

Not that he could blame her. Their first night together in the same bed was bound to be somewhat awkward. However, they'd been laying in silence for two hours and neither of them had succumbed to slumber. Dashed inconvenient, that, especially when he'd dreamed of reclining in a soft bed such as this for what had been years. The bed at the inn had been better than a prison cell but not as luxurious as this. Perhaps it was the company that added comfort.

"Caro, why did you name the house Scoundrel's Trespass when that was the name of my ship?" It had been a question at the uppermost of his mind since returning.

She sighed into the darkness but remained silent for so long he feared she'd never answer. Finally, she said in a whisper, "You are the only scoundrel I know who might have attempted to trespass on this island." A faint laugh escaped her. "I wanted it known far and wide. You and you alone would know what the message meant had you attempted a return."

"Aye." She was clever, his Caroline. He liked that. "I would have at that."

"I thought if you did come back, you might think twice about coming home to me." The bedsheets rustled. "The man you were, the man I married, he was a bastard, I don't mind telling you." She huffed out a breath. "My parents were leery of the match, as was Paul even though he'd introduced us; the courtship was so sudden, so intense."

Adam snorted. "We were that together. Always like sparks to kindling." He reached out a hand, hoping to touch her, needing to feel the warmth of her skin. When she shied away, he bit back a curse. Why wouldn't she trust him? Resentment stirred in his heart. How did she give Paul her affection so easily but not her own husband? Granted, from everything he'd gathered from his friend, he'd had a hard time of it too. As the old anger threatened to surface and the reflex to bellow grew, he tamped it. The thoughts were unfounded. If he wanted her trust, he'd have to earn it, show her he was in earnest. "I'm not that man anymore." He didn't know if he said it for her benefit or his.

"Anyone can say those words." The bedclothes rustled again. Then the soft breeze from her breathing tickled his shoulder. She was so close but so far away. "If you want me to believe you, show me that you've changed."

"I can do that." However, having Paul underfoot so often would be detrimental to his efforts. "Regarding your feelings for Paul…"

"Oh, Adam, right now?" Irritation seeped from her voice. "I already told you, he was here when you weren't. Yes, I'm close to him. Yes, I love him. Am I expected to forget about him simply because you've returned?"

"It would be nice." Hurt stabbed his heart. She'd never said those words to him.

She sighed. "I don't know if I can do that. There's too much history there, too many feelings. It would be like asking me to choose which arm I'd like to lose."

"I understand." He reeled when he realized he truly did. When looking at the situation from her point of view, he admitted it would be difficult to cut someone out of her life she'd depended upon in the absence of her husband. "I want to know you better as a person, a woman—my wife. But I can't do that while you're distracted by him. That's not fair to me or to you if you want to give me a second chance."

"This is true." Silence stretched between them and he could swear he heard her mind working. "What do you propose?" Wariness had crept into the words, but at least she hadn't outright refused to hear him.

"On the days he's on the island to visit, I promise to stay out of your way. You may spend your time with him as you did before. I won't question you about those days or what they contained." His gut clenched. Could he trust Paul to remain a gentleman? He didn't know, yet something had to be done. None of them could move forward while at this deadlock. Perhaps he should rely on trusting Caro more. "On the days he's not here, you must promise to spend your time with me. No distractions."

"And then what? Where will all of this go? I refuse to live my life in a quagmire of sorts." She propped herself up against the pillows. "I rather doubt my confusion between you two will go away with this new arrangement."

"You will ultimately need to choose." As much as he hated to contemplate the words, they were true. He couldn't force her to love him, even if he hoped she'd pick him. He rolled onto his side and searched out her eyes in the darkness. "Let's give it to the first of next month. You can have your answer to me then, and if Paul has won your favor," Adam forced a swallow, nearly choking on the bitterness of those words, "then I will grant a divorce and walk away. You'll no longer need to be plagued by my unwanted attention." Could he truly do that? It would be leaving everything he'd ever known or wanted, trying to forget everything that had kept him alive when all he wanted was to end it.

If I survived the British, I can survive this. As much as he assumed Paul would try every trick in his arsenal to win Caroline's affections, he would too, and he'd always been more adept at flirtation than his friend. Plus, he already knew that Caroline enjoyed the bed sport between them. *I will win.*

A sob left her throat. Was it of horror or relief? "And if I choose you?"

His chest constricted. The tension between them grew. "Naturally, I'll ask that you limit the time when you're in Paul's company. I won't forbid you to see him since he is a dear friend, just know that you'll probably not want to be alone in his company once a commitment to me is renewed."

Her breath hitched. "Because you'll put on another show of possession and jealousy like the one you enacted in the parlor earlier?"

"No, because you'll feel as if you've betrayed me once I solidify myself in your affections again." He grinned in case she could see the gesture, but it was a dismal affair. Honestly, he didn't know if he could win her back after all this time, not when she'd already admitted to feelings for his rival, not when so much had happened to both of them. "Betrayal is difficult to move past."

"I'd forgotten about your rampant confidence," she said on the heels of a chuckle. "You always caught me up in that and made me feel daring."

Adam relaxed slightly. If she was laughing, there was hope. All through dinner, she'd barely talked to him, and he'd let her carry on conversation with Paul merely to give him a chance to watch her, study her, size up his opponent. Never had she engaged him with questions, and she'd fled shortly afterward. Was she embarrassed about the display of passion she'd greeted him with? Just when he would have made an overture to show her exactly what being in such close proximity did for him, he stopped himself.

She had to be the one who asked or gave permission. Even so, he couldn't resist baiting her. "I hope you haven't also forgotten about another rampant part of me."

"How can I forget when I've thought of nothing else since yesterday?" The whispered words surprised him. "That was the one thing about your absence I had the most trouble overcoming — knowing I'd never have another chance to feel your body against mine. At times I'd wished to die as a reprieve from the need, the horrible want in me you left behind."

Relief swept through him on a warm tide. At least he had her spoken admission no other man had been in her bed. "We never had issue when it came to bed sport. That connection between us, at least, was — is — as certain as the North Star." Adam bent his arm at the elbow then propped his head in his hand. "I apologize I left you to a lonely existence. If I had the opportunity to live everything over again, I would have never departed."

She snorted. "I highly doubt that. The sea is in your blood and you were mad with wanderlust once my dowry was settled."

"True, and I cannot apologize more for that." He sighed. "The sea was in my blood." The statement came out harsher than he'd wanted, so he tempered his tone. "I enjoy having it near, but I will never again uproot my life for the sail. Having said that, if I were to return to the sea, I would only do so if you were by my side. I rather think you'd be a welcome and ravishing sight out on the ocean."

"You would ask me to go with you?" A hint of wonder underscored the question.

"Aye. After the trials I've been through, I came to many a decision, one of which was life isn't worth it unless the love of a good woman is involved." Damnation. He hadn't meant to say anything of the sort, but it had slipped out. Did he love her? He'd certainly held her in high esteem those long years. Despite his spotty memories, she'd become his hope, his muse, the goal to ultimately claim once he'd quit the British. But love? He didn't know, for she certainly didn't return the sentiment if he did.

Maybe he enjoyed the idea of loving her and the hope therein.

Perhaps it was too early for him as well. Even if he did, how the hell was he supposed to express that or any of the softer emotions when he'd been too well schooled at hiding even a tiny bit of weakness? His stomach twisted. Add to the strain the fact she and Paul shared feelings for each other, and the gulf between them widened. It seemed the path he needed to trod just grew triple in length.

"That's nice to know. Thank you for sharing it with me." Was that a smile in her voice?

Never one to let sleeping dogs lie, Adam gave in to the worry sitting uppermost in his mind. "During my absence, did you, ah, ask Paul to take my place in soothing your need?" He hated that his curiosity to know outweighed his caution not to upset her.

Instead of the ire he expected, Caroline lightly touched his chest, which was bare, for he'd never grown accustomed to sleeping with a nightshirt and neither was there that luxury during the last five years. However, he did wear his small pants since Caroline would no doubt kick him out if he'd shown up to her bed naked.

Too much of a temptation for me. "Caroline, please tell me." Agony propelled the words from his throat. "I have to know, regardless of your earlier admission." He cleared his throat of excess feeling. "I promise it won't anger me." If he accomplished nothing else, he would show her he was a changed man.

She brushed her fingertips along his collarbone, which left him tense and harder than ever. If she didn't leave off, his cock would be beyond rampant and she'd be on her back, legs wrapped around his middle before either of them could draw another breath, vow be damned. "I never did, though I was sorely tempted at times." She found a round scar near his shoulder where he'd been pierced with a hot poker early in his captivity. Adam held his breath. Would she ask about it? Those tales weren't the best for pillow talk with near strangers. She didn't, but she did keep circling the area with a fingertip. "In the end I chose to remain true to our marriage vows, even if you did not."

He captured her hand and pressed it to his chest. The heat of her seeped into him and further aroused him. "What makes you think I didn't?"

"Adam, please. You were the captain of a privateering vessel, away from home, adventuring, presented with scores of women all over the world. Plus, you being the sort of man you were, I didn't expect you to honor me."

At least she'd used "were." "Oh, Caroline." Gently, he squeezed her fingers. "I can set your mind at ease. There were not scores of women. In those days, I was no doubt busy with the needs of the ship and its crew. Everyone assumes a ship captain has loads of free time at his disposal, when the opposite is true. Privateering or adventuring isn't so glamourous as the stories make it seem." He chuckled. Some might be content enough with handing out responsibilities to other officers, but he'd never relinquished what were rightly his duties. "And now? Do you believe I'm a changed man?"

"The more I see of you, the more overwhelming the evidence."

He released her hand only to caress a path up her arm to her shoulder then back again. The long-sleeved night rail she wore did nothing to add to his lust, and for that he was grateful, but he did wish to feel the satin glide of her bare skin. *Easy, Adam. Go slowly.*

"I would enjoy a few words of comfort, though." The words, so vulnerable and small in the darkness, spoke of everything she left unsaid.

"In the last five years, I can promise you I wasn't with a woman of any sort. Before that, my memories are sketchy as you know, but I'm fairly certain there was not a female in my life." He would have remembered that, wouldn't he? Try as he might, the only woman's touch imprinted upon his mind was Caroline. "I cannot say such a thing didn't happen, I'm only saying that I don't remember, don't *feel* that it did. You can choose to believe me or not." Annoyance for the British rose again. Because of them, his life would forever be altered. He'd always wonder what occurred in those lost years and if he'd really remained true to his wife. Perhaps the memories would flash or return. And what then? He didn't know. "I suppose if I ever do remember and it turns out I'd been the rake you thought, you can offer that as cause for divorce."

"Shh." She scooted closer to him, found the scar at his temple then smoothed her fingers over it. "It matters not. You came home."

His brow furrowed with a frown. Where had the haughty, angry woman gone? Their bodies almost touched. If he took a deep breath, his chest would brush her breasts. Though words hovered on the tip of his tongue, he uttered none of them. Instead, he closed his eyes and kept his hands to himself. "What… what difference does that make now? At tea you wouldn't have anything to do with me."

"Jealousy is always a strong motivator for a man, don't you think?" She giggled. "Honestly, you didn't have to come back. That's how I know you're more than likely telling the truth. Had you been whoring or carousing or spending more coin than you had, you would have remained away. After all, what can this life offer that the world cannot?" Her voice wavered. "At least, that's what I'm choosing to believe." She cupped his cheek. "That alone is a good start in showing me you are no longer the man I married."

"It's enough." Daring to rush his fences, he slid an arm beneath her then pulled her close. "It gives me hope, and that's more than I had this morning." With her pressed against him, he buried his nose in her still-bound tresses and inhaled. Faint notes of roses assailed him.

"Adam, no." She struggled in his embrace, planted her palms on his chest and went stiff, her muscles bunched and readied for flight. "Coming to terms with you on one level doesn't mean I'm ready to invite you between my legs right now."

He bit back his frustration. Would they always be more strangers than friends? Under no circumstance would he accept that he'd come home for naught. "Calm yourself, woman. I'm not forcing myself on you. I merely wish to hold you." Truth be known, if given even the slightest encouragement, he'd take full advantage in claiming her tight heat. But he wouldn't. "I meant what I said. No more relations unless you grant permission." At times, he wanted the affirmation that only the touch of a compassionate human being could give. There was too much hatred in the world already; he didn't need it from his wife.

And that would probably be the last promise he ever made, for it would kill him not to love her the way he'd dreamed of all those years.

Long seconds dragged by then, finally, Caroline relaxed a fraction. She glanced her lips along his jawline but ended the gesture too abruptly for him to lose control. Still, his pulse pounded in time to his throbbing cock. "I don't know how long it will be before I allow intimacy between us again. What happened yesterday was an aberration, at best. I knew a moment of insanity that only being with you could abate."

"No explanation is necessary." Though, he couldn't help the smug grin that tugged at his mouth. He'd been able to quiet the storm inside her. It was the conversing and providing emotional support that he'd failed miserably at.

"I'm glad you understand. Intercourse requires more trust than I'm willing to part with at the moment." The whispered words in his ear sent hot need crashing through his system, but he ignored it the best he could. Did she feel the insistent prod of his length on her thigh? Would it give her pause that she denied herself as much as she did him? Then another thought blotted out all others. When they married, she'd allowed him access to her body. She'd trusted him when he'd been that ogre. His chest tightened. If she trusted him then, he could surely win her trust anew, for the man he was now.

"Fair enough." Trust he understood, perhaps more than she'd ever know. "If you believe nothing else of me, I am a man of my word."

She slipped a hand around his waist then brushed her fingertips up and down his spine. Every pass, every fleeting touch sent him closer to the inevitable. "I will promise you this: I intend to give you your answer in two weeks' time, though that is scandalously short and certainly doesn't equal a ten-year absence."

"No, it does not, but I'm of the opinion that any man worth his salt can court a woman well enough in that time frame." A courtship? Is that what he wished from her, from himself? Perhaps. Only time would tell the rest.

Though he couldn't hear her amusement, he knew she smiled, felt the movement of her cheek against his chest. "I thank you for allowing me the choice. I haven't had much of that in a long time. Between Father's dictates and Paul's, this is much welcomed."

Adam couldn't imagine what her life had been reduced to, all those years, waiting on word, never knowing what had happened to him. It must have been hell. No wonder she'd turned to Paul. At least she had him for comfort and support and guidance even if she chafed under that. He'd had no one in those stinking years of torture and punishment.

"Thank you for naming our child after me." It was moot at this point, and an obvious change in subject, yet he wanted to make certain she knew he appreciated the honor.

"You're welcome." She traced one of the whipping scars that crisscrossed his back. "No matter what you were then, you did father the babe and deserved a modicum of respect."

Adam flinched, as much from her words as her touching the overwhelming history of the British brutality on his skin. His breath shallowed, and with every inch of scar she followed, the horrors of how each one came into being surfaced, some still crowded by shadows. What woman would choose a broken man—in both body and mind—when she could have a fully capable gentleman in Paul? His stomach clenched with a knot of worry.

"There will be other children, Caro." The unspoken emotion clogging his throat made it difficult for the words to squeeze out past the tightness. Though, would they be with him?

"Perhaps, but for now, I cannot allow myself to dream." Strain lingered in her voice. She continued to trace his scars. "How did you come to be so marked?" The whispered question rasped in his ear, sounded harsh in the oppressive silence. Now it was she who changed the subject.

"Suffice it to say the British naval officers are skilled in wielding the cat-o-nine tails among other sorts of torture." He couldn't expand upon the subject. No woman of gentle breeding should ever hear the stories, and he didn't wish to win her back through pity or a misplaced sense of responsibility. Disgust for himself and deep-seated hatred of the British roared to life, swamping everything else. "Leave off, wife. I desire sleep."

Before she could reply, Adam released her then turned away to recline on his opposite side. He stared into the room and watched the play of deeper shadows and the snow at the window. As much as the pastoral scene should lull him into calm, his thoughts and long-buried emotions churned just beneath the surface.

How could a man so damaged in form, mind, and psyche hope to return to a normal life of love when he couldn't forgive himself for leaving in the first place?

⨯⨯⨯ Chapter Nine ⨯⨯⨯

The next morning, Caroline hadn't made it twenty feet from the house before Adam caught up to her, albeit somewhat awkwardly on the teardrop-shaped snowshoes. "What are you doing?"

She stifled a sigh. He might not be the same arrogant bastard that he'd been when she married him, but the man he'd turned into was as difficult to understand. Just when they'd been in the midst of sharing the night before, he'd cut her off under the guise of sleeping.

Why wouldn't he — or couldn't he — share what had happened to him in the years he'd been away? Was he hiding something he didn't wish her to discover? Or worse, perhaps he couldn't bear the pain, the memories. Damn him. How could she help if she didn't know how?

"I'm accompanying you to wherever you're going," came his slightly breathless reply. One of his snowshoes dangled from his foot. When he tripped over to her, he bent and retied the leather strings around his calves. "As our agreement states, today is my day with you. I refuse to waste a minute of it."

"Very well."

"Where are you going?"

She rolled her eyes. "To visit my parents. I haven't seen them in a couple of weeks." It felt exceedingly odd to traipse through the woods with a companion. Though she'd made this same five-mile trek to the lighthouse countless times, usually she did so by herself. It afforded her plenty of time to think about her life or perhaps dream of the future. When Paul visited the island, he usually stopped by her parents' first before coming inland. His companionship was lovely, but sometimes she craved solitude. She was good at being alone. It was having to be *something* to another person she failed at, for she usually failed to come up to the other person's expectations. At least nature never disappointed her or let her down or demanded anything from her. She could never frustrate it either. "Did you eat breakfast? Trekking through snow will make even the heartiest man famished on an empty stomach."

"I did not. By the time I realized you were up and about, I had to scramble for clothes if I wished to catch you." He grunted as they set into motion. Their puffs of breath clouded in the chilly air.

Caroline refused to let her mind dwell on him waking disoriented, perhaps stretching while the muscles in his chest rippled. It had taken all her willpower not to do more than lightly kiss him the night before. "I see." Even though he was covered with the shabby clothes and a well-worn greatcoat, his form still sent tendrils of heat through her veins. Damn him.

Though he limped, he matched her stride. Apparently, he'd taken to snowshoeing with alacrity. "Do you normally make a habit of walking so early?"

"Early?" Her laughter echoed off the trees. "It is already eight, Adam. I rose before sunrise for tea and a nice hamsteak and fresh bread with honey. Mrs. Abbottson is quite a cook." She gave into a giggle. "We have to smuggle in the honey and some of the other ingredients thanks to the naval blockades, but Paul is quite skilled in procuring anything I wish."

"I'm sure he is." He grunted. "You do not tend to your own meals?"

She glanced at him, but there was no censure in his expression, only curiosity. "I do on the days Mrs. Abbottson doesn't come out." With a shrug, she pulled her cloak more tightly about her body. "It's lonely cooking for only myself or perhaps Jane. So, I joyfully let Mrs. Abbottson fuss over me. She lives about a half mile south on the island. Most of the servants have their own cottages there. Sometimes Paul dines with me, or sometimes my parents join me."

"Are your parents enjoying good health? I seem to recall your mother experiencing palpitations shortly after we married."

"As she tells me regularly, she's getting older." Anxiety squeezed her chest. "In recent years she's grown more frail. She rarely accompanies Father when he ascends the lighthouse. She says the stairs tire her." Her parents were in their sixties and she was their only child—the one baby who wasn't born dead. As a consequence, they weren't young anymore, and she worried about them alone. "Beyond that, her mind isn't as sharp as it used to be. She forgets things often, things we'd discussed not two weeks before." Her throat tightened.

"I'm sorry to hear that." When she stumbled over a snow-covered tree root, Adam grabbed her arm and kept her upright. He didn't release his hold even after she'd recovered. "I hope I have the opportunity to further my acquaintance with both her and your father soon."

"That's a nice thought, but you'll need to convince Father of your sincerity first. He wasn't exactly your biggest supporter when we wed." She liked that he kept his touch on her. It was a comfort, as was his desire to visit with her parents. Perhaps he'd changed after all.

"I'll trust you on that for I don't recall it." A chuckle rumbled from Adam's throat. "Honestly, I was surprised he didn't run me off the island at gunpoint if he hated me so much."

She nodded. "The only reason he did not was at my request." When she attempted to pull away, he tightened his hold. Unwilling to argue, she decided to enjoy the warmth his body imparted to hers. Having a companion at her side did indeed make the trek more bearable. "It should be interesting to see his reaction at your coming back from the dead. I should have gone up alone and prepared them, but there wasn't time and you're very insistent."

"No time like the present."

"I suppose." Glad for the light-hearted banter, she linked her arm more comfortably with his then patted his gloved hand with her mitten-clad one. "Do go easy on them. Mother, especially. I'd rather you not argue with my parents like you did with Paul. Your history doesn't matter, not in their lives."

"For you, I shall."

They walked along in silence for the next few miles. The crunch of the snow beneath their shoes, their breathing, and the soft fall of snow from the tree branches the only sound to break the peace. It wasn't an awkward, uncomfortable sort of quiet, but more a companionable sameness shared by two people comfortable in each other's presence.

Which was odd. Shouldn't she feel anxious being alone with him? Caroline kept her focus straight ahead on the pristine path, for if she allowed awareness of her husband to creep up on her, she'd lose control. How often did a woman tackle a man on a lonely path in the woods? If they both tumbled into a snow bank, would someone come along and observe them in a compromising position?

Warmth slid through her body. The remembrance of him taking her hard and fast on the kitchen table floated to the forefront of her mind, quickly followed by how she'd felt when he'd paddled her with the hairbrush. She sucked in a breath. Did it make her desperate that she wanted him again in a carnal way? Well, her body did. There simply wasn't another experience like indulging in intercourse with a man who knew exactly how to pleasure a woman. Her mind and heart weren't so certain. She didn't wish to be hurt so deeply again. After all, they'd barely begun renewing their acquaintance. He'd paid her lip service, nothing more.

Except... the man she used to know certainly wouldn't have tolerated trekking through fresh snow while sharing silence with a woman. If anything, he would have ordered her to make the trip alone or demanded her parents come to him. Caroline stole a glance at him and she frowned. He deeply inhaled gulps of air then slowly let them out again.

"Are you all right?" Tendrils of alarm slid through her stomach. Had he not acclimated to land as well as he'd thought? Were his insides damaged too much from whatever had happened to him while in British custody? She pulled them both to a halt. "Adam? Should we go for the mainland and a doctor instead?"

"No, truly, I'm quite fine." His eyes glowed a clear gray beneath the brim of his battered tricorne hat as he faced her. "I just now realized how glorious it is to be able to breathe deeply and not smell piss or sickness or death." He caught her by the waist, lifted her off her feet then twirled around in a fast circle and ended up faltering slightly due to his injury. "Do you know how lovely it is to enjoy the sharp scent of pine or the crispness of snow?"

When he set her back on her feet, she stared at him with her jaw slightly agape.

"Think of it, Caro." He bent and scooped up a handful of the powdery snow then threw it above his head. The flakes drifted through the air around them, each one sparkling like diamonds in the morning sunshine.

"I adore how it twinkles." That was all she had to say when he was fairly bursting with awe for the world around him? What had happened in his life to make him revel in the ordinary now? She rapidly blinked when a couple of the flakes alighted on her eyelashes.

"Oh, aye. I never thought I'd see snow again much less the outside world or have the opportunity to walk about unfettered like this." He repeated the gesture and this time tilted his chin so the snow fell upon his upturned face. His lips parted with a wide grin. "The heat of the sun on my skin, the cold sting of the snow, the vast stillness of the wilderness here, the honor of walking with you by my side." He slid his gaze to her. Wonder and gratitude shimmered in the stormy depths. "I took so much for granted before. I was an arse, plain and simple, thought the world owed me something, didn't think I had anything to learn. Never will I make that mistake again."

"I'm glad to hear it." Her mind spun and her heart skipped a beat. This man, so lost in abandon, and dare she say innocence, stole her breath and made butterflies tickle her belly. His joy was almost palpable. "If you like the forest, you'll adore seeing the sea from the lanthorn—

the lantern room of the lighthouse." She grabbed his hand and tugged him along the path. "In the summertime, the sea is blue, a cold blue and so pretty, but in the wintertime, it's a gorgeous blue-gray. I like to think there is mystery down in those depths. I can pretend that if I held my breath long enough or dove deep enough, I'd unlock those secrets."

Why did she tell him something so silly that she'd kept to herself all this time? He didn't want to hear the blathers of a woman.

Adam stopped once more, and this time he put a gloved hand beneath her chin and lifted it until she met his gaze. "I believe you could." His eyes darkened. "You and the sea share an affinity. I'd give many things to see you, wild and abandoned, on the deck of a ship."

She forced a swallow into her tight throat. "I've often wondered what it would feel like, on the open sea with no land in sight, just me and the wind and the water." What would he look like with the breeze clawing at his hair and his skin glistening with sweat in the high noon sun? Her core throbbed and she clenched her thighs together to prolong the sweet sensations.

"It's one of the most freeing things a person can do." He brushed a thumb along her bottom lip, and she wished he wasn't wearing a glove. "It's the closest a person can be to flying."

"That must be wonderful." Her knees trembled. With the stark white backdrop and the rugged countenance of her husband, her heart pounded as she waited on his answer. So much potential for magic in this moment. And that had been sorely missing from her life for a while now.

"Aye." Then he lowered his head and kissed her, their lips barely touching, the whiskers from his beard sending prickles of awareness over her skin.

"Oh." Caroline surrendered with a shuddering sigh. She crushed the lapels of his greatcoat in her fists. Where she'd expected his typical storming the castle type of boldness, this embrace was nothing but tender and gentle. The feather lightness of his lips caressing hers overwhelmed her with sweetness. She melted against his strong chest and moaned when he slipped his free hand to the small of her back and fitted his lips more firmly over hers. He took again and again from her, tasting, teasing, searching, but not once did he probe with his tongue or even push to deepen the kiss, he merely made love to her mouth. The tickles in her belly doubled. Perhaps having her husband home wasn't the burden she'd first thought.

All too soon he pulled away, but the heat he'd ignited lingered. Her balance wobbled as he pinned her with an inscrutable look. Then he tucked her hand through the crook of his bent arm and continued their forward motions along the path as if nothing had occurred.

"No matter how lovely being on the sea is, there is nothing quite as beautiful as being able to kiss a bewitching woman in the midst of a snowy morning."

"I think you must be touched in the head as much as you talk gammon." Yet, she couldn't help the smile curving her lips. Finding herself enjoying banter with her husband was an unexpected surprise.

The burst of genuine laughter that left his throat had her reeling into confusion once more. The Adam she'd known had never laughed unless in mockery. "I speak the truth, woman. Accept it and move on."

Mayhap she should accept things as they were now and not question them or try to find a reason why she shouldn't. But, in her heart of hearts she refused to fall completely beneath his spell for fear this was all a cruel joke at her expense. She'd had too many years to hate him for his absence, and only a few days to acclimate to his return. Thank goodness her parents would be there to act as chaperone. Otherwise, she could easily throw her doubts aside and attempt to seduce the man who accompanied her.

Don't be a ninny, Caroline. Guard your heart and tell your body no.

Not long afterward, they reached the tiny, four-room cottage where her parents lived. It sat on the same plot of land as the lighthouse, the only difference being the lighthouse had been built on a slight hill. In the summertime, the path leading from the cottage to the lighthouse sparkled with crushed seashells. Now, one set of boot prints marred the pristine blanket of snow. No sooner had she reached for the doorknob of the cottage did the door swung inward and her father stood in the frame, his lean body stooped slightly and the shock of white hair fringing his mostly bald head.

"Caroline." His blue eyes lit with relief. "Perfect timing."

"For what?" She frowned while he stepped aside. Why was he dressed to go out? "Are you going somewhere?"

When she went past him and Adam followed, her father gasped. "Good Lord."

Caroline spun around in time to see her father clutch his chest. "Are you all right?" Her pulse pounded hard. Had it been his heart again? She rushed to his side. "Father?"

"I'm fine." The older man waved a hand toward Adam. "Your husband has returned." He peered more intently at him. "You're marked with experience and sadness. I can see it in your eyes." He stumbled toward her husband. "I'm a big enough man to admit I thought your hasty wedding or that you abandoning Caroline before the bed grew cold was the worst idea I'd ever heard of, but now that you're here and in my little girl's company without her shredding you to bits, I have to say, I'm mighty glad to lay eyes on you."

For the second time that morning, Caroline's jaw dropped in astonishment. "I wouldn't have shredded him to bits."

"Not that she didn't try," Adam added with a laugh.

Her cheeks flamed from her father's frank words. *This* was her father, the man who hadn't thought twice about saying cutting things about her husband in the years he'd been away? *This* man who was currently pumping Adam's hand and slapping him on the shoulder was the same parent who'd told her multiple times she should forget about the sea captain and learn to love another?

"Father, please!" She shot a glance at Adam, but her husband wore a wide grin and his eyes twinkled. She didn't trust that gleam one bit.

"I appreciate your approval, Mr. W…" He narrowed his eyes. "I want to say Winchester, Windemere, Win—"

"Winslow." Her parent finally released him. "Come in, come in." He waved Adam toward the cozy common room and the comfortable, old leather chairs. "It's a pity Mother and I are heading to the mainland and can't visit."

Caroline startled out of the haze she'd fallen into. "What do you mean? You never leave the island. What about the lighthouse? Have you made arrangements with Paul?"

The men exchanged a speaking glance, no longer than a second, but both seemed to find amusement in her questions. Her father shook his head. When he looked at her, his eyes were sad. "Your mother has taken a turn for the worse, Caroline. I need to have a doctor in Portsmouth attend to her."

"What?" When her knees would no longer support her weight, Adam was there with an arm around her waist, leading her to a rocking chair and showing her into it. "Tell me what happened."

Her father shrugged. "Her mind isn't as strong as it used to be. She's slipping more and more into the past. Some days she's herself, but others, she thinks she's the woman she was twenty-five years ago." He rubbed a hand along his angular jaw. "Today's a good day. I'm just afraid she'll wander away when I'm minding the light. There are too many obstacles on this island that can harm her." A sigh escaped him. "I can't do it on my own."

"I should have been more attentive." Tears misted her eyes. Again, she'd been a failure as a daughter. "I should have spent more time here." She offered a wobbly smile when Adam patted her shoulder. "I've been selfish, and I'm sorry." And she didn't know how to relate to her mother when she was lost in the memories. Perhaps she didn't have the patience needed to care for a person suffering like that. "I'd asked her so many times to come stay in the house with me, but she always refused because she didn't want to leave you."

A faint smile wreathed his face. "We've been together a long time. Perhaps I should relinquish my claim on the light."

"No!" Both she and Adam protested at the same time. Caroline coughed and modulated her voice. "I mean, it's been in the family since Grandfather's boyhood. I'd hoped to pass it down…" Tears pricked the backs of her eyelids.

"Yes, sir, you really should keep it in the family," Adam continued. "Way too many British supporters out there who are hungry for the light. No doubt if England knew the light was for sale, they'd jump on the chance. You can't let that happen."

"Perhaps." Her father nodded.

Caroline relaxed, but only marginally. "I'm sorry you are taking care of Mother alone. I should have—"

"Enough of that, Caroline." He slashed at the air with a hand. "I didn't want her to be away from me either. When a man finds the right woman, it'll take an act of God to part them." Her father's sharp rebuke cut into her dismal thoughts. "She knows you love her and she knows you also have weathered your fair share of hardships. The last thing she wanted to be was a burden to anyone. I was going to ask Paul to mind the light and send you word, but now…" He looked at Adam. "I need you to take over operations, son, until I can get back here."

"But, where are you taking Mother?" Caroline interrupted.

"Always too headstrong, girl." Her father huffed. "After the doc checks her, I'm going to take her to your Aunt Lynda for a spell. I think a nice, leisurely visit would do the trick. She keeps talking about her sister anyway." His jaw worked. "I'm hoping it might help bring her back to me."

For the first time she saw her father in a different light. No longer was he merely her parent and the man she'd looked to for wisdom and with admiration. Now he was her mother's lover, her life mate, and at one time, they'd had a grand romance and courtship. As much as she herself mourned the loss of Adam, losing a partner piece by piece with agonizing slowness right in front of his eyes must tear her father up inside.

"Take as much time as you need." She swallowed around the lump of unshed tears in her throat. Love was vital to every aspect of life, and when two people found it, no one should attempt to rip it apart. Her chest tightened. Would she ever know that deep, abiding love such as her parents had? "No doubt Adam will be happy to mind the light."

"Aye, sir. I will and shoot a British intruder dead to rights if he steps too close." Determination graveled his voice.

"He can certainly do it until I can ask Paul to take over duties here. Maybe he and Paul can fight over their political differences then." Her father flashed a cheeky grin. "Because I'm sure the two of you have other things to work on, and none of them include keeping a lighthouse running. Paul will be happy to help."

Heat flooded Caroline's cheeks as Adam shared a purely masculine laugh with her parent. Help in what way? Why had her father never told her he'd hoped for a reconciliation if Adam ever returned? It would seem her whole family had failed, at least in communication. "I'll just go say goodbye to Mother." She stood, glad that her strength had returned.

"Good, and don't take it personal if she only remembers you as a little girl. I'll take your husband up to the light and show him how to manage the lanterns and teach him how to clean everything."

"Oh, and Mr. Winslow," Adam interrupted. He removed an envelope from his greatcoat pocket. "Would you mind terribly mailing this letter for me?"

"It'd be my pleasure, son." Her parent accepted the offering then glanced at it. "Washington, D.C., eh? That's high company you keep if you're writing to the president."

A faint flush washed over Adam's cheeks. "I'm merely replying to a request from him. I... have information he'll want. No doubt sooner than later."

"Then the post will be my first order of business." Her father tucked the missive away.

What was that about? She glanced at Adam, but he gave nothing away. More secrets. What did it mean? Before her father could take his leave, she pulled him aside and whispered for his ears alone, "I thought you didn't care for Adam. Why the change of heart?"

"Honey, sometimes circumstances shift and a man has to learn how to navigate in a different direction out of necessity if he wants to keep a good attitude."

"But I told you of my plans with Paul. You were going to let him take care of the light. I don't understand."

He slipped an arm around her shoulders. "I was used to being your protector and champion, but now your mother needs me more. Yes, I thought Paul would be good for you, but now, I think things have changed. Adam returned at the right time, and I'm glad to hand over the responsibility to him." He looked down into her face and met her gaze. "Don't punish him too long for being away. Life goes by too quickly at times for petty bitterness to fester. Work things out the best you can with everyone involved."

❦ Chapter Ten ❦

Adam stood on the gallery that surrounded the lantern room, his hands clasped behind his back. From his perch at sixty-one feet up, he watched as the ferry with Caroline's parents aboard pulled away from Gull's Island. He searched the nondescript dock and easily found her form, so stark against the gray sea and snow-blanketed world. A gust of wind blew and battered the hem of her black cloak about her legs.

Damnation, but the woman was a challenge, and he thoroughly enjoyed keeping her off-balance as he had during their trek to the lighthouse. When he thought about the kiss they'd shared, his body tightened. He hadn't lied when he'd told her he refused to take his life for granted any longer. Courting Caroline was now the most important task on his agenda, well that and taking care of the lighthouse in the absence of her father.

When he focused his gaze on the dock once more, Caroline had left the area. He turned away from the breeze as he walked the galleries with a frown. Though he'd assured her father he'd be honored to oversee the lighthouse duties for as long as needed, Mr. Winslow was adamant that he'd mention the need to Paul. If the other man wished to have the keeper position, he could. Yes, it would free Adam's time, but having certain responsibility again gave him a sense of purpose.

Perhaps that was the key to happiness—a man needed purpose. He hadn't had one since he'd escaped the British for the last time. Sure, wishing to win back Caroline's affections was a nice goal. If only they didn't act as strangers or mere acquaintances and more like a wedded couple looking forward to raising a family or growing old together. Once the president wrote back and invited him to visit and tell his tale, he'd have another purpose, but until that time, his life was here on Gull's Island.

"Adam."

The uttering of his name in her soft voice halted his restless pacing. "Did you see your parents off?"

"Yes." She joined him on the gallery but leaned her forearms on the white-painted railing. "Mother was somewhat lucid. At least she knew me as the current me." The breeze tore at her braid and long, red strands escaped their bindings. In profile he caught the fear and worry in her expression. Her throat worked with the force of a hard swallow. "Father isn't sure how long they'll be away or if he'll return without her, though he says it'll be at least a week before I hear from him."

"Your aunt is equipped to care for your mother in this altered state?" The human mind was fascinating—he'd give anything to remember his lost memories while Caroline's mother would probably give the same not to be stuck in them.

"Oh, yes. She has three grown children, all of who live within a stone's throw. Her home is a newer build and design; there is no upper floor. Plus, there is a high fence surrounding the property because the previous owners kept dogs. If Mother manages to escape the house, she won't go far."

"Everything will work the way it should, but I'm glad they're still around. Your father is good people." He stared out to sea. "I often wonder what happened with my parents."

"You don't know?" She glanced at him, her brow furrowed.

"I'm afraid not." He faced her then tucked an escaped strand of hair behind her ear. "When I sailed with Paul as a young man, they were very much a part of the London social scene. I lost touch with them. Obviously, the post isn't reliable while moving from port to port." He shrugged. "Hell, I don't even know where my brother is." An unexpected grin tugged at his lips. "Clar... Caleb? Lud, but I don't recall his name." *Damn injury.*

"Clinton," she provided in a soft voice.

"Yes, Clinton is only ten months my elder. We were often mistaken for twins growing up. I don't know if he's alive, as he was a privateer like me, and if he is, would he wish to see me again since it's been so long?" His chest tightened. "My distaste for the British might put us at odds."

A man was nothing without his family and roots. What did that make him? It had been his business to move around, to create havoc, to disappear, to forget, all in the name of protection.

Caroline smiled and it was as if the world ceased to exist except in her twinkling eyes and the labored thud of his heartbeat. "As luck would have it, you did receive word from your brother a few days ago. I opened the letter, for you hadn't returned yet."

"And?" He grasped her hand. The poor thing shivered with cold. "Do you want my coat?"

"No. I'll be fine."

Stubborn woman. "Is my brother well?"

She nodded. "Not only is he well, but he's apparently about to be wed. He did mention you should come. Of course, he doesn't know about your issues with the British."

Both of his eyebrows rose. "What? My brother, married?" Astonishment gripped him. Another flash of memory asserted itself. "Clinton, the man who'd been a confirmed rogue and lover of women, has pledged his troth to just one?" *How amazing.*

"That's the news I ascertained from his letter. I kept it for you, in my top bureau drawer." She smirked. "I guess both the Montmorency men have experienced willingness to change in recent years, huh?"

"Perhaps, but I still cannot believe it." He shook his head. "Did you know that I have a cousin, too?"

"No, I had no idea. You have never been the most forthcoming man." Slight censure rang in her voice, but she hadn't lost her smile.

Bits and pieces of his early life poured in, one on top of the other. "From what I recall, Francis—he goes by a different name but I cannot recall it—holds the title of viscount or something of that nature. Granted to him by the Crown for acts of bravery or some gammon." He shrugged. "As if that sort of buggery matters in the world right now."

"I suppose it does to the upper crust of England." Her laughter sent a shiver up his spine. "He is like you and your brother? A pirate?"

"Privateer." His chuckle blended with hers, and for one moment, everything was right in the world, and he could forget the troubles swirling about them. "I would have no idea anymore. He's around my age though. Our fathers were brothers. I often wonder what became of him and if he is a man of the marque." He threaded their fingers together. "Once, long ago, when Clinton and I were just young boys causing havoc in the English countryside, there was a rumor."

"Oh?" Curiosity hung on that one word.

Why couldn't life always be this halcyon with his wife? He nodded. "The servants talked, as servants do. It was hinted that my uncle fathered a child with my cousin's governess."

"Was it true?"

"I would have no idea. Even if those memories weren't muddled, I never heard anything more substantial than rumors. Anything is possible, I suppose. Uncle was a bit of a rogue, even after he married."

"Runs in the family." She laughed again. "Such arrogance you still possess, Captain. This talk of servants and illegitimate siblings as if it's commonplace." She tugged on his hand. "Come back to the house. It's rather chilly up here."

"I could warm you. Just say the word." The teasing words fell from his lips without thought, and for one long second he thought she'd drop his hand and march into the lighthouse staircase without him, but she merely looked over her should at him, her gaze inscrutable. "Or perhaps I could make tea."

"Perhaps." Eventually, she did release his hand in order to press the door, which had a tricky handle. "And over tea you can tell me about those scars on your back. Don't assume I'm a delicate flower or that I won't be able to bear whatever horrible story haunts the depths of your eyes. I'm made of sterner stuff."

Adam gaped at the empty spot she'd just vacated before stumbling after her. He caught up to her on the twisting metal stairs as she paused by one of the thin, rectangular lookout windows. "I never doubted your constitution." Damnation, any woman who could retain her composure after surviving the abandonment of her husband as well as the loss of a child had his respect.

"Show me you haven't." She faced him with her back pressed against the window glass, her neck craned to stare into his face. The sunlight streaming through the pane illuminated the richness of her blue irises. "Share your horrors with me."

"So you'll understand me better?" He couldn't hear for the erratic pounding of his heartbeat in his ears.

"That, and so some of the pain will leave you." She held up a hand, palm outward, when he would have closed the small distance. "You might have changed from the man you used to be, but that infinite sadness and hatred I see in glimpses terrifies me, Adam. What will that eventually drive you to do? I cannot abide another parting, not now, just when I'm growing accustomed to having you back." Her eyes filled with tears. "Not now when I'm losing my mother. Not having you around through another tragedy isn't to be borne." Without another word, she ducked around him then whipped down the spiral staircase. The hem of her cloak billowed behind her and her boots rang on each step.

He laid a hand over his heart where the dull ache he'd carried around since his hatred of the British lived. Did she fear he'd leave again if the rigors of daily life grew too great? Devil take it, but this wasn't how he wanted her to view him. He wanted her to see him as a man fit to carry her heart and make all of her dreams come true. And, damn it, he couldn't do that by shutting her out. His gut roiled. It had been so long since he'd trusted another person, he had no idea how he'd go about letting Caroline inside that part of himself he didn't even relish revisiting.

Filled with a sense of renewed purpose and spirit, he chased her down the seventy-one steps—he'd counted them on his previous ascent—to the wood-paneled service room. She waited near the clockworks and a table where the cleaning supplies were laid out, ready for use on the morrow. In cupboards to one side of the octagon-shaped room were extra lanterns, wicks, oils, and everything needed to maintain the lighthouse. A pleasant enough area to play.

His mouth went dry as he looked at her, so hopeful yet vulnerable as she touched a finger to one of the clocks. The folds of her black cloak fell gracefully over the fabric of the sapphire wool dress she wore. The color drew out the deeper hues in her eyes and left them breathtakingly enchanting. What should he say to her? How could he start such a conversation that would end up stealing another piece of his mind? Would she still be there when the heartache ended, when he'd bared what was left of his soul and gave her everything the British hadn't taken from him?

Could he let himself be that vulnerable?

Adam forced down a hard swallow. Without breaking his promise, he'd do what came natural, what he and Caroline did when conversation wouldn't come—he'd seduce her. Only this time he'd do it with words. What she chose to do afterward would be her decision.

Seduction would lead to talking. Among the pillows and twisted sheets they could be themselves—or at least the selves they allowed each other to see.

Surely that would work again, and if it didn't… He shook his head. That couldn't be contemplated. There was precious little time alone with her as it was. All too soon and she'd be with Paul. No doubt he'd be obliged to take over manning the light in order for them to spend time together. He had to make headway, and fast.

"Come, Caro. Indulge me." He stood in the middle of the room with a hand extended.

"In what?" She faced him with a frown marring her highly kissable mouth.

"A dance, or a waltz, specifically." He wriggled his fingers. "I find I miss the niceties in life."

"Here?" She glanced about then landed her bright gaze on him once more. "There isn't sufficient room, nor is there music, and won't your heel bother you? You try to hide it, but I see you stumble and falter. Don't think I haven't."

"Let me worry about that." His chest tightened that she'd remembered his injury.

Her brow furrowed. "Are you mad?"

"Sometimes, I wonder." He refused to drop his hand. "However, it doesn't negate my want for this dance." *Or for you.* "Perhaps pretending is the best course of action that will help us cope with reality."

"But, if we chose to hide from our lives as they are, what sort of people will we become?"

"We become what we've always been meant to be: resilient, the type who will bend but not break. The sort of people who've had to be strong because we've had no other choice." Would she accept what he didn't say and understand his point? "We belong to the race of people who still believe in fairy tales and the good that's in the world even if we haven't had cause to witness it much in our lives."

"I think you're right, but how would you know when neither of us has mentioned fairy stories?"

"Everyone wants a slice of happiness and good things."

"True." Slowly, she crossed the room then laid her hand in his. She gasped as he tugged her into a close embrace. "This is hardly the proper form for a waltz." Yet, she slid her palms up his chest then locked her hands around his neck.

"Ah, but then I'm not the proper partner." Adam set them into the first steps of the dance while humming a few bars of a popular song. "I don't think that word and me have ever graced the same sentence, unless someone has called me a 'right proper arse.'"

She peered into his face with the hint of a smile. "As they say, if the shoe fits…"

Ah, the cheekiness of his wife. Thank the heavens she hadn't lost her sense of humor. He pulled her closer still and their bodies fit tightly together as a hand to a glove as they performed the steps in the cozy confines of the service room. "If I had your attention in a proper ballroom, you wouldn't receive proper conversation, either."

"Oh? Then what would you entertain me with?"

"Blatant flirtation bent on seduction." There was no need to lie to her. "I'd tell you exactly what I planned to do to you the second we quit the event."

"Ah, I see. Such as going to a tavern and having a pint or taking yourself to the dock to commune with your ship?" Did she mean to goad or tease him?

"Something infinitely better. Something to whet your appetite and make you pant with want. Something to have you spreading those pretty legs and begging me to join with you."

She let go a throaty laugh. The sound of it grabbed him by the neck and wouldn't let go. "If you think you're that skilled with mere words. I haven't met a man yet who wields that much power."

"I do and I am." He hummed a few more bars then said, "I'd whisk you away to a private room, even a shallow nook would be acceptable, and kiss the breath from you, gently at first then with ever increasing intensity, for that's the way you enjoy being kissed."

"Arrogant man. I like many styles of kissing." Rosy color infused her cheeks. "Just because you employ one way doesn't make it my favorite."

"How silly of me to assume." But he knew. She was a terrible liar; her eyes showed every emotion. He slowed their turns about the room in order to concentrate on his tale. "Then I'd pay court to every delectable inch of your satiny skin with my fingers first. Then I'd lick every

131

sensitive spot, tease every place on your body that brought you pleasure. Imagine the heat of my mouth on your pebbled nipples, circling, suckling until you arch your hips." He put his lips to the shell of her ear. "I'd slowly slide down your body, kissing a path along the way, and when I reached your mons, I'd part your thighs, look my fill, and ever so slowly spread those gorgeous lower lips before delving my tongue into your hot, wet pussy and feast on your cream until you give into release."

"Oh." That soft utterance was issued on the heels of a moan. The sound held him captive and he wished to say something else merely to hear it again. Her hands trembled at his nape.

"Indeed, and when I was finished, I'd suck your swollen button into my mouth and torment your sex until you cried mercy."

She attempted to stifle another moan, but it escaped anyway. Did she wobble in her steps or was it his that faltered? "What would you do then?" Was it his imagination or did she gently grind her hips into his? His cock certainly felt the increased pressure. "That's hardly enough to stop me from walking away and leaving you wanting. Must be horrible to have a member so thick and needy."

Minx. He tamped his grin. Could he drive her into desperation? "Aye, and what sort of woman would be content with coming undone one mere time?" It had been thus between them. He was never happy until he could send her flying twice or more each session, with the exception of having his way with her on the kitchen table upon his return. That hadn't been well done of him. "Once I'd thoroughly pleasured you with tongue and teeth, I'd take you on the floor, perhaps from behind if passion consumed us both to prevent finessing."

"And?" She slid a hand down the length of his back, not pausing until she'd gripped a buttock and gave it a squeeze. His prick jumped in response. "Sounds a tad boring."

Oh, he'd give her boring. "Then, I'd order you onto all fours and fuck you hard and show you exactly who was in control of your pleasure. I'd fondle those lush breasts of yours and if you still weren't near release, I'd pinch and pluck your hardened nipples. I know well how you crave the pain-pleasure cycle." As evidenced by her affinity for the hair brush he'd employed.

"Not enough." But her breathing sounded harsh and labored. Her eyes had darkened near to the share of her gown. His lady wife was sufficiently aroused.

As was he. Lust shivered up his spine and lodged deep in his gut. "Aye, if you didn't succumb to those tactics, I'd slather your juices over your arse then work two fingers inside that tempting dark hole. Oh, it would be such a tight fit, and so foreign you'd gasp your surrender before you could offer protest." He blew out a breath to temper his reaction. "You've never known bliss like that, I'll wager. The pressure employed from my fingers and my thick cock in your sheath will have you screaming my name in no time."

Bugger. His prick throbbed and pressed painfully against the front of his trousers. Perhaps his teasing had gone too far, for he was ready to explode.

"Damn your eyes, Adam. You don't play fair." That was all the warning he had from her before Caroline pulled his head down to hers and claimed his mouth in a searing kiss.

"I never claimed to be fair," he whispered against her lips, and then hunger and need took control. He devoured her as if she held the last breath of air in the world. Caroline returned the favor with as much enthusiasm as he, and it was he who gasped for breath. Desire licked through his veins and set his blood aflame. He refused to break his promise, no matter that every kiss, every meeting of their tongues, every caress from her hands on his body made him regret every word of that vow. "Do you want me, Caro?" He rested his forehead on hers. "You have to say it. I'll not dishonor what I told you before."

Damnation, but he'd walk away right now if she ordered it, no matter how difficult it would be, no matter that he'd no doubt spend in his pants before he could gain privacy.

"Yes." She bit his bottom lip. "Dear Lord, yes I want you." She nibbled a path beneath his jaw, in the place that always drove him wild. When she met his gaze, her eyes were heavy-lidded with passion. "You're a sickness in my blood that I cannot fight. Take me to bed, Captain. In this, we are of an accord."

"To hell with a bed," he muttered as he propelled them both over the wooden floor to the nearest wall. When her back connected with it, he grunted. "Once again, there's no time for proper."

"From your own admission, you've never been that," she reminded him as she fumbled with the buttons at the front of his trousers. When the placket fell open, his engorged cock sprang free. He held his breath when she wrapped her hand around his girth then squeezed. "I certainly wouldn't want you to be. This version of you is quite agreeable."

She pumped his length until he flicked her hand away. "Leave off, woman." Adam lifted her, levering her against the wall. "Legs around my waist." He rucked her skirts up the best he could in the precarious position. When she did as instructed, he leaned in and ravaged her. By the time he allowed them both air, their shallowed breathing rang in the silent room. "My God, Caro." He slid the head of his cock through her drenched folds. "I can't get enough of you." Then need guided his actions and with a flex of his hips, he penetrated her heat and didn't stop until he was fully seated. "Every time I look at you, I forget all else except being with you." It was as close as he'd come to sharing anything soft.

"Oh." A moan dragged the word out. She gripped his shoulders, her fingers digging in through all the layers of his coat and clothing. "Adam, now. Make me fly." She tilted her hips and he went in further still. "I need this." Her gaze captured his. "I need you."

Never had a statement been as sweet. He grasped her thighs, holding her steady, and thrust into her passage over and over, as deep as he dared, and as hard. Just as he'd tormented her with his words earlier, he delivered on the teasing now. Each stroke heightened his passion. Faster he worked into her pussy. With each drive, he watched her. A flush colored her cheeks. Her eyes closed and the red sweep of her lashes against her skin fascinated him. A gentle smile curved her kiss-swollen lips.

That gesture broke him. She should always look like that in his company, yet figuring out how to do that beyond the carnal escaped him.

All too soon, she stiffened. Her back arched and she clutched at him. "Adam. Oh, oh yes!" Her inner walls fluttered then contracted hard around his cock. They greedily gripped him as she tightened the lock of her ankles around his waist, which in turn dragged him into the vortex of darkness and light.

He couldn't last any longer. Seeing her hit release with all the fervor she did everything else brought him undone. With a curse, he thrust deep into her body. Then his prick pulsed and he came fiercer than he could remember. Stars erupted behind his closed eyelids. He ground his hips into hers to prolong the sensations.

Limp and sated, he slumped into her, and she looped her arms around his shoulders, hugging him close. While his pulse thundered in his temples, he turned his head and kissed the side of her neck. His chest heaved as he came back to himself. "Why can we not deport ourselves as a normal, genteel couple?" Though, what they did have was fine with him. It worked, after a fashion.

Caroline's laugh held a decidedly exhausted edge. "Perhaps that isn't the type of people we are. What is wrong with coming together like a thunderstorm?"

"Nothing, I'll wager." Though, was sharing only the physical enough to satisfy her? "Storms can be beautiful when they're not destructive." What would happen if passion faded?

"This doesn't exempt you from telling me the stories of when you were gone," she admonished in a quiet voice. "I still want to know."

"Aye." Apparently the physical wasn't, and he'd need to come to grips with that soon. "I promise I'll tell you everything once I square with it in my mind."

And he hoped to hell it wouldn't be too late.

❧ Chapter Eleven ❧

A low, eerie moan awoke Caroline during the early morning hours. She struggled into a sitting position while ever-plagued by the feeling something wasn't right. As her heartbeat thumped hard through her veins, she glanced through the gloom at the comforting room, but this wasn't her home.

Then the remembrance came tumbling back. No, she wasn't home at the Scoundrel's Trespass. Instead, she and Adam had decided to stay the night at her parents' cottage, for after their bout of passion, neither of them had wished to part, though nothing of import had occurred between them during a simple tea and a country dinner made from the meal her mother had already set aside for whomever would have minded the light that night.

The moan sounded again and she directed her attention beside her in the bed. Adam lay on his side, his back to her, but he shivered as if he'd been outside overlong. She put a hand to his shoulder. He didn't burn with fever and neither did he feel chilled, but he flinched and tried to shy away from her touch. Before she could do anything else, he thrashed his head on the pillow and mumbled, the words low and too unintelligible for her to distinguish.

"Adam." Caroline shook his shoulder. If he was locked in a nightmare, perhaps all he required was to be awakened.

He flopped onto his back, but his eyes remained closed. The filtered illumination from the light through the lacy curtains at the window gave away his agitation. It continued so much that fear and pain lined his expression. The more he moved, the farther the bedclothes slid down his bare body. He'd come to bed naked, apparently, after he'd tended the light for the last time. She'd been so exhausted she hadn't woken when he'd joined her. "No more. Please, God. Stop." The soft entreaty rang with desperation, his voice raw and thick from emotion.

"Adam, wake up." She raised her voice in the hopes that it would penetrate the nightmare. When that didn't work, Caroline leaned over him. She jostled his shoulder with more force than before. "Adam, you're dreaming. Wake up."

His eyes popped open and he stared with a wide gaze up into her face. "You can torture me all you want, but it will gain you nothing."

The taste of sour bile hit the back of her throat. Good Lord, he was still dreaming even while awake. "Adam." She tapped his cheek, but he closed a hand around her wrist, squeezing tight.

"You're no better than the French scum you claim to hate." He yanked downward and she came more fully over his body. "I will kill you if I have the chance."

A cry left her lips, and when he didn't release her, she climbed on top of him, straddling his waist. Her heart pounded with fear. Wherever he'd lost himself, he needed to return to the present before he put her at risk. "Let me go. I'm not them." She wrenched from his hold, but instead of fleeing the area like any sane woman would do, Caroline held his face between her palms. The coarse hairs from his beard rasped against her palms and sent a wave of need flowing through her. "Adam. Wake. Up." With a sense of regret, she drew back one hand and swiftly slapped his cheek.

The sound echoed in the silence. He gasped. His whole body stiffened. For one, heart-stopping second she thought he'd deliver her a facer or attempt to harm her another way, but he blinked, shook his head then stared at her. Horror and confusion dawned over his face. "Caro." He looked about the immediate area. "What are you doing?"

"Trying to calm you." Her chest heaved with relief, but her racing pulse didn't quiet. She stroked a hand along the side of his face. "You had a nightmare."

"Did I hurt you?" He pressed a hand to hers and held them both against his cheek. "Forgive me for anything I did while lost."

"No, not really." She flexed her other hand. Her wrist, though faintly sore, didn't appear to have suffered damage. "Though, you did frighten me."

"I apologize." Adam turned his head then pressed a kiss to her palm. His whiskers tickled her skin. "It happens at times. The horrors creep into my dreams. I can't escape it." When he shifted his gaze to hers, shadows still lurked in the depths. "To spare you, I shall endeavor to sleep elsewhere."

"It's not a bother. Perhaps," she forced a swallow into her tight throat, "perhaps it's good that I'm here and will remain with you. Do these dreams happen frequently?"

"At times." Exhaustion threaded his voice. "I often wonder if or when that darkness will win."

She bit her lip. "It won't. I don't want you lost permanently to the nightmares either."

"There is always that threat, but for now I'll keep fighting." When he made to pitch her off him, she resisted and remained sitting at his waist. "Caro, please. I need to tend to the light anyway."

"It will keep." This was the first chance she'd really had to question him about his history. "Tell me where you were just then. Let me help you through it."

He shook his head. "It's too ugly for a lady to hear."

"Try me." She situated herself more comfortably on top of him, only belatedly conscious that his cock hardened and grew, hot and ready at the crease of her rear. Awareness skittered along her nerve endings. The scrape of his body hair on the sensitive skin of her inner thighs and her folds shot heat into her core. She bit back a moan of pure desire. Now was not the time.

Adam drew in a shuddering breath but gave a curt nod. "I was on the British frigate, *Monitor*. They'd taken me and the few survivors of the *Scoundrel's* wreck aboard following the battle."

"Yes, I remember you mentioning them." She spoke in a low voice she usually reserved for small children or frightened livestock. Barely did she wish to breathe for fear of scaring him into moody silence.

"For a few days, I was grateful, even to the English, but once I'd recovered my strength, it became all too obvious why they'd rescued me and kept me alive." The muscles in his chest went taut beneath her hands. "The British aren't known as benevolent in the navy. They have a nasty habit of kidnapping sailors then pressing them into service for their own ships. Such was my new life."

"I assume you fought them?" As much as she wished to know, a part of her did not. If she wasn't told of how life really was, she could keep on pretending war was a little boy's game and not the horrible, life-threatening stupidity of men.

"Aye, and then my existence became worse." Adam ran his hands up the side of her legs, beneath the bunched night rail she'd borrowed from her mother to settle at her hips. He traced abstract circles on the skin there. Shivers chased up and down her spine. "Every refusal brought a session with the cat-o-nine-tails. Sometimes, if I was

140

especially quarrelsome, the captain would employ the whip on my back."

"Oh, Adam." Nurturing instincts kicked in. She wanted so much to put her arms around him, hold him and protect him, assure him everything would be all right now, but she knew he'd hate her for it, would assume it was pity that drove the emotion. So, she sat as still as she could, waiting.

"Eventually, I lost count of how many lashes I'd received during those long weeks. Those men tried to break my spirit, oh how they tried." His voice, ringing with hate and tinged with despair, lowered. "That wouldn't happen until much later."

"What did you do?" Tears stung the backs of her eyelids. She blinked them away. If she showed emotion, would he stop talking?

"Honestly, I grew tired of the pain and grew bored from inactivity. I agreed to their terms and eventually went on to captain the *Monitor* once various battles wiped out the attending officers." He shook his head as if wishing to clear his thoughts. "In those three years, I committed atrocious acts in the name of the Crown. They used my act of pardon against me. I killed men from whichever nation didn't fly England's colors, all for the sake of upholding Britain's might and showing her power. Filling her coffers was an added bonus. As long as I took in a certain amount of coin each month, I was allowed to remain alive."

She flinched from the bitterness in the words, and giving in to the daring, she leaned over him then kissed his forehead. "I'm sorry you had to suffer."

"I hated myself—still do—for what I did merely to remain alive until such time that I could escape." He fisted a hand. "I hear the dying screams and desperate pleas for mercy each time I close my eyes. It's something I alternately wish to forget but hope I never will, for the remembrance forces me to be better, to never return to those days. To never be that man again." He gripped her hips so tight his fingers dug into her skin. No doubt she'd be bruised later.

But she didn't protest. Caroline's attempt to stifle a sob resulted in a gasping sort of sound. Finally, he'd shared a part of his torment with her and what did she do? Turn into a watering pot. "You did what you had to do until circumstance could change," she murmured, but it wasn't enough. Nothing she could ever say would ever be enough, would never heal those wounds she couldn't see. For the first time in her life, she began to understand the man her husband had become.

Perhaps he needed her more than he'd ever say, and what was more, mayhap she needed him to fill her too long empty arms, to show him his struggle hadn't been in vain, that she finally understood what had kept him away and still did to a certain extent.

The knowledge rocked her to her core.

Caroline did the only thing she knew that would comfort him. She rose to her knees and slid a hand between their bodies. When she found his rampant cock, she wrapped her fingers around the turgid girth.

"What are you doing?" Strain graveled his voice.

"Showing you how grateful I am that you came back to me, no matter how many pieces you've returned in." And that was it—no longer did it matter that he'd been gone for so long or that there was still an enormous gap between them. In this moment, they needed each other.

"Caro, this is hardly the time…"

Before he could further protest, she impaled herself on his rigid member. Her moan of appreciation blended with his. He filled her channel completely, and at this angle, his thick girth hit every pleasure point she had. Caroline wriggled her hips for a better fit, grabbed hold of his shoulders to anchor herself, then slowly moved up and down on his cock. The wet, sucking noises of their joined bodies was the only sound in the room.

And still she played him as a violinist wielded a bow. It was different, this tender coming together, from anything she'd experienced with him before. Those other times, he'd commanded the coupling; he'd been the one to initiate intercourse. But now, she held control, held both his pleasure and hers, and she could draw it out for as long as she chose.

Feminine power was heady stuff. A grin pulled at the corners of her mouth. It was wonderful. Flutters danced through her core. Coiling heat built in her lower belly.

She said nothing. Neither did he. Words weren't appropriate in this early morning communion. The lantern's light bathed his face and showed the stark craving and confusion in his stormy eyes. Those emotions were echoed in her chest, but she wanted more—she wanted all of him. When would he give her what she needed? No matter that her heart was greedy, her body recalled her to the moment… and it was greedier still.

Her movements grew more frantic as great waves of throbbing desire held her. She gyrated her hips against his after each down stroke. It wasn't enough. Longing welled from deep within, a gnawing, nagging void that she couldn't seem to fill, yet she remained locked in the ageless dance and she didn't slow in her quest for release.

As in everything carnal between them, he sensed her want. Adam gripped her hips tighter. He caught her gaze with his then thrust upward, meeting each of her strokes with one of his own. They moved in a rhythm they'd perfected years ago.

She concentrated on the heated pleasure overtaking her senses. His labored breathing mirrored hers, and all too soon the shivery tingles gave way to the all-consuming contractions through her core. Caroline didn't bother to stifle her scream as release caught her in its voracious tide. She threw back her head and let the undulating bliss break over her.

"Devil take it." Adam's soft cursing preceded his own release. His cock pulsed and warm jets of seed flooded her passage. "Good God, woman, you wear me out." Emotion rasped in his voice, but she couldn't identify it; she was surprised it was there.

"Stop complaining," she gently admonished as she came back to herself. She collapsed on top of him and breathed in his earthy, manly scent. "Just take the gift as it was given and be grateful." Her smile deepened.

For the moment, she certainly was.

Caroline frowned as she walked through her snow-covered garden hours after she'd lain with Adam. She set her gaze east in the direction of the lighthouse. What was her husband doing at this moment? Pleasant warmth slid through her body. Her husband, the man who guided her pleasure and satisfied the basest needs of her body. He was nothing if not a thoroughly intense lover, and the fact that she came together with him with all the force of a hurricane should either make her happy or terrify her. A shiver raced up her spine as she remembered the hurried lovemaking in the lighthouse as well as their gentle coming together as she'd soothed him. There was something about him she couldn't deny. Perhaps she shouldn't try.

And yet, he wasn't by her side this midday. Adam maintained that he wouldn't break his promise—today Paul was due to visit and he'd give them their privacy. Her heart had gone out to him at the admission. What must it be like, knowing she might choose Paul over him, the man she'd wed all those years ago, as well as the man who'd been broken too many times?

After their passionate coupling following his early morning terrors, they'd walked the shore, and she'd told him the history of the island or identified a few animals they'd seen. Mostly, they communed in silence. He hadn't mentioned his past again and neither had she.

It wasn't a bad thing. Strength and support had passed between them in the quiet. They might not have shared anything with words, but perhaps what each of them needed didn't rely on conversation or the noise of talking.

How strange, yet somewhat freeing.

The little tug at her heart troubled her. Incredibly, she missed him. His big, rugged presence, his haunted eyes, and even his penchant for avoidance filled the emptiness her life had fallen into, but she still couldn't figure him out. Why was he so reticent? Should it bother her he didn't wish to open up to her fully, or should she accept him as the man he was now and not worry she'd never know all of his secrets? Then again, he'd never been very verbose.

Except, it's so hard to read him. Would closeness spring between them that had nothing to do with carnal intimacy? She worried her bottom lip. *Can I live the rest of my life with a man who dwells too much in his own head, a man who has seen too many terrible things that he may not ever be able to function in society?* The nightmares would surely see to that. Her pulse accelerated. If gripped by the memories too long, would he leave as an escape? Then she gasped.

145

Perhaps by pushing her away and not sharing with her, he meant to keep himself safe from being hurt again.

How well she understood that. But what was life without opening the heart again? Wasn't that why she hadn't exactly been as forthcoming in sharing with him as she could be? She didn't invite emotional intimacy with him, even if he never offered.

Aren't we a pair?

"I'm surprised to find you out here, my love."

The soothing tenor of Paul's voice yanked her from her musings. The endearment warmed her. It was good to hear such things. She glanced up as he slowly approached her. "You know how walking my garden helps me calm my mind." Though, his presence did wonders for that as well. Dressed impeccably, as always, his buff-colored trousers, gray wool greatcoat, and beaver felt top hat gave him the air of a fine English gentleman. There were times when she'd love to knock off that hat and muss his golden hair merely to see if he'd become flustered. She bit back a giggle at the uncharitable thought.

"No doubt recent events have thrown you off-kilter." He closed the distance then slipped his arms about her waist. His brown eyes in the sunshine were the color of molten chocolate. "Perhaps we should talk of other things."

She smiled as he placed a fleeting kiss to her forehead. Gentle warmth flowed through her. He was such an anchor in her life and never failed to lend her support whenever she needed it. "What other things do you hint at?" But, she knew, of course. As with Adam, who wanted nothing more than to best Paul, this man would feel the same about her husband.

"For one, where is Adam? Can I be so lucky to find he's given in to the lure of the sea?"

"The captain is at the lighthouse and will be there until you depart this evening." She fought the urge to roll her eyes.

"Oh?" Surprise infused the word. "I'd happened across your parents as they arrived into town. When your father told me of the need here, I couldn't believe he'd actually asked Adam to take responsibility for the light."

"Well, I'm certain he thought you'd need to prepare, and someone had to mind the light until you came. In truth, I believe it's good for Adam. Keeps him connected to the sea he still loves." When she'd come upon him on the gallery yesterday with the sea and gray skies as backdrop, the sense of power he exuded had been amplified. He'd never go far from his first love, and if minding the light kept him home, who was she to dissuade him?

"It's only a matter of time before he seeks adventure again." Paul released her but only as much as to guide her through the snow-covered garden rows and to a wooden bench at the rear of the oasis. He peered into her face, his gaze searching hers, for what she couldn't imagine. "He's a wanted criminal for crimes against the British navy. From what I understand, there's a bounty on his head." His eyes twinkled. "It wouldn't do for you to become too much attached to him again when he's at risk of being away for one reason or another."

She glanced sharply at him. "How do you know that?"

"I've heard gossip around town. Adam himself told me about the bounty."

"Well, he didn't inform me." *That bastard.* Why wouldn't he share such an important detail?

Paul shrugged. "Perhaps he didn't wish to worry you." He shifted his attention to the bench as he dusted the covering of snow from the weathered wood. "Come and sit with me for a while. I'd enjoy having your attention all to myself." A good-natured chuckle rumbled up from his chest. "I suppose I should thank your reprobate husband for being such an upstanding gentleman and allowing us this time."

"What Adam proposed is fair — to me, not really to him, which speaks volumes. He's given me two weeks to choose between you and him." Caroline frowned when he sat before she did. He must be truly aggravated if he'd forget ingrained manners.

"How magnanimous. And if I win, what's to say he'll play the gentleman over landing me a facer?" His eyes flashed, his expression pinched.

"He's not that man anymore. He's different, yes, and definitely broken. At times he's lost in the nightmares of his time with the British."

"Fascinating." He crossed his arms over his chest and raised one to tap a finger to his chin. Today, he'd neglected to wear gloves. "But he could be portraying that persona to have you fall for him again."

She shook her head. "I'm not in love with him." Though she sucked in a shallow breath and let it out again. She wasn't. *I'm not.* She loved Paul, didn't she? Yet, she felt *something* for her husband as evidenced by their continuing return to intercourse. "He might not be ideal, but he's not the person I married ten years ago." A smile curved her lips. "He's… interesting." What kind of man would lead her into an impromptu waltz then still ask her permission before he let lust consume him? The old Adam would have plowed ahead whether she'd agreed or not.

"Devil take it, Caroline." Paul narrowed his eyes. His lips thinned when she gasped. "I beg your pardon. I don't wish to talk about Adam." He tugged on her hand, and she tumbled awkwardly into his lap. "I want to talk about us. More specifically, what I can't wait to do with you once you're finally mine."

Heat shot into her cheeks. She struggled into a more proper position, but even then she sat across his legs with hers off to the side. He supported her with an arm around her back. Such close quarters had her confusion flaring and awareness skating through her body. "What are you doing?" She glanced around. The high evergreen shrubs shielded them from the house while wilderness greeted her from the other side. Nothing else stirred in the garden.

"Taking a few liberties." Paul placed a row of feather-weighted kisses along her jawline. When he reached her ear, he lightly bit her lobe. "Will you indulge me?" He trailed his free hand down her leg.

Had he planned ahead of time for the tryst? Never had she known him not to be proper. "Ah, that depends on what else you intend." Shivers danced down her spine when he drew his hand up her leg then walked his fingers up her torso to linger briefly at the curve of her breast before continuing on to the clasp of her cloak. The heat from his hand seeped into the skin of her throat. "Anyone could come upon us."

"You said yourself that Adam will remain at the lighthouse. And don't your cook and maid visit the mainland today for their monthly trip to the market?" He manipulated the clasp with ease and the cloak fell open. "Or, if you'd rather, we can move inside." He drew the tip of his index finger along the lace edging of her scooped neckline while he grinned. His expression brimmed with a wickedness that had previously been foreign to him. Her breath caught in excitement. "It matters not to me. I merely want you and wish to show you how much."

"Oh." She barely needed to lift her face to his and he claimed her lips with a gentle kiss. So courtly, so courteous, so different than Adam. Her heart felt light when she was with Paul. Interaction between them was effortless, comfortable from years of friendship. A tremor rocked her core and she shifted on his lap. For the second time that day, a man desired her—a man she could so easily envision her future with. In him, she'd always know what to expect. There'd be no puzzling behavior, no struggle for sharing. She took in a quick gasp of air as her heart pounded. Was he what she wanted? Then she drew her tongue along his firm bottom lip before kissing him. Perhaps she needed to find out. "It's a nice day if you can stand the chill. Ever since you had pneumonia two winters ago…"

"I'll be fine and have never enjoyed better health."

"Then, why waste the sunshine?" How far would he take the tryst? How far would she let him, especially when she was just beginning to understand Adam? She sent the thought to the back of her mind. She owed it to herself to figure out which man she wanted above the other.

"Why waste it indeed?"

⨪⨪ Chapter Twelve ⨪⨪

The thrill of victory lanced down Paul's spine when he heard the sweet words of her acceptance of his rather unorthodox plan. Desperate times called for desperate measures, and if he had to go outside the normal bounds of proper courting, he would. Adam thought he'd gain the upper hand by sneaking into her parents' good graces, did he? Not unless he wanted a war. Who'd continued to bring them supplies and help with minor repairs around the island for the last ten years? If the Winslows treated anyone like a son of the family, it would be him.

And he'd gain the damn lighthouse in the bargain. That alone would find him favor with the British admiralty and ensure his holdings were unmolested during the damned war. Hopefully, it would also mean the ships connected to his shipping company would be given unrestricted passive into Portsmouth once British presence increased. According to his contact with the navy, they'd been sweeping the coast on the search of lighthouses in the quest to control all the harbors. What his countrymen would do with the light didn't concern him. Wreck American vessels or only let England's through, he didn't care. He merely wanted Caroline and the light, and he'd gain it once he married her.

"Paul? Is there something wrong?" Concern rang in her voice as she arched her neck, giving him easier access to her warm flesh.

"No, darling. In fact, everything is wonderful." And he'd do his level best to keep it that way. He slid a hand to her nape, cupping the side of her smooth throat and rubbing the hollow with his thumb. When she shivered, he replaced his thumb with his lips and gladly teased the spot with his mouth and tongue. She was an enticing bundle on his lap, for certain, and he couldn't believe he hadn't had the courage to compromise her before. How silly to think giving her physical affection might scare her away. "Dearest Caroline, how happy you make me."

She stroked a hand down the side of his face and he glanced up. "You make me happy as well." Her blue eyes sparkled in the sunlight, and with her lips parting with a smile, she was easily the most attractive women he'd seen. Of course, ever since he'd realized his feelings for her, she'd been the only woman to exist in his world.

"I'm glad." He claimed her lips, slanting his mouth overs hers again and again. Every taste of her sent his desire soaring. For so long he'd waited to show her how he'd felt. Now, when he had the chance to completely ravish her, all he wanted to do was go slow and savor each moment. He pulled slightly away. "You should give up this silly idea of letting Adam attempt to woo you." He tugged the bodice of her modest dress down. More and more of her creamy breast was exposed. A tiny bit more encouragement and the mound was bared to his hungry gaze.

"Don't you think it's only fair? I am married to him." Yet, she turned into his touch as he palmed her breast. A shuddering sigh left her lips when he rubbed the pad of his thumb back and forth over the rosy nipple until it puckered and hardened. "If there is still a hope our marriage can be salvaged, I owe it to him and to me to try."

Paul grunted and he stilled his fingers on her warm flesh. "He deserves nothing except to be treated as he's treated you." Her loyalty to Adam both made him proud but also struck fear through his heart. If she chose him over her husband, would she remain faithful to him since apparently she enjoyed gracing his rival's bed?

"No, he doesn't." She turned his face toward hers and held his gaze. "That is the same as saying you don't deserve my love and affection because you're a British supporter." A small smile curved her lips. "I need to do this, Paul. I have to attempt to decide if I want to spend the rest of my life with Adam or with you."

"What's difficult? You love me. You don't love him." Why couldn't she see her reprobate husband was all wrong for her?

"I do love you, but I'm not sure what I feel for Adam. He's... persuasive and completely makes me forget myself." She shifted her gaze to his cravat. "As difficult as it is, there is no option that would allow me to have you both, so give me the freedom to explore. Please."

Her ability to remain levelheaded was just one of the reasons he loved her. "Very well, but do consider I can make you feel the same if given the same chance." He resumed manipulation of her breast. "Bear in mind that I've waited a long time indeed to be with you in all the ways a man should. I won't take kindly to being shoved out by a man whose only connection to you is through a signature on a scrap of paper in the eyes of the law and God." But then, her words truly sank into his desire soaked consciousness.

...there is not an option that would allow me to have you both...

Interesting concept, especially since he and Adam had often shared women in the past. He stilled his ministrations yet again. *But no.* Even if he wished to consider such an intriguing possibility, he refused to share with or play second fiddle to Adam. His friend forfeited the right to Caroline's smiles, her touch, her body and even her company when he'd sailed away with her not a new bride more than a few months.

"Paul?" Caroline huffed with annoyance. "If you persist in woolgathering, I'm returning to the house." She made to wriggle off his lap.

"You're right. I apologize." He gave her the smile he reserved only for her. "I've been remiss in letting my thoughts claim my attention." He resituated her so that she now straddled his lap. A shudder moved through him at the acute awareness that her legs were splayed and only a few layers of fabric separated her heat from his aching cock. "How would my lady enjoy being pleasured?" Strain graveled his voice.

A throaty laugh left her lips. "Mmm, I heartily approve of this playful side of you." Her eyes sparkled and she wrapped her arms loosely around his shoulders. "Why don't you leave it to chance?" She arched an eyebrow. God, how much did he adore that vibrant shade of red hair or that cocky tilt to her head? "Perhaps you should do something that will leave an indelible impression on me. After all, you have my undivided attention for today."

For today. Not a lifetime. At least not yet. It just meant he'd need to work harder. "This is true." And it was all the permission he needed. With her kiss-swollen lips slightly parted and her nipple still erect from his play, she was the very essence of a woman ready for a tumble. "Let's see what mischief I can get up to." So saying, he tugged the remainder of her bodice down, freeing her other breast. The sunlight caught the blue-green sea glass pendant and his chest tightened. Another reminder she belonged to Adam. He shoved the thought away. "You're as beautiful as I've always imagined." He cupped both fleshy mounds and gently squeezed. When she moaned and her eyelashes fluttered, he chuckled. "And oh so tempting."

He couldn't deny himself any longer.

Paul bent his head to first one breast and then the other. He lifted them, trailing kisses along the upper slopes of each. So warm, so satiny soft. The faint scent of roses drifted to his nose and spurred his actions. After covering one turgid tip with his mouth, he suckled the pebbled bud and ran the tip of his tongue over it, which elicited pleased gasps from the woman on his lap. "Like that, do you?" He looked up into her face.

"Yes." She wriggled and pressed herself more firmly into his hands. "Don't stop."

The hunger in her eyes and the abandon in her actions thrilled him. He knew she'd be receptive to his advances. Always when he'd dreamed of being with her, she'd been calm and gentle, waiting for him to initiate all acts or teach her the different ways of pleasure. He slid a hand to her nape, holding her steady. How much he wished her hair was unbound, but now was not the time.

Of course, she was no shrinking virgin. No doubt Adam had thoroughly put her through her paces and taught her all manner of erotic acts. With a growl, he shoved those thoughts aside. No matter. His skill in the bedroom might not match his friend's, but he wasn't a complete lack wit.

With renewed vigor, he continued to suck her nipple while he rolled the neglected bud with his free hand. Her soft moan slid over him like a silk garment and he increased his pressure. She let her head loll back onto her shoulder. He knew the swift urge to throw her on the ground, remove her clothes and claim her body, but he tamped it. That wouldn't be well done, not when the garden was snow-covered and cold. Yet, his cock thrust hard and tight against the confines of his trousers. Devil take it, he wanted her.

Not now. Not here. Their first time together should be in a proper bed.

So, he would do the next best thing—he'd send her soaring. With a grin, he moved his hand from her breast, through the many folds of her bunched skirting, then finally between her splayed thighs. Her warmth sank into his skin, and as soon as his fingers glanced along her already damp curls, she shivered.

"Paul, never say you intend to..." Her words trailed off when he, indeed, slid his fingers through those precious curls then along her slick folds. "Oh, God." Her eyes fluttered closed and she fell into his chest. "Make me fly, my love."

His heart squeezed. Yes, he would win the day from that bastard Adam. Biting back a chuckle, he spent a few moments strumming his fingers along that wet flesh. What would it be like to replace his fingers with his cock? He swallowed around the ball of emotion in his throat. Soon, he'd claim her as a man did his wife. Now, he'd make certain she'd not forget him even when she was with her husband. "I adore how ready you are for me, and we've done naught but talk and kiss."

"I think we've both thought about this moment for a long time." Her whispered words steamed his ear.

"Yes, we have." Emboldened by her acceptance, he slipped first one finger into her tight, drenched heat then added a second. "Would that it was my tongue dipping into your honey, then my cock moving in and out of your passage," he said in a soft, strangled voice while he worked her dripping channel.

A shiver ripped through her. She fairly hummed on his lap. Her breathing shallowed. "It can be so soon—" Whatever else she might have said disappeared beneath a long moan. She wriggled her hips and pressed her sex tighter into his palm. "Paul, please."

"Gladly." As he finger-fucked her, he flicked her swollen bud with his thumb until it came further out of hiding. "Would that I could see you, eat my fill from your wonderful body." He imagined what she'd taste like, both tart and sweet, pretended what that slippery nub would feel like against his tongue, what she'd sound like if he teased that bit of flesh with his teeth.

"Oh, you naughty boy." She gasped. "You'll send me over with your words alone." She purred. "Adam uses vulgarity to arouse me, but your genteel way of doing things is just as effective."

"Then I shall endeavor to try harder." His chuckle sounded forced even to his own ears. God damn Adam anyway. No gently bred woman should be subjected to a sailor's vocabulary. He clenched his jaw and attempted to ignore the throbbing pain in his cock as well as his friend. "So many times I've dreamed of claiming you, of making love to you throughout the night until you're sated and happy and looking at me with such love in the morning that you refuse to leave your bed." *Refuse to leave me.*

As he talked, he continued to work her channel. Her juices coated his fingers, helped him slide faster and harder into her while he kept increased pressure on her button. Soon enough he found a rhythm that he liked and she seemed to enjoy. Caroline gyrated on his lap. Each movement of her hips was in time to his strokes. So easy it was to imagine his cock moving within her, thrusting again and again deep inside her, making her hips arch and her eyes glaze with passion.

"Paul," she hissed. Her eyes closed and her desperate moans filled his ears. "Oh, oh." She bit back another moan only to utter a sharp, "Ah!" Her body stiffened while the walls of her core fluttered and tightened around his fingers. Then she gave into a shudder. "Oh, Paul." She squirmed then flung her arms around his shoulders. "Thank you for the wonderful gift." She placed a kiss to his cheek as she melted into him.

He withdrew his hand from beneath her skirting then held her close, for if he moved at all, he'd explode. The sounds she'd made, the reactions of her body, the heat and very essence of her had him aroused beyond measure. There was nothing he wanted more in his life than her. Too many years he'd loved her from afar. Now was the time to do something about it.

"Caroline." He drew in a deep breath then pulled back in order to peer into her faintly flushed face. "Come to the mainland with me this evening. I'd like to take you to dinner." How many times had she told him she adored an evening out at one of the nicer eating establishments? He wished to have his contemporaries see her on his arm, wanted to know the pride of showing her about Portsmouth, mere days away from being able to shout from the rooftops that after all this time she was finally his.

Surprise widened her eyes. "Truly? You remembered!" When he nodded, she bounced on his lap, much to his horror. A groan tore from his throat. As she realized why, she snickered. "I'm sorry." With a kiss to the tip of his nose, she eased from his person to sit beside him on the bench.

Paul pasted a rueful grin to his face. "Yes, well, it's no secret how much I'm affected by you." Still, he was grateful for the greatcoat that hid the obvious evidence of his regard.

"You're adorable." She wrapped a hand around his upper arm and squeezed. "Yes, I would love to join you for dinner."

A few hours later, Paul escorted his lady along the weathered boards of the dock. The ferryman had just pulled up, since it was the regular time that Paul usually took himself back home. "Evening, my good man," he called as greeting to the grizzled fellow. "You'll be taking both of us to the mainland then we'll return with you on your last trip of the evening."

The afternoon had passed in comfortable ways. He and Caroline had read to each other from books of poetry. She'd made them popping corn on the hearth. Then they'd spent a delightful interlude while he "helped" her dress for dinner. Again, he'd resisted the temptation of having her naked and willing beneath him. There was plenty of time for that, and he did want their first time together to be romantic, not borne of opportunity.

"Matters not to me who I take," the ferryman replied with a grin. "The coin for passage is the same."

"That it is." Paul handed Caroline into the longboat then made to follow when an agitated shout froze him to the dock.

"What the hell do you think you're doing?" Adam bounded over to them from the direction of the cottage, his limp more pronounced. His expression was as dark as a thundercloud. "You will not take my wife to the mainland!"

Paul bit back the smug grin he desperately wished to show, for this was truly his victory over his rival, but it didn't halt the annoyance. Why couldn't the man leave them be? "I can and I will," he said in an even voice once his friend drew abreast of him. He held the other man's gaze even as ire rose in his chest. "After all, isn't this my day to be with her?" He lowered his voice lest the ferryman hear. "And the day isn't over. Not until midnight."

Adam's only answer was a growl and the fisting of his hands.

"However, if you wish to accompany us, you may. I'm certain there are a few folks in town who are anxious to make your acquaintance." And if they weren't alerted to Adam's presence through their spy network, he'd sent a runner to the closest naval office to make sure they were. How lucky would it be to have finally secured Caroline's affections and rid himself of his rival in the same day? "The choice is yours." This time, he let his full cheeky grin unfurl.

"I don't know what game you play, but I don't like it." The breeze whipped Adam's longish hair, tearing it from its leather tie. Behind him, the setting sun into dark storm clouds further added to the tension between them. The man resembled a storm-tossed god of the sea in his dark anger and shabby clothing. No wonder Caroline remained conflicted by him. Any woman would.

He hated the grudging respect that gripped him. "You don't have to like it, but you did make the rules." Paul narrowed his eyes. He risked a glance over his shoulder at Caroline, now sitting on one of the benches with a wide, worried gaze. When he gave Adam his attention once more, he said, "All's fair in love and war, my friend. You've had your chance, now it's my turn. And if I happen to win in both this night, so be it."

Adam brought a fist up. "What the devil does that mean?"

"Nothing that concerns you for as long as you keep to the island." Let Adam think what he would. Perhaps that would tip things into his favor.

"I should land you a facer right this instant." A tick in Adam's cheek flared just under his left eye.

"Then do so." Paul shored up his stance as he awaited the blow. It wouldn't be the first time his friend and he had fought with fists and punches.

"Prick." He shifted his gaze to Caroline then frowned and let his hand fall to his side. A bit of softness entered his expression and stole the edge on his anger. That emotion troubled Paul. Could it be that he truly cared for Caroline and he really wasn't the man who'd left the island ten years before? "Very well, but I will be waiting for your return. See if I don't, and as soon as the clock strikes midnight, you better hope your arse is in that ferry."

Wanting nothing more than to infuriate Adam, Paul sketched him a mocking bow. "To the victor goes the spoils, eh Montmorency?" With that, he turned his back on his friend then joined Caroline in the boat.

She immediately grabbed his hand. "What was that all about?"

Paul sent one last scathing glance at his rival then pointedly ignored the bigger man standing on the dock with his arms crossed over his barrel chest. "Nothing important. Merely your husband attempting to assert a claim." A claim he desperately didn't wish for his rival to have. He patted her hand as the ferryman set them into motion.

The sooner he gave the captain up to the British admiralty, the sooner he could begin the life he'd thought he might have with Caroline. So then, why did his stomach clench at the thought of betraying his best friend?

⨳ Chapter Thirteen ⨳

Adam checked the vents once more. The damn wind had changed direction since the sun had set, which didn't bode well for the coming night. Yet another storm brewed, and the bulk of it would be upon them in the next couple of hours. For the moment, the lanterns remained lit, though their wicks flickered wildly with each gust and push of snow flurries. She'd hold, but it would be a battle. He'd need to make certain he kept coffee on the stove.

As he completed another round of the galleries, the flash and glimmer of light on the water drew his attention. It bobbed as if floating on the waves. He squinted through the snowflakes and hunched his shoulders against the gusts. The ferry had returned. One glance at his scratched and battered pocket watch revealed it was half past ten in the evening. After shoving the watch into his pocket, Adam slammed through the door and made his descent down the seventy-odd stairs. His footsteps rang on the metal. By the time he'd gained the service room, his temper had risen to a frenzied pitch.

What had occurred between Caroline and Paul while she'd been in his company?

He clenched his jaw so tight pain glanced up into his temple. Caro was his wife, damn it. This deal he'd struck with her was insane. Why couldn't she realize she belonged with him?

It took all of a few minutes to exit the lighthouse then make his way to the dock. The snow had picked up in intensity and swirled in eddies about the weathered wood. He waited for the two of them to disembark while agony held him captive. Every grip of her hand in Paul's, every giggle she uttered, every soft look she directed his way speared his heart with tiny needles. By the time the duo reached the head of the short path at the dock's end, Adam's temper had churned into a veritable storm inside him.

"About damn time you brought her back," he grumbled when Paul moved into earshot.

"And a good evening to you as well," his friend responded with uncanny cheeriness. He halted before Adam then gave Caroline's hand a pat from where it rested on his forearm. "If you were wondering, dinner in town was as lovely as my companion."

"I don't give a fig about your dinner," Adam muttered. He glanced at his wife, who wore the beginnings of a scowl. "Are you quite finished?"

Caroline narrowed her eyes. "Don't do this, Adam. You promised you wouldn't interfere."

"Tell me how inquiring if your evening is finished construes interference? If I wanted to make a nuisance of myself, I'd demand to know what the two of you did throughout the day." That not knowing was killing him slowly. Did they sleep together? Did his friend put his hands on Caroline? Did she give him access to her intimate parts, which should only be reserved for her husband? The urge to bellow grew strong, but he tamped it. He grabbed her upper arm then pulled her to his side. In the gloom and snow, he couldn't ascertain the emotions in her eyes.

"Yes, in fact, we've decided the evening has drawn to a close." Paul took possession of her other arm. "I was in the process of escorting Caroline back to the house before you rudely waylaid us." Annoyance wove through his tone even though his expression remained placid.

"Like hell." Adam tightened his hold. "You've done your duty, now be off. I'll walk Caroline home."

"What about the light?" Paul jeered. "Surely you don't mean to disappoint Mr. Winslow the second night you're on the job? Because, if so, he did ask me to do the job. It's almost as if he expected you to fail." He looked about through the snow. "Looks to be a bad storm moving in."

"That is none of your affair," Adam replied.

Paul's lips tightened into a thin line. "It is, for the Winslows have been a second family to me during the years of your absence. They treat me like the son they never had. It appalls me to know how little you think of them if you're willing to abandon the light as easily as you've abandoned everything else in your life."

"God damn you." The statement slid out with rage clinging to each word. "You'll answer for that slight. This lighthouse belongs to me now anyway as part of Caroline's dowry. You will never again need to set foot in it."

"That is a wrong assumption, and one I've already corrected for you," she inserted, no less angry than she'd been before. "My father made certain it wasn't included in the dowry. While everything on the island might have been, the lighthouse is his alone, as it has been for generations." She shook her head. "It will pass to me upon his death. Neither of you will own it. The law and what's expected of a woman and her alleged rights can go hang. I will never give it up to either of you."

Adam frowned. At least Paul would never gain it. "Too bad, Paul. Looks like you're thwarted again, in case you wanted such a thing. Would have been quite the jewel for you to give to your precious British."

"Things can change with enough incentive," the other man murmured.

"What the bloody hell does that mean?" Adam bellowed.

"Enough!" Caroline wrenched out of their hold. She popped her hands on her hips. "This posturing between the two of you has to stop." Her glare encompassed both of them. "I refuse to be seen as an object to take possession of, as chattel. I am my own woman, a person with needs. I have feelings and know my own mind, and right now, I'm disgusted by both of you."

"I beg your pardon, Caroline. I let pride and jealousy get the better of me," Paul replied with nothing but consideration in his voice. How could a man such as him be that sincere? "Pray, forgive me and let me take you home." He reached out a hand to her.

She skittered away a few steps. "Of course you're forgiven." For a second her soft gaze lingered on him, which sent pain through Adam's belly as if stuck by a hot poker. Then she snapped her attention to him, and blue lightning blazed in her eyes. "However, there is no call for your behavior. You promised and you broke that promise. After everything, you're reverting to your former self." She shook her head then drew her cloak tighter about her frame. "I will walk home alone."

Adam's protest blended with Paul's.

"But, the snow is picking up intensity." He couldn't shake how much her disappointment weighed on him or the self-loathing his failure brought to the forefront. Why the hell couldn't he just act like a civilized person around her?

"It's dark and it's late. Let me accompany you." Paul's soft-spoken offer grated on Adam's nerves. No matter that he'd had the same thought, he'd never be able to voice it wrapped in niceties like Paul.

"Stop! I won't stand here and listen to the two of you bicker — over me." Her voice wavered, but she retained control. "Both of you mean too much to me and I refuse to have a friendship as strong as yours used to be felled due to jealousy."

"Caroline, darling, if you'd but send him—" Paul interrupted.

"I will not choose right now! I cannot." Desperation rang in the exclamation. She held up her hands, palms outward. "I'm not a delicate piece of china, Paul." Her livid gaze landed on him and Adam snickered. "My pace, when needed, can be quite brisk. I can navigate the path in my sleep." Then she looked at Adam. "I've lived in the District of Maine all my life. I well know how the weather is and I've been out in snow before. Don't disrespect me by thinking an incoming storm will be a match for the heat of my temper."

"I understand that, but what about your snowshoes? The snow on that particular path is still deep. You know how it drifts."

If possible, her glare strengthened. A lesser man would have mumbled an excuse and run away. "I detest that you're right." She clenched one of her hands into a fist. "However, there are snowshoes around back of the cottage. I'll borrow a pair." She stormed past them and into the cottage. The sound of doors slamming reached his ears as they waited. A quick minute later she returned, stomping over the earth with the snowshoes strapped to her boots. She yanked up her skirts so he could see that she'd done it. "Satisfied?"

"In that, yes. The visual wasn't needed." Adam knew enough not to attempt to stop her as she swept past him once more. That he remembered well, the blazing temper she fell into when pushed into a corner. Hadn't she run him out of the barn with a pitchfork a week after they'd wed when he'd teased a horse into rearing? His chest tightened and he rubbed a finger in a circular pattern over the old scar at his temple. Why now did that old memory come back to him?

However, perhaps his rival hadn't had cause to witness Caroline in her full glory. Paul rushed after her then dared to lay a hand on her shoulder, halting her forward progress. She turned on him like a caged tiger. With jerky movements, she shook off his touch, and from the hand gestures it appeared she was telling the man what he could do with himself. Paul, to his credit, argued his case, but the wind whipped their words away and prevented Adam from hearing the whole exchange. Finally, she shot out a hand and slapped him. Good God she had a temper and for once he was glad it wasn't directed at him. Then she resumed her angry march down the path, her skirts snapping about her ankles. Adam followed her progress with his gaze until the night and the forest swallowed her.

"Damn fool man." He pivoted to return to the cottage, but a hail from the ferryman stopped him.

"Water's getting angry. If you don't have need of me, I'll go back now." The man's longboat bobbed with force on the waves.

"That's fine," Paul said as he approached. "I'll ask Mrs. Montmorency for a room tonight. If the weather turns tomorrow, I'll row myself back."

"Suit yourself and good luck. She's in a right good temper." The ferryman threw himself fully into the boat then began the laborious task of the return trip.

"You will *not* stay beneath my roof; not as long as I have breath," Adam stated to his unlikely companion before turning away and heading toward the cottage.

"I beg to differ," Paul said in a dangerously soft voice. "You're no longer onboard a ship, Captain. You gave up the right to command anyone when you left."

Before Adam could answer, Paul bolted at him from behind and they both tumbled to the snow-covered ground in a heap of limbs, but Paul squirmed until he faced Adam.

"Why did you have to return? We were all happy enough here without you," his friend demanded on the heels of a punch to Adam's jaw.

Pain exploded through his face. What the devil was he about? "Are you mad?" With a grunt, Adam heaved Paul off his frame then staggered to his feet. If it was a fight he wanted, fine. "Why wouldn't I come back to Caroline? I didn't survive the horrors of the British navy and their stinking prisons to be forced from the only life I want now." He delivered a punch of his own once Paul gained his footing. Unlike the times in his past when all he could do was fight to survive, lashing out now wasn't as satisfying. "Last time I checked, you didn't command my life."

"You've ruined everything." Paul rushed him again. He shoved against Adam's chest, and when he couldn't topple him, he threw an uppercut, which merely clipped Adams chin as he dodged the blow. "She was almost mine, finally, after all these years of carefully cultivating her affections."

Adam ignored the pain in his friend's voice. "She was never yours, and she still belongs to me." He aimed a jab at Paul's midsection. It connected, and the other man grunted, but between the solid muscle and the winter garb, it didn't do much damage. "Caro is my wife. Why can you not let me show her that I'm not the man I once was?"

After everything, would the opposition be too much to overcome?

"I don't want to take the chance and see her hurt again." Paul huffed and his breath crystalized in the cold air. "After the death of your son, and when it became apparent you weren't coming back years into your stint at sea, I feared for her life." He threw another punch, but Adam was too slow to block and it connected with his shoulder. "There were times when I thought she'd throw herself into the sea. Her father and I watched her like hawks those long months, and where the hell were you when she needed you the most?"

"I don't remember." A cold sliver of fear lodged in his heart. He hadn't been there when she'd needed support the most. If he was given the chance, he'd spent the rest of his life making up for that.

"Convenient." Paul's next jab clipped Adam's jaw. Another round of pain ricocheted into his temple. "However, I believe she's better off without that constant reminder. Let her live, man. Do the right thing and bow out."

"I can't." How did he explain that winning Caroline and finding peace in his existence was of paramount importance? How did one tell a man who knew nothing of the horrors of war that Caroline's memory and image kept him sane and gave him hope when it would have been too easy to succumb to death merely to make the nightmare stop? "I want a life of domestication, Paul. I want everything a good man should have."

Paul grunted. "Too bad you're not that man."

A red haze fell over Adam's vision. "You have no idea why I want what I do or what sort of man I am. It's not for you to judge." He sprang at his friend and knocked the other man to the ground. "You have no right to meddle." He straddled the other man and pummeled his fists into him. All the rage and frustration he'd held on to fueled his actions.

"I love her to distraction." Paul crossed his arms over his face. Not once did he defend himself. "She loves me."

The quiet words, as well as Paul's refusal to fight, cooled Adam's anger. He immediately stopped his attack. "But *I* love her." In his own way, not that he'd said the words to her. Did her enthusiasm for their couplings indicate a mutual return of the sentiment, or was she simply using him for the needs of her body alone? The latter was a jagged pill to try and swallow. "You'd expect me to give her up anyway?" He rolled off the other man then collapsed, sprawled on the snowy ground.

"I expect you to do what's best for Caroline." Paul expelled a long breath as he retained his position beside Adam. "Life is too short to be unhappy, even for you. And you are like an overly large, hulking thunderstorm because of this—because of this situation."

"Something must be done. I agree." Yet why should it be him who exited? Did his feelings not matter? Perhaps his bitterness had damaged him so much he couldn't function around people any longer. *When will I finally have the life – the love – I deserve?* When would someone want him, the scarred, broken man that he was without expectations and conditions?

"But, I will say that it won't be decided overnight."

"No. It won't." He frowned into the falling snowflakes. "What happened to us, Paul? When did we become enemies?" For once, it would be nice to have a friend instead of someone he antagonized. "I thought I'd come home from the horrors I'd lived through to a wife and a best friend who both gave me undying support. That hasn't exactly been reality." He refused to give up any more of himself to the conversation. After all, Paul was still his rival and anything might be used against him.

"I don't know." The other man was silent for so long, Adam thought that was all he'd say, then, "There was a time when I honestly thought you and I would continue the friendship we started before..."

Adam heaved a sigh. "...before the advent of Caroline."

"Yes. Never did I think a woman would come between us. We used to be more cavalier than that." His laugh was forced. "Used to be that if we squabbled over a bit of skirt, we simply shared, thus keeping the friendship intact." He huffed. "I suppose that wouldn't be acceptable off a privateering vessel."

Was that a note of wistfulness in his voice? "I don't suppose it would be." Adam frowned. "You love her too." Instinctually, he knew that. Even though Paul had introduced them and stood by with enthusiasm and smiles while Adam had wed her, there had been no light in Paul's eyes and no warmth in the obligatory congratulants. Perhaps the man had loved her then but hadn't realized this.

"Yes. Caroline has been the only woman I've felt this way about. She's different than the others." His friend slowly stood then dusted the snow from his clothing. "But that's neither here nor there, and it certainly doesn't help the current problem."

"You're right." Adam gained his feet as well. "One thing I learned while incarcerated is that life's short and shouldn't be spent clinging to bitterness and hate." He faced Paul then held out a hand. "I grow weary of the fight and would rather have a brother not of blood again than an enemy." Would the other man accept the peace offering or would they forever be at odds?

After an interminable hesitation, Paul clasped his hand with Adam's. "I'd like that as well." His smile was tentative, but at least it wasn't a glower and his grip didn't waver. "Despite everything, I am glad you're home."

That brought out a bark of laughter from Adam. "Even though you'd rather gouge out my eyes then toss me into the sea if it would win favor from Caroline?" He released Paul's hand then spun and headed up the path to the lighthouse. His bones ached from the tussle. No doubt he'd sport impressive bruises in the morning.

"Well, I'd let you keep your eyes," came the smart reply. "Where are you going?"

"To check the vents and the lanterns. The wind is wicked bad." Adam grinned. Perhaps he remembered more of the District of Maine cant than he realized.

"I'll come up too."

"Oh?"

Paul chuckled as his footsteps rang on the metal stairs behind Adam. "Why not? I have nowhere else to go. I'd planned to ask Caroline to stay over, though in light of our contretemps, I'm no longer sure."

That was true. Once in the lantern room, he busied himself by checking all four lanterns. Only one would require an oil refill before the dawn. When the wicks flickered with a particularly stubborn gust, Adam adjusted the vents until the wild dancing flames stilled. As he made a round of the room, bobbing illumination on the water caught his attention. "What the hell is that?" He squinted, then went outside to the gallery.

Paul joined him. "Looks like a longboat, fully manned."

"Does she bear a flag?" Who would be coming to Gull's Island at this late hour and in a snowstorm to boot?

"Yes." The wind snatched Paul's response.

"And?" Adam gripped the metal railing hard. He already knew the answer.

"It's clearly a British flag." Something akin to guilt coated the admission.

What did Paul have to feel remorseful over? "God damn it." There was no time to quell the lanterns. No doubt the occupants of that longboat had already caught a glimpse of the island. "What the hell do they want?" Were they the faction he'd seen at the tavern that night?

"I would have no idea." Paul directed his gaze over the water. "Perhaps we should sneak down close to the shore. Maybe it's just a patrol, though this area isn't occupied. Doubtful they'd actually disembark tonight."

Adam stared at his friend's face in profile, but the light revealed nothing of his thoughts. "Very well." A sluggish memory surfaced in his brain. "I'm remembering something about Jamaica and a situation like this."

"Indeed." Paul led the way into the lantern room then further into the stairwell. "We'd managed to woo the governor's youngest daughter on our last night in port. After a wild romp, we deposited her, rumpled and quite ruined, back on her doorstep, much to the censure of everyone in the household, who'd thought she'd been kidnapped."

The metallic ring of their boots blended with the echoes of their voices in the tight, spiral stairwell. Adam grinned. "Aye. We barely reached the docks that night with our lives. If I recall correctly, in addition to the governor's own men, members of the British navy hunted for us."

"We were damn lucky we were able to board our ship that morning. If it hadn't been for a more hated pirate turning up an hour before and deflecting attention, our arses would have been in prison for certain."

"Not for long. Everyone has a price." Some of the tension left Adam's shoulders. Perhaps there was hope for them after all—as long as they didn't speak of Caroline.

They kept to the shadows as best they could. The driving snow gave enough cover if they didn't move too fast. On shore, he and Paul crouched behind a grouping of tumbled boulders and other sea debris that had washed up then frozen. They'd be out of sight from the men in the boat, but near enough to hear any conversation. Of course, the surf and wind might thwart the plan.

Adam kept a finger to his lips as the vessel drew even with their location.

"Gull's Island light operational, sir," someone in the boat said.

"Still owned by a Mr. Jonah Winslow?" another man inquired.

"Aye, though I'm told he's visiting on the mainland at the present time." A space of low conversation ensued, too garbled and scattered by the wind for Adam to make out. Then the same man continued, "I received word the fugitive has taken up residence here. Is apparently wed to Winslow's daughter." A throat cleared. "Shall we go ashore and apprehend?"

Adam's heart raced. His chest tightened. How the hell did they know he was here? Though, no doubt it was inevitable they'd find him. He leaned into Paul and whispered, "Is there a store of weapons nearby?" If they wanted him, they'd have to take him after a fight. No way would he let them harm Caroline.

Before his friend could answer, another man on the boat said, "In this foul weather? Not likely. I don't want something as trivial as snow to let him elude us again. We'll return when the weather clears. Meanwhile, keep close to the shoreline and do a pass around the island. I want to see what else is visible. If we take the island, perhaps they'll finally see how valuable these shores are up here."

"Aye, sir."

Laughter sounded, and with it a definite note of victory. "We've tracked him to earth. You'll see extra silver this month, I'll wager, and he'll see death for his crimes." The slap of oars hitting the water and the groans of the oarsmen drifted to their location.

Finally, the longboat pulled away, but Adam and Paul remained hidden for several moments afterward.

"In answer to your question, yes, both the cottage and the house have enough pistols, rifles, and bayonets for defense." Paul stirred then stood and brushed the blanket of snow from his clothing. "You do know willfully causing death to a British navy man will likely result in you being hung, right?"

"As if they would afford me that luxury," Adam said in a soft voice. "They'd as soon put me in front of a firing squad. Hanging would take too long and has questionable results." He raised his gaze to his friend's. "Whatever else you might think I am, I will defend this island, that light, and Caroline until my dying breath."

And he would. If he found himself back in British custody, the life he'd leave behind wouldn't be safe or free of English domination.

He'd gone through too much. "I refuse to die a prisoner. But at least alive, I can try to make certain those I leave behind might have a shot at freedom." Then he sent a speaking glance to his friend. "We've had our differences, and in light of our truce and the present circumstances, I want you to take care of Caro. I'm bowing out." His chest was on fire with the words. He wanted to rip his heart out. At least then he'd cease to feel.

"What?" Paul's jaw dropped. "You cannot be serious. Not ten minutes ago you fought for her."

Adam took deep breaths and let them ease out until some semblance of calm was restored. "I am. I don't want to bring her additional grief if something should happen to me at British hands. If I bow out now before her feelings grow deeper, it will be easier." *On her.* Inside, he died a little more with each passing admission.

"Thank you." The other man caught him in an embrace. "I'll try to be worthy of you."

"I'd expect nothing less." He pulled away as soon as he was able. "I plan to remove to the cottage until her parents return. Then I'll make plans from there."

For her, he'd sacrifice everything. His motives didn't have to make sense to anyone else.

❧ **Chapter Fourteen** ❧

Caroline peered into the darkened night, but only the driving snow met her anxious gaze. What had happened between Adam and Paul? The storm was bad enough. Leaving two jealous, angry, competitive men alone together was worse. Now, she'd been sitting in bed for nigh onto three hours and still had no idea what had occurred.

She glanced again at the Officer's Clock resting on the fireplace mantle. It had been the one thing Adam had sent back from his travels she'd made use of. The needle hadn't moved much since the last time. Quarter to two in the morning. The wind still blew in a squall while snow hurtled past the window glass in an unrelenting blur.

When she thought about Paul, a sweet smile curved her lips. She loved him; that much was true. He'd been her friend for many years and her silent strength for the same. More than anything she wanted to be with him, grow old with him. Then there was Adam. Her smile faded, but her heartbeat accelerated. What she felt for her husband might not exactly be the deep, abiding love she held for Paul, yet it was exciting and all-consuming. She was fond of him, certainly, but without being able to share everything with him, that affection wouldn't grow. Perhaps she'd too long held onto the memory of the man he'd been and hadn't learned to appreciate the man he was now.

After all, neither was she the same woman she'd been ten years ago. Back then, she'd been a naïve young girl, intent on her first courtship and in love with the thrill of landing a husband after a whirlwind romance. Ah, and mayhap that made the difference, that silly little idea of what love should be, what it had to be. But what if love was bigger and encompassed two men?

Which one should remain in her life? Because, when all was said and done, once she chose, the other wouldn't be happy. Her heart ached. It was madness to let the problem take hold of her mind. There simply wasn't an option to have one without the other. "I want them both," she whispered to the shadows. How scandalous such an admission was and something she couldn't say to any of her friends or even her parents. What sort of woman did that make her? No doubt a horrible sinner in the eyes of decent folk. What would happen to her charity work if word escaped she harbored thoughts of having two men in her life, and worse, having them both in her bed?

Was that the crux of her problem? She sucked in a sharp breath then let it ease out between her lips. She, who'd been left alone without physical love for ten years, contemplated a highly illicit relationship after she'd welcomed relations three times now from her just returned husband? A wave of heat washed over her as she thought about finding herself, naked and willing, beneath both Adam as well as Paul. Would it really be so bad? They were often together in her mind and her heart. Why should her body be any different?

"Don't be a lackwit, Caroline. Neither man would offer or agree to such an insane plan." As it should be. Whatever else both men were, they would abide by the law.

The sound of the front door opening then closing met her ears. She slid from the bed, and not stopping to don her wrapper, padded into the hallway. "Adam?" Never had she flown down the narrow staircase so fast. Was he all right? And how interesting this feeling of missing him was.

"Caro." His expression conveyed exhaustion. He had an arm around Paul in support. "Help me get him into bed."

For one horrible second she thought real life had fallen into her woolgathering. It was on the tip of her tongue to ask the question burning through her brain, but she tamped it, saying instead, "What happened?" She hurried to Paul's other side and took some of his weight on her shoulders. In the dark, they walked the other man up the stairs then into the spare room across the hall from theirs. As Adam guided him to the bed made up with a bright quilt, Caroline darted across the room. She lit the oil lamp on the low bureau. Immediately, golden light flooded the room and cast shadows over the floor.

"We, ah, engaged in an unfortunate bout of fisticuffs after you left us." Adam tugged off the other man's boots then let them drop to the floor with a heavy thump. When she would have dressed him down, he shook his head. "After that, we came to a tentative truce."

"Even regarding me?" Her heart pounded so loud she feared it would echo in the silence.

"No." He turned away from her in order to help Paul off with his greatcoat then jacket and finally his waistcoat. Then he urged the other man beneath the bedclothes. "We spoke of many things, but where you are concerned, more negotiations will be needed. Though, I have made a decision."

She crossed the room then sat on the side of the bed. "Is he hurt?" She brushed back a damp lock of his blond hair. "He's wet."

Paul struggled into a reclining position against the pillows. "Leave off, Caroline. I'm fine. It's nothing more than a poor excuse of a ruse by my rather obvious friend."

"In case you haven't noticed, love, there's a right good storm going on," Adam said with a trace of humor clinging to the words. He acted as if he hadn't heard anything Paul said. When she eyed him askance, he snorted. "No, he's not hurt. Could be suffering from prolonged exposure. He'll be fine."

"What were you doing out in the snow? Why were you not taking refuge in the cottage?"

Adam cleared his throat. "We spied a British longboat that came close to the shore."

"A bold action in such a storm." When she drew her fingers along Paul's chest, hoping to comfort him, he captured it in his hand. A thrill raced down her spine. She'd never seen him in such an undressed manner. Her thoughts went to the light and her father's staunch insistence it not come under British supervision. "Though, it's worrying. There is not an active campaign in these waters." She met Paul's brown gaze, which he then fixed to a point over her shoulder.

"Caro." Adam dropped a hand on her shoulder. "They're searching for me. Said they'd return once the weather clears. Somehow, they've found me."

She frowned. "Here in the District of Maine, that could be months from now." Her pulse wouldn't settle. "That bounty must be excessive for the British navy to set hands from the fleet to chase you." What would they do with him once—if—they caught him? Sour bile rose into her throat as she thought of the torture he'd already endured.

"Perhaps." Lines of stress appeared on his face. He dropped his hand. "I'm sorry I brought the British scum to your door."

"They haven't arrived yet and when they get here, I'll be right by your side, defending what's mine." She widened her eyes and hoped she conveyed what she felt. *You are mine.* She glanced at Paul. Caroline peered at Adam. "What happened after the boat went away?"

"Paul helped me mind the light for a few hours. We had a bad time of it at one point when the wind shifted directions and blew two of the lanterns out." He clasped her hand then gave it a squeeze. "Caro." His throat worked, and though pain and resignation lurked deep in the depths of his eyes, something softer shone there as well. "Why don't you lay down with Paul and spend some time with him?" His voice broke, but with his next swallow, he'd regained control. "I'd rather him not pass the night alone."

Asking her to do anything with Paul was odd, even for Adam. She rose swiftly to her feet and missed his warmth when he released her hand. "What are you saying?"

"Darling," Paul entreated. He reached for her, but she scooted away and his fingertips grazed her night shift. "It's all right. Adam and I discussed things."

"What things?" Foreboding sizzled along her spine. She gazed at Adam. The despair in his expression pierced her heart, so much that she bit back a sob. "What did you do?"

"Please." He shook his head then moved to across the small room to hover in the door frame. "Accept the gift and remember me fondly. Just know that I..." Adam shoved a hand through his wet hair. "Well, it doesn't matter now, does it?" He stepped into the hall, made the short trip into their room, and then the soft click of their door rang in the silence.

Caroline stared at the space he'd previously occupied. She faced Paul, who still wore that glint of anticipation, though now it held a bittersweet edge. "What else happened out there at the light tonight?"

He waved her over to the bed. "Let me explain."

Adam spent endless moments packing the bag he'd brought with him a handful of days ago when he'd reentered Caroline's life. Just across the hall, his wife was no doubt sharing her charms with his rival and best friend — and he'd given his permission. It was his gift to them and would keep her safe more than his presence in her life would. The rise and fall of low conversation from the other room troubled him. What if Caroline refused the plan? Would she argue too much with Paul before he could convince her to join him? Once his friend finally coerced her into his bed, they'd be fine.

Devil take it. He gritted his teeth against that image.

The arrival of that longboat worried him more than he'd let on. He'd seen the brutality of the British navy and had cause to fear them. If his exit from Caroline's life would keep her safe, he'd follow through with his insane plan. The last thing he wanted was for them to torture her until he gave himself up. Of course, there was every possibility they would anyway. Confusion blanketed him, but he refused to land back in their clutches. And, as much as it hurt him on every level, he'd given her into Paul's care because the other man could be everything she needed. He could protect her.

I don't have the capacity for the softer emotions, for the support she deserves.

In many ways, he was too broken to be of any use to her. The answer had come to him as he heard Paul's confession of loving her for so many years. It made sense. They were a good fit, and he was a better mate for her than Adam would ever be. He was such a bastard that he'd planned to drag out the silly competition until the month's end then make her choose. Instead, he'd made the choice for her — his parting farewell. Hopefully, she'd not protest and he also hoped his friend would convince her this was the best way all around. No doubt Paul would convince her to file the papers claiming his desertion and she could be free of him. With Paul, she'd experience everything a woman should from the man at her side: conversation, emotional support, bed sport, and hopefully children.

Children she deserved and would love to distraction. He died another death at the thought of those future offspring who would take after Paul instead of him. His throat tightened with the urge to rage at the heavens. Perhaps it was unfair, but it had to be this way.

Once he'd completed the packing, he buttoned the flap, hefted the strap to his shoulder then crept quietly from the room and into the hall. The golden glow of lantern light spilled into his position, but it was the soft sounds from within that arrested his attention. One peek, then he'd be off, he promised.

As he did so, he cursed himself for a fool. Caroline's creamy pale skin met his hungry gaze as she lay naked beneath Paul. Her eyes were closed, but the tiny sounds of enjoyment she made told the tale. From all accounts, Paul had just begun his conquest, though he was as naked as she.

At the doorway, Adam smirked while his friend tenderly, almost reverently paid homage to Caro's erect nipples. *Damnation, man, she doesn't enjoy gentle.* His wife usually demanded hard and forceful lovemaking. She liked feeling everything her partner did to her, wanted all the sensations he could invoke at a level that she'd break apart several times. She craved knowing her man had to work in order to bring her to release.

Sex should be a celebration, Adam. A woman waits her whole life to share herself intimately with her husband, she'd said shortly before he'd gone off to adventure. *If it's not loud and messy and breath-stealing, there is no point. When a woman makes love, she wants to feel alive, not like she's but a chore to take care of.*

Out of all the things he'd forgotten about her, why he should remember those words, he had no idea. He bit down on his fist to stifle the anguish he wished he could indulge in. He'd taken her for granted, had no idea the treasure he gave up for the sea.

Yet, now that he knew her worth, here he was, giving her up again, and this time to Paul. Was the sacrifice worth it? Would she finally know how much she meant to him?

The sounds in the room recalled his attention. Perhaps Paul would learn, but Adam knew instinctively he was too much a gentleman and had chivalry and decorum in his blood. She might come undone, but it would be a poor affair. Shattered memories of their early days of sailing together drifted into his mind. He'd teased Paul about his unwillingness to dominate a woman's body, and Paul had always answered lovemaking was more about the finesse than the force.

Perhaps so, but she'll always remember my hands upon her body, my skill between her thighs, the way I made her feel instead.

Small comfort when he stood there torturing himself by being a voyeur to their private moment — the last time he'd likely see either of them.

She attempted to guide Paul with little nudges and soft instruction. His Caro was nothing if not relentless on how she enjoyed being pleasured. Memories from the night before when she rode him flashed. His cock hardened. He willed away the reaction, but God, she'd been beautiful taking command, chasing her own bliss even as she'd brought him comfort.

Finally, Paul came into his own. He slid a hand between her thighs and must have found her button, for a keening cry left her lips. "That's it, my darling. Just like yesterday, only this time I'll finally claim you."

That bugger. Adam grinned. Had Paul trysted with her while he'd been catching up on sleep from minding the light? *Of course he did.* Any man would.

She came undone at the same time Paul penetrated her with a flex of his hips. He encouraged one of her legs into the air as he moved within her. Adam stepped away from the doorframe. He leaned his back against the wall and closed his eyes. He couldn't watch, couldn't bear witness to seeing his wife find pleasure in another man's arms. Even still, he couldn't escape the sounds of their mutual enjoyment.

"More. I need more, Paul," Caroline gasped on the heels of a moan. "Touch me, yes there. Like that. Harder, I—" Another cry stole away the remainder of her words.

God damn it. Adam clenched his jaw so hard his temple throbbed. *I'm not strong enough for this.* In an effort to ensure their privacy, he ducked into the room and pulled the door quietly closed. *Fair thee well, wife.* It had been a long time indeed since he'd remembered the Creator, but he mumbled a silent prayer that Paul would give her everything she could ever want and that Caroline would finally find the happiness and peace she deserved.

Then, he hustled along the hallway and down the stairs, taking care not to make too much noise. Just like he'd arrived mere days ago, he let himself out with quiet dignity. The storm still raged around him, but it didn't have near the intensity of what tore through him. Leaving Caroline this time would kill him for certain. When he'd walked out of her life ten years ago, he'd been an arrogant, smug bastard, full of himself and longing for adventure. He'd thrown away the best thing that ever happened to him. This time, he'd feel the loss until he drew his dying breath.

She was his hope, his muse, his reason for existing through the last five, tortuous years, and now she belonged to Paul.

Adam staggered through the snow toward the barn. He'd borrow a horse and return to the cottage since a return five-mile trip by foot would take an eternity. Halfway there, he fell to his knees and let the sob that had been building take control.

"What do you want from me?" he implored the heavens. His only answer was the inky sky and the furious drive of snow. He pushed back his tricorne hat and gave himself over to the cold, stinging precipitation. "Wasn't five years of torture enough penance?" Not to anyone had he admitted that those years he'd felt punishment for the crimes he'd committed in his days as a man of the marque, not to mention atonement for how he'd treated Caroline. "How much more will I need to give?" The wind snatched his anguished cry. "I have nothing else left." He bowed his head as the tears on his cheeks caught the chill in the air. "I am nothing more of value."

Adam shook with the throes of emotion, he knew not how long. Eventually, once he was spent and drained, he clambered to his feet, marched dutifully to the barn then methodically saddled one of the two horses once he'd removed the heavy blanket from its back when he didn't find a groom or a stable lad. Didn't the family have help with the livestock? He shoved feed into a sack as well as a blanket and a brush then slung that over the pommel with his bag. After that, he mounted the steed and took himself off to the cottage and the lighthouse.

For the moment, keeping the lanterns lit and preventing maritime deaths was his only purpose. He wouldn't fail at that too.

Chapter Fifteen

One week later

Caroline shook the worst of the snow from the hem of her dress and cloak before unlacing the snowshoes. Brilliant sunshine flooded the world and made the snow sparkle like millions of diamonds. The sky of robin egg blue was a tease. If one only looked up, they'd never know it was still winter until they caught sight of the wealth of fresh snow from two back-to-back storms. The only saving grace was the wind had blown itself out and the temperatures weren't frigid. Perhaps they'd experience a break in the harsh weather they'd had recently.

She leaned both snowshoes against the side of the cottage. Then she quietly let herself into the dwelling. Once inside, she dropped her worn leather satchel, removed her shoes, mittens, muffler, and finally her cloak then moved briskly across the room with a sigh. A cherry fire blazed in the hearth. *Thank God.* That meant Adam was still in attendance.

Her heart skipped a beat as she thought about him. She hadn't seen him in nearly seven days, not since his cryptic entreaty that she be with Paul. Forcing a swallow into her suddenly tight throat, she draped her wet cloak on the grate then found places for the damp clothing. Her stockings soon joined the collection. Paul had explained why Adam did what he did—well, explained to the best of his knowledge, for Adam had not given him much to go on—and she'd lost another piece of her heart to her husband.

It was a nice gesture, this need to protect her from whatever the murky future held, but she refused to let any one—man or woman—make that sort of sacrifice on her behalf without first consulting her. She hadn't protested before for the mere reason she was selfish. She'd wanted to know what sexual congress with Paul would be like. If either of the men found her actions offensive, so be it. Sometimes a woman had to take care of her own needs and soothe the angst in her own mind any way she could.

Taking care not to step into puddles of melting snow her footsteps had left, she retrieved her bag then crept down the hardwood hall. Since it was midday, Adam would no doubt be sleeping. And if she was lucky, she'd catch him unawares. Perhaps if he was surprised, he'd be more open to hearing what she'd come to say.

The moment she stepped into the bedroom, her determination wavered. Adam wasn't in bed as she'd expected. Oh no. Her husband stood at the washstand with his back to her, completely naked as he drew a wet rag over his face and neck. Yet, it wasn't his muscled, firm physique or broad shoulders that held her attention, it was the network of scars marring the skin of his back—the same scars and raised flesh she'd felt that night in the dark. Seeing them, those angry red welts and furrows of skin that had been shredded and never healed quite correctly, was much different than tracing them with her fingertips.

"Adam." The whispered word cut the silence more sharply than a knife.

He didn't answer her. In fact, he studiously ignored her while he continued to wash his face.

No matter. Caroline swept her gaze over his form. His skin, from the waist down, was pale, made even more so because the rest of his body was tanned golden. The play of his muscles beneath that glorious skin shallowed her breath. The toned, firm buttocks and his narrow waist had her fingers itching to explore. It had been ages since she'd caressed his flat stomach and ridged abdomen or traced a path lower with her tongue. Tingles moved through her core. Since he'd been home, their couplings had been swift and fast and mostly with some sort of clothing still intact, and he was a beautiful man.

"Adam." She tried again and this time entered the room, only pausing to toss her satchel on the still-rumpled bed. "I'd like to talk to you."

"Why? To tell me how incredibly happy you are with your chosen man?" He finished with the rag, tossed it onto the basin's edge then faced her. "To ask me how soon you'll be free of me?" Annoyance and a hint of despair tinged his lovely tenor voice. "Now that we're experiencing decent weather, I'd like to leave Gull's Island. Perhaps I'll lose myself in Portsmouth or book a stage to a destination far away from here. When travel is allowed on the seas, I might return to England to visit my brother. Cornwall is well enough removed that it's doubtful I'd be pursued to the end of the world there."

"No." *He can't leave!* Her throat went dry when she caught sight of his impressive cock—his cock that grew more erect the longer she stared. "Quite frankly, I'm not as happy as I could be, and Paul isn't my chosen man. The two of you decided between yourselves that I should be with him exclusively. I was never consulted."

Yes, indulging in a bout of lovemaking with Paul had fulfilled a long-held fantasy and had brought them closer, but it hadn't satisfied her soul.

"Why are you here, Caro?" Adam closed the distance between them so quickly she didn't have time to move. "Why the devil are you here if not to torture me?" He pressed his body into hers, trapping her between the hard length of him and the wall.

She might jeopardize everything, but she refused to abandon her secret hope of being with them both. "I needed to see you."

"And you thought to 'talk' to me, the same way we always do?" His eyes were a stormy sea of clouded emotion. He grabbed her hands then shoved them over her head, securing them in one of his large ones. A tiny moan escaped her and she arched into him. Her breasts thrust forward and brushed his chest, but that casual friction didn't provide the relief from the ache building inside.

"Adam, that's not it." Though, she *had* come with the hope they might indulge. He had forever been her obsession, even in those long years of waiting and wondering. Always, she'd wanted him. Locked in an embrace, they were everything, no talking needed, every broken part sealed together.

"Is it bed sport you crave, wife? Is that all I've ever been to you, a means to trigger the release of your body, because I'm certainly not capable of being anything else?"

"That's not true." She attempted to come up with a more in-depth answer, but he swiftly claimed her lips. Again and again he slanted his mouth over hers, taking what he wanted, receiving everything she gave. He cupped the side of her face with his free hand, slid his fingers into her hair and worked out the pins holding the knot in place. When the tresses tumbled about her shoulders, he cradled her skull and held her so tightly to him that she ceased to be herself as he deepened the kiss. The rigid length of his cock jumped along her belly. His strength wrapped around her, powerful enough to carry her to the heavens. Her breath was his and his was hers. In that one moment, they were the same entity, living for each other with a hunger she'd only experienced with him.

When he finally pulled away, she gasped, her chest heaving and heart aching for something only he could give—something he didn't want her to have—but she'd keep trying for it anyway. And she knew, in that one heart-stopping second, she loved him. That either made her the biggest idiot in New England or the most powerful woman, because hadn't he left her before when she thought she'd loved him? She shook her head, but the thoughts wouldn't clear and neither did the wonder of the realization. This time was different. This time she came at the problem with a woman's maturity instead of a girl's naïve dreams. She knew what it would cost her this time around. And she couldn't live without him.

"Why did you come, Caro?" The soft question slid across her consciousness. A plea rested in the deepest depths of his eyes though he didn't speak it. He released her wrists then turned away.

She sagged against the wall as her pulse frantically pounded and heat swirled around her. While he rooted about the floor for his breeches and slid them on, she gazed at him mutely. Her mind shouted at her to say the words, the keys that would keep him with her. They tingled on the tip of her tongue, but she hesitated. What if he hurt her again? What if she couldn't recover this time?

"I came because…" She licked her lips. It was a complicated thing. "I came…" *Because I need you so much it frightens me.* In the end, she uttered the truth. What point was there in telling a lie? She had nothing to lose, but everything to gain. "You bedevil me at every turn, Adam. I alternately detest it and relish it." He finished buttoning the flap but didn't look at her. "You might think Paul is the best man for me, but you'd be wrong. You are. Yet, you're not, perhaps." Tears prickled the backs of her eyelids. She wasn't making sense. "You make me feel things so intensely, so big, so much, that I fear breaking

191

apart, but just when I think I will, I fly instead. You send me higher and deeper into everything."

"That's how it's always been between us." He faced her. "Whatever else we were, when we came together in a carnal manner, passion would never be denied."

Her hand shook at his use of "were." *This isn't over.* "Yes, it has, but now it's more." She swallowed past her tightened throat even as panic rose and threatened to choke her. "I need someone who'll shelter me, protect me, make me feel like things will be all right even if they won't. I want a man who will support my dreams or let me do whatever I wish without argument."

"That's why you have Paul. He'll spoil you soon enough, and he certainly won't argue, the besotted fool. He'll treat you like a queen, like you deserve."

"I don't deserve to be set on a pedestal or left on a shelf because you're fearful I might break!" She raked her fingers through her hair then flicked the mass over a shoulder. "I want to feel loved and needed. Cherished even, but I want it equally at the side of my man." *Men.* "I want to experience whatever befalls me—us—together. Don't shut me out."

He snatched up a shirt then savagely pulled it over his head and smoothed the linen along his torso, effectively hiding his tempting chest from view. "I gave him to you for all of the reasons you stated, yet here you are. Badgering me." His gaze roiled with indecision and…

Was that hope buried in those handsome gray-blue depths?

"Why?"

Her spine tingled with a dose of courage. If she wanted this life for herself, it was up to her to fight for it. If he wished to be stubborn, fine, but she'd been called obstinate before as well, and she wasn't married to him for nothing. "I'm tired of knowing you're here, hiding away, sulking, shutting yourself in this cottage thinking you've done the greater good by giving me up."

"Is that what you believe I'm doing—sulking?" He shoved by her then snatched up an emerald green waistcoat embroidered with orange flowers.

"Aren't you?" She approached him as she would a scared and injured colt. "Seems to me you've given up. And I've never known you to run from a problem."

"No." He struggled with the garment. "I'm trying to keep you safe, damn fool woman. Why must you constantly mistrust me?"

"There isn't a threat here yet. I don't need your protection." Caroline swatted his hands away. She helped him into the vest then came around and fastened the buttons. His citrus and cloves scent teased her nose. "If there is a threat, I certainly know how to fire a rifle or pistol. And I'm certainly not chattel for you give to whomever you choose."

He rolled his eyes. "You have no idea what the British navy is capable of—what the most black-hearted people are capable of. That's why I want you safe, and you will be—with Paul."

She ignored that. "No, I don't what they can do. Why is that? Because you refuse to share with me what happened to you at their hands."

"I did share."

"Not all of it. Perhaps it's you who mistrusts me."

"I shared what I could. The rest…" He shook his head. "I'm not ready for that right now. I don't know if I'll ever be."

Some of her ire faded. The poor man. Life would always be difficult for him. "Adam." She stood a hand's breadth from him yet still held his gaze. "Regarding Paul—"

"I don't wish to hear about how wonderful life is with your lover." There was a decided growl in his voice. When he went to turn away, she stopped his momentum with a hand to his shoulder. "Caroline, don't."

She trembled at the use of her full name from him. "Captain, if you do nothing else, please have the courtesy to listen to what I need to tell you now." She tipped her head back to peer into his eyes. "If you care for me at all, I'd like you to hear this."

His shoulders slumped. Resignation roiled in those gray depths and he gave a slight nod. "Very well."

Caroline stifled a sigh. She'd fully expected him to turn her away or close her out. Since he did not, perhaps it was a victory indeed. Still, the need for caution had never been greater. "Before we go further, I want it abundantly clear that Paul and I were only together the night you left us." It was important Adam know this. She wanted him to know she hadn't given up on the idea of having him in her life too.

"I gave you to him. You should have taken advantage—"

She held up a hand. "Once again, I am not property. *I* decide where my life goes from here on out. *I* control who I want at my side into old age. *I* command who I wish to have in my bed and when." She narrowed her eyes. "Do you understand?"

He stared back at her, tenacious to a fault. "All too clear." The corners of his lips curved into a grin. "Your spirit hasn't dimmed."

"No, and it only grows more animated when dealing with posturing, insistent males. Unfortunately, I have two such men in my life." But that grin allowed her to relax a fraction and sent warmth through her limbs. It was one of the first things she'd noticed about him before their whirlwind courtship had even begun. "In any event,

I wish to remain your wife." She cocked an eyebrow when he tried to protest. "I care for Paul. I love him, this is true, and I'm not ashamed of it. I can't help how I feel. However, I love you too." With a palm to his cheek, she kept him from looking away. The muscles beneath her hand went taut. "I hadn't realized it until you kissed me just now. Sometimes, clarity comes upon us from the least provocation."

"None of that changes our situation." He moved around her with ease. When he gained the low bureau, he rooted around in a bag then withdrew a pair of worn socks. "I'm wanted by the British navy. It's only a matter of time until they collect me." His voice was flat and devoid of the bluster and arrogance she'd become accustomed to from him. "I'd rather not have you put in harm's way when that happens."

"That may be so, but I have no intention of letting them do that."

"It's not that simple." His shoulders sagged.

"Perhaps not, but if you don't let me in, how can we present a united front? How can we hope to have a chance?" In fending off the British but also in their relationship.

Her optimism flagged at his silence. Didn't he care at all for her—for them? She fought back a sob. Perhaps she was the fool for wanting a man who wouldn't let her in past the physical. As he sat on the edge of the bed while drawing on his socks, she fought against the wave of panic that built in her belly. She took a deep breath and let it ease out. *I'll either lose him or win him forever.* "For what it's worth, I wish I could have both you and Paul—in my home, my bed, and my life. That very idea has been uppermost in my mind since you returned home, perhaps longer, and it leaves me in the depths of despair because what I want simply cannot be condoned by society." Her voice wavered and she fought for control. "Please don't leave me. I cannot bear that again."

Not now, especially not when she'd just figured out what he meant to her. Broken or not, she wanted whatever he could give.

Adam tugged on first one boot then the other. He didn't look at her, didn't say a word, merely remained the same emotionally stunted man she'd married.

A piece of her heart cracked. "I'll take your silence as your answer." Caroline swept across the room as tears stung her eyes. She couldn't let him see her cry. *I thought he'd changed.* "Goodbye, Adam. As you said to me, remember me fondly."

The moment she stepped a foot over the threshold, he spoke. "I spent two years in the belly of a British prison ship after my usefulness at the sail was over." A bitter laugh escaped him. "Of course, my sinking a few of their ships along the way when I doubled as a privateer for America didn't sit well with them either. Thus the need for punishment."

Caroline froze. "Oh?" She feared saying much more of anything in the event he'd shut her out again.

"The British have a nasty habit of stealing sailors from other ships all over the world then making them sail beneath their colors — whether the victims want to or not."

"This you've told me." How did someone force Adam, her strong, mulish, arrogant husband, to do anything against his will?

"I had no choice. They would have put me to death, but if I did what they asked, I had a chance of escaping." Another wash of silence flowed between them. "I committed many terrible crimes in the name of the Empire as I told you, and took many innocent lives of the British in retaliation, but none of that weighs equally against what they did to me." Bitterness rang in his voice and brought her turning around to face him. "Two years I suffered humiliation after humiliation. Eventually, the lashes of the whip didn't matter as I retreated further into myself. I learned not to show emotion or even a reaction of any kind. It was the only way to survive."

"Oh, Adam." She dashed across the floor and the sound of her feet rang on the hardwood then she stumbled to an awkward halt in front of him. "What did they punish you for?"

"Anything. Everything. Most times they didn't need a reason." He raised his gaze to hers. Desolation lurked in the stormy depths. "Once, I was kicked multiple times in the side for no other reason than I asked for water. We'd had none in three days. I suffered through two broken ribs alone. To complain about an injury from their hands would have meant worse treatment."

Worse than that? A shiver lanced down her spine. "How *did* you manage to keep living?" She knelt in front of him, scooting between his splayed knees and grabbing one of his hands. "These stories of yours tell a different tale. You weren't spared and you're certainly broken."

"Aye. I am." He threaded their fingers together. "I kept the image of you in my mind. Whenever horrors were visited upon me, with every bite of the whip, every jab from a baton or a hot poker from the fire, every kick from an officer's boot, every day I went through without food or water, I recalled how you looked the last time I saw you and I fixed that picture to my consciousness. I concentrated on how you smelled, how it felt when we made love, what you sounded like, how soft your skin was." His throat worked with a hard swallow. "I remembered all of that until the pain, the torture, the horrible things went away and the mental anguish couldn't touch me. That part of me I escaped to, they could never breach or take away from me. It was mine alone.

That part was where you were, and I wanted to be there more than anything."

Despite her resolve to remain strong, tears welled in her eyes and spilled onto her cheeks. "I never knew I meant that much to you."

"I had no idea until the night I lost the *Scoundrel*. My memories were compromised as a result of the head wounds, but I had flashes, snippets that haunted me." He cupped her cheek and caught one of her tears with a swipe of this thumb. "Only one brought me comfort though I didn't deserve it. The one that kept flashing in fractured pieces every time I closed my eyes was you—and then I hated myself all over again."

"Why?" Did he go mad simply from the thought of her?

"Because I didn't deserve you, didn't deserve to think of you as mine, not after everything."

She held tight to his hand. "Adam—"

"No, you need to hear it. I need to tell you." Agony laced his voice. "I treated you as if you didn't matter. I left you when I should have been by your side, giving you everything you needed, being the only man you could ever want." The bitterness increased with each word. "I was a fool and now I'm paying the price." His eyes bore into hers, held her gaze with such intensity she couldn't look away. "Sometime during those hideous years, I fell in love with you or at least the woman I imagined you to be. Hard. Completely. Hopelessly." He severed their connection and stared at a point beyond her shoulder. "And now I'm too broken to be of use or value to you, to the woman I'm glad to see you've become. I've lost you to Paul, and that shatters me. It seems I never did have a chance to make things right between us and now it's too late." His words sounded forced as if from a tight throat.

"No. Oh no, Adam, it's not too late at all." Her heart fluttered. When she blinked, another few tears fell. "Ten years is a long time to wait to hear those words, but they're no less sweet. Believe me when I tell you that broken things still work perfectly."

He shook his head and the shaggy length of his hair floated about his face and shoulders. "I don't understand."

"Look at me." With her free hand, she moved his face until their eyes met again. "Does not sunlight still come through a cracked window? You can still see your reflection in the shards of a broken mirror. Spilled ink can still be used in a pen head. You can continue to eat soup from a spoon with a bent handle." She searched his gaze as she dropped her hand. The urge to sob flooded her. There was so much despair and bitter self-loathing there. In many ways, he lived locked away in his mind, keeping himself from hurt. Perhaps he'd never come fully out into the light again. Only he could work through those demons. "You might be broken, but you still have the capacity to love and be loved in return."

"Oh, Caro. How amazing you are. How surprising." Adam took her free hand in his then raised her knuckles to his lips. With tender care, he kissed each one. He turned her hand over and just as gently put a kiss into her palm then closed her fingers around it. "I had many, many hours to reflect upon my life in that stinking prison. All around me, men died from starvation, dehydration, infection, disease, or simply despair. The last condition was always the harshest. When a man no longer has hope, he has nothing."

"But you had hope?" She couldn't imagine the things he'd suffered.

"Yes. The thought of you, of us together." He released her hand. "I refused to give the British the satisfaction of me dying, and so, I remembered you, invented the conversations I would have when I returned to you in the hope you'd forgive me — love me."

Her stomach clenched. All those years, he'd fostered hope, which turned into love and apparently grew with every passing day, and what did she do? Each of those years, she'd nurtured annoyance, only remembering the horrid parts of him until they blotted out everything else. "Adam, I don't…" Her words trailed away as guilt crept in. What could she say that he'd believe when everyone else in his life had betrayed him or lied?

"If I had known that day I walked out of your life was the last time I'd see you, I would have striven to make you smile so I could remember that too. Lord knows I didn't make you do enough of that." His expression grew soft and some of the angst left his face. "If I had known I'd not be able to kiss you for ten long years, I would have spent endless moments finessing my embraces, learning the secrets of your mouth, courting your lips, drawing those precious seconds out so you'd remember me differently than you no doubt did."

Dear God, could he now read minds? Her tears fell in earnest. Where had this man come from? But then, she supposed after going through the horrors he had, anyone would change. No one would come out of those things the same. "Oh, Adam, I'm so, so sorry."

"It's not your fault, love." He didn't protest when she burrowed into him and wrapped her arms around his waist.

"I'm sorry all the same. I hate that you had to go through those terrible trials." His waistcoat muffled her reply.

"Perhaps I had to endure them to throw my life back into perspective." The rumble of his laughter resounded in her ear. "I suppose even the Creator thinks I'm a right arse sometimes."

An unexpected giggle left her lips. What had it cost him to share all that he had? Would he shut her out again after this? "You survived. That's the important thing. Adam," she pulled back and peered up into his face, "you lived when others died. But, if you waste the rest of your life in resentment, jealousy, and hating yourself, what was the point? You do injustice to their memories."

"Indeed." Hope brightened his eyes. "Memories should never be allowed to be forgotten."

"I'm so glad to have you here, in my life. I'll strive to be worthy of the woman you remember me to be." What if she could never live up to that ideal?

"Aye. I'm glad too, but Caro, you are already worthy. You always have been." He leaned down then placed a kiss upon her forehead. "Don't expect a turnabout overnight. I can only survive one day at a time."

"That's more than I had a month ago." Caroline scrambled to her feet just as Adam brushed his hand over her satchel. "As are you."

"What is this?" Without waiting for a reply, he undid the buckles then plunged in a hand. With a puzzled expression, he withdrew her silver-backed hairbrush. "You came to bring me this?"

Heat flooded her cheeks and pushed away the heavier emotions they'd shared. "It was, ah, an incentive, so to speak, in the event you were recalcitrant." Not for worlds would she admit she hoped he might use it on her again.

"Your propensity for naughty never ceases to astound me." His eyes darkened as he shifted his gaze between her and the brush. "I would enjoy plaiting your hair, but all other uses for the brush should be confined to our bedroom, and not the one your parents share." He winked and returned the implement to the bag. This time he pulled out an envelope of ivory vellum. "And this?"

"A letter from the White House. Look at the seal." She gestured to the back of the envelope even as he turned it over. The brown wax seal remained unbroken. "For you. The ferry man brought over a special courier just yesterday once the sea calmed. Paul went back to the mainland as well." Though her curiosity for what the letter contained grew with each passing second, she refrained from inquiring. He would share when he was ready.

She hoped.

"I pray this means I've been granted an audience with the president." He folded the envelope into thirds then slipped it into the pocket of his waistcoat where his watch fob would go. "Thank you, Caro."

She didn't know whether he said that for bringing the letter or for listening to his story. "Will you come home, husband?"

"I will, until the light needs tending again."

"And." She stood, emotions roiling through her chest, but uncertainty won out. "You won't leave?" She bit her bottom lip. After all he'd said, would he still believe he wasn't wanted?

He stood. "I won't leave." His voice softened to a whisper. "As long as you have need of me, I'll remain."

"Thank you." Another few tears fell and she scrubbed them away. What a watering pot she was becoming. "Adam?"

"Yes?" He moved across the room then retrieved his jacket from a hook on the wall.

"Even though he was a babe, our son took after you in many ways. Looks and temperament, for certain. He would have been fearless and brave, like you, I think. Would have grown up to be a good man, as have you." He deserved to hear nice things about himself and this was but one gift she could give him.

He fisted his hands in the fabric so hard his knuckles showed white as he turned slightly back to her. "I appreciate that." As she left the room, she caught sight of a tear as it rolled down his cheek and into his beard.

Perhaps being broken and then finding solace in someone equally broken was the only way to heal.

❧ Chapter Sixteen ❧

Paul drummed his fingers on his thigh as he waited for his audience with the commodore. No one else waited in the makeshift office, except the commodore's secretary. That short, lean man sat scribbling in a ledger while studiously ignoring him.

As if I don't matter.

In the whole time he'd lived in Portsmouth, he'd remained loyal to England. When his friends and neighbors had talked about throwing over rule from Massachusetts and wanted to stop relying so heavily on goods from England, he'd staunchly touted the benefits of keeping ties to both healthy. His shipping business was as strong as ever, thanks to his relationship with both, but now, he pondered if he'd done the right thing by only looking after his own interests. Should he have only been loyal to one?

He stilled his fingers only to drum them again when the office door remained firmly closed. To curb the restlessness, he peered out the nearby window. The wharves and docks were busy at this hour. Nearly tea time, various fishermen returned with the day's catch while shopkeepers attempted to snare last minute transactions before they closed in a few hours. Beyond that, the scarlets and navy blues of the British naval uniforms blended through the chaos. There was no official occupation to be sure, and the navy had set up offices here as more of a way to manage shipping channels and trade relations, yet more and more of them arrived daily. That was suspect. Rumors abounded that a contingent of them was planning something on a large scale, and though Paul could guess what that plan would be, he hoped Portsmouth wouldn't be overrun with them. Closing the harbor would be devastating to local commerce.

His chest tightened with irritation. He needed to secure the promise that his ships would still be given free passage in and out. Giving up Adam's whereabouts to these men had been contingent upon that one vital concession.

Yet, here he waited.

Discreetly, he cleared his throat until the secretary glanced in his direction. "Pardon me, but will the commodore be much longer? I do have other business to attend this afternoon." Try as he might to keep the annoyance from his voice, it rang in his ears.

The other man lifted a black eyebrow. "I'm certain he'll be with you as soon as he has a moment. After all, you didn't have an appointment." Censure dripped from his tone.

"Yes, thank you for reminding me of my horrible manners." That couldn't be helped, for this mission was of some import.

As the secretary resumed his scribbling, Paul shifted on the hard, straight-backed chair and returned to woolgathering. Adam was the reason he'd called upon the commodore — and the reason for the emotional morass threatening to pull him beneath its murky surface.

A week ago, he'd thought all of his dreams had come true when Adam had more or less given him permission to bed his wife. Then, when the captain had walked out of the house and kept himself at the lighthouse, Paul had assumed the man had given up all claim to the woman they both loved. That one glorious night of passion with Caroline had been everything he'd hoped, and the next morning, when he'd tried for a repeat of those relations, she'd begged off, and continued to do so with more than a bit of what seemed like *ennui*.

Until he'd finally asked her if she was happy. There'd been hesitation on her part, but she wouldn't be the woman he'd fallen for if she'd lied. She admitted that while their coupling had been everything she'd hoped for, she missed her husband, and that it was unfair he and Adam had made a decision for her that only gave her one man and that she couldn't help she cared for them both. Until something changed and she had the opportunity to speak with Adam herself, she couldn't move forward in her relationship with Paul.

He'd understood, of course, but her continuing unhappiness only increased his guilt because he knew the answer to the riddle plaguing them all: the three of them needed to come together as a unit. It would be illicit in every sense of the word, but the connection between them couldn't be denied. He'd been a fool to think he could take Caroline away from his friend without consequence and a bigger one to ignore what had been right in front of his face all along. If the reason for her unhappiness hinged on not being with both of them, why not broach the subject of a ménage with her posthaste?

Because… he was afraid. Fearful that somehow her feelings for her husband would overshadow what she felt for him, and once more, he'd be on the outside looking in after all these years.

He gave his head a shake to clear the thoughts. Yet, despite that, there was no jealousy on his part. After he and Adam had fought that evening, he'd understood more of what drove the other man. How could he deny Adam the one woman who'd seen him through his terrible trials? Not that he knew in detail, but he could guess. There were always rumors in town, whispers of the horrors shared in the taverns about the atrocities the British navy gleefully inflicted on their prisoners. Paul's chest tightened. In order for him to have Caroline in his own life, he had no choice but to accept his rival, not only as part of Caroline's world, but into his — in all aspects.

Though he hadn't broached the subject for a ménage to Caroline, he and Adam had hinted at it each in their own way. Gah, how stupid he'd been not to pick up on that! But, would the other man agree now? He understood Adam's want to lay all claim to his own wife, so would he be willing to share in this type of a scenario? Sure, they'd often bedded the same woman back in their privateering days. The difference being Adam had never wed any of those women. Now? Paul didn't know. He glanced again at the silent secretary across the room. Of course, all of those plans hinged on the commodore agreeing not to take Adam into custody like they'd originally planned. They couldn't have a threesome with only two.

His belly roiled with his deception. Sooner or later, he'd need to confess all to not only Adam, but also Caroline. Would his betrayal — or near betrayal — affect how his end of the relationship went forward? The knowledge of Paul's duplicity would destroy Adam even further, if the British navy didn't put him to death. Either way, Caroline would never forgive him. How could she when he'd be the cause of wrenching her husband from her life this second time? He rubbed a hand over his eyes. That one night of passion seemed so far away, yet it wasn't enough to justify the enormity of what he'd done.

Bugger this. If I tell Adam everything right now, perhaps we can form a plan to circumvent the worst. Providing his best friend didn't land him a facer then put a ball through him before he could fully explain.

Paul shot to his feet. "Excuse me, my good man, but I really must be going —"

The office door opened at that moment and a man stood in its frame. He stood at average height, but the way he carried his fit form made him all the more imposing. His short, black hair, styled a la Brutus, gleamed in the weak afternoon light that slanted through the windows and his crisp, navy blue uniform with its brass buttons and piping work proclaimed his rank and influence before he even spoke.

"Mr. Douglas? If you'd be so kind as to step into my office." Commodore Matthers stepped aside. "We have much to discuss and to finalize."

With nothing left to do, Paul did as instructed, but his movements felt stiff and awkward, when all he really wished to do was run out of that office then plead his case, on his knees if need be, before Adam and Caroline. Perhaps the commodore would listen to reason.

Once inside the small room, the commodore closed the door behind him then he edged around a large, cherry wood desk. "Please, make yourself comfortable, Mr. Douglas," the other man invited as he took his seat. The springs of his leather chair briefly protested. "To what do I owe the honor of this unexpected meeting? I had assumed after our last one, everything that needed to be said had been."

Paul forced a swallow into his suddenly tight throat as he settled on a leather winged-back chair facing the desk. "I came to open a discourse regarding the fate of Captain Adam Montmorency."

"Ah, yes, our mutual adversary." The commodore took up a pen, dipped the tip into an inkwell then scratched a few lines on a piece of vellum. "You need not worry on that account. I've made the necessary arrangements. The man should be out of your life and mine in short order."

The sour taste of bile crept up the back of Paul's throat. "About that, I'd hoped we could discuss it before the plans were set into motion."

"No need. I believe the arrangements are satisfactory to all parties." Finally, the other man glanced up. He held Paul's gaze and his hazel eyes were hard. "Thanks to your intelligence, we're ready to deploy a contingent of men to Gull's Island. We'll apprehend the traitor. Then, most likely, he'll face the hangman's noose — if we don't send him back to England and have him tried there. In the end, it will matter not what becomes of him."

"About that, Commodore Matthers," Paul shifted. "I'd think the captain has suffered enough at the hands of the British navy. Why not just exile him to England or even elsewhere the Empire has holdings? Force him into hard labor. Is it truly necessary to put the man to death?"

With a huff, the commodore rested his pen in its holder then sprinkled sand over the lines he'd just written. He trained his gaze on Paul. "Is it necessary to put a man to death who has caused multiple deaths not only against our navy but also against various other members of our military during his rampage through the seas? Not to mention the enormous treasure he's stolen that we've yet to track down." He moved the document to one side of his desk then folded his hands upon the empty space. "I think it is. Even death would be too good for the likes of Montmorency. The man is little better than a pirate."

Would that his friend had turned to piracy. He'd not now be in such peril. "Perhaps he's a changed man. Perhaps he did those things out of desperation instead of hatred, but I'm sure you don't care either way." Though, truth be known, if he were Adam, no doubt some of those murders were done in the heat of rage.

"Be that as it may, we must make an example out of him for the rest of the prisoners and those who defy the

Empire. This is a new, precarious world we live in, Mr. Douglas. England has been given a figurative black eye by these upstart Americans and we must move swiftly to quell continuing dissention. The trade relations between all of us are at stake. Any man who resists deserves his fate."

"I understand that, of course, but I—"

The other man's gaze bore into his. "Never say you sympathize with the traitor? You were anxious enough to give him up a week or so ago."

"Yes, I was." Paul clasped his hands together. Beneath his greatcoat, heat rolled over his body. A week ago, he could think of nothing more than ridding his life of Adam. Now… "However, I'm merely thinking it would go a long way to furthering public relations with the townsfolk if you were to magnanimously pardon him before sending him into exile." At least with exile, Adam would still be alive and perhaps, since he escaped the English prison once, he could do it again.

I'll do everything in my power to assist.

"Perhaps." The commodore sat back in his chair with a finger over his lips. He leaned on one elbow for long moments, then he edged forward and again rested his hands on the desktop. "However, we've been hunting the captain for a long time and have been embarrassed in too many instances to let him walk away from here under his own power." He drew his abandoned document to him, shook off the sand then gave the paper a tri-fold. "If it offends your sensibilities, you don't need to come to the ceremony. Many a man outside of the military is squeamish at the sight of justice being carried out. We won't hold it against you." His lips quirked into the ghost of a smile. "In fact, I can send a courier when the deed is complete."

While the knot in Paul's stomach grew, he watched helplessly as the navy man heated a stick of wax in the candle's flame at the corner of his desk. He dabbed a blob of the red wax onto the paper then quickly used a wooden-handled stamper to imprint an official seal in the pool. "Thank you, but I think I will skip bearing witness. I do not need the details."

"Very well. It is your choice, after all." Commodore Matthers opened a drawer in the desk and withdrew a brown leather folio. "My contingent will lay siege to Gull's Island in two days in a bid to win favor from the Crown, so it would behoove you not to be in the vicinity." He gestured to the letter he'd just sealed. "This is an official order for Mrs. Montmorency, informing her we will take possession of the island and the lighthouse unless she can meet our rather high monetary donation."

Hope flared in Paul's chest. "If she meets the demand, will you let the captain go free?"

"The lighthouse and the captain are two separate issues, Mr. Douglas." A snort of derision issued from the other man. "The letter is a mere formality, for the navy desires full use of the lighthouse anyway."

"The lighthouse belongs to Adam. It came to him upon marriage," Paul reminded him.

"True, and this is merely for records. Once we have the captain in our possession, all of his holdings become property of England. Consider it the price of doing business." He arched an eyebrow. "There is an official set of paperwork we do need to necessitate. We are, after all, gentlemen. In issuing the order, we've done our duty." He looked at Paul, his expression amused. "It is a rather high sum, I will admit. No ordinary person could produce that much wealth on the spot."

How much did they demand? "Yet, if she would somehow manage it?"

The commodore sighed. "We'd renegotiate, perhaps, but that doesn't negate the captain's guilt, as I said before. We'll claim the island and take Montmorency into custody. As is our right."

"And Caroline?" Paul's gut clenched. "Will she be a prisoner as well?"

"We have no use for the woman beyond the property." He laid the pouch on top of the letter. "For your excellent service to the Crown, I'm authorized to gift you with our infinite thanks for a job well done."

Paul rubbed a hand along his chin. Good God, they were rewarding him for betraying his friend and taking away the only home Caroline had ever known? The urge to retch grew. "I don't require reward for his blood."

"That is not for me to say. I'm only following orders." The commodore shrugged. "I'm told the Prince Regent himself has taken note of your activities over the years. He detests being made to look the fool, and Montmorency has made our navy resemble a laughing stock as well as killed his own brothers-in-arms, which makes the Regent by extension an object of mirth. He arranged this reward for anyone who could finally put an end to using our naval resources in his hunting. So it was good for us all when you contacted us. In exchange for your continued loyalty to the Crown and of course our appreciation, the Regent will award the small courtesy title of baron upon your person as well as some property, should you so desire." He gestured at the leather folio. "You merely need to confirm with the Regent, and his people will make arrangements for the official ceremony. All the information you need to accomplish this is contained herein."

Oh, dear heavens. Paul briefly closed his eyes. "This is all too much and surely unexpected." A title. Property in England. Elevation to a proper British gentleman. An under the table entry into the world of the *ton*. He wouldn't need to worry if his shipping business ended in a dismal failure, but at what cost? Would it mean the same thing if he didn't have Caroline by his side, or if he had to live knowing his duplicity sent Adam to his death and destroyed her life? How did a man weigh each against the other? He nodded. "Thank you so much. I don't know what else to say."

The commodore smiled, revealing a line of crooked teeth along his bottom jaw. "The Crown knows how to take care of its own, Mr. Douglas." He stood, which forced Paul to do the same. "I believe this interview has concluded. If there is nothing else?"

"No. Nothing else." After all, what could he say that would change the commodore's mind? Everything had been set into motion too well from that well-placed whisper he'd initiated over a week ago. From his bloody irritation and jealousy. Guilt speared through his chest.

"Very well then." Commodore Matthews picked up the two items from his desktop, came around that piece of furniture then handed them to Paul. "I appreciate your devotion to the cause."

Paul headed toward the door. As he put his hand on the knob, he paused. "Oh, one more thing, commodore." He looked over his shoulder. "Will the ships belonging to my company be granted continued unrestricted access in and out of the harbor and the British controlled waters beyond while the war rages?"

"For the time being, yes. Do make certain your captains carry the letter of pardon I've already given you with them at all times though." His brow creased. "Even I cannot say what will happen tomorrow. These are uncertain times."

Which meant his ships would be guaranteed safe only for the foreseeable future. If the commodore was promoted or reassigned to a different area of the country, all previous arrangements would be rendered void. And his betrayal of Adam would again be worth only the cost of the new title alone. "Again, thank you." Paul wrenched open the door. He stepped into the outer office, nodded at the secretary then exited the building, all to the accompaniment of his pounding heart.

What to do now?

By the time Paul arrived on the island, it was past tea time, but he knocked on the front door anyway. Many times, Caroline would take a nap or wander through her garden after tea. Since the sun still shone, it was entirely possible she'd chosen to take in the crisp, winter air. Perhaps he'd join her and maybe they'd repeat their session from the last time he'd met her in the garden. His groin twitched at the thought. The maid opened the door on his second knock and sent his thoughts scattering.

"Hullo, Jane. Is Mrs. Montmorency receiving by any chance?" Briefly, he touched a gloved hand to the breast pocket of his greatcoat. The parchment crackled and the weight of the leather folio reminded him the documents still rested there. "Actually, is the captain at home?" Given Caroline's frame of mind regarding her husband, he had every confidence she'd convinced him to return home. He may as well confess everything to Adam, and if he survived that encounter, he'd plead his case to Caroline.

"The captain and Mrs. are both at home. Captain Montmorency is in the front parlor, Mr. Douglas." She stepped out of the way so he could enter. "Do you wish for me to announce you?"

"Yes, thank you." Today, he simply wasn't in the mood to show up as a surprise. His gut tightened. Would this end his friendship with Adam? Of course it would. Most people cut all ties with people who betrayed them. With heavy steps, he followed the maid down the hallway. He stood sweating beneath his greatcoat, as she stepped over the threshold.

"Captain Montmorency? Mr. Douglas is here to see you."

Adam's voice rumbled out. "Show him in. And Jane?" he added as Paul crept through the doorway. "We won't have need of you anymore tonight. You're free to go home early."

"But dinner, sir?" Confusion filled the maid's inquiry. "Should I ask Mrs. Montgomery if she'll need my assistance?"

"No need. Caroline is even now in the kitchen and she's perfectly content in trying her hand with a chicken, if I remember right." He chuckled as if the thought of that amused him. "If you should need help through the snow, please ask the groom to assist you." As per his habit, he'd check on the cluster of buildings where the staff lived to see if they were in need of supplies or anything else.

"Very well." Jane turned to him. "May I take your coat, Mr. Douglas?"

"No!" Not while the paperwork still resided in his pocket. He'd need to introduce that subject somehow. "Er, I mean, no thank you. I most likely won't stay long."

The servant nodded. "Captain, shall I refresh your tea?"

"Mention it to my wife on your way out. If she thinks it's needed, she can bring in a fresh pot."

"Very well, sir." Then with a questioning glance back at Adam, Jane departed the room.

Paul stood with more than a little uncertainty as Montmorency looked back at him with varying degrees of interest. At least Caroline wasn't in attendance for the time being. His nerve would have no doubt left him if he'd found himself in her presence. He swallowed hard when Adam stood. This man, who'd once been his closest friend, was now the same man who'd given his blessing for Paul to sleep with his wife. He was also the man he'd betrayed and for what? Good standing in the titled world of a country he didn't know if he wished to return to? "I realize I need to explain why exactly I'm here."

"That would be nice since Caro and I weren't expecting company."

He nodded. "Yes, I suppose you weren't. In fact, I wasn't truly certain you would have returned with Caroline." Damn, this was deuced hard.

"Yes, indeed." His friend gently cleared his throat. "She convinced me, last night, in fact. My wife and I came to an understanding of sorts. You and I might as well discuss how things stand while she's otherwise occupied."

"Ah." Paul's heart seized. This was the beginning of the end. "I take it you've gone back on your promise that Caroline and I should be together?"

"In a manner of speaking, that's something you and I need to discuss." Adam sent him a speaking glance. "So, please, have a seat. I'm anxious to gauge your reaction to what I'm about to say."

Oh, God. Paul shrugged out of his greatcoat then approached the grouping of furniture. He laid the garment over the back of a leather chair. "Adam, you should know..." Know what? That his oldest and most trusted friend was nothing but a traitor and had more or less signed his death warrant? Because he'd been mad with jealousy and acted like a hurt school boy? With his stomach clenching and his throat dry, Paul slunk around the chair then slumped into it. "You should know that I—"

"Paul. I know." Adam held up a hand.

Damnation, he's going to kill me.

216

✎❧ Chapter Seventeen ❧✎

Adam narrowed his eyes when the color leeched from Paul's face. What the hell did his friend think they were talking about? "Relax. It's not like we've never done such a thing. Though, it is different and daunting when the potential has Caro in the mix."

"I beg your pardon?" Paul stared at him as if he'd suddenly grown two heads. "What does she have to do with it?"

"Well, she'll need to be a part of the whole plan. You know, sharing a woman usually entails having the woman present." He shot him a sharp glance. "Are you feeling quite well? You look a bit green, man."

"I'm fine." The other man straightened and some of the color returned to his cheeks. "Ah, *that's* what you know." A relieved smile parted his lips. "A *ménage a trois.*"

"Yes, of course. What else did you think I was referring to?" He'd never seen Paul so discomfited.

"Nothing. Forget it."

"All right." He'd been acting strange the last time they'd interacted too. "Should we discuss what's bothering you instead?"

"No." The word rushed from his friend's mouth. "I'd much rather talk about this." Paul gestured between them. "Er, the three of us, that is. My issue will keep." He threw a glance over his shoulder, at what? Something beyond his sight? His coat slung over the back of the chair?

"You're acting deuced strange." The instinct that had always guided him flared strong now. He studied his friend, took in his hands clasped tightly on his knees, the lines of strain around his mouth and on his brow, the clouded emotion in his eyes, and he frowned. Was Paul hiding something, or was he merely thinking the worst based on past experience?

"Suffice it to say, it's been a rather trying day." Finally, Paul met his gaze square on. "Then, coming out here, hearing that you and Caroline had reconciled, I fully expected to be tossed to the proverbial wolves once more."

"Perhaps a week ago that would have been so, but my wife is stubborn and her feelings run deep." For the love of Caroline, he'd do anything to keep her happy. If she wanted both of them, then that was what he'd make happen. It could be worse. The third could be a virtual stranger instead of the best friend of his youth. "You are aware that she loves you and that she also holds the same affection for me."

"Yes. She's always been very open and adamant regarding both of us."

Adam nodded. Caroline's ability to remain forthright in the face of what had to be a morass of confusion for her stunned him. How would he have reacted if faced with the same scenario? "I refuse to lose her again." When the other man would have spoken, he held up a hand. "I also understand you're unwilling to bow out or watch her be torn away from you." He paused, choosing his next words carefully. It was, after all, a rather delicate situation. "We are all in a unique situation and the common thread holding us together is her. In order to keep her happy and make her feel secure and well-loved, I'm inquiring as to the possibility of shifting the relationship to include you."

"You intend to remain married to her?" There was no animosity in Paul's voice, only curiosity.

"I do. I'd thought about going through with having a divorce enacted. However, it would look suspicious and get tongues to wagging when I remained on the island." He sat back on the settee. "I know you looked forward to wedding her, and I am sorry about that. I just don't see any other option that won't garner undue attention." At least in this, she'd keep his name. That small fact brought him peace with the situation.

"Then, any children she might bear will also have your name?"

It was eerie how well his friend's thoughts mirrored his own. "Yes." Adam's chest tightened. He still hadn't recovered from the insight she'd shared with him regarding the child she'd—they'd—lost. To think and hope that they might have more children together seemed a temptation of fate, but he'd enjoy that above all things. Even now, Caro could be with child from the three times they'd already been together since his homecoming. He stared back at Paul without guile or victory. "If such an event occurs, the child or children might be fathered by either of us. You have to square with that." *As do I.* As he'd told Caroline yesterday, all of these changes wouldn't happen overnight. He'd need to work through them in time. "Any child will be part of her and will be loved…" He choked back a sob. Would that he'd been there to hold his only child, and now it was too late.

The other man visibly swallowed. "You would have been an outstanding father," Paul whispered.

Belatedly, Adam realized his friend would have been around Caroline after the birth, would have seen the boy Adam had only dreamed of, would have perhaps held the babe. And in his jealousy, he would have had the man banished from Caroline's life. Paul, another connection to the past he'd mucked up. "I've spent years being a bloody fool. Forgive me."

"There's nothing to forgive. Especially in light of..." The other man shook his head, his eyes haunted once more. "In the course of loving Caroline, anything that brings her joy will be my joy as well, be that you or another babe." He coughed then cleared his throat. "It matters not who will father a child." He fixed a hard look upon Adam. "As long as you won't leave her again." He cleared his throat yet again. "Leave us, I suppose I should say. Of course, everything depends on your understanding and forgiveness of certain other things..." His voice trailed off and a trace of red infused his cheeks.

Adam's jaw slackened. God, perhaps he didn't know his friend as well as he'd thought. What the hell was he going on about? "I hope I haven't given you an erroneous impression. This proposed relationship will be for Caro—her needs and desires. I will not be pleasuring you or vice versa." He glanced away, suddenly landing in an awkward situation he'd rather not broach. That coupled with Paul's strange behavior was enough to make his head pound.

"Oh, Lord." Paul's bark of laughter cleared away the tension and brought back a bit of his friend's old humor. "My sexual preferences don't run to men." He shook with silent mirth. "I very much want Caroline in my bed. However, I meant what I said." His laughter died and his expression sobered. "You might not believe it, but I did miss you when you left. Sure, I hated what your callous treatment and absence did to Caroline, but that bond we'd formed during our early adventures will never be forgotten." His voice faltered and he dropped his gaze. "I'd enjoy a return of that comradery. If we can do that with Caroline as the mediator, then I'm all for such a relationship. Even after you realize that I..."

Emotion clogged Adam's throat. "You're a good friend. I'd enjoy that as well."

"I don't know how good of a friend I am," the other man mumbled.

"Because of our posturing over her?" When Paul remained silent, Adam forged ahead. "Think nothing of it. In some ways, I'm glad you were here for her when I could not be. And, you're able to give her what I cannot." He clenched his jaw then reminded himself to relax. They weren't enemies any longer. They had the same goal: keeping Caroline happy and feeling loved. "I have a tendency to get lost in my own head too often. She'll need to rely on you more then. If I go off by myself during those times, you need to provide comfort and assurance."

"Don't put the responsibility on me, Adam. I'm not the sort of man you think I am." Paul struggled to his feet. "I don't deserve your regard or hers." Guilt was etched into his expression. "I need to tell you…"

Again, this new annoying habit of letting his words trailed off flared. Adam frowned. What the hell was wrong with the man?

"What does that mean?" Caroline's question shattered the at times strange conversation between them as she came into the room with a teapot in one hand. Her eyes were round.

It was now or never. He shot a glance to Paul, but his friend had his gaze directed at her with an almost pleading look in his eye. "Paul and I were discussing you because we've come to an agreement and hope you'll find it favorable as well." He stepped forward, took the teapot from her grasp then laid it carefully on the tray next to the cold one. "Caro, we both want to—"

"Yes!" She threw her arms around his neck and hugged him close.

"But, you haven't heard me out," Adam protested.

"I don't need to. I can see it in your eyes. Oh, this is just what I've hoped for and wanted but was afraid to broach the subject with you, either of you, for fear of losing you both." Yet, when she pulled back, concern clouded her blue gaze. "It's not legal. You'll think I'm depraved. We'll be ostracized or worse. Between the townspeople here and the increasing British presence, I just don't see how we can keep a secret like this." A mist of tears welled in her eyes.

Paul muttered beneath his breath, his words to garbled to make out then he said clearly, "There is something I should say before any plans are made—"

She spoke over him in apparent excitement. "I refuse to indulge, even if for one, illicit time, if it will sacrifice what we currently have, as broken and strained as it is."

Good God, she would cry again? It tore him up inside to see her upset and he didn't know how to comfort her. Didn't she know how they felt? "It's a damn island, Caro. All we have is privacy. Ninety miles of it."

"But, what about my parents? Do we tell them? Plus, the servants." Her eyes widened. "Of course we won't be able to hide such a thing from them and they'll talk…"

"I…" He hadn't thought that far ahead. He sent a frantic gaze to Paul and mouthed the word, "Help."

"I cannot." Paul looked as if he could retch at any moment. "I shouldn't, now when I've—"

"God damn it, Paul. Whatever it is you have on your mind, we'll get to that in short order. Right now I need you. *We* need you." The authority in his voice couldn't be denied.

Immediately, his friend took control and his bearing changed. Adam hoped he'd come back to his normal self. He closed the distance between them and drew Caroline into an embrace. "We'll make certain to be discreet." He pressed a kiss to her forehead. "I'll remain in my residence on the mainland and conduct my life much the same way I do now. No one has questioned it yet. They'll have no reason to assume anything else is afoot." He followed the pronouncement with a kiss to each of her cheeks. Finally, he framed her face in his hands as he peered into her eyes. "You'll need to trust us to make it work. Whether you wish to inform your parents or anyone else of our arrangement is up to your judgment."

Caroline stood peering up into his face with a wide smile and adoration in her eyes. Adam's heart squeezed. Did she look at him the same way? "I don't know what to say. So long I've hoped for this." She twined her arms around Paul's neck then touched her lips to his. "I have my two men."

The other man groaned as he tightened his embrace and pulled her against him. He returned her kisses, moving over her ripe mouth with all the grace and elegance Adam remembered from him.

Frozen in observance, he knew a moment of panic even as his cock awakened. Was her affection for Paul greater than what she felt for him? After everything, would she prefer if he quietly melted from her life? Then, she broke the kiss long enough to glance over her shoulder at him, her eyes full of questions and dark with desire. He expelled the breath he'd held. "Caro." The word was a mere whisper as he joined them, fitting his body to hers and pressing his front to her backside. This, he remembered from the murky, disjointed depths of his memory, this sensation of having a woman between him and Paul, this competition of sorts yet the knowledge of working together to bring the lady to dizzying heights of pleasure, which had only enhanced their own.

"Adam." She wiggled her backside against his burgeoning length. "Make love to me." Her voice, husky with need, washed over him. "The way only you can."

"There's not enough time to properly manage such a thing," he said as he pressed his lips to the soft skin of her nape. Though, he did take a smattering of pride that she enjoyed his style. "Sunset will be upon us in an hour, and I do need to get to the light. Too many men depend on that beacon." Her disappointed sounds had him reconsidering, but in the end, he'd always be a sailor. He had to do right by his brothers on the sea. "However, Paul and I can give you a taste until tomorrow, perhaps." God, could he survive that long before being able to bury himself in her heat?

"Or we can taste you," Paul murmured against her throat.

A thrill of dark anticipation lanced down his spine at the thought of watching his friend with his mouth between Caroline's thighs. "Yes." He gripped her hips and ground his hardening erection into the small of her back. "Perhaps we'll send you flying before I must depart."

"I hope you're not teasing."

Some of Adam's humor returned. "Does this feel like we're teasing?" He slid his palms up her ribcage then cupped her breasts and squeezed.

"Mmm." Her head lolled back, and he took full advantage by nipping her earlobe while Paul leaned down and licked the swell of her breasts above her neckline. "Being here, with the two of you, I never knew..." Awe wove through her voice, and she trembled in his arms. "I never thought it would happen."

A growl escaped him as he tugged the fabric and her bodice slipped down. The beautiful globes of her breasts popped free. "Shh. Don't talk. Enjoy." He rolled one turgid nipple while Paul sucked the other into his mouth. Every sound she uttered, every shuddery intake of breath seeped into his consciousness and sent his desire soaring. "Paul, remember that trick we used to do with the chair?" Once, onboard ship, there hadn't been a chair available so they'd used a water barrel. Why he recalled such a thing was beyond him. Maybe his current occupation jogged his brain.

The other man raised his head. His eyes twinkled. "Capital idea." He gestured with his chin. "Just there should work."

Adam disentangled himself from his wife. She protested and he grinned. "Patience, woman. You'll be rewarded shortly." A few stumbling steps took him to the chair Paul had occupied earlier. He fell into it with more haste than dignity, and the greatcoat along the back slid down beside him. "Come. Sit on my lap." He held out a hand to her.

Hunger blazed in her gaze. With her breasts hanging out of her gown and high color in her pale cheeks, he wanted nothing else but to bury his face between those mounds and lick his fill. She had the look of a woman on the cusp of spending. "Will you spank me?"

He grabbed a handful of her skirting and reeled her in, turned her about, and then planted her on his lap. When Paul's eyes went wide, he said, "Our Caro has a fondness for a little domestic correction, especially with a hairbrush."

"You don't say?" His friend knelt in front of them. He shoved her skirts up her legs. "Straddle him a bit, darling." When she did as instructed, Adam splayed his thighs, which opened Caroline to Paul's perusal. "Ah, God you're beautiful."

Adam knew exactly what his friend meant. It was what he'd felt when seeing her lovely pink, glistening bits on his first night back. His chest swelled. "She's gorgeous and tastes sweet." His mouth watered. "Yours is an enviable position."

"You'll have your turn." Paul smirked. He caressed the inside of her thighs. "This is the finest tea treat I've ever been offered."

Caroline gasped. "You are both very naughty. Perhaps I shouldn't have agreed to this plan." She wriggled on Adam's lap and moaned in encouragement.

He groaned as his engorged cock protested. "Leave off, my girl, else I'll embarrass myself."

"Give me an incentive not to move then, husband," she taunted.

Was there any wonder he loved her to distraction? When he buried his nose into her hair and inhaled the rose scent of her, felt the heat of her body sink into his and spied the smattering of freckles across the bridge of her nose, he knew with more certainty than he knew a storm was moving in that he loved her more than life itself.

"Wench," he whispered and took her breasts in hand once more. This time he squeezed with more force. "Is this what you want? Pleasure or pain today, love?"

She slumped into his chest. Breathless laughter escaped her. "What do you think?" The laughter vanished beneath a squeal of delight the second Paul's head disappeared beneath her skirts. "Oh!"

Putting his need to the back of his mind, he rolled her nipples then plucked them with firm pressure. When she moaned, he continued the cycle while kissing the sweet spot where her neck and shoulder met. Soon, the soft sounds of her moans blended with Paul's hums of appreciation. Adam groaned. He shifted to accommodate his abused cock and the greatcoat tumbled down further.

Caroline listed to the left as Paul no doubt plied her button with attention. Would that he could see such an occurrence, but given his current state, it was good he could not. Seconds later, she sprang upright on his lap. "Ouch!"

"What?" Paul came out from under her skirts. His lips and lower face shone with her juices. "Did I hurt you? I swear I didn't mean to. I assumed that since you'd hinted at pain, you'd like a bit of teeth in our play..."

She waved a hand then rooted around the mound of fabric. "Something dug into my side and is just uncomfortable enough to ruin my concentration."

"Uh, Caroline, please don't—" Paul's protest was cut off at the same moment she withdrew crumpled paperwork and a leather pouch from the coat. His eyes rounded and something akin to fear shadowed them.

"What's this?" She held up the pouch. "Is it part of your surprise?"

"Caroline, that's private—" Paul reached for the pouch, but she held it out of reach.

Adam snatched it from her hand. "Allow me." His curiosity was piqued. Did this folio hold the key to Paul's odd behavior? He nudged his wife. "You look at the other one."

She sucked in a breath. "Why does this have my name written on it?"

"For the love of God, if you two have ever had a care for me at all before, please don't read those documents." Slowly, Paul rose to his feet. Fear, dread, and resignation lined his face. "Please."

Adam's gut tightened as he slipped open the folio then withdrew the few papers residing within. "What did you do?" Then his heart dropped into his boots as he read the first line of the official decree on royal letterhead. *For turning in the fugitive known as Captain Adam Montmorency, the Crown recognizes your bravery and heroism by the award of the title of baron...*

He stopped reading as the sour taste of bile rose up the back of his throat. He encouraged Caroline none too gently off his lap. Then he stood as his chest heaved and the red haze of anger slid over his vision. "What the hell did you do, Paul?" Another glance at the papers in his hand didn't reveal anything different. "You betrayed me? You? After everything we've been through? *You* gave me up to the British?" His voice rose with each question.

"Paul?" Caroline's hushed voice cut through some of Adam's anger. He glanced at her, took in the pallor of her face and the slight wobble in her chin, and he braced himself for further emotional outbursts. The tendons in her throat worked with a hard swallow. She glanced at the other man. "Why are the British demanding the island as well as the lighthouse? They've never bothered me before."

"I can explain." Paul wiped his face on his sleeve, which was a shocking act for one as fastidious as he. "I tried earlier, Adam, but the words wouldn't come or I was interrupted and then you demanded I help with Caroline." He blew out a breath. "I told you I didn't deserve anything you bestowed upon me. This happened at your return, and I'd honestly thought you weren't what Caroline needed. We were at odds then and I didn't think we'd ever reconcile." His words tripped fast and furious out of his mouth. "I was annoyed you'd come back. I'd thought it was an easy way to see you gone, and —"

"I will kill you with my bare hands," Adam forced out from around clenched teeth. His chest ached as if he'd been stabbed with a heated fire poker. "Never did I think that a trusted friend, the man I allowed into my house, fucking my wife, inviting you back into my life, would betray me." He threw the papers and folio into the chair then lunged at his former friend. The last thing he remembered hearing was Caroline's screamed entreaty not to hurt him.

❦ Chapter Eighteen ❦

The official letter fell from Caroline's hand and fluttered to the floor. She yanked her bodice back into place as she flew across the room in pursuit of Adam. All thoughts and remembered sensations from their dual pleasures vanished. His expression and the livid glint in his stormy eyes terrified her as much as his attack on Paul. "Adam, stop!" She reached him at the same time he slammed Paul's back into the wall and pressed a forearm to the other man's throat. "Don't do this. You're not that man anymore."

"This doesn't concern you, Caro," her husband growled. He never looked away from his adversary, who struggled for breath and clawed at Adam's arm.

"Like hell it doesn't." She gripped his arm with both hands. Tight muscles flinched beneath her fingertips, and after a couple of attempts she managed to wrench Adam off Paul, who then slumped against the wall, his breathing labored, while Adam seethed. After slipping between the men, she planted her hands against her husband's chest and pushed him. He stumbled back a few steps then simply refused to move any more. "I'm your wife. That alone means whatever happens to you happens to me."

"Don't patronize me. You know nothing about this."

Tendrils of hurt wrapped around her heart and tears pricked the backs of her eyes. She understood why her husband wished to kill Paul, but that wouldn't change what his friend had done. She shoved her annoyance away. "I know you and that's enough. You should know me as well. Violence won't solve this."

When Adam would have stepped around her, murderous intent still gleaming in his eyes, she matched him step for step. "Damnation, woman! Leave off." His torso fairly vibrated beneath her palms. The stormy depths of his eyes promised retribution for any who opposed him. It both terrified and awed her.

"No." Her own chest heaved from the force of the emotions roiling through her. She couldn't fathom why Paul had done whatever he'd done, but her first concern was that the men she loved didn't kill each other. "If you want a more substantial argument, consider this: Gull's Island is my home, it's my father's legacy. That light represents hope to our navy men and any man sailing a ship for trade, smuggling or for whatever reason—even the British—and it gives hope for each and every resident of Portsmouth who sees it, who looks upon its light for comfort through the storm. I refuse to let this property be lost to a war that's merely based on men's bruised egos."

"You know nothing of betrayal," he spat out.

"Don't I?" She popped her hands onto her hips and glared. Behind her, Paul's wheezing echoed in the silence. "How do you think I felt when you went away? How do you think I felt when our son died under my watch? How do you think I felt when I thought you'd died, leaving me a barely bedded widow with no future unless I had proof? How do you think I feel when fate is taking my own mother's mind and strength? You think on that then ask again if I don't know what it feels like to know betrayal." Even though her fingers itched with the need to slap him, make him see sense again, she conquered the urge. Violence wouldn't end with violence.

"This isn't the same thing!" His roar bounced off the walls and she cringed at the power he commanded. In that instant, she saw what everyone else did — the indomitable sea captain, the man who'd survived years of torture by his will alone, the man who was a tyrant but had forged that steel of his soul into something different, something fierce that would never again be broken. A tremble moved down her spine and she remembered when he'd been locked in a dream and tried to harm her. "Move away, Caroline. Paul has to answer for what he's done."

A frisson of alarm worked through her chest at his use of her full name. "No." She crossed her arms beneath her breasts. "I know Paul, mayhap better than you do. Yes, what he did is despicable, but at least let him explain. Just as you have changed, perhaps so has he."

"Dammit, you don't understand." But some of the rage had faded from his voice.

"I do. You thought never again would someone betray you, let alone someone close to you, someone you opened yourself up to and trusted again." She glanced over her shoulder at Paul, who stood tensely, ready for flight no doubt, his gaze anchored on them, self-loathing and despair in those depths. With a sigh, Caroline returned her attention to her husband. She touched his chest. "Don't let all those who've died before you do it in vain. You are better than your circumstances, more than your past. Just as you warranted understanding so does he."

She and Adam locked gazes, and for one tiny second she fully believed he'd shove her aside and go after Paul anyway, but then, his shoulders sagged. He drew in a deep breath then let it ease out between his teeth. More of the anger dimmed in his eyes. Finally, he cupped her cheek and brought his forehead to hers. "More than ever it's obvious I do not deserve you."

A sigh of relief escaped her. He was back, the man she knew he could be. "You deserve so much more than you think."

"Perhaps." He pulled away then shoved a hand through his hair. Sometime in the struggle, he'd lost the bit of leather he usually tied it back with. It gave him a roguish air, more pirate than upstanding member of society. "Paul." A muscle in his jaw ticked. He curled a hand into a fist. "I'd hear your explanation now. Then we can decide on our next action of defense."

Her eyes stung with tears, both grateful and irate. Adam would stay instead of stick to some antiquated notion of giving himself up for their safety. Even though she'd calmed him, she rounded on Paul. "How dare you think to make it possible I'd lose my husband yet again when you already know that was my biggest fear."

It was Adam's turn to calm her. "Caro, if I'm to let him talk, perhaps you should as well. There will be plenty of time to rip him to shreds later." His deep voice washed over her, soothing as a balm.

"This is all too much." Quickly, she blinked her tears away as she glanced to the other man. He'd paled but seemed less conflicted than before. She didn't know how to help either of her men, especially after something as big as this. "Paul, you not only betrayed Adam but me as well. I… I don't quite know how to act toward you now."

Paul implored her with his gaze. "If you'll but hear me out…"

Adam clenched his hands into fists. "Because of her I won't draw blood on you, but I cannot guarantee I won't once out of the house. You've hurt her and for that I cannot forgive you."

Her chest tightened. How much did she adore him championing her? Unbidden, her father's words from days ago came back to her, reminding her that life was indeed too short. If she wanted her dream, she'd have to fight for it. "Come." She held out a hand to Paul. "Let's see if our connections can be salvaged." When he grasped it and Adam growled, she pinned her husband with a look then drew Paul over to the settee. They sat at the same time, and once Adam stood nearby, for he refused to sit anywhere, she nodded. "Go ahead."

"I never meant to hurt you, Caroline. I didn't think how this would have affected you, never counted on the fact you would have worked things out with Adam, that you would forgive him…" His throat moved with a hard swallow. He swung his gaze from Adam's frowning visage to her. "Yes, I was annoyed when Adam returned, the perfect image of a dashing sea captain, back to claim his wife and the life he'd left—the life I desperately wanted."

"So you thought the answer was to expose my presence to the British navy, after what you knew they did to me?" The question, in Adam's quiet voice, showcased his banked fury.

"You never spoke definitively about your experiences."

"Yet even if I didn't, betraying someone close to you is never a decent thing to do!" Adam's shout echoed off the walls.

"I know. What I did was appalling no matter the reason." Paul shook his head. "That's beside the point. I only knew I wanted you gone. I was blinded by jealousy, by hurt. If handing you over to them meant I'd have Caroline to myself, that was all I desired—at that moment." He shifted his attention to Caroline. "Then, I saw how much he'd changed and I caught glimpses of our old friendship. You were once more smitten with him, perhaps even more so now than you had been back then."

His voice caught. "Then Adam made the sacrifice to protect you. He allowed me to be with you and I broke…" His words fractured.

"I know. Everything was already in play and you were caught in the tide." Caroline patted his hand. She looked up at her husband. "Say something."

"What words of comfort would you have me utter?" A warning underscored the question. "A traitor isn't given concessions."

"But at one time, you were the traitor and wished for the same," she said in a soft voice. The act of forgiveness was such a huge thing. She'd never thought she'd give the same to him when he'd come back, let alone allow him close again. But she had. Trust was a powerful weapon as well as a key. Everyone deserved it. Even Paul, even in the face of his enormous betrayal. "Adam—"

"No. He's right," Paul interrupted. He scrubbed a hand over his face. "I don't expect you to understand or even forgive me." He struggled to his feet. "However, I'm not proud of what I've done. I knew how wrong it was that night I laid with Caroline, the night you walked out of our lives making what was probably the biggest sacrifice you've ever put forth."

"I thought I could trust you," Adam returned with more gruffness than before. "I'd hoped you'd be the man of honor and integrity you'd always been."

"I am. You can." He faced her husband, his expression earnest and tinged with embarrassment. "The Adam of old would never have done, or even allowed, anything that has transpired these past couple of weeks. I'm amazed at the change in you and in seeing that change, it puts my life into sharp relief, makes me want to be a better man as well."

"Yet, you betrayed me anyway."

His throat worked. "You know what they say about hindsight." He shook his head. "I could never forget about my conversation with the commodore, but had not the chance to ask him to reverse the plans."

"Not even when we witnessed the scouting party come to the island?" Adam asked in a voice that brimmed with animosity. "It didn't occur to you then to make a damn appointment?" Rage quivered through his words.

"I know. I was lax. I was an idiot." He shrugged. "I was quite occupied with other things. It's not an excuse, but it's a reason." When he passed a glance to her, Caroline's body heated.

"Sometimes navigating through life's pitfalls is a difficult prospect." Listening to him, watching the emotions cross his face, gave her a greater understanding. Put in his position, she'd be hard pressed not to do the same.

Maybe.

"Ah Caroline." A ghost of a smile touched his sensuous lips. "Love makes a person do horrible, stupid things, I suppose. However, this afternoon I went into the commodore's office, intending to make this right. I'd hoped he'd call off his plan and merely exile Adam if he wouldn't change his mind."

Her husband snorted. "Oh, because being exiled by the British to another part of the world controlled by the same is such a better life?"

"It's a hell of a lot better than being put to death, don't you think?" Paul's spirit returned in that exchange. A touch of anger strengthened his voice. He stood taller and prouder with his back ramrod straight. "I tried to make things right once I realized how very much hinged on that betrayal. I thought if you were at least alive, I could break you from whatever prison you landed in. We could all still be together and wouldn't that be better?"

Adam snorted. "The British would never consent to exile. They've wanted me dead for too long."

"There was a chance…"

"There was, but it would take us all from Gull's Island." Caroline stood. She smiled at Paul. "Your heart was in the right place though you realized it too late." With a look to Adam and the murderous intent still blazing in his eyes, she said, "What now?" When her husband didn't answer immediately, she walked across the room, retrieved the abandoned letter then returned to her two men, who were staring at each other, not a grin between them. *Oh, good God.* Men and their egos. "Gentlemen, I'm not about to let the life I've dreamed of slip through my fingers because of this damned misunderstanding," she slid her gaze to her husband, "or your hurt feelings," then she looked at Paul, "or your misplaced intentions. Though, I must state right now I *am* angry and I will be for a while. The British will take this island and its light because of your actions, Paul. My life will change yet again just when I'd hoped it would settle."

Paul held up his hands. "I know and I cannot apologize enough to both of you. If the commodore would take my life instead of his…" He looked to Adam, who didn't yield. Paul's shoulders sagged.

"Well, we won't solve anything by talking." And neither would the hurt dissolve now that there was a rift in the trust. "You'd best start formulating a plan, or I will. I'm bloody tired of having my life dictated by men."

"Like hell you will, wife," Adam rejoined. He crossed his arms over his broad chest and glared. "You'll remain here. We'll take care of things. If Paul," she thought he might spit after he uttered the name, "wishes to remain alive, he'll help run the British off when they arrive. But knowing you, you'll rush into the fray to

237

defend us." He rubbed his chin. "Perhaps I'll lock you in the cellar."

"You wouldn't dare." Something about the cellar tickled the edges of her memory, but she didn't know why.

A hint of a grin teased his lips. Some of the anger faded from his eyes. "I'd dare anything where you're concerned."

Heat slipped through her veins. Whatever happened, they were going to survive together. She'd accept nothing less, not when the life of her dreams was so close.

"I second the sentiment," Paul added. "I don't want you anywhere near harm's way."

Adam glared. All softer feeling fled. "You do not have any right to make demands of any kind for her. I have not forgiven you. The trust is gone."

"I hate to say it but Adam is correct." She frowned. "However, I refuse to sit at home and fret while men seek to decide my fate. And if that's what you think, neither of you know me that well. In case you need proof of my ability, here's an abbreviated list: I've fought off a black bear," it was a cub, "shot a bobcat who tried to eat my chickens," her shot went wide and the cat ran off, more scared than she was, "and I lived after I lost my son." That had been that hardest test of all. She owed Paul the credit for bringing her back among the living. "I even lived after I thought I'd lost my husband, so do not assume I have nothing to offer, that I'm not strong enough, especially when its every bit my life hanging on the balance."

The men still offered protests. Ignoring them, she skimmed through the letter.

Dear Mrs. Montmorency,

The British Navy requires full, complete and immediate use of Gull's Island as well as its lighthouse. In accordance, we are asking for your removal from the area within the next forty-eight hours, unless, of course, you can procure the sum of two thousand pounds. This will only buy you a grace period while I bring this issue to the attention of the admiral.

I will be in touch soon.
Regards,

Commodore Nigel Matthers.

When she glanced up from her perusal, both men had their gazes fixed upon her. "What?"

Adam focused his attention on the paper she held. "Well?"

"They want two thousand pounds, which will only buy me a tiny bit of time before they take possession of the island and the light anyway." As much as she intended to fight, dejection still rang in her voice. "Essentially, I'm paying them to take my home and everything I hold dear." Most likely, they'd take the island as well as Adam. "I cannot..." She forced a swallow. Not until right this moment did she realize the enormity of the situation. "If Paul hadn't done what he did..." A near hysterical laugh rose in her throat and broke the air.

"Damn the British. A pox upon all of them," Adam muttered. He shot a speaking glance to Paul. "Some more than others."

"You conveniently forget *you* are British, husband." Despite the situation, a tiny smile pulled at the corners of her lips.

"That is different. I've made a conscious effort to not deport myself like my countrymen. After all, I married

a fiery American, even sailed for their interests for a time."
Then he eyed his friend askance. The anger was still
present in his eyes, but it wasn't as horrible as it had been
before. "I suppose present company excluded," he said in
a grudging voice.

Paul inclined his head. "No offense. Even if you did
mean it, I'd agree. I deserve everything you throw at me
and will understand if I'm never granted forgiveness by
either of you."

Her heart trembled for her two broken men. She
wished Adam would wrap his arms around her, offer her
some sort of comfort for the upcoming ordeal, but he
didn't. Neither of them did. Damn them both. "Comfort
and words would be most welcome at the moment," she
hinted. It was Paul who slipped an arm about her waist
and squeezed. She glanced into his face and smiled as she
tamped on the urge to cry in frustration. "Thank you."

"As always, it's my pleasure." For a moment, she
rested her head on his shoulder but watched her husband.
Was this their future then even if Paul's betrayal could be
overcome? Adam not providing emotional support and
Paul's skill in bed not nearly as fulfilling as Adam's? She
bit her bottom lip. Perhaps, between the two of them
they'd provide everything she'd need.

And, God how she wanted the chance to explore
the opportunity.

Adam's eyes softened as he returned her regard. "I
must go see to the lighthouse, but this is not over," he told
Paul as he flicked his attention to the other man and the
harsh gray of a roiling sea returned. "I won't soon forget
it's your fault that hell will soon spew its minions upon us
or that all of our lives are in danger."

"Adam…" Caroline took a step toward him.

He shook his head. "I understand he's contrite now.
That doesn't negate the wheels that are already turning.

These are facts. Also a fact is betrayed trust won't heal quickly, at least it won't with me." When she closed the distance then stood on tiptoe and pressed a kiss to his cheek, a shuddery exhalation left him. He tweaked an escaped lock of her hair. "Please promise me you'll be careful and stay safe no matter what happens."

"You can assure yourself of that, for I'm going with you to the lighthouse."

"Caro, please, for once follow my dictates." No anger lingered in his voice, only exhaustion. How much had this night cost him?

"No. If you wanted a docile bride, you should have chosen differently. Finally, I'm going to have an adventure of my own!" She flashed a grin as her confidence soared. "Besides, according to the letter, we have two days to prepare. We'll be ready and I'll be damned if I let the British walk away with everything." Then she flicked her attention to Paul. "And, you're wrong. Love makes people do truly wonderful things. Let's see what we're all capable of. Allow your actions to rebuild what you've destroyed."

By the time the three of them arrived at the light—Adam by horse and she and Paul under their own foot power—the short twilight had given way to the inky darkness of night. Since Adam had arrived ahead of them, the golden glow of the light already cut through the darkness.

After removing their snowshoes, Paul chose to speak with Adam in the light while Caroline pushed open the door to the cottage. Lord, but she hoped Adam would be in the mood to listen. Those two needed each other. The robust scent of strong coffee met her nose and pulled her out of her thoughts, as did the rich aroma of her mother's buttery crumb cake. Often, she'd bake the goodie in the evening so her father could snack on it during the long night tending the light. She looked about with a frown. "Mother?" Wasn't she supposed to be with her sister? "When did you return?"

"Caroline, how lovely you've come for a visit. We only returned a couple of hours ago." Her parent came into the tiny living space from the equally tiny kitchen. "Your father didn't tell me you'd intended to drop by."

"I didn't know myself, but there's been an issue with Adam, and I—"

"Oh, and I met your husband a bit ago." Her mother grabbed Caroline's hand and pulled her toward the worn sofa then tugged her down next to her. "I'm so glad the captain has returned. I always hoped he'd come back. Such a charming man. Much different than the man you married."

"As am I." Thank God her mother was lucid. There were times when she'd demanded to see Adam and couldn't understand why he never accompanied Caroline when she visited. "Why are you here? I thought you were staying with Aunt—"

Her mother's expression went soft and her faded blue eyes sparkled. In the low candlelight, Caroline could easily imagine what her parent had looked like as a young woman. "Well, your father only wanted to stay through this afternoon. I couldn't bear to be parted with him, so I told him I was coming with him."

"And he let you?"

"He doesn't 'let' me do anything." A low-pitched tinkling laugh escaped the older woman. "Sometimes, my girl, a woman has to stand up for herself, even if that's not what her man wants." She clasped Caroline's hand tighter. "You father is a good husband, but there are times when he's so stubborn that I just want to—"

242

"Stand up to him toe-to-toe and argue him down?" Caroline interrupted with a smile. She had no idea her mother had been so much like... her. Or rather, she was so much like her mother. There was a certain amount of pride in the knowledge.

"Yes." A smile curved her parent's lips. "I think," she giggled, "I think he likes me to argue."

"I don't doubt that." Caroline bit back a grin lest her mother think she laughed at her instead of the irony of the situation. She rather thought Adam enjoyed verbally sparring as well.

"When we were younger, after such arguments, we'd end up in bed and—"

"Mother!" The heat of embarrassment flooded Caroline's cheeks. *I do not want to know.*

"What?" Her mother smiled. "I'm not ashamed that we have a satisfying married life outside—"

"Enough." She held up a hand. "Where is Father?"

"He and your husband went to tend the light, but I think they want to share an ale there instead." The older woman giggled again at the shared confidence.

This time she did smile. "Men will be men." She drew in a shuddering breath as she studied her mother. Gray streaked her once bright red hair and blue veins crisscrossed the backs of her hands. "Paul came with me as well. He went to find Adam. They've, ah, recently come to a disagreement. And they should talk, but I fear things will come to violence between them."

"They'll work things out to a reasonable solution. They're fast friends beneath everything. Eventually, they'll remember that." She nodded. "Oh, I do so love Paul. He's a good man." She cut a sly glance to Caroline. "But Adam is also a fine man, and he's your husband."

"Yes." How much of what had recently occurred in her life could she share with her mother? Would she remember it anyway, and if she did, would she blurt it out at an inopportune time?

"A woman who has the love of two such men is fortunate indeed."

She peered sharply at her mother. "I'm hardly a young woman any longer. Most of my youth was spent waiting." For the love of each of those men.

"Perhaps there was a good reason for that." Her mother released her hand then sat back into the cushions. "Are you happy with your life, Caroline?"

"Yes." She clasped her hands together to still their shaking. "At least, I think I am, but that happiness might be taken away when the British navy arrives to steal the island from us." Her voice wavered. "To take Adam from me. To take away our home. Yours as well."

"The island is the only home I've known since I married." Sadness entered her mother's eyes. "Don't let any of it happen. You deserve this place and both of your men." Her steady gaze landed on Caroline. "Life is too fleeting to let worry steal your happiness."

"Your happiness as well." Her stomach clenched. So many lives beyond hers would be broken if the British won the island. "But what if what makes me happy is wrong in the eyes of everyone else?"

"No one will know if you're careful. And it's no one else's business beside." Her mother waved a hand. "Just don't tell your father."

"Why?" Was that her mother's subtle way of saying she approved of the unorthodox relationship? The thought took away some of her anxiety. "Will he be angry?"

"Yes, at me." Another giggle left her parent's throat. "I told him years ago that if Adam did return, you should keep them both for your own pleasure. He staunchly disagreed, saying you'd remain true to Adam, but he did so like Paul too."

Heat blasted through Caroline's cheeks. There was something decidedly odd about skirting around her romantic life in conversation with her mother. "Oh, my."

Further talk was prohibited by the arrival of Paul and Adam. Both wore expressions of alarm and concern.

"What's wrong?" Caroline sprang to her feet as her pulse accelerated. "Have you been fighting?"

"Not physically." Adam leveled a speaking glance at her. "Though we have declared a tentative truce in light of more important things. We sighted a long boat approaching. It bears a British flag."

She sucked in a breath. "They're early."

"Bastards," Paul breathed. When everyone looked at him, he gave a sheepish grin. "Never trust a British officer. They'll cheat every time." He approached her mother. "Why don't you come with me? Your husband asked that you lock yourself into the service room of the lighthouse. At least you'll be out of range of the fighting."

A shiver shot down Caroline's spine. She forced a swallow, but kept eye contact with her husband. This was her life and she'd fight alongside her men to keep them. "Come with me. I'll show you where Father keeps his small store of weapons."

⚝ Chapter Nineteen ⚝

Adam barely listened to the soft cadence of Caroline's voice as she went through the trunk of weapons at the foot of the bed. After this night, he'd either be dead or he'd never see his wife again.

And he couldn't bear that. Of course, he'd defend her and the island until he had no more breath, but there was every possibility they might not win.

"I don't know if I'm strong enough to lose you again," he whispered as surprise and fear gripped his chest. He'd been so long without the want to show softer emotions that he didn't know how to properly portray his feelings. He kept his gaze on the pistol in his hand then shoved the weapon into his coat pocket.

"Pardon?" She glanced up at him from her position of kneeling on the floor before the trunk. The hood of her dark cloak fell back and the paleness of her cheeks stood stark against the fabric. The wool pooled around her like spilled ink. She almost had the look of a supplicant at prayer. Fitting on this night.

He bit back a sigh. "I walked away from you the first time. Then my fractured memories nearly took you the second time. I thought I'd lost you to Paul, which would have been the third time. Now, faced with a fourth possibility of losing you again," he blew out a breath, "I don't know that I can survive such a thing." His heart squeezed as if a vice were placed over it. He didn't care for the feeling.

"Oh, Adam." The words were borne on the wings of a sobbing sound and she came to her feet in one smooth motion. "I promise not to let that happen." Her eyes sparkled in the light that filtered into the room from the lacy curtains. "I expect you in my bed once this is over. Don't disappoint me." She flung herself into his arms careful to keep the dagger clutched in one hand away from his flesh.

A grin curved his lips. Adam kissed the crown of her hair. "Aye. That is one set of orders I'll make certain to fulfil." He pulled back and peered into her face. "Caro, I..."

Caroline shook her head. "It's all right. You don't need to say it." She cupped his cheek with her free hand. "I know."

"That very well may be." He placed a hand over hers then moved them both and pressed a kiss into her palm. "But it needs saying now." The longer he stared into her eyes, the more he wanted to drown in those bright blue depths. He framed her face in his hands, his fingers fanning into her hair, then kissed her. It wasn't a lover's embrace, merely an attempt to convey the complexity of his regard, but he drank from her sweet lips as if it would be the last time he'd do such a thing. When he allowed her breath, he said, "I love you. Never think I do not, even if I'm not the best at showing it."

She nodded. "I appreciate every effort you make." As she stared at him, she sucked in a breath. Excitement lit her eyes. "I have it!"

"You have what?" Immediately wary, Adam tensed.

"The coin needed to buy us more time. Though in light of the British showing up early, I don't guess it matters now." She sent him a grin brimming with hope. "In the early years of your voyages, you used to send me back parcels of treasures and things. I," her voice faltered, "I never used them, with the exception of the clock, never even unpacked them because I didn't want anything from you." She met his gaze and tears lingered there. "But I'll gladly relinquish those things now to keep you."

He released her hand then put it to his heart, where that organ threatened to jump from his chest. "I barely remember I'd sent you those things." They must be worth several times the bounty, surely.

"You did." She blinked away the moisture. "They're somewhere in the cellar at the house. If I can return there quickly, I—"

A scratching sound at the doorway interrupted the interlude. As one they stared at the newcomer. "Paul. I suppose it's time?" It took every ounce of willpower Adam had to even talk to the man, let him come near Caroline, but the sting of the betrayal paled in the face of the upcoming battle. At times, a man's priorities shifted whether he wished them to or not.

"Yes." The other man came further into the room with a glance to Caroline. "I'm afraid a trip to the homestead is out of the question now." The buckle on the belt slung low over his hips jingled. He wore a light officer's saber at his side. A rifle was slung crossways over his back both from the stored weapons cache. Adam had seen many such weapons employed at the hands of the British. "There is other bad news."

"Of course." He looked at Caroline as she drew up the hood of her cloak. His heart squeezed. Why was it a man never realized how valuable something was until he was on the verge of losing it? And yet she intended to fight by his side with naught but a dagger for she'd refused a gun. *What did I do in my life to deserve such a fine woman?* He swung his attention back to his friend. "Tell me."

"There are two longboats. Nine men in each. Moments away from docking."

Adam briefly closed his eyes. He ignored the swift intake of Caroline's breath, but to her credit, she didn't fall into hysterics. It was one of the things he appreciated about his wife. She was steadfast in the face of any crisis. "Eighteen against the three of us. Plus Caroline's parents. Her mother refused to be taken away for her own safety." Much like his wife. Already, the odds weren't in their favor. "I've fought worse."

"We fight together. If you'll have me." Paul extended his hand.

"Aye. I won't say no to friends at a time like this." Adam clasped the other man's forearm. "This is by no means forgiveness, and quite frankly you arse can damn well help us get out of the drink you landed us in, but still. I suppose it's a start." They held the pose for several seconds before releasing. Life was too precious to lose it to bitterness and strife. "Good luck."

"And to you." Paul faced Caroline. "You're certain you don't wish to join your parents?"

"Don't insult me, Paul. I love you, but my patience with overprotective males grows thin." She rapidly closed the distance between them then kissed him with some measure of passion that Adam had to look away with a grin. "As I told my husband, I expect you in my bed at the end of this, so please manage to remain alive. I've looked forward to that moment for a very long time."

His friend gripped her hand. "Is there any wonder why I love you?"

Her throaty laughter filled the small bedroom. "This is merely the beginning." She caught Adam's eye. "Ready?"

"Yes, but I'd prefer if you armed yourself with more than a dagger." Dear God, she needed more protection than that.

"I am." She pulled back the folds of her cloak. A belt similar to Paul's encircled the enticing curve of her hips. A saber rested at her side. "Let's go." She pushed past them and her boot heels rang in the hallway beyond.

"Damnation," Adam breathed. He grabbed a Baker rifle from the trunk.

"Indeed." Strain filled Paul's chuckle. "Something tells me she'll lead us both by the nose after this."

"As if she's not already." Adam couldn't halt his grin as he followed his wife out of the cottage. "Would you want it any other way?" She was fearless, his wife. She was the sort of woman a man would love waking up beside every morning. Hopefully, fate would let him do just that.

Some minutes later, he and Paul crouched behind the same breakers they had that seemingly long ago day when they'd spied upon another such longboat. "Recognize any of those men?" The weak illumination from lanterns bounced golden arcs over the water as well as the sand. The dark greatcoats of the navy men made them appear more like a somber religious order congregating on the shore than members of the military.

Paul's soft snort sounded in his ear. "Commodore Matthers is the one leading the landing party." He spat upon the ground. "That bounder looked me right in the eye and lied to me regarding when his contingent would begin operations."

"Are you more upset that he lied or that you believed one of your countrymen?" Though he had no love for the horrors the British were capable of inflicting upon their fellow man, he ached in sympathy for Paul. He was only beginning to find out what Adam already knew.

"Both. I realize this is wartime, but I did expect a man's word to be sound. And he's no countryman of mine. Not anymore."

A snort escaped Adam. "I never figured you for an American."

"Sometimes a man is capable of great change."

"You there." The commodore pointed to the men disembarking the first longboat. "Split up. Search the beaches. Go around the perimeter if need be. Make certain the fugitive has no means of escape."

Adam stiffened. Beside him, Paul clicked his tongue. "Easy. Should I fire a shot?" The soldiers split into two groups then marched off.

"Hold. No need unless they fire first." He reeled. Even in this he'd changed. Before he'd come back into Caroline's life and she into his, he would have fired non-stop until every man was felled.

A soft whistle cut through the silence, and three men from the rear arc separated from the company. The commodore's voice sounded as clear as fine crystal being struck. "Find the homestead. Burn it to the ground if there's resistance. Don't shoot to kill. Bring anyone you find to me." They marched off into the scraggly brush before gaining the path that would lead eventually to the house.

"Damn." Paul's soft utterance summed up the situation. "I hadn't counted on this."

"The British have no regard for anyone who doesn't help their cause." A trace of bitterness clung to his voice. "I hope the others are either well-hidden or well-armed." Belatedly, he should have brought the rest with them, but as it was, he'd only had time to give a quick warning.

"The grooms will keep the women safe. They know what to do, as we've long discussed the possibility of a raid since the trouble at sea first began. They know how to hide the cellars. In the event there is no time, they'll flee to a safe point along the southern shore. There's a hidden longboat there they can use for escape."

"I see." Of course, Paul had been here for years, taking up responsibility for everyone in his stead. Another debt Adam would not be able to repay.

"We can't worry about that now." The other man shifted onto his knees. "What was Caroline's position supposed to be?"

"She told me she'd guard the path to the lighthouse. Why?"

His friend gestured to the tableau rapidly assembling before them. Men filed out of the longboats. They fanned out in formation on the beach in two arcs with the commodore holding court in the middle. And damn it all if Caroline wasn't marching across the sand to meet him.

"The woman is a plague," he muttered as he rose to his feet, with every intention of defending her.

Paul snickered, following suit. "Well, you married her, so what does that say about you?"

"Perhaps I enjoy the challenge." He cast a sideways glance at his friend and gave a tight smile. He adored that Caroline wasn't one of those women who sat at home with embroidery and who didn't follow orders well — if at all. "Of course, you bedded her too. What does that say about you?"

"That I'm bloody lucky to be anywhere near her and I'm going to keep it that way." Paul dug an elbow into his side. "Let's go."

Adam didn't need a second prod. He and Paul dashed from their hiding spot and sprinted down the beach. A few soldiers ran to intercept, but an order from the commodore halted them. By the time they reached her location, she was neck deep into a diatribe, taking the commodore to task, her speech peppered with words he hoped to God she hadn't learned from him. He cringed with some of the more colorful language. He leaned closer to Paul. "Where the devil did she learn that?"

"I have no idea. This is a side to Caroline I've never seen before." Paul's pistol dipped as they stared. "Perhaps those trips to the mainland when she does her charity work warrant a second look."

"Perhaps." As much as he wished to leave her to it, he approached her as she continued.

"What sort of vile person are you?" She took a step forward and drew her saber. The remaining soldiers either drew similar sabers or pistols. "How dare you come onto my island and threaten me? You have the gall to intimidate me into giving up my house and the lighthouse that's been in my family for generations? I thought the British could at least appreciate tradition. Apparently, not."

"Mrs. Montmorency, if you'll just—" The commodore attempted to interrupt, but Caroline kept going.

"—I can damn well assure you, you bastard, that you'll have to kill me before I'll let you one step further onto this property." She stuck the tip of her saber into the sand and rested her hand on the hilt.

"Caro, I rather think the commodore has gotten the gist of your ire," Adam said in a droll tone as he rested a hand on her shoulder. Not for worlds would he tell her how much he admired her courage right then.

She sent him a half glance. "Well, you two weren't doing anything productive, so I had to take matters into my own hands." Her huff of irritation clouded on the chilly air. "Plus, he just annoys me. My parents could be hurt," she ended in a small voice that held the hint of a waiver. "Or you could…"

That tiny slip in her armor nearly sent him to his knees. "I know, but I won't let that happen."

"Neither will I," Paul whispered from behind him.

"Enough of this drama." Commodore Matthews cleared his throat as he stepped forward. The breeze ruffled the capes of his greatcoat. He snapped the fingers of one hand and two men came forward, holding lanterns aloft. The golden illumination threw the long features of his face into sharp relief. "Don't make promises you won't be able to keep, Captain."

"What makes you so certain?" Adam asked, his tone carefully modulated. "I believe you know of my record. This small contingent is merely an appetizer, Commodore."

The navy man jerked his chin to one side. The two men not holding the lanterns marched up the path toward the lighthouse. Caroline let out a cry and made to follow, but Adam held her arm then handed her into Paul's keeping… except, Paul wasn't there. *Damn his eyes.* Hopefully, he'd gone to defend the light and keep his promise. A rifle shot echoed in the night, quickly followed by another off toward the direction of the lighthouse. Who had engaged and who defended?

"It's always a struggle, making certain those you love are safe, isn't it, Captain Montmorency?" the commodore drawled. He brushed nonexistent lint from one sleeve. "At any moment, your in-laws will be taken into custody and—"

A rifle shot rang out, cutting through the silence. Caroline's cry of alarm came hard on the heels of that report. Adam's chest tightened. "There will be no escape for you or your men if you kill them." He'd put an end to so many others in his past, what was the death of the commodore on his conscience?

"Oh, I don't believe you have the right to make threats here."

Before either man could continue, Caroline yanked her arm from Adam's grasp. "Leave them alone! They have been loyal to the light all these years. Your fight is not with them."

"You are partially correct, Mrs. Montmorency. However, nothing is fair in this life. And, we'd like to have control of the lighthouse for plans down the line. You have no say in this." The light of victory gleamed in the commodore's eyes. The subtle flicker of his gaze over Adam's shoulder unnerved him. Cold sweat slid down his spine. Did the soldiers return from the homestead? "Your husband has been an embarrassment to our navy for quite some time. It's now over, so resistance really isn't a logical choice."

Despite Caroline's tense body and her itch for a fight, Adam drew an arm around her waist, put his lips to her ear and said, "Run. Whatever happens, do not come back to this beach. Do you understand?"

"But—"

The commodore's conversational speech interrupted what Adam would have said. "Perhaps I should give you the credit of bringing the traitor to my doorstep, ma'am. I should give you the bounty that's on his head instead of to Mr. Douglas."

That gave both her and Adam pause. "Why don't you just keep the coin and let go the lighthouse?" Caroline countered. "I assume the price on my husband's head is exorbitant; otherwise, you wouldn't waste time attempting to capture him. And you said in your letter that if I procured the money — extortion, really, but then I wouldn't be surprised with anything from you — the lighthouse could stay in my family's control."

"No, I said the coin would buy you time until I had the final order, which I did receive anyway. You have no bargaining power," the commodore stated in a steady voice.

"You are a dirty cheater and a bald-faced liar." She spat at the commodore's feet. "You will not prevail."

Adam's jaw dropped open slightly as he beheld his wife in action. Beautiful, fiery, intelligent and crafty. *And mine.* "Caro, perhaps—"

"No, Adam, I'm beyond annoyed at his tactics. If he wants to play dirty, so be it." She broke away from him and took a step toward the commodore. Then she hefted the saber and poked the point of the blade into the man's torso. Of course, it didn't penetrate the commodore's greatcoat, but the fact she had the gall to do such a thing tightened Adam's chest. "Well?" She stared at the military man while the men holding the lanterns shifted on their feet, obviously waiting for orders.

"God, I detest you bloody Americans," Commodore Matthews muttered. He moved her blade away from his person with a gloved finger. "We'll take the island regardless of what you want. You're married to a traitor, which makes you guilty by association, as it does Mr. Douglas. Continue to resist, and you could easily find yourself and Mr. Douglas locked in a prison cell." He arched an eyebrow. "Will there be anything else? I have a warm bed to return to tonight."

Bastard. Adam shook his head. He tugged on Caroline's cloak, reeling her back to him and out of reach from the commodore. Above everything, he had to keep her safe. She was his life, and if she remained alive, so would his hope. He wrapped his arms around her and held her backside tight against his front. "I'd like to discuss new terms."

"There will be no more negotiations." The jingle of hardware on belts and uniforms sounded in the distance. No doubt part of a contingent was returning.

Adam calmed his breathing. "I'll give myself up, but in return, I want your promise you'll let Caroline, her parents, and Paul leave the island unmolested." At least if they were off the island, they had a chance at remaining free.

"No," Caroline breathed. She struggled in his hold.

Silence reigned for several long moments. Adam heard nothing except the frantic beat of his heart.

"That is acceptable."

"I want to see them leave. Then you can have at me." He ignored Caroline's whispered protests.

"Done." The commodore executed a slight bow from the waist. He gestured toward them with a hand. "Seize them."

Adam shoved his wife hard from him. "Go to the light. Find Paul, but for the love of God, run. Get off the island. I don't trust him to keep his promise."

For perhaps the first time in their married life, Caroline followed instructions. As the two men flanking the commodore set down their lanterns and moved in on Adam's position, he prayed that he'd see her again, prayed that she'd survive and know happiness and peace in her life if he didn't.

Then, his attention was taken up when the men took hold and hauled him in front of the commodore. The military man backhanded him across the face. Pain exploded through Adam's jaw, but he didn't fight back. Not now. Not yet. Not until Caroline had time to make a good lead.

Commodore Matthers loomed over him then drew close. "I'd put an end to your miserable life myself if that wouldn't warrant a court martial." He spat upon Adam's cheek. "One of the guards you killed on that prison ship was my brother, so I'll have some fun with you before we hit the mainland." He gestured at his compatriots, and when they renewed their grip on Adam's arms and hauled him to his feet, the commodore delivered a hard jab into his midsection. "First, you'll answer my own personal charges off the official record. My superiors can have what's left."

Adam fought off nausea as waves of pain rolled over him. He might hate the British, but he loved Caroline more, and if every crime against him bought her more time, he'd survive it. "Nothing you can do will ever equal the atrocities of what I was treated to on that ship."

The commodore's harsh laughter echoed eerily in the still winter air. "Where do you think my brother learned those skills?"

Oh dear God. An icy shiver shot down Adam's spine. Never did he think he'd return to such torture. Was he strong enough to survive this time?

❦ Chapter Twenty ❦

Caroline pelted along the path to the lighthouse even as the sickening thuds of blows landing on human flesh rang in her ears. She wanted to remain, to fight alongside her husband, to protect him from further harm at the hands of people who hated him for simply being him, but she couldn't. Not yet. She needed a rifle. Then she'd return and pick them off one by one.

I need Paul. I need my father. I need ammunition.

That was her mantra as she ran over the snow-covered path. So great were her musings that she didn't see the figure coming at her on the shadow-shrouded path until it was too late and she plowed full on into him. A shriek left her throat when he closed his hands around her upper arms.

"Quiet, Caroline," Paul hissed in an urgent whisper. "You need to come with me right now. We're losing time." Strain and sorrow clung to his words. "Quickly."

"But Adam needs our help." Her attempt to pull off his tight grip on one of her arms went unsuccessful.

"He's not dead yet. He can wait." As they gained the service room door, they passed the bodies of three British soldiers. "I apologize for not shielding you from the carnage. There's no way around it."

Despite Paul's steady hold, she slowed long enough to give a long stare. Two men lay on their backs—both shot in the chest. Dark wet splotches stained the blue of their greatcoats. The third man had crumpled onto his side, a hole in his forehead the only evidence of his demise. Scarlet seeped into the once virginal snow beneath him.

Her stomach heaved. She swallowed heavily a couple of times to keep the contents down. "Did you shoot them?" The hilt of the saber felt awkward in her hand — an instrument of death. Had she really thought to use it against another living person?

"Two of them. The body across the threshold is a product of your mother." He pulled her onward then preceded her through the open doorway.

Caroline picked up her skirts as she stepped over the young solider. A shiver wracked her shoulders. "Do you mean my mother killed him?"

"She's up top with your father, but you need to prepare yourself, Caroline." A warning, softened with concern, rang in his voice as he led the way into the curving, metal stairwell.

"Why?" The base of her spine tingled with foreboding. A knot formed in her belly when he didn't answer, merely continuing up.

When they reached the lantern room, Paul halted at the doorway. "I apologize for being so blunt and not preparing your properly. Your mother is dying and doesn't have much time. Make your words count."

As he stepped aside to let her pass, horror rose in Caroline's throat. "No." Her mother sat on the floor, propped against her father's chest while he pressed the bloodstained length of his cravat against her side. Her eyes were closed and her breathing was shallow. "No!" She rushed across the short expanse of floor then tumbled to her knees at her mother's other side. Her saber clattered to floor beside her. "What happened?" Tears flooded her eyes. She blinked and they fell to her cheeks.

"Your mother never did anything for her own good," her father said softly with a slight smile. "Refused to hide in the cottage. Was adamant she defend the light—our life—with her own two hands by my side. I tried to keep her out of harm's way, but she never did listen to me."

"They shot her?" Panic spread through her veins at the very real possibility her mother wouldn't be there any longer.

"No, but one of 'em sure jabbed her good with a bayonet. The bastard." Remarkably, his smile widened. "You should have seen her, Caroline. Fought like a tiger when she realized she'd been run through. Madder than hell." When her mother weakly shook her head, he crooned into her ear until she quieted. He raised his agonized gaze to hers. "Held out her hand as bold as you please. She wiggled her fingers until I gave over my pistol regardless of the fact we were already engaged in fighting." He stroked her mother's gray-streaked hair with a shaking hand. "You should have seen her, the damn fool woman I married. Never did care for the rules. Always giving me another reason to love her. Independent until the end." His voice broke on the last word.

Caroline bit back a sob. She cast a glance to Paul, but he stood stone-faced near the door, a rifle locked in one hand. When she returned her attention to her parents, her heart broke. The two of them had been her strength over the last ten years, even if she didn't rely on them most of the time. "Mother." She grasped one of the older woman's cold hands. "I'm so, so sorry I haven't been around lately."

Her mother's eyelids fluttered. Then she stared at Caroline with glassy eyes. "No remorse. I only want happiness... for, my baby." She drew in a shuddering breath and again thrashed her head on her husband's chest.

"I should have visited more." Even though most times her mother barely remembered who she was. If it hadn't been for her own fears, her own inability to deal with the disease that ravaged her mother's mind, she would have—should have—been at her side. "Especially after…" Everything. Life had gotten in the way. Many days, she'd preferred her own grief and anger, cherished solitude or Paul's company over being with family.

"No." The word came out stronger than the others. Her mother's chest labored with her breathing. Her eyes went wide. "My role in your life… was never to be overbearing or intrusive." Her eyes closed, and for long moments Caroline thought she'd not say anything else. Finally, she said, "Don't waste life, darling." She gasped in pain and her body stiffened.

"Elizabeth, save your strength," her father cautioned.

"No." Her mother shook her head, defiant to the last. "Chase love. Enjoy it when you capture it. Let it consume you." Another ragged breath followed. Her grip on Caroline's fingers weakened. "It's the only thing… worth… living—fighting—for." She gazed up into her husband's face and her grin could have rivaled the light's illumination. So much love shone from her pain-darkened eyes. "Tell me about the stars, Jonah." A horrible rattling sound issued from her chest as she struggled to breathe. "Tell me about the children we will have. I do so want a large family."

"We just have the one, Elizabeth," her father replied in a patient tone Caroline knew only too well.

"How do you know? We only succumbed," gasp, "to passion," a wet cough interrupted her speech, "once." She giggled, a weird sort of sound mixed with the gasping. "Mother will be cross when she finds out you ruined me."

And once more, her mother was no longer in the present. Perhaps that was for the best.

Her father met Caroline's gaze over her mother's head even as her cheeks blazed from her mother's brazen subject matter. "She always did love the stars. It's why I brought her up here for her last…" His jaw worked and moisture welled in his eyes. "So she'd see beauty instead of—"

"I know." Caroline stood, for in her mother's mind, she didn't exist anyway. Her heart clenched with despair. "I'll just be over there." She slipped to Paul's side, and when he wordlessly wrapped his arms around her, she sobbed into his shoulder. "I cannot believe she's leaving me."

"I think perhaps she left a long time ago," Paul whispered and held her tighter.

"I know, but it's still a shock." Caroline quieted enough to catch her father's soft words as he pointed out the various constellations in the clear night sky. Every so often, he'd whisper of his love and their life together. Minutes later, mayhap it was hours, even days, her mother's ragged breathing ceased. She pulled out of the protective circle of Paul's arms and looked toward her parents; her mother body's still cradled within her father's embrace. "Is she…?"

"Yes." Her father nodded. He pressed a kiss into her hair. "If you don't mind, I'd like to stay here a while with her." He coughed and cleared his throat. "I just can't let her go so soon."

"Of course." Paul put a hand to the small of Caroline's back. "Come. There is still much to do this night."

She nodded and forced a hard swallow into her tight throat. "Will you be all right here alone?"

"Aye," her father confirmed, but his gaze was far away as he regarded the ocean beyond the glass. "At least for tonight. Those British will have a surprise if they come up here and bother me." He patted a rifle on the floor next to him. "I won't soon forget what they did."

"Neither will I." Seeing his heartbroken expression, listening to the pain in his words, something inside Caroline snapped. She rushed past Paul and took the metal stairs at breakneck speed.

"Caroline?"

She ignored the concern in his voice. "These horrors are supposed to happen on a dashed battlefield. Not to my parents. Not on my island. Not to the men I love." She gathered her hands in her skirting and lifted it out of the way of her pounding feet. The ache in her chest grew as another realization gripped her and nearly had her stumbling headlong down the remaining twists of the staircase. "I didn't remember to tell Mother I loved her, and now it's too late."

Paul was right there behind her with a steadying hand on her elbow. "She knew, sweetness. She knew."

"That may be, but it won't dissolve my guilt in the lapse." She blinked away the tears blurring her vision. The time for crying had passed. Now, rage filled her being—harsh, hot and all-consuming. "I refuse to lose another person I care about tonight. If the damn British think to take my husband away from me too, they can fight alongside me into hell, because that's where I intend to drive them."

"Hand me a rifle, and for the love of God don't argue with me," Caroline whispered as she and Paul hid behind a low stone wall on the path midway between the lighthouse and the beach. Down below on the sand, Adam knelt on the ground, his shoulders slumped, his hands tied behind his back, the snow-covered sand dotted and sprayed with blood. Was it his? Was he even now hurt and injured? Her stomach clenched as Paul put the barrel of a rifle into her gloved hand. "How many?"

Paul grunted softly beside her. "Three directly around him. Two with the commodore. Three more making one of the longboats ready. No doubt the other contingents tasked with checking the beaches are still well away from here." He stroked a hand along the barrel of his own rifle. "You'll have little time between firing and reloading before they're upon us."

"I know." In her mind, she went over the motions involved. She touched the pouches on her belt where the necessary pieces rested. Her fingers brushed the hilt of the dagger, her only other weapon since she'd left the saber with her father. "If we both get off two true shots, that will at least confuse them long enough for a reload. If luck is with us, we can fell two more before the others render assistance. Beyond that, I'd rather have the feeling of sinking my blade into their black hearts."

"Very well." He kept his focus on the scene below.

For which she was grateful. He didn't censure her or provide her with lectures that it was too dangerous or a fool's errand. She already knew all of that. But then, war wasn't a product of a logical mind. War and fighting with the intent to kill your enemies was borne of a primal instinct to rid the world of people one didn't think like. That gave her pause. *Have I become as them?*

"Ready?" Paul's whisper snuck past her thoughts and scattered them.

"Yes. Let's rescue my husband." She rose then fit the rifle to her shoulder. Paul did the same. Some of her confidence wavered. "Paul?"

"No talking until we're done. Remember, I'm scheduled to make an appearance in your bed afterward."

A grin curved her lips for the first time since the defense of the island began. "Yes. Yes you are." She took up position once more. "First men to go down are the ones surrounding Adam."

Paul didn't answer with words. Instead, the cracking report of his rifle split the silence of the night. Seconds later, one of the soldiers fell to the snowy ground. As he lowered his weapon and began the routine of reloading, Caroline took her shot. The second soldier staggered then ultimately fell atop the first.

After that, their presence was made known to the remaining men on the ground. The commodore shouted, pointing to the path, and the three soldiers around him ran in their direction. Paul put his rifle to his shoulder once more while Caroline struggled to reload her weapon. The report of his discharging made her start.

"Two incoming." He tossed the rifle away. "No time for more. It's hand to hand from here on out."

"Right." Caroline abandoned her half loaded weapon. "Occupy them. I'm going for Adam." At least if he were free, he'd be another ally on their side.

"Be visually aware at all times," he said as he darted from her side with his saber drawn. Seconds later he engaged the two men with the clash of steel on steel.

Caroline sprinted down the remainder of the path. She kept her attention trained on the commodore. He'd gone a small way down the beach in order to speak to the three men near the longboat. With one sweeping glance around the area and confirming Adam was alone, she hurried to his position while drawing her dagger as she ran.

"Adam," she said in a frantic whisper. She dropped to her knees behind him. Two swipes with the blade and the ropes fell free. The damn men hadn't bothered to tighten the bonds or even make a proper set of nautical knots. "Sloppy work will get you nowhere, gentlemen," she muttered. Her husband grunted. "Quickly, now. Time is of the essence." When he didn't rise immediately to his feet, she tugged at his shoulder. The breath hissed between his teeth. "Adam, he's coming back." In the distance, cries from soldiers rent the silence, but she couldn't determine if they came from the longboat or Paul's position.

Finally, he moved, heaving into a standing position, and that's when she had her first real look at him in the lantern's light. Bottom lip bloodied, his left eye swollen nearly closed, he clutched his ribcage with his right hand while his left arm hung awkwardly at his side. "I won't be of much use, love." He raised his stormy gaze to hers. "Once again, I'm too broken to be of value to you."

"No, you're not. I'd want you no matter what." She hesitated to touch him for fear of hurting him, even though he said nothing of his injuries. "We have to run, get away—"

"Oh, too late to provide rescue, Mrs. Montmorency," the commodore said in a sickeningly sweet voice. The unmistakable cock of a pistol echoed in the air around them.

She swung around with the blade of her dagger leading the way. "Let him go." As the commodore approached with his pistol trained on Adam, the three other soldiers circled them. In order to keep an eye on all of them, she went back to back with her husband.

"I'm getting bloody sick of the American spirit," Commodore Matthers said. He wasn't without battle wounds either. The whole right side of his face was streaked with red from a decent cut on his forehead.

"Then leave. Nothing's keeping you here," Carolyn shot off. The rage she'd left the lighthouse with still remained intact. Was that a chortle from Adam? She couldn't tell.

"I won't leave without your husband. He's way too valuable to me."

"How curious that we have something in common, Commodore," Caroline spat out. "He's too valuable to me to let go, and since your people have already killed my mother, you won't have the luxury of depriving me of another loved one."

The inhale of breath from Adam was the only outward sign he registered her words.

"I rather think you're not in the position for compromise." He gestured at the solider nearest him. "Bring them to the longboat. We've wasted enough time here."

Activity exploded around them. Seconds before her arms were seized, Adam whirled around. He yanked the dagger from her hand, held it by the blade then threw it in the commodore's direction. The sharp metal thudded into the man's right shoulder, easily cutting through the layers of his clothing and close enough to a vital area that he might not survive. The commodore staggered and stumbled to his knees. The report from a rifle sounded and seconds later, the man struggling with her grunted in pain. Warmth splattered onto her cheek as he went down, the whole side of his face slick with blood.

"Take cover," Adam urged, and with a push at her back, he followed after the commodore the best he could while the remaining two men returned fire toward the direction of the lighthouse path.

"No, thank you, you pigheaded man." Caroline jerked the saber from the belt of the fallen man at her feet. She spared a second to glance at the path. Paul had managed to put one man down, but he struggled with two others. Behind her, Adam and the commodore fought in a bizarre, lopsided sort of dance, since each of them was heavily wounded. She left them to it then chased up the path to assist Paul.

By the time she arrived, one of the soldiers had pinned Paul against the stone wall with his rifle pressed to his throat. Caroline's pulse, already beating out of control, accelerated. She rushed at them, her saber point trained directly on the back of the man threatening Paul. At the last second, the other solider turned. He neatly blocked her stroke with his own blade. Her wrist shook. Tingles raced up her arm from the unfamiliar sensations. Regardless, she thrust again, but the result was the same. Another block. They repeated the dance until Caroline's strength flagged and she was forced to retreat down the path.

The man followed her, the light of victory in his eyes. "Why don't you surrender?" he asked with a particularly vigorous thrust.

Caroline didn't step away fast enough and the blade caught her right forearm. She hissed at the nick of the metal bit her skin. "Why don't you go bother someone else? You're trespassing." She stepped backward and her foot rolled on an abandoned pistol. With a curse, she stumbled, and for one weightless second felt suspended in the frosty winter air before she landed so hard on her bottom her teeth jarred together. The saber flew from her hand on impact. It fell with a muffled thud in the fluffy snow.

"Ha. You're mine now." The solider came at her, his saber raised.

"Actually, she's mine." Paul appeared behind the soldier's shoulder. When the man swung around, Paul threw a punch to the younger man's jaw. The soldier grunted then slid to the ground. He stirred but didn't rouse. "Are you unharmed?" Paul offered her a hand and when she slipped her fingers into his, he hauled her to her feet.

Her heart fluttered. Concern gripped her as she caught sight of a cut on his left cheek and another on his neck above his now soiled cravat. "Nothing that a hot bath and a cup of tea won't cure." Now that some of the urgency had left her body, the cold seeped in. God, how long had it been since she'd last indulged in anything without worries at the back of her mind?

"It's over." He escorted her along the remainder of the path. "With the exception of the contingent searching the shorelines." Exhaustion rang in his voice. "I'll meet them in short order."

"No." She squeezed his hand. "Adam needs help." That useless arm of his meant trouble. "His shoulder is dislocated, I think."

"Aye. It won't be the first time I've had to pop it back into place."

There were so many stories she still needed to hear from both men. Would they have time? Adrenaline and worry propelled her steps as she matched Paul's stride. By the time they reached Adam's location on the beach, she wished to drop on the snow-covered sand and sleep for a week. Caroline remained standing, mostly for the bald fact that if she gave in to the urge to collapse, she wouldn't be able to stumble home. She was nearly upon Adam before she realized he stood alone. "Where is Commodore Matthers?"

Her husband pointed to a longboat on the ocean. It contained two men, one of whom was the commodore. "There. One of his men carried him away. God knows if he's more dead than alive." Weariness underscored his words. Strain lined his expression and framed his sad eyes. "Bastard."

"You didn't kill him." It wasn't a question.

"I might have. The blade found its mark too well, but in the event he does live, it would be fitting. Sometimes a man needs to think about what he's done. At others times, a man has already thought about what he's done and chooses to walk away from that old life in order to be more in a new one." He swayed on his feet. Before she could assist, Paul was there, lending his shoulder and supporting her husband when he would have fallen. "Give me a moment and I'll catch a second wind."

Paul snorted. "You'll catch your death, perhaps, but you're in no condition to do much else. Let's put you in front of a fire then go over options." He looked at Caroline. "You too. You're ready to drop. For the time being, the danger has passed. I'll let you rest a few minutes then we'll take care of the rest of the men."

She nodded and let the men precede her as she gazed after them with heavy-lidded eyes. They were both heroes in their own right and she couldn't be more proud.

 Chapter Twenty-one

Four days later

Paul approached his friend on silent feet. The fresh layer of snow on the sand muffled his boot steps, but he found Adam easily enough. But then, he knew his friend as well as he knew himself, and in times of confliction, there had only been one thing outside of Caroline that would calm his mind.

The *Scoundrel's Trespass*.

Clear late afternoon sunlight filtered through the skeleton-like remains of the once proud frigate. Tilted on its side for what would be eternity until the earth reclaimed it, the ship was a mere shadow of its former self. The main mast, long fallen, dug deep into the sand. The fabric of its sails a tattered and ghostly remnant of the proud glory it used to be. Every so often, the sea breeze would catch parts of the dingy white cloth and a flutter would ensue then die as if it couldn't retain the needed energy any longer.

As if completing the scene, Adam's broad-shouldered figure appeared much like the specter of death with his black greatcoat, trousers, and boots. The battered tricorne hat sat on his dark hair just like Paul remembered him as a younger man, and his hands rested clasped behind his back as he peered out to sea. Did he remember times gone by, spent on those decks of the once beloved ship, or did he mull over more recent matters, which no doubt bridged both halves of the man he was now?

Paul rested a gloved hand against the sun-bleached and well-weathered wood that used to serve as the bottom of the vessel. "How long have you been here?" he asked in a soft voice. He didn't wish to startle his friend, but the man did need to know he was there and not intruding.

"Since sun up." Adam faced him and the afternoon light framed him, blocked him out until he was but a dark outline — a genuine angel of death or perhaps a demon from the depths of hell no man should have cause to experience. He came forward, closing the distance, and when he drew abreast of the ship, the brilliant light pulled away and left him mortal once more. "How was the service?"

"It went well. A small gathering of friends and family attended. Then Elizabeth was interred in Caroline's garden near your babe."

His friend flinched. "Thank you for standing with her. I trust you sent my condolences?" His gaze held a world's worth of sadness. Paired with the bruises and lacerations on his face, he resembled a champion of old.

"Yes. She would have loved having you by her side. I understand why you didn't come. I think you're wrong, but I understand." Adam had fled before Caroline had risen for the day. "None of this was your fault." His chest tightened. "It was mine."

Adam waved a hand. "It's safe to say we're both guilty. And what's more, we affected Caroline's life." He thumped a fist against the ship's remains. "My fondest wish is that she'll not hold my absence against me."

"She will not. Caroline loves you, even if you do not believe it or think you deserve it." Paul bowed his head. Adam was certainly not the friend he'd known before. That man's arrogance assumed every woman fell under his spell. Now, his past had broken him, left him vulnerable, stole his inherent confidence. When he returned his gaze to his friend, Adam regarded him with a frown. "In fact, it was on her advice that I come find you."

"To fetch me back like a wayward hound?"

"No. To return you to the bosom of family and love where you belong." When his friend didn't answer, merely stared with unblinking stormy eyes shadowed by the hat, Paul sighed. "Believe it or not, you are a vital member of our circle. After the service, there was a brunch, where Jonah shared a few favorite stories about his wife. Caroline remained mostly silent. I couldn't determine if it was grief making her hold her tongue or worries about you."

A bark of bitter laughter left Adam's throat. "I'm not worth any thought she might have. If it wasn't for me, her life would be perfect, happy, ideal."

Paul tamped the urge to rail at the other man, talk some sense into him, make him see that he wasn't the worthless bounder Adam thought of himself. "That's not true. Once the brunch was over, I sent everyone home. Jonah retreated to the lighthouse and Caroline went to lie down, pleading a megrim. These last few days have taken a toll on her, I'm afraid." No woman should ever have been subjected to what Caroline had been. Except, she was no ordinary woman.

"For the rest of my life I'll know remorse for that." Adam leaned an arm against the ship then rested his forehead upon it. "Leave me, Paul. Go to Caroline and soothe her soul. I'm not fit company."

"You can be if you pull your head from your arse." After the fight for the lighthouse, the three of them had more or less collapsed in the cottage. Near dawn, the remaining contingent returned to the beach. He and Adam encouraged them to return to the mainland, letting their rifles do the speaking for them.

Adam shoved off the ship and faced him. "Is there something you'd say to me?"

Ah, the arrogance had returned. Which meant his friend was coming around. "There is. We have precious little time together and I, for one, would rather not spend it conversing in this deuced cold when there's promised bed sport in the offing." Though the three hadn't talked about their coming together over the course of the last few days, it had been uppermost in Paul's mind. They owed it to themselves to seal their pact and take that next step into their future.

"Precious little time? Are you going somewhere? I thought you'd be by Caroline's side until the end." Adam cleared his throat. "In fact, I expected it. Hoped for it, actually, since—"

"Leave off with the martyr bit, Adam. It's a tired act." Paul rolled his eyes. "I've pledged my life to Caroline, as have you. I'm not leaving, but you are. You and your wife, to be more specific."

One of Adam's eyebrows rose. "How do you figure?"

So, he'd be stubborn, eh? "I'm having one of my merchant ships readied to make a quick voyage south... to Washington if you must know specifics." He couldn't contain his grin. Those safe travel vouchers were still in effect, at least he hoped. If they'd weren't, well, he and Adam had fought their way out of worse. "It's imperative you meet with the president, isn't it? Also, it will remove you from this area for a time. Commodore Matthers is near death."

"As he should be." Finally, a genuine chuckle left Adam's lips. "Though, why would you risk so much for me? Your loyalties don't exactly align."

Embarrassment burned up the back of his neck. "Perhaps a man can change after all." Would Adam know that he meant him as well and that he recognized the marked difference in his friend? "I've come to realize that perhaps the British are high-handed when dealing with this country and I don't wish to be associated with the Empire any longer, even if it does mean the demise of my shipping business. I want to forge my own path without reliance on an old way of doing things."

"Interesting." The light of humor gleamed in Adam's eyes. "I suppose your new title in the *ton* has been shot to hell as well?"

Paul waved a hand. "Overrated, don't you think? All those lords and ladies doing little to grow as people and nary a callous on their hands to signify an honest day's work?"

"A bit." The other man's lips quirked with a grin. "What will you do now? Once the commodore decides on revenge, your shipping business will suffer."

"There will be other opportunities." As much as he believed that, it didn't stop his stomach from clenching. "The future belongs to those who are fearless."

"Are you fearless?" Adam's query was quiet as his grin faded. "A man has to be in this day and age. Caroline deserves no less."

"True. I believe I am, and if I'm not, there's no one better to learn from than you." He pinned his friend with a direct gaze. "Come home, Adam. Caroline needs you." He forced down a hard swallow. "I need you." When surprise flickered over the other man's face, Paul continued quickly before he could interrupt, "It's true. I've missed you over the years."

"I'm not the same man you once knew."

"You're not, but perhaps I'm not either." He crossed his arms over his chest. "Life changes a man — if we're lucky. But I can't be everything Caroline needs by myself. I have limits, the same as you. This won't work if we're all three not committed and together."

Adam remained silent for a long time. Finally, when he did speak, the words were so soft, Paul strained to hear over the crash of the waves and the breeze whistling through the slats of the ship. "When the *Scoundrel's Trespass* went down in the storm, I thought I wanted to die with the ship. Stupidly, I'd assumed it was the most important thing I could ever know." He brushed snow from one of the weathered ribs. "In the following years, enduring everything I did at the hands of the British, I thought I wanted to die merely to escape the pain. In that stinking prison ship, I erroneously believed my anger and hope for revenge was what would bring me happiness."

"Yet?" Despite himself, Paul couldn't pull himself away from the hypnotic sound of his friend's voice. There'd always been something about Adam that demanded attention.

"In the darkest moments of my life that I inexorably did live, the thought of Caroline brought me back from the brink." He shifted his focus from the ship to Paul. "I wanted her more than anything. I desired her above the pitiful existence my life had become, but," his gaze softened, "at the back of my mind, I wanted a return of the friendship you and I shared once upon a time. The love of a good woman is essential to life, but the comradery between a man's close contemporaries is equally vital."

"What are you trying to say?" He wanted no misunderstandings. "In blunt words, if you please."

A cocky grin spread across Adam's face. The scar at his temple stood in stark relief in the sunshine. "I need you by my side as much as I need Caroline. We go into this as a partnership. I am no more important than you, and we are there to make her happy and keep her that way. And if we both find satisfaction in the same, that's all to the good. Savvy?"

"Aye." An answering grin parted Paul's lips. "You'll accept that Caroline and I both love you and we accept you for the man you are—scars and all?"

"I accept the idea of it, yes." His humor faltered. "It will take some time for me to be free enough of my past that I can exist outside my thoughts, but I'll get there." He stuck out a hand. "With your help." His jaw worked. "Whatever else has happened between us, we now lay it to rest with the *Scoundrel*. I'm weary of the fight."

"Agreed." Paul clasped the other man's forearm. "And with your help, I can realize my own potential. Wherever that will take us."

When they pulled away, some of the lines of stress left Adam's face. "I suppose you want me to return to the house now?"

"That would be helpful if we were all together." The relief flowing over his body surprised him. He hadn't realized how tense he'd been for so long. "How's your shoulder?" When Caroline had been occupied with making tea after they'd wandered in from the battle, he'd tackled the unsavory task of popping Adam's shoulder back into place. Even now, he could still feel the movement of bones in his fingertips, hear the echo of Adam's agonized cries in his ears, but then, it hadn't been the first time he'd done such a thing.

"Still sore, but it's nothing that will prevent me from doing other things." Heavy meaning hung on the words.

"Excellent. Shall we inform Caroline?" Anticipation warmed his blood. They were on the verge of seeing a dream come to fruition.

"Yes. However, I'd like to make one stop first."

Adam followed the snow-covered paths through Caroline's garden. Footprints marred the pristine surface, evidence that others had trod before him this day. When he arrived at the back where his child, and now his mother-in-law, were buried, he paused as mixed emotions fought for dominance in his chest.

"You're paying your respects?" Incredulity clung to Paul's question.

"Aye." He reached into a pocket of his coat then withdrew a bracelet. The bright coral beads were interspersed with pearls. "I sent this in a package years ago to Caroline." He turned the bauble over in his gloved palm. "This piece I'd selected specifically for Elizabeth because I thought she'd adore showing it off to her friends." A half-grin lifted one corner of his mouth. "Can you imagine this bracelet on her wrist at a dinner party?"

Paul chuckled. "She would have flaunted it about, but when she was home, she would have kept it in her jewel box because it was special. Or way too valuable."

"True enough." He knelt at the mound of fresh-turned earth then laid the bracelet on top. "I found this in Greece at one of the open air markets."

"Yet Caroline hid it away all this time?"

"Apparently. She had some notion she'd rather be independent than rely on the treasures I'd sent her." He bowed his head. "In one, I'd sent her a ring I thought she'd like. Many nights I envisioned it on her finger, but she never took anything out for herself."

Paul glanced sharply at him. "Did you carry it out with you along with the bracelet?"

"Yes. I'd hoped she might accept it—"

"Bring it to bed with you." Excitement wove through his friend's tone. "She already loves you but play to her romantic side. You might be uncomfortable, but it's not about you."

Adam snorted. "Isn't this sort of thing your forte?"

The other man nudged him with the toe of his boot. "Don't be an arse."

He attempted to contain his smile. "Very well. I only just unearthed the parcels she'd hidden away in the cellar. Who knows what we'll do with those things now." At the moment, every piece rested in a trunk at the foot of their bed.

"Does any of it hold sentimental value?"

"No. They are merely things. People have value. You and Caro are what I want in life." He reeled as he realized it was true. He'd been all over the world, seen many grand things, accumulated more wealth than a man could ever need in a lifetime, but none of it meant anything if he didn't have love.

"Hawk most of it. Barter with it. Pick up and start over somewhere." Paul touched his shoulder. "Escape the British, buy some property in the country, any place in the world, and live your life the way you wish."

"You make it sound like a fairy tale." Adam wiped the thin covering of snow from the brass plate where his son rested. His chest tightened. Would they have another child? Finally, when he was so close to the dream of his heart, he couldn't help but think something would occur to yank it all away. He struggled to his feet with a muted groan. He wasn't a young man any longer, and the various aches and pains in his joints were compounded by the cold. Perhaps retreating to warmer climes would be beneficial. "Is there any such place that won't be tainted? I wonder."

"If you don't wish to remove permanently, why not visit your brother?" A chuckle left Paul's throat. "I realize there's no love lost between the whole of the Empire and you, but a man shouldn't shun his brother if there's no true need. You two were thick as thieves at one point before you and I took up the adventures."

"Aye. We were." Adam adjusted his hat. "Everyone no doubt breathed a sigh of relief when the two of us went to sea permanently. We were rather obnoxious regarding property, spirits, and women." That life seemed so long ago, but he could honestly say he didn't wish for that anymore. After a man went through his trials, he came to realize the only things he wanted were a wife, a good friend close by, a space to put up his feet, and a view of the sea.

"Now that you're somewhat domesticated, I imagine you're no longer a threat." A thread of sarcasm clung to his friend's words. "At least to strangers."

It was eerie how well Paul's spoken thoughts mirrored his. "Perhaps." He shot what he hoped was a cocky grin at his friend. "True. I'm only a threat to my wife. As are you."

"Indeed." Paul looked back with an equally smug smile. "Are you interested in vexing and teasing said woman?" A hint of desperation tinged the words.

"I am." He clasped the other man on the shoulder. "Thank you for your patience in this. You've waited years for the next part of your life to begin and I apologize for having a hand in that, both directly and indirectly."

Paul nodded. "That's in the past." A muscle in his jaw jumped. "There are many things in the past that should stay there. Put it from your mind."

"I will, if you'll do the same." The niggle of responsibility grew in Adam's gut. "Come with Caroline and me to Washington."

"Why?" Incredulity brimmed in the other man's eyes.

"You are part of what we are. I'd like to have you along, and if we have the chance, perhaps we can sail to England from there. Leave off with this country for a bit until the navy can finally rid the harbors of the British." Other, deeper words danced on the tip of his tongue, but he couldn't say them. Not now. Mayhap in the future when more growth had changed him. "Circumstances on the island have changed. The British heavily active yet that far south."

Warmth shadowed the brown depths of Paul's eyes. "I appreciate that and will think upon it seriously. I don't know that I could leave Caroline's father at a time like this."

"Fair enough." Though, Caroline's aunt had grown children. Surely, one of them could be convinced to help out with the light. Adam set off toward the house. "When will your ship be readied?"

"By dawn tomorrow most likely. Midday at the latest."

"Then I'll try my best to convince you in that short amount of time." And he would. Now that the growing pains of the new relationship had passed, his confidence rose. They could do this. They could finally have the life they'd dreamed of. "I hope Caroline reacts with enthusiasm," he mused as they let themselves in through the side door.

"Has she ever acted without some level of passion in any of your dealings?" Paul's chuckle followed him as he went through every room in the lower level on the search for her.

"This is true." In the kitchen, he encountered Jane, who'd just arranged a tea towel over a basket of the molasses cookies he favored. "Where is Mrs. Montmorency?"

The maid's eyes rounded as she looked between the men. "I drew her a bath not thirty minutes ago. She told me she wasn't hungry, and she gave me and Mrs. Abbottson the rest of the day off. Told us she wanted to be alone."

"Understandable," Adam murmured even though disappointment crashed into him.

The young woman gestured to the door. "If you can spare Henry, we were going to take a sleigh ride before his chores of the evening come due." A faint wash of color filled her cheeks.

"Henry is?" He turned to Paul.

"Your groom's apprentice." His friend's lips twitched. "You really should take an active interest in your staff, man."

"Ah." Adam nodded. "Go ahead and enjoy yourself. I'll look after my wife and see to her every need." It took all of his willpower not to look at Paul. "She probably wants to be alone after the events of the day anyway."

"I'm sorry for your loss," Jane murmured with a slight curtsey. "Cook left cold cuts, boiled eggs, and pastries from brunch. Will there be anything else?" Already, she was edging toward the side nook where her cloak hung on a peg.

"No. Go ahead. I don't expect we should require assistance until the morrow." And even then, they'd do well to remember not to sleep in, especially if they ended this day in a tangle of limbs in the same bed.

Paul cleared his throat and sent a speaking glance Adam's way. "If you'll excuse me, I'll just wait for you and Caroline in the parlor. If she's not up to visiting, I'll return tomorrow."

"Very well." Adam swallowed down the laugh that welled in his throat at Paul's obvious attempt at deception to keep up appearances. "I should know the status of her mood momentarily." Once Paul departed and Adam had seen Jane out of the house, he did another search to make certain the cook had taken her leave as well. No doubt the two servants were fatigued from the added guests from brunch. Doubts assailed him as he climbed the narrow back stairs two at a time. Perhaps Caro wouldn't want to indulge in bed sport so soon after she'd said goodbye to her mother.

Every thought left his head the moment he opened the bedroom door and spied his wife. She lounged in an oval-shaped wooden bathtub someone had placed close to the fireplace. Cheery flames danced in the hearth and lent pleasant warmth to the room. But it was Caroline who caught and held his attention. Naked, of course, and her skin pink-tinged from the heated water and the fire, she'd piled her glorious red hair loosely atop her head. It gleamed a burnished copper in the firelight. One slim leg rested along the lip of the tub, moisture clinging to her skin and faint steam rose from the limb.

"Caro." The whispered word left his throat in a rush. He couldn't move; his feet felt glued to the floor. He quickly snatched his hat from his head.

She glanced up from the book she held and a soft smile parted her lips. "Hello, Adam." Her smile widened the longer he stared. The sea glass penchant reclined between her breasts as if it was the most natural thing in the world. "Did you need something?"

"No." *You, it's always been you.* "I mean, yes, er…" It was as if he'd been hurled back through time and he stood before her a young man with no sexual prowess at all. He forced a hard swallow into his suddenly dry throat. "That is, I'd hoped your disposition was such that you would welcome a round of…" God, why was this so difficult? It was highly inappropriate for a man to ask his wife for such a thing after what she'd just been through. "Ah, I understand if you wish to be alone due to recent events, but I did wonder if you wouldn't mind company. In bed. Mine." He cleared his throat. What the hell was wrong with him? "Er, that is mine and Paul's."

Finally, he stumbled to a halt as he crushed the hat's brim in his fingers. *That wasn't well done of me at all.* Doubts crowded his mind. Why would she want to welcome such an ordeal? She should be in mourning and properly distraught. Of course she wouldn't—

"Yes." She stuck a finger into her book and closed it then hung that hand over the lip of the tub. "Yes. I want you. In my—our—bed." She flicked her gaze beyond his shoulder and her expression went from humorous to smoldering and hungry. "With Paul."

Adam half-turned to catch his friend standing in the doorway. A certain level of relief swept through him. "She has agreed."

"So I surmised." Amusement lingered in his voice. "And, by the way, smooth. That's exactly how I'd attempt to romance my wife, with stuttering and staring as if I'd never seen a woman before." Paul clapped a hand to his shoulder then came further into the room. He approached Caroline's tub, leaned over her upon arrival, and planted a gentle kiss to her lips as she lifted her face.

The levity and heart-breaking tenderness shown by his friend was exactly what he needed to shake off the momentary doldrums and confusion. He tossed his hat into one corner, but before he removed his greatcoat, he took off his gloves, withdrew the ring, slipped it over his pinky finger, and threw the coat after his hat.

"Before we begin, I need to ask you a question that's been on my mind for quite some time." Adam sank to his knees at the side of her tub. Paul went to the opposite side and assumed a similar position once he divested himself of his outer wear. She was so beautiful, his wife, inside and out. A sprinkling of freckles lay like a veil over her cheeks, her upper chest, and down her arms. He adored every one of those beauty marks, but as she focused her big, blue eyes on him, even going so far as to drop her book and cup his cheek, his heart squeezed.

What had he done right in his life to deserve such a woman? Would fate realize the oversight and take everything from him?

"Caro." He removed the ring from his pinky and held it aloft. Much to his dismay, his hand shook. The ruby glowed a deep claret color in the firelight. "After all these years and all the trials we've been through, would you do me the high honor of being my wife?"

She glanced from the ring, to Paul then back to his face with bewilderment in her eyes. "We're already married."

"I know. You've never had a ring. I never cared enough to realize what you meant during our nuptials. Now I do." He captured her hand and pulled it away from his cheek. "I mean, I would like you to be my wife in every way that matters." Before she could protest, he slipped the ring over her fourth finger. The candlelight twinkled off the delicate silver band. "Will you let me have that favored place by your side for the rest of my life?"

And his pulse thundered in his ears as he waited for her reply.

❧ Chapter Twenty-two ❧

Caroline feared that she gawked at her husband more than she should have. There was an intensity in his stormy eyes she'd never seen before, an earnestness as he held her gaze, but uncertainty also waited in the darker depths, as if he expected her to refuse, to cast him aside as unworthy, just as everyone had done so many times these last years. She sat up straighter and in doing so, put both her legs back in the water.

Her hand trembled; but then, so did his. She peered at Paul on her right. His soft expression and the passion in his brown eyes convinced her more than anything else. When he pressed a kiss to the scabbed-over cut on her forearm where she'd been bitten with the saber's blade, she stifled a sigh. Did any woman have any right to feel so surrounded by love as she did right now?

Well, yes, she did, in fact.

She squeezed his hand then returned her attention to her husband. "Adam." She brought his hand to her lips then kissed his palm. Unshed tears welled in her throat. In the ten years she'd been separated from him, she'd never lost hope he'd come home to her, that he'd figure out they could be so much greater together than apart. Now, here he was, vulnerable before her, waiting, perhaps hoping just as much as she had. She drew in a shuddering breath and her bath water rippled. How bizarre it was to have such a serious conversation with two men while she was naked and ensconced in a tub full of water.

"For the love of God, Caro, don't drag this out." Emotion graveled his voice. The muscles in his arm tensed. "Please, just put me out of my misery..."

The rest of her heart she'd guarded from being hurt burst free from its shackles and swelled with love. She looked at the square-shaped ruby nestled in the delicate silver filigree and how the light caught the stone, and she smiled, grinned, actually as a wave of happiness propelled that gesture. "Yes, I will be your wife." She leaned slightly up from the tub and captured his face between her palms while pinning his gaze with hers. "I want everything this life with you can give; I want everything loving Paul will add."

"I cannot recall the last time I've known such happiness," he whispered seconds before he claimed her lips in a searing kiss that set her blood on fire.

Caroline clung to him even as he pushed her back into the water. The firm press of his mouth as it moved over hers, the steady hold of his hands as he cradled her head, all worked to ignite the desire she'd always held for her husband. And she wanted so much more. Eventually, common sense penetrated the haze of passion surrounding her brain. "You're ruining your clothes." Already, his jacket sleeves were wet to the elbow.

"The only remedy is removing the offending pieces then," he growled as he pulled away. He shot a burning glance to Paul. "Ready?"

"I've thought of nothing else for days."

As one, the men stood, unbuttoning clothing as they went. Caroline shivered in her bath even though the water was still warm. She was moments away from having both of the men she loved in her bed, their hands on her body, and she could hardly wait. "I'd hoped Paul would be successful in retrieving you," she said into the silence while jackets were shed and cravats were unwound. "It's why I sent the staff home and put forth the idea I wanted to be alone." She stopped talking, mostly because they weren't listening anyway, but also due to the fact she simply wished to watch them disrobe.

Waistcoats were discarded. Boots were toed off. Linen shirts came away with alacrity. Then Caroline had nothing else to do except feast her eyes on two taut male torsos as both men approached the tub once more. Adam's broader chest with its heavy mat of black hair spread over his skin in a butterfly-shaped pattern made her fingers itch to comb through those curls. A dark ribbon of hair enticed her gaze downward, and heat awakened in her core, but his breeches prevented a more thorough investigation.

Then she glanced at Paul. Slighter in build than Adam, he was no less spectacular. Where her husband's skin was still tanned golden from his time at sea, Paul was paler. A sprinkling of blond curls decorated his frame, but his flat abdomen was bereft of hair, which was just as mouthwatering as Adam's rugged look.

When they resumed their positions on either side of the tub, she gave into the tremors playing her spine. "Shouldn't I at least get out and dry off before we begin?" Her voice sounded small in the sudden silence of the room that had shrunk in size with the presence of her men.

"For the moment, I want you right there," Adam replied with a twinkle of mischief in his eyes. He touched her knee then slid his hand beneath the water and caressed the sensitive skin of her inner thigh. "No going back from this point onward, love. Are you certain you have the fortitude?"

Goose flesh popped over her skin. Anticipation tightened her nipples. "That largely depends on how well the two of you perform, doesn't it?" Oh, how she adored teasing them.

Paul's snort from her other side brought her attention to him. "How commanding you've become, darling." He moved to the head of the tub then slid his palms along her shoulders. "One might erroneously think you're descended from royalty." With the ease of a consummate charmer, he worked his fingers along the kinks in her neck while Adam stroked his fingers along the curls shrouding her sex. "Or perhaps you're merely imperious when it comes to bed sport," he murmured near her ear as he feathered those magical digits lower over her chest.

She sucked in a breath. He was so close to where she wanted him. So was her husband. It was glorious having them both pleasuring her. Her breasts were heavy with aching need and she arched her back, hoping to encourage him to touch her when her painfully erect nipples broke the water. "Why shouldn't I be?" With a slight tip of her head, she peered into his dear face. The fire in her blood went molten as Adam stroked along her folds. As much as she could in the narrow confines of the tub, she spread her legs in accommodation. "I do so enjoy lovemaking."

"That you do." Adam slipped a finger into her channel the same moment Paul cupped her breasts and squeezed. "For me, there's nothing in this world as fulfilling than seeing you come undone, knowing that you found pleasure at my hand."

A soft cry escaped Caroline's throat. Oh, was there anything more decadent than having two men's undivided attention? "I'd really love to be out of this water and in more of a position to touch you."

"Not just yet." Paul nibbled the curve of her shoulder where it joined her neck. Something about that tiny stretch of skin sent ripples of desire coursing through her body. "We want to should you how earnest we are."

"As well as make certain you're well and truly ready for us," Adam added as he pumped that finger in and out of her.

"I am," she insisted then let the feelings they invoked within consume her. She no longer registered the water she reclined in. Oh no. How could she when Paul pinched and plucked her nipples? Pain-tipped pleasure zipped from between her breasts to her swelling button. She squirmed with their ministrations, and Adam withdrew from her passage only to flick her nub and rub his fingers over it in a firm rhythm. Awareness of them both intensified.

"We'll decide that." Paul's smug chuckle reverberated in her chest and added to the sensations swamping her. He added tiny nips and bites to the side of her throat. Heat burned through her veins with each prick of pain.

Caroline's only answer was a breathy moan. Tremors chased over her skin and gentle tremors rocked her core. "I really want to move to a bed and… oh." Both men increased the friction. They plucked and pulled, teased and agitated in tandem. Pressure grew and coiled in her lower belly. Her back arched, but that didn't alleviate the terrible need that gripped her. "So close." She grabbed Adam's hand and pressed him tighter to where she wanted him and did the same with Paul, guiding their fingers, encouraging them both to do greater things to the responsive parts of her they pleasured.

Then her world shattered into a million pieces of light as the release caught her in its storm. Her eyes fluttered closed and she slumped against the back of the tub. Throbbing need skittered through her core in time to the thrumming ache in her breasts. "That was lovely." But not nearly enough.

Adam withdrew. He rose to his feet with a groan. "Now, you're ready, love."

"I concur." Paul dropped a kiss to her forehead then stood as well. "Come."

"Well, since she just did, perhaps we'll make her spend again." Her husband held out a hand to her with a chuckle. "Another couple of times."

She put her fingers into his then did the same to Paul. They brought her upright, Adam grabbed a cloth and dried her quickly then Paul scooped her into his arms. He carried her the few feet across the room. When she settled onto the quilt amidst the pillows, another shiver swept over her, this one from the cool temperatures in the air and the wetness on her skin. "Join me. I'm cold."

"Gladly. In a twinkling."

She uttered a small sound of protest when he left her, but the visual delights more than made up for her momentary loneliness. As her pulse accelerated and heat swept over her body once more, the men shucked out of their remaining clothing. As soon as Adam's breeches fell away and he disposed of his small pants, Caroline released a sigh of appreciation. It was the first time she'd seen his fully naked form since he'd returned, since their prior lovemaking was either conducted with clothing on or in the dark. Except that one time when she beheld the horrible scars on his back.

Shoving those images away, she said, "I'm so glad you're home." She licked her lips as she looked her fill of his cock. It jutted proudly rampant, veined and undeniably thick. It had been a long time since she'd taken his member into her mouth, but she'd remedy that soon. Liquid heat tickled her folds. She couldn't wait until she could feel the impact of that length in her core. "I'll never have enough of you," she whispered as he prowled toward her.

"Hmm. Somehow, I think you only appreciate me for this." Adam fisted his member and she moaned. "Objectifying your husband isn't well done of you, my love."

A laugh escaped her throat. "I'll never feel shame for admitting I admire your form as well as adore being satisfied by your cock." Was that purring sound really her? She shoved self-censure to the back of her mind. Nothing could dim this moment. She made a shuddering sigh as he joined her on the bed then fit his body over hers. The hot, hard insistence of his erection rested against her thigh. "But I'm grateful for much more than just that and I rather suspect you know it."

"Aye, but bantering with you is something I never thought I'd have an opportunity to do again." Genuine affection shone from his eyes. "The fact I can hold my wife in my arms again is miracle enough." His body tensed. Seconds later, he flipped onto his back and took her with him so that she tumbled haphazardly over his chest. The sea glass pendant swung from the valley of her breasts to thump against his chest. "If you'd like, I can arrange walking about the house in naught but my skin so that you might appreciate my body at your convenience."

Ah, some of his arrogance remained, it seemed. She didn't mind that in the least. "No doubt the servants would object." As would she.

"Let them look."

"You are hell bent on trouble and are not a proper gentleman."

His grin made her heart skip a beat. "Aye, but then I never claimed to be a proper anything."

"Except a proper arse," she whispered in a conscious echo of the words he'd said to her days ago when they'd waltzed in the lighthouse. When his grin widened, Caroline leaned down and kissed him with every ounce of feeling she had for him. This man, who'd survived so many things and still had trouble relating to people, had stolen her heart back piece by piece. Slightly breathless, she said, "No one is allowed to view your naked form except me."

"Well, and perhaps me," Paul added as he approached the bed, his grin no less large than her husband's.

She glanced over her shoulder at him. Another round of pulsing need shot through her. Paul's cock, though longer and slightly slimmer than Adam's, was no less impressive. The large head beckoned, as did the impressive set of hair-covered stones. What she wouldn't do to suck his equipage into her mouth and pleasure him as he'd done to her that horrible day they found out about his betrayal. The unrestrained member curved toward his stomach, twitching as she stared.

"Darling, I can't use this to its full potential if you'd rather ogle it instead of having me deploy it." Humor clung to Paul's voice as he joined them on the bed and crept up behind her.

When she caught Adam's knowing gaze, heat flooded her cheeks. "You two will be the death of me." The firm pressure of Paul's hands on her back sent a shiver down her spine.

"We might at that, but I rather think you'll die a happy woman." Her husband chuckled. He slid a hand behind each of her thighs then encouraged her up his legs as she straddled him. The rigid length of his cock rubbed against her swollen nubbin. A host of tingles ripped through her belly and her nipples tightened. A strangled sound escaped her and arousal sprang to voracious life once more. "However." Adam pulled her over him until he could put his lips to her ear. "If you go and expire on me before I've had, oh, thirty years or so to enjoy your company, I will be extremely put out." Then he cupped her face and applied himself to the task of kissing her senseless.

Caroline melted into his embrace. The rasp of his beard heightened her need. She met each thrust of his tongue with one of her own and soon they both gasped for breath, their chests heaving together. When Paul reached around her and she pulled slightly back, he fondled her breasts, she didn't bother to hide her moan of appreciation. "Please, just begin already. I cannot wait any longer." If that made her appear the wanton, so be it. She'd passed too many lonely nights these last ten years.

Both Paul and Adam laughed, then her husband said, "I suppose we have no choice but to follow orders."

"Perhaps she's the Montmorency the British navy should fear the most," Paul rejoined with a firm pinch to her nipples.

A flood of heat drenched her folds and she squirmed on Adam's lap. Was it possible to come undone merely from expectation?

"Aye." Adam claimed another searing kiss before he delivered a smart slap to her buttock. "Lever up for me, my girl. This will require a bit of rearranging."

Her pulse raced. It was too scandalous how much she enjoyed being spanked, but she did as instructed, while Paul eased off to the side. When Adam propped his back against a wall of pillows, he reached for her, spreading his legs and bending them at the knee. His cock sprang proud and ready. She frowned. "What should I do?" For the first time since she'd dreamed of such a scenario, she considered the logistics of such a joining. How would it work?

"Sit between my legs. Face Paul. I'll hold you steady for the first part." Stark hunger darkened his eyes. What did it cost him to delay his own gratification in deference to Paul? As soon as she did so, Adam cupped her breasts. He plucked her nipples into hard, aching buds, which pulled a moan from her throat. "Draw up your knees and let Paul see how beautiful you are," he whispered against the side of her neck.

Caroline did so and Paul didn't disappoint. He nodded with approval. The same hunger in Adam's eyes mirrored in his. "Please." She squirmed in Adam's hold, but he increased his ministrations on her nipples and pleasure-pain sensations swamped her.

"I adore how impatient you are." Paul scooted forward on his knees. The tip of his cock brushed her folds. He tormented her further by sliding it through her juices then rubbing that wide head over her swollen button. "That heightens my arousal."

"Paul, for the love of God, stop prattling!" These men of hers would truly cause her early expiration. Was she expected to ignore the insistent prod of Adam's member against the small of her back?

He chuckled. "Very well." Even closer he came. He gripped her knees, spread her wider then entered her with one smooth flex of his hips. "Damnation, you feel good."

She wanted to give him a compliment as well, but she had no voice to spare as all of her concentration went into the enjoyment of having his length fill her completely. "Mmm," she mumbled, and when he pulled out, an incoherent protest burst from her lips. He didn't leave her to suffer, for he pushed back in then moved into a slow, even rhythm.

"Enjoy, love," Adam whispered into her ear. He never stopped playing with her nipples. Every twist and pluck added to the exquisite pressure building in her core.

Her eyelids fluttered. She wanted to close her eyes and give herself over to Paul's lovemaking but feared if she did, she'd miss the most wonderful thing that had ever happened to her. There she was, sandwiched between her two men. Every inch of her touched some part of them and they were both bent on her pleasure. A sigh escaped. She wrapped her hands around Paul's muscled thighs then slid one up and squeezed a tight buttock. "I'll never have enough." She tilted her hips to receive even more of him. A moan fell from her throat. With every stroke of his cock, his flesh brushed her nubbin; the head of his member slid over a spot deep inside her that sent shivery sensation through every nerve ending.

"Watching him fuck you is one of the most erotic things I've ever seen." Adam bit her earlobe. "Later, we'll take turns tasting your pussy until you beg for mercy."

Need rippled over her from his hands on her body as well as the dark vulgarity. The first tendrils of release spread through her consciousness. "I'm almost spent." How was it possible they'd barely started and she was ready to shatter?

"Let me help you with the fall." Adam slid a hand between her body and Paul's. Easily, he found her button and when he rubbed his fingers over the slippery organ, her grip on sanity faltered.

Paul gasped. Tension lined his face. "Caroline, I'm there." His thrusting turned frantic as his hips pistoned and his fingers tightened on her knees.

The friction from Adam's fingers combined with Paul's penetration beat down the dam holding back the bands of pressure. She didn't just break. Oh no. Caroline exploded as wave after wave of bliss swept her away on their tide. Her chest heaved. Sweat coated her back where Adam pressed against her. A keening cry left her throat as her body stiffened then went pliant. Her inner walls contracted around Paul's length, pulling him deeper, as if loathe to let their joining end.

"Nothing I could ever dream was this sweet," Paul whispered. He ground against her while warm seed jetted into her channel with each pulse of his cock. "You were wonderful, my dear." He leaned into her and dropped a kiss to her forehead. Seconds later, he collapsed onto his back. The harsh rasp of their breathing filled the sudden silence.

Caroline trembled in the wake of the release still moving through her body. "I never knew how good it would feel." Though they both weren't in her body at the same time as she'd dreamed of, just being surrounded by her men left her in a cocoon of joy.

"You're not done yet, love." Adam dragged his lips along the side of her neck then he gently urged her toward Paul. "On your knees. I want to see that gorgeous arse of yours."

Too tired to ask about his request, Caroline pushed herself into the required position, while Adam went behind her. The touch of his hands on her hips, the rough scrape of the calluses on his palms spiked her desire into being once more. Paul rearranged himself and slid beneath her so that his head aligned with her breasts. He took one in hand and guided the nipple into his mouth. A shaky sigh mingled with a moan. Caroline's arms went weak. "I don't know how much longer I can—"

Her words were lost on the heels of a cry as Adam shoved into her channel with all the force she'd known from him. Instinctively, she pushed back against him and his thick cock was sheathed more deeply than before. The different angle—the different man—had tremors dancing wildly through her core. Her breasts tingled. Every pull, each suckle of Paul's mouth on her nipples worked to build up the bands of pressure he'd just released.

Caroline rocked and met each of her husband's thrusts. "Adam. I'm almost... Oh." She and Adam and

Paul ceased to exist, and she became a product of feelings and sensations only.

"There is one thing I promised that I want to give," Adam murmured. He paused in his conquest, but he didn't withdraw and having his cock still embedded within her body teased even more than his love making did. "Don't tense."

She nodded. The few pins holding her hair up let go and her tresses tumbled down over Paul's head and chest. Adam slipped a hand around to fondle her button. Once he'd rubbed his fingers through her slick folds, he spread her juices at her back passage. "Adam?"

"Remember what I told you that night at the lighthouse?" Gently but firmly, he pressed his index finger against her puckered rosette.

"Yes, but why — ?" The last of her query was lost to a cry of both delight and pain as he penetrated her dark opening.

"Shh." Adam smoothed his free hand along her buttock. He withdrew his cock halfway then slid more fully inside. "This will give you more pleasure than you've known before and is but one way I can show my regard." With steady pressure, he worked his finger further into her hole and past the first ring of muscles. "When you are accustomed to this, we'll replace fingers with cocks in the future."

"Dear God, I won't survive this." Already, the tightness grew overwhelming. Having both passages filled left her on the brink of coming undone harder than she ever had before.

"You will," Paul crooned. He cupped her cheek and brought her head down for a kiss. The second he claimed her lips, she relaxed and Adam's finger slipped in all the way.

"Ah, Caro." Admiration threaded with desire through her husband's words. "I love that you're so adventurous." He wriggled his finger inside her back passage and she nearly launched off the bed. "You truly are my muse, my lover, my wife." Strain graveled his voice. He slid the finger from her rear only to slow insert two this time, stretching her, filling her, ready to light the fuse that would send her sailing. "You are my hope and my dream."

Tears stung her eyes, from his words or his ministrations, she couldn't say. Didn't want to try. This moment would bind them all together. "Finish me, husband." The exquisite torture of having him fill her whole body cracked. Tremors grew and multiplied into swelling need. She shook in his hold. *I won't survive.* "Quickly."

He didn't waste time and set a hard and fast rhythm between his cock and fingers. The slap of his balls against her backside resounded in the air. Each stroke of his fingers pushed her higher, every thrust of his cock multiplied the pressure, each bite and nibble of Paul's mouth on her nipples sent her hurtling into a vortex of light and joy. Paul moved beneath her then the hot, wet heat of his tongue on her nubbin added the last component to the coupling and shot Caroline into clouds of bliss.

Never had she come as violently as she did now. She vaguely heard Adam's shout of completion, barely felt the jerk and jump of his member within her passage as she surrendered to the pure pleasure of being thoroughly and completely loved.

Then her strength gave out and she poured herself onto the bed, half on top of Paul. She uttered a brief protest as Adam slid out of her body in both places and the mattress depressed when he left. Her eyes slid closed.

Paul wrapped his arms around her. The splash of water from the basin nearby rang in her ears. Residual trembles played her spine and circled through her insides. She smiled and gave into the pleasant lethargy that weighted down her limbs.

"You've never been more beautiful," Paul whispered. He pressed a kiss to her temple.

"Aye. She hasn't." Adam rejoined them on the bed. He pulled them both into the shelter of his arms, which smashed her once more between the two men. "Thank you." He covered her lips with his in a feather-light kiss.

"For what?" Though she wanted nothing more than to let sleep claim her, she struggled to open her eyes and look at her husband.

Was that an actual tear glimmering in his eye? He blinked and the moisture was gone, but the softer emotions in his stormy gaze remained. "For accepting me as the man I am. For making me feel I'm finally home where I belong."

She drew in a shuddering sigh and nestled deeper into his embrace. *Home*. It wasn't a physical location or a place. It was the people one surrounded oneself with that made the difference. "I know exactly what you mean." After ten long years, she'd finally come home as well. Most folks wouldn't understand the life she'd chosen for herself, but then, most folks didn't matter; only the love in her heart and the men she shared it with did.

Minutes passed, perhaps hours before they stirred and disentangled from each other. The shadows of twilight were beginning to creep in through the window. Paul left the bed first. He retrieved his trousers then shucked into them. "Do you need help with the packing?"

"Packing?" Caroline frowned as she pushed into a sitting position. "What for?" She shoved a lock of hair from her face as she glanced between the men. "What have you done now?"

Both Adam and Paul grinned, but it was her husband who answered. "Paul's readied a ship, which will leave near dawn. We're going to meet with the president."

"All of us?" Her heartbeat kicked up. How could she leave Paul behind when she'd only just won him?

"Yes. All of us," Paul answered. He moved to the window and peered out. "I should go. I'll need to pack as well."

"You'll meet us at the docks in Portsmouth?" Adam asked as he, too, left the bed. Gone was the intense lover and in his place came the inherent sea captain bent on a mission.

"I will." Paul came across the floor with a hand extended.

Adam growled. He bypassed the hand and instead embraced the other man despite still being naked, slapping him twice on the back before releasing him. "We'll be prompt."

"That is best." With a wink in her direction, Paul gathered the remainder of his clothes then left the room. Seconds later his footsteps thundered down the stairs.

Caroline stared at her husband in open-mouthed astonishment. "We're sailing to Washington." It wasn't a question. Her mind whirled with the possibilities.

"We are." Adam snagged his breeches from the floor. He struggled into them, tucking his flaccid cock into the fabric before doing up the buttons.

"And then?" What if all of this had been a wonderful dream? All remnants of sleep were banished beneath the worry.

The grin he bestowed upon her warmed her to the depths of her being. "And then I thought we'd take a voyage to England as a belated wedding trip. I'm feeling the need to reacquaint myself with my family. Perhaps I haven't missed Clinton's wedding after all." He bounded across the room then flung himself onto the bed, where he tackled her to the mattress and pinned her under him as he rested his weight on his forearms. "Does that sound agreeable?"

"Very much so." She squirmed in the attempt to extricate herself, but he captured her lips, moving his mouth over hers in a kiss that shoved all other thought from her head. When he allowed her air, she sighed and gazed into his eyes. "Paul will go with us on this adventure?"

"Absolutely. It was his idea." Adam rolled them over and once again, Caroline sprawled across his chest. "Between the two of you, I'll have no choice but to forget the atrocities I've lived through and walk in the light."

"That's as it should be." She pushed up and her breasts jiggled. He followed the movement with his gaze. A frisson of renewed desire bloomed in her core. "When will we return to Gull's Island?" Though excitement gripped her at the thought of sailing at her husband's side as well as with Paul, she hated leaving her father right after her mother had died. "I need to tell my father goodbye, make certain he's cared for in my absence."

"We will. As for our return, I suppose that depends on many things. None of which you need to worry about at the moment." He delivered a smart smack to her bottom that sent the slow burn of need through her veins. "Go dress. We have much to do this night."

Slowly, Caroline slid off her husband, being sure to let certain points of her body scrape against certain points of his. "Will we have time for—?"

"Caro." He cut her off as he came to his feet. "I'm not a young man anymore. Didn't that session satisfy you?"

"Very much." She couldn't help her grin. Already, slight soreness infused her muscles. "But, as I said before, I do so enjoy lovemaking, even more now that the dream of my heart has come true."

His jaw worked then he hid his expression in the act of retrieving his shirt. "That will largely depend on how much packing you have, wife."

Oh, she'd show him just how easy it would be to fill a trunk. "Hmm, I wonder if I should have need for my silver-backed hairbrush?" she asked in a nonchalant voice as she crossed the room to the armoire. "Perhaps my husband would dare use it?"

"Woman, you're playing with fire." Adam closed the distance between them. He trapped her between the hard wall of his chest and the cool wood of the cabinet door. When he put his arms around her middle and his lips to the shell of her ear, she shivered with desire. "How many times do I need tell you that where you're concerned, I'd dare anything, survive anything to keep you by my side?"

"I wouldn't want it any other way," she whispered seconds before he spun her around and claimed her lips in a kiss.

As long as she had Paul on one side and Adam on the other, her life was perfect.

The End

Rake of the Seas
(Men of the Marque, book three)
Coming late 2016 or early 2017)

Never come between a pirate and his ship…

Viscount Crestline, or Captain Alec Francis Montmorency to those who know him well, can't wait to leave Marshalsea prison behind him. He has plans to go after the man who stole his ship, as well as the highly lucrative cargo she held, and then return to his privateering life. Kissing a beautiful woman while inside said prison only heightens his quest for adventure.

Theodosia Reddington has been left literally, at sea. When the ship she was on sank after a pirate attack, she was tossed in prison on charges of smuggling. Now, in the confusion of a prison break, she's stunned to learn the unkempt scallywag who had the audacity to kiss her is none other than the man she gave her heart—and innocence—to years ago, the same man her father had told her was dead.

…but death to anyone who comes between a pirate and his woman.

Stuck in a sticky web of obligations and double-crosses to everyone he's ever known, Alec embarks on his journey—with Theodosia and her near-fiancé in tow. His own guilty secrets aside, her goals of going back to India won't return his ship and neither will his lingering feelings for her. Love is the treasure, but bloody vengeance lies in wait and the pair will need fancy maneuvering to steal it.

Stay current on Sandra Sookoo's latest releases by subscribing to her monthly newsletter. Send an email to sandrasookoo@yahoo.com with SUBSCRIBE in the subject line. Every month features an exclusive contest.

Or, like her Author Page on Facebook, join her private Facebook group, SHENANIGANS WITH SANDRA, or find her on Twitter, Instagram and Pinterest.

About the Author

Sandra Sookoo is a bestselling author who firmly believes every person deserves acceptance and a happy ending. Most days you can find her creating scandal and mischief in the Regency-era, serendipity and happenstance in Victorian America or snarky humor in the contemporary world. Reading romance is a lot like eating fine chocolates—you can't just have one. Good thing books don't have calories!

When she's not wearing out computer keyboards, Sandra spends time with her real life Prince Charming in central Indiana where she's been known to goof off and make moments count because the key to life is laughter. A Disney fan since the age of ten, when her soul gets bogged down and her imagination flags, a trip to Walt Disney World is in order. Nothing fuels her dreams more than the land of eternal happy endings, hope and love stories.

Coming June 2016
The Widow's Maestro

Wishing for change…

Five years of widowhood and the imminent marriage of her son as well as her daughter nearing college age have left Josephine Prescott at loose ends. When a golden-haired rogue, thirteen years her junior, propositions her, she immediately dismisses him. She's a proper Victorian lady after all, yet a lady can only protest so much.

Playing for pleasure…

Benedict Fitzgerald, talented pianist and maestro, wants a new lover and Josephine is ripe for seduction. The age difference intrigues him as does her willingness for sexual adventure, and as the relationship deepens, it plays out like the notes in a beautiful waltz.

Thwarted by circumstance…

Their busy lives don't lead to the scandalous liaison either of them envisioned, and Benedict doesn't count on being so captivated by Josie, or that the stunning widow would embody his musical muse. Stolen moments together, even quicker sexual trysts don't satisfy. They both want more, but gossip and familial interests oppose their possible match.

Bound by love…

Will their relationship end in a discordant disaster or culminate as a pleasing symphony? Only they can decide.

www.ingramcontent.com/pod-product-compliance
Lightning Source LLC
Chambersburg PA
CBHW071103250626
47159CB00002B/574